Chalk Hearts

Emma Whittaker

SRL Publishing Ltd

SRL Publishing Ltd
London
www.srlpublishing.co.uk

First published worldwide by SRL Publishing in 2022

ISBN: 978-1915073-10-5

1 3 5 7 9 10 8 6 4 2

A CIP catalogue record for this book is available from the
British Library

SRL Publishing is a Climate Positive publisher offsetting more
carbon emissions than it emits.

To my wonderful dad,
Thank you for filling my world with inspiration
I will love and miss you forever x

One

Concealer and a brave face. The two magic ingredients that always kept scars at bay. Amy twisted the box in her hands, reading the words as they caught the sunlight. *Buildable coverage with 24-hour staying power.* She touched a fingertip to her jaw and coated a blemish until it was camouflaged.

As the sliding doors parted for the hundredth time, she could hardly look up to see whose movement had opened them. From where she had parked in the layby, the flipflops and tanned legs of women in shorts flickered across the wingmirror and trolleys clattered into the realms of the unknown.

It would only be a quick dash inside. Just a handful of items to whizz through the checkout and then she would go straight home, knowing she had finally done something normal again.

She counted to five and swivelled from the driving seat, feeling naked as the pavement scorched through her sandals. Approaching from the side, she peered beyond the closed glass where a flower display and newspaper rack partially masked her from view. The aisle ahead was clear, leading all the way to a deli counter where no customers lurked.

A clumsy lunge at the stack of baskets sent the doors shooting backwards with a bang and an elderly man nodded to let her in ahead of him. She edged over to the crates, tasting the scent of ripe fruit as she panted it through her lungs, wishing that the leafy layers of salad would stretch out to obscure her face.

'You're in for a shock.'

The low voice made her freeze.

'Imagine how it feels to be grabbed around the throat until you choke.'

Amy turned to leave and knocked a jar to the floor, amazed that it hadn't smashed to pieces. She bent down to pick it up, her eyes dragging over the back of a toned body, tightly clothed in gym gear, and a young child sucking an ice pop.

'A bit of spice doesn't scare me,' replied the woman as she stabbed a square of cheese with a skewer.

'That's what they all say at first.' The assistant grinned from behind the stand. 'But the chilli in this recipe is a long, slow burn. Once you're in its clutches, you'll never escape!'

The little boy gazed up at Amy and stuck out a blue tongue. Tossing the jar in her basket, she took off towards the bakery.

She grabbed something from a shelf without reading the packaging. Teacakes of some sort, with raisins speckling through. They squished under her knuckles at the footsteps passing by. The rustling in the bread stacks and the distant thumping of freezer doors.

Shuffling around the corner, she came to the far end, losing focus as the drinks blurred in a giant wall of plastic. A bottle fell into her modest nest of shopping. The water she would soon be swilling around her dry mouth.

Checkouts beeped. She ducked into the self-service queue behind someone buying a paddling pool and eyed the bodies passing by as the box blocked out their faces. Crop tops. Carrier bags. Phones in hands. She watched every pair of feet leaving the tills and stepping back out into the freedom beyond the exit.

A green light flashed at the next free space and she kept her head down, packing the food like lightning and tapping desperately at the screen, imagining that all eyes were burning through her.

'Please scan your PlusPoints card,' demanded a voice

from the machine.

But she had done that at the start. Quickly grappling with her purse, she pulled out the card and waved the code at the scanner. An error message dimmed out the payment method icons and the pulsing light of doom crept into the corner of her eye.

'Be with you in a minute, love…' called the attendant, who was busily unpacking an entire bag of a neighbouring customer's shopping.

She felt all attention on her. Heard the impatient sighs huffing through the queue. Frozen on the spot, there was nothing she could do but wait.

Then a phone rang out from across the store. An unmistakable drone of the Dread Head theme tune. The old horror film he had made her watch time and time again in their early days of dating. He had set it as a ringtone months ago, laughing whenever someone called. Stomach-churning… blood-curdling… the noise grew louder as the phone was retrieved from a pocket.

She eyed the kiosk, fighting for breath at the side view of a familiar yet stubbled jawline. Hand raised with the phone to his ear and a glint of white teeth as he spoke.

'Sorry to keep you waiting!' The attendant marched over and tapped in a code to correct the error before cancelling the transaction. 'Not working, I'm afraid. Just pop over there and I'll put it all through for you again.'

The woman gestured in the direction of the kiosk and Amy felt the room swaying. The noise of the supermarket whooshed past her ears and she reached out to grab the nearest surface.

'No worries, I'll just… I'll just leave it thank you.'

'Not feeling well?' The attendant frowned and rushed to the loudspeaker. 'Let's get you some help.'

As the call for First Aid sailed out around the store, Amy paced backwards before sprinting past the photobooth and straight out of the door. Battling the sweltering street, she dodged her way through pedestrians and dogs on leads, hazard cones, and pushchair wheels until she was back at her car.

Wheezing, she locked herself inside and waited behind the shield of her sunglasses until she felt calm enough to drive. The supermarket doors were restless in the mirror, every so often spitting more people out. Refusing to focus on any one of them, she skidded away from the layby and plunged through the traffic lights just as they turned red.

Sweat and teardrops stung her cheeks as she left Popplewell High Street, following a trove of spiky evergreens and rooftops that shone saffron in the sunlight. The lush soil played host to a myriad of colour, with flowers hoisted high above their peaty roots and copiously plump crops swelling from every vine and vegetable plot. As always, the sky seemed perpetually blue and the stream bubbled away in the breeze as it wafted through her window.

Arriving at Larkspur View, she turned into the lane of neatly thatched dwellings and parked outside a cottage clad in a fudgy coating of stone. A narrow path led her through a lawn garnished with forget-me-nots and mottled sprays of cowslip.

She stepped shakily inside and made her way through to the kitchen where her housemate, Colin, was unpacking bags and filling the cupboards with food.

'Thank goodness for that, I was getting worried about you, darling!'

Amy said nothing and sank into a chair.

'And I see that you've already had breakfast.' He nodded at the plate of toast crumbs that was still on the table from earlier. 'I'd made a fresh batch of Dewberry Drizzle for your porridge.'

'I just wanted to try something crunchy… you know, to see if it still hurt.'

'So, does it?'

'Not as much as it did, I suppose.'

'Well, that's progress, right?'

His beam disappeared. There was a visible tremble as she

4

dabbed away more tears.

'Darling, what's wrong?' Colin sprung over to the table and lifted her face into his hands. 'Whatever has happened?'

'I was in Freshway and… I saw him, Col.'

'Oh, God.' He pressed her head to his chest and his voice vibrated in her ear. 'What the hell did he do? Did he see you?'

'I don't think so,' she mumbled into the tea towel that was hanging over his shoulder. 'I left straight away.'

A relieved sigh heaved through him.

'Well, at least that's something.' He kissed her forehead. 'But darling, it's too soon. You shouldn't be out on your own.'

'I was only in there for a minute.' Amy pulled away slightly, releasing the strands of hair that were sticking to her cheeks. 'I just thought if I could manage that then… then I wouldn't have to feel like this anymore.'

Colin used the tea towel to wipe around her eyes.

'Shhhh… I know, sweetheart, I know. Of course, you won't feel like this forever, but it's going to take time.'

'No…' she wailed. 'He'll always be here. Every time I set foot out of that door, he'll be wherever I turn.'

'Darling… please listen to me. You're going to heal, inside and out, and eventually all your fears will melt away. And you know you've always got us.' He squeezed her shoulders. 'Yes?'

Amy glanced out of the window, trying not to blink. Apart from the distant birdsong and a butterfly on the ivy, all was still. Her eyes trailed across the lichen-laced birdbath to the foxgloves flocking beyond the fishpond. Living in picturesque Popplewell was the only thing keeping her going.

'Come on…' He lifted her chin. 'What can I do to make it better?'

'Nothing, really.' She shrugged him off softly. 'I'll be OK.'

Colin caught sight of the furrowed margarine. 'Is toast all you've had?'

Amy nodded solemnly.

'You need something more substantial, now you can eat comfortably again.' He got up and rummaged through the shopping. 'What will it be? Eggs Benedict... Omelette... Croque Monsieur?'

'I'm really not hungry.'

'Well, perhaps you will be after a nice, relaxing bath. Why don't you go and have a good soak for a while? Then come back down and I'll rustle you up some lunch.'

'I suppose so,' Amy agreed reluctantly and pushed her chair under the table. 'See you in a bit then.'

She headed into the hallway and started to climb the stairs.

'Before I forget...' Colin passed her a padded envelope. 'Postman Pat couldn't be arsed to knock so he dumped it at the gate instead.'

The parcel felt thick but easy to bend. Turning it over as she went upstairs, she recognised her father's handwriting. He always sent her letters by post whenever his emails weren't working.

Amy put the envelope down on the bed and picked up her wash bag. She closed the bathroom door and her reflection was unavoidable. Her ash-blonde hair spilled flatly onto her shoulders and her blue eyes sat like sapphires in her pale, milky skin. She touched the faded scratches on her jawline. Four weeks had passed since the attack and the bruises were evaporating to yellow on her flesh, yet still a wave of coldness swooped over her. She swallowed hard, refusing to let the tears fall. Then she filled the bath with lavender-scented water and allowed her thoughts to puff away into the gentle clouds of steam.

Lying back in the foamy haven, she felt the bubbles swirling between her toes, knowing inside that she had to get away. That no matter what anyone else said, or how much time went by, Nathan would always be there, breathing down her neck.

In the weeks since her night of terror, she had begun the daunting search for another job, but nothing seemed to match what she already had as a teacher at the quaint village school. She had been first to move into the Larkspur View cottage, which she now shared with Colin Cleaves, a bookshop manager, and Rosie Willis, a hotel receptionist. The three had stuck together through thick and thin, and the thought of leaving them filled her with sadness.

After well over an hour, Amy emerged invigorated and headed back downstairs in comfy clothes, at least feeling hungry enough for one of Colin's blueberry muffins. Rosie was at the kitchen table, sipping a foamy cappuccino as Colin stood over her expectantly.

'Amazing,' she purred. 'What have you put in it?'

'That'll be the cinnamon syrup. A symphony on the tastebuds.'

'Well, you've converted me. I thought I hated cinnamon.' She took another slurp and looked up as Amy entered the hallway. 'I've just heard. Thank God you came straight home, babe.'

'I've filled her in.' Colin winked. 'She's been frantic.'

'You should have rung me!' Rosie embraced her anxiously. 'I was only down the road at the dentist.'

Amy shook her head. 'I drove off there and then… just wanted to get away.'

'Scum of the earth.' Rosie glared. 'What was he even doing in there?'

'No doubt contaminating the aisles with his presence,' replied Colin, shooting a look of disgust. 'Anyway, you need to stay put for now, sweetheart. No going out except straight to work and back.'

'Unless she's with us.'

Colin frowned at Rosie's response.

'It's not safe, dearest. You never know what that creep is going to do.'

'Oh, stop it, Colin. She'll turn into a nervous wreck.' Rosie's hazel eyes reached out to Amy's. 'Now, I know you're upset. I know you're… hurt, but you can't let this stop you having a life.'

'I thought I was ready.' Amy shrugged helplessly. 'Then look what happened. I can't even be in the same room as him.'

'Which is why you're not doing it alone,' urged Rosie. 'But if you stay locked inside forever, you're letting him win. Why should you hide away at home while he's allowed to cruise around as if nothing's happened?'

'We wouldn't be having this conversation if you'd just go to the police,' said Colin. 'There's still time, you know.'

Amy shook her head. 'You heard what I said. I can't unearth all the gory details again, it's just too much to take. So, I'll have to face the fact that he's always out there somewhere.'

'Then the only thing to do is look at the positives.'

Colin and Amy glanced perplexedly at Rosie.

'What I'm saying is,' she continued, 'you only saw a glimpse of him. He didn't actually do anything, did he? I mean, he didn't even see you.'

'No, I suppose not. But…'

'But nothing, babe. Show him. Show the whole world that you're not going to be intimidated like this.'

'Rosie, dearest.' Colin winced. 'It's too early for all that. She's had a nasty shock today and she needs to take her time.

'The pub.' Rosie clapped her hands together, not listening to Colin. 'Let's go down to the Frog and Fiddle tonight.'

Amy crumpled her face.

'Don't give me that look! You'll feel amazing once you've done it.'

'Nonsense. She'll be better off staying in with a good film and a slap-up serving of my Sweet and Sour Surprise.'

'They do bar food, dear.' Rosie snapped bluntly.

'That is not the point!' cried Colin. 'She's hardly cut out for a night in the pub if five minutes in the supermarket is too much to take.'

'Staying in will do more harm than good. Do you want this morning's blip to be ingrained in her mind?'

'Well, obviously not, but…'

'So, let's just do it and have a nice time. Besides… your favourite barman might be working tonight. Wouldn't want to miss out on that, would you?'

'How shallow do you think I am?' Colin almost shouted. 'Amy's wellbeing is far more important.'

'If you care so much, you'll agree with me.' Rosie squared up to him with a spatula. 'And I know deep down, you would kill for a pina colada. Especially if he's the one sticking an umbrella in it.'

'Resorting to bribes now, are we? Well, you can stick them where the sun doesn't…'

'Perhaps she's right.'

They both turned to Amy. Colin's face filled with horror while Rosie shot her a delighted smile.

'That's the spirit! I promise, you won't regret it.'

'Don't feel pushed into this darling,' Colin warned. 'You've had enough worry for one day.'

'I can't go on like this. If I'm not running away, then I have to be able to do ordinary things without feeling terrified every time I try.'

'Exactly.' Rosie put an arm around her. 'We'll be back here before you know it, and you'll feel so much better for getting all done up and going somewhere without anything disastrous happening.'

'But only an hour or so,' replied Amy. 'And a quiet table at the back.'

'If you're sure,' Colin sighed. 'I suppose it's a chance to wear my new shirt.'

'I knew you couldn't resist, Col,' Rosie patted his arm. 'And as for you…' She gripped Amy and guided her out of the kitchen. 'You're going to look so sexy tonight, you'll forget that dirtbag ever existed.'

***

They chose a table tucked well away in the cosiest corner of the Frog and Fiddle, and, after two drinks, Amy started to unwind. Her eyes were rimmed with metallic liner that matched her shimmery top and Rosie had helped her to expertly cover every last trace of her scars.

Colin leaned against the bar and ordered them two gin and tonics along with a Singapore Sling for himself. He locked the barman in a seductive stare while he tapped his card on the machine and slipped it into his pocket. Then he left with the drinks, throwing a sultry glance over his shoulder.

'He wants me,' he declared, placing the glasses on the table.

'He's not even looking at you.' Rosie frowned.

'It's called being subtle. Ever heard of that, darling?'

'You haven't,' she scoffed.

'And what is that supposed to mean?' He looked wounded.

'Perhaps she's got her eye on him too,' joked Amy.

'Oh please.' Rosie rolled her eyes. 'Somehow the five layers of fake tan don't quite do it for me.'

'You have no taste, dear, that's your problem,' Colin retorted.

'Taste?' She nearly choked into her glass. 'I'm more than partial to peanut butter but not when it's airbrushed onto someone's skin.'

'A newly-qualified accountant.' He sighed, indulging in another look towards the bar. 'And I know just the bookshop that needs one. Next round's on me again, girls!'

'Good thinking. Give it half an hour and he'll be gagging for your bleary eyes and inability to walk in a straight line.'

Narrowing his eyes at Rosie, Colin turned back to Amy with a defiant smile. He cocked his head to one side as if to examine her in more detail.

'Darling, darling, look at you.'

'What?' She was suddenly alarmed.

He put his hand on hers and squeezed it.

'Not only do you look like a goddess tonight, but you're

smiling like one. Wonderful to see you happy.'

'I second that,' Rosie agreed wholeheartedly. 'You're smashing it, girl!'

'Never let anything – or any*one* for that matter – get you down.'

Amy felt grateful as she sat snugly between them. It was uplifting to be facing the world again, somewhere outside work. To relax in the humble surroundings of the pub, hearing the clinking of glasses as the crowds laughed and chattered, was an unexpected tonic. Like a flame on a lighter, a tiny glow was beginning to take effect.

'Another drink, ladies?' Colin drained his glass and swiftly stood up. 'That sly little fox has his eye on me again.'

'Don't push it.' Rosie pulled him back down. 'There are plenty more nights for the rest of the cocktail menu.'

'I beg to differ.' He laughed. 'One Bloody Mary and he's mine.'

As Rosie continued restraining him, Amy's phone began buzzing on the table and an unknown number filled the screen. She frowned, then answered.

'Hello?'

There was silence.

'Hello…?'

The sound of wind or traffic blustered in her ear. Then she stiffened.

It was someone breathing.

'Have you…' she stuttered. 'I think you might have the wrong num…'

'I can see you.'

Her heart pumped with the weight of a brick as she eyed every area of the room.

'Nathan, how did you get my…'

'I have my ways,' he replied casually. 'Can't stay away from me, can you?'

'How do you know where I am?'

She could barely grip the phone for shaking. Rosie and Colin had stopped arguing and were firmly rooted either side of her.

'Now that would be telling.'

'What do you want? Why are you doing this?'

There was a long pause.

'I'd take care getting home if I were you.'

'I don't understand…'

Chills paralysed her spine and the whole pub seemed to be blacking out as his whisper echoed sharply down the phone.

'You might not be as lucky next time.'

'Please,' Amy begged, trying not to cry. 'Don't do this, Nathan.'

The line went dead.

'Nathan!'

She clambered to her feet, clutching the table as her eyes darted once more around the room. Then, barely able to see for the tears, she wriggled across Colin's lap and stumbled over to the door.

'Wait!' Rosie grabbed her from behind. 'You can't just leg it outside on your own. You don't know where the tosser is.'

Ensuring that Colin was by Amy's side, she stepped onto the street and checked in both directions.

'Come on.' She beckoned. 'He's not here.'

Colin walked Amy out cautiously with his arm around her shoulder. They carried on in silence until they turned a corner.

'It's all right, darling,' he said calmly. 'The brute is nowhere to be seen.'

'This whole thing is my fault,' Rosie cried. 'I shouldn't have made you go out.'

'Never mind that,' directed Colin. 'Let's just get her inside.'

As soon as he unlocked the front door, Amy headed upstairs.

'Oh, don't go straight to bed, sweetheart,' he whined. 'Come and talk to us.'

'Please, Col, I just need to sleep.' Amy fought to sound upbeat.

'Night then,' called Rosie up the banister. 'But tomorrow, you tell the police.'

The tears fell uncontrollably as soon as she was out of sight. She huddled up in bed while her mind replayed every minute of the phone call. It had all crashed down around her in one split second. She still couldn't escape from Nathan.

As she rolled over to face the wall, a papery thud hit the carpet and she switched on her lamp to investigate. It was the forgotten envelope from her father. She slid it back up on the bed and tore away the seal.

Through her watery vision, she pulled out a scribbled note and a folded copy of the Flintley Gazette. Blue tape marked a page where an advert was ringed in yellow highlighter. She wiped her eyes and scanned the words in bold:

Year Four Teacher, starting September. Experience necessary.

Then she read the small print below and stopped at the third line down:

Woodbrook Primary School, Flintley.

Two

It was well after midnight when she flopped onto the pillows, too tired to rinse her face. From the moment she closed her eyes, the dull walls of the classroom surrounded her once more. The plastic chair dug at her spine and the pencil in her shaking hand was sharpened and unused. There were pages of unanswered questions. Percentage signs and fractions turning to liquid in the dim light.

Laughter came in spasms, swishing like a stormy sea that she was incapable of navigating. Children huddled in their same tight groups, having kicked her to the kerb.

She looked down at her shoelaces. The ones they said were *thick, like her.* As chatter swirled in the distant playground, she pulled yarn from the stripe around her cuff, awaiting another breaktime of being pushed into walls.

A pen squeaked blue to scrawl the letters of her name, right up there with rats and slime on the list of class dislikes. She watched the teacher's statuesque frame leaning across the whiteboard, and the movement of her corkscrew curls as she drilled down on the nib. The eyes and smirks of turning heads as they focused on the loser.

Tears bled out making holes in the lined paper. She covered them with an arm, too small to hide the damage. The teacher's sight fell on the mess and her coral lips quaked with a roar. High heels hammered the wooden floor and the sculpted cheekbones swooped up close, cheered by a band of voices.

A hand clapped down like a gunshot on her desk and

harsh light streamed into the room.

Amy woke sharply and her body thudded on the mattress. As her heartbeat steadied, she forced back her puffy eyelids and raised herself up against the cushions, a relentless pain clamping her forehead. Slumped on the bed, she stared at the frayed newspaper as the pictures of the night fluttered away into fragments.

With a morsel of energy, she flipped off the duvet and let the breeze fan at her through the window as the copper sun kissed the clouds. She bent out beyond the glass, feeling the balmy air bathing her face yet clashing with the dryness of her throat.

Slipping quietly into the bathroom, she cleaned her teeth and freed her skin from the smudges of make-up. Then, in the nearest clothes she could find, she crept downstairs through the dormant hallway and out of the front door.

A twisted road led away from the garden. The old stone houses slept on as dawn slashed its way through the fading coat of indigo. Shade dripped down over the fuchsia-fringed walls and sunlight stretched from each gate in thin slivers on the pavement.

Echoes of the stream murmured gently along the footpath. The belt of water scurried past as she crossed the bridge, ushered by the weeping willows that bowed along the bank. She trod gingerly up the tree root steps and through the gap in the hedges which opened out onto the park.

Its grassy ring circled around a sloping rockery that was deftly cultivated and spilling flowers from its pockets. Flat pathways traced the outer edges and an army of trees guarded the far corner like soldiers. By now, the sun's yolky sphere had cracked into the cloudiness as Amy neared a hilly mound and settled under the branches. The playground's woodchip oval stood dead like a graveyard and the ghostly slide hung heavily in the middle like a huge, lifeless tongue.

The words of the advert bounced off the paper. It was like a knife, slicing down and splitting her mind in two. She thought of Flintley and the grey erosion of shops and buildings running through its centre. The idea of moving back to her hometown was hardly appealing. Aside from the lack of friends, she would possibly be doomed in a dilapidated flat if she didn't find luck in its prettier northern border or somewhere along the peaceful coastline. It was tired, gloomy, and completely devoid of anything that could be considered useful.

But she could live with all that and more, if only the school in question wasn't Woodbrook.

She had escaped like a bird from a cage on the day she'd last walked from its doors at eleven years old. Those cold, lonely times were forever stacked up like a collage in her memory. The bullying, the seclusion and her reputation as a hopeless case all came straight back in a moment's thought.

Dread flooded through her as she imagined being recognised. Still strung up as a failure and scrutinised for her faults. She wondered if they would laugh at her for trying to claim their respect. Those years were planted firmly in her soul, bearing a lifetime of insecurity.

As she sat in the heart of Popplewell now, she wondered how she could leave it all behind. The three towers of the ancient school were just visible beyond the fuzz of the trees. Tomorrow it would be full of life again as the children pulsed through, cheerfully boisterous from the weekend. The stately structure and all that took place within its walls symbolised everything she had worked for since dragging herself up from the pit of her own schooldays.

From the challenges of the lessons to the happy lilt that frequented the staffroom, she couldn't think of a better place to be. Staring into the calm treetops, she scanned the bright stretch of grass, the wildlife waking around her and the petunias swaying like bonnets in the breeze. Surely she couldn't let it all slip away?

But there was a major flaw. What had once set the scene for a budding romance now only reminded her of everything she had lost. Each piece of it was a different painting of the past. Like the coffee shop in the alleyway, which had been a top spot for lunch, or the bus shelter under the cape of jasmine, where they had met for their first date.

The wounds from that last black night with Nathan were fading on the surface, but a future in Popplewell would etch it eternally in her mind. She could try all she liked to carry on as normal. She could say things were fine until she was blue in the face, but it wouldn't change the facts. If she chose to stay, she chose to keep him near her. It simply couldn't be done.

Flintley beckoned again and Amy squinted up at the mystic sky, no longer able to back down. There was only one way to shake off her past for good.

To return to Woodbrook as a total stranger.

If she could step inside those walls as a new, competent teacher, her history as a hopeless case would be dead and buried forever. An instant escape from Nathan might just heal her childhood wounds.

In twenty years, her name had changed due to her parents' late marriage. The staff would all be different and perhaps even Woodbrook itself.

As the glimmer of hope sparked again, she got to her feet and stood tall with the tree trunks. Then she walked off briskly down the pathway.

Upstairs in her room, Amy unfolded the newspaper. There was a website address at the bottom of the advert, so she went online to browse. It was only a basic layout but the building on the home page was unrecognisable. Aside from brief details of the uniform and awards scheme, there wasn't much else to go on, but at least there was a staff list.

She waited with intrigue as it loaded and was relieved when only strangers filled the screen. There were even blank spaces where some pictures were missing, each one labelled with the words, *To be updated*. Perhaps these were other vacancies to be filled by more new people.

It was as if something else was controlling her body as she began to type her covering letter. The words seemed to flow effortlessly and she rounded them off with a strong and confident finish.

As she turned away from the screen and put the paper to one side, her father's note slipped out from the pages and she picked it up to read again. It was just a few words about the advert, but she felt a warm rush as she saw his quirky handwriting. That was the one good thing about Flintley – her family were there. Her parents still lived in the same house, high up on the northern border, and her younger sister, Vanessa, shared a flat with her boyfriend in the next town. She hadn't considered how good it would be to have them nearby again.

Amy's tired eyes started to close and she crawled into bed. As soon as her face touched the pillow, she was far away in a long and peaceful nap.

It was five in the evening when she woke. Salmon clouds gauzed over the violet sky and covered the walls in a shadowy darkness. The air was cool and the muggy day had been quenched by the restful evening. She padded downstairs towards the muffled sound of the TV in the living room, where Rosie was flicking through the channels.

'At last! You must have been out like a light.'

'I was.' Amy stretched. 'What are you up to?'

'Choosing something decent to watch. Colin's out so I'm taking full advantage. I don't think I can face another seal getting eaten by sharks.'

'Where's he gone?'

'One guess.' Rosie glanced from the corner of her eye.

'Not the pub again.'

'He's gone to ask Mr Mixology to do the bookshop accounts,' sighed Rosie dramatically. 'He thinks it'll be an ice-breaker.'

'Well, let's hope it's not overkill already.'

'Believe me I tried to stop him, but he was having none of it.'

'You should have woken me. I'd have talked some sense into him.'

'I thought I was doing you a favour. He wanted your advice, but I told him to let you sleep.'

'It's all going to end in tears again, just like the rest of them.'

'Fear not, babe.' Rosie tapped a tissue box. 'I am more than prepared for the waterworks.'

They made a bowl of popcorn and relaxed with a bottle of rosé wine to watch one of their favourite films, but halfway through, Rosie's eyes widened and she hit the mute button on the remote.

'It's him,' she said in a hushed tone before turning the volume back up. 'We're in for a long night.'

Colin's crestfallen figure appeared at the lounge doorway.

'Oh no!' Amy turned to face him. 'What happened?'

He stared at the opposite side of the room, as if he couldn't look at them.

'Come on then…' Rosie waved a tissue in his direction. 'Let's hear it.'

'It's a tragedy. That's what it is, a tragedy.'

'Why?' asked Amy. 'What did he say to you?'

'Nothing. Absolutely nothing at all.'

'So, he ignored you, did he?' Rosie chipped in. 'Well, I wouldn't worry, babe. He probably spends all day on his calculator so he wouldn't have enough time left for you. Besides, I've seen better biceps on a…'

'Thank you, darling, but what I mean is, he wasn't there.'

'What a relief!' mumbled Rosie.

Amy whacked her softly and quickly interrupted. 'That's good then. At least there wasn't some terrible…'

'Embarrassing showdown,' Rosie cut in.

'What are you suggesting?' Colin glared over at her. 'Do you honestly think I would have walked in there and blown it?'

'Have some wine,' Amy interrupted. 'Try a glass of this, it's gorgeous.'

'Might as well.' Colin's eyes brightened. 'Just a tiny tincture of the pink princess.'

'Now, don't be disheartened,' Rosie soothed as Colin sipped away. 'Just get an early night and wait for the next time you see him.'

'That's if I ever do.'

'You will. I mean, you never know, he might end up fancying *me* instead.'

She grinned smugly between mouthfuls of popcorn.

'We'll see about that, young lady.' Colin drained his glass. Then he shot her a sour look and glided up the staircase.

***

As the foil-studded night sky spread across the window, Amy read through her completed application. It sounded impressive enough and she had presented it neatly with no obvious errors. Finally satisfied, she closed her laptop lid.

Despite her earlier sleep, she was still exhausted from the drinks, the sticky heat and a mind crammed with too many thoughts. She sprawled out under the covers and lost herself in a dream.

Soon she was running faster than she had ever done in her life. Yards of fresh grass flew past in a blur as she tore unstoppably through an endless field towards a disc of scorching sun, flashing out ahead of her in the steel-blue air.

She could see nothing else. Her eyes were transfixed on the summoning light, surrounded by a mass of soaring sky. Nothing had ever felt more urgent and necessary. Voices echoed behind her and clawed shapes disintegrated as they tried to pull her back. She just ran at top speed, leaving it all to crumble behind her. Now, just one thing was clear and true as she sprinted for her life, never to stop until she reached her destiny.

Three

The shrill notes chimed from inside Amy's handbag as if clamouring to compete with the choral birds above. Not far along the shortcut on her way home from work, she rummaged through her pens and make-up, finally gripping the phone.

Squinting under the alcove of leaves, her skin turned cold as the blank caller details lit up in the palm of her hand. Fighting to control her breath, she slowly pressed the answer button and waited for the moment when she would hear Nathan's voice.

'Hello?'

'Good afternoon, is this Amy Ashcroft?'

'Yes, speaking.'

'Ian Farley here, Headteacher of Woodbrook Primary School. I hope I'm not calling at a bad time.'

'No!' She struggled to hide her flustered tone. 'Not at all.'

'Well, we received your application and we would very much like to meet you, so I wondered if you'd be free on…'

Amy waited while he shifted about and rustled something into the receiver.

'Oh, I can't see my calendar. Please bear with me, I do apologise.' His voice was obscured for a few seconds. 'Sue, where in the world is the calendar app?'

A woman's mutter was just audible and soon Ian was back on the phone.

'Sorry about that, I'm not used to this technology. Would next Tuesday morning work?'

'That sounds good.'

'Wonderful. I'll confirm it in an email for you. There'll be full directions and where to go once you've arrived.'

'Oh, I know where to...' Amy stopped mid-sentence. 'I mean, thank you, that will be helpful.'

'Would nine be convenient?'

'Yes, that's fine.' She winced, hoping he had missed her stumble.

'We'll see you then. Goodbye for now.'

Amy made sure she had cancelled the call before cursing herself for nearly saying too much. She had muddled through that quick exchange, but the interview would be worse.

Setting a reminder on her phone, she wondered if she was doing the right thing. It had been unnerving to take a simple phone call from that place, never mind committing herself to another lifetime there.

She had almost given herself away in the first conversation, so how long would it be before she really put her foot in it? Walking off down the lamp-lit cobbles, her mind misted with doubt. It was too late to back out now. She had got the interview and she was going in at the deep end.

The following days seemed incredibly long, giving too much time for contemplation. Every hour she spent in Popplewell made her wonder what was possessing her to leave. She was spellbound by the silence in the streets, broken only by the echoes of the cool, frolicking stream. Vanilla clouds churned over a quintessential sky and the crusty village brickwork was lathered in wisteria.

But something marred the scenery now and chased her far away. She felt cold to the bones at the slightest reminder of him.

On the eve of the interview, she barely slept as nervous thoughts took her all over Woodbrook. Her mind painted pictures of the library, the top unit classrooms and the big assembly hall, just as she remembered them, until her alarm rang at the crack of dawn like the piercing school bell.

After a warm shower, she slipped into some figure-hugging trousers, a cream blouse and a tailored jacket to smarten up the outfit. She applied perfect make-up before giving her hair a final spray and driving out of the village.

Her heart beat low and deep in her chest as she arrived in the visitors' car park. Children were playing their early morning games and making the most of the fresh air before lessons started. It was such a familiar scene, but the surroundings had changed beyond recognition.

A whole new block sat in a bold oblong to the right, with scatters of painted handprints decorating the windows. The main entrance had been rebuilt with a wider path and curving archway, and the small outdoor swimming pool was now covered by a roof. A cabin-style creation had replaced the old canteen which was crumbling when Amy had been at school there.

She scoured every corner, dreading a familiar face. Praying she could get through this trial without anyone blowing her cover.

A smiling secretary introduced herself as Sue and dialled an internal phone number. Two minutes later, another woman strode up to Amy at the desk. She had a neat black bob and a forehead dented with lines. Glancing at Amy up and down, she pursed her lips into a tight smile.

'Sorry to keep you waiting.' She stretched out a hand, embellished with a gaudy emerald bracelet. 'You must be Amy.'

'That's right.'

'Welcome to Woodbrook. I'm Penny, the Deputy Head. I'm afraid Ian's caught in traffic so we'll have to start without him. Can I get you some tea or coffee?'

'Tea would be good.'

Penny turned to Sue, who was busy on the phone, and scribbled out the order on a sticky note. She slapped it on the screen and swept out of the room with Amy following behind her.

They walked into a small office and sat down at the desk.

Amy waited in silence while Penny scrolled through the files on her computer.

'Right.' She clicked open a document and Amy could see it was her application. 'So, you're at... Popplewell, is it?'

'That's correct.'

'Funny name. I've not heard of it before.'

'It's one of the oldest villages in the country, very tucked away. Apparently, it's been the subject of a few famous paintings.'

'Sounds idyllic.' Penny's face broke into a grin. 'Why ever would you want to leave a place like that?'

Amy hesitated for a moment. The fact that she was desperate to get away from her violent thug of an ex-boyfriend wasn't going to go down well.

'I want a change,' she answered adamantly. 'I've been there for a while and I'm ready for a new challenge.'

She rolled her eyes as Penny continued to peruse the credentials. The biggest cliché in the book, but she couldn't think of anything else on the spot.

'And you've stayed at the same school for the last four years?'

'Yes. It's been a great experience.' Amy's heart sank as she thought of her days there coming to an end.

'Rolling hills, babbling brooks, that sort of thing?'

'Something like that. I must admit, it's a lovely place.'

Penny sneered. 'So, what makes you think you can handle this?'

'Sorry?'

'Woodbrook, is an entirely different kettle of fish. The Mary Poppins effect won't win these kids over.'

Amy laughed. She was joking of course. Wasn't she?

She wasn't.

'This school is seriously hard work. We need a candidate with an iron backbone to manage these children. Someone with experience of this kind of school and area would be a distinct advantage.'

'Yes, I'm sure.' Amy hoped she sounded positive. 'But I

do know this area.'

'Oh?'

'I mean, I grew up somewhere… very similar.'

'So, where would that be exactly?'

As Amy opened her mouth to reply, the door swung open and a stout, middle-aged man with dark grey hair glanced at the two of them.

'Morning, Penny.' He frowned. 'Is there a problem here?'

'Not at all. We were just having a little chat, Ian.'

There was an uncomfortable pause.

'If I could have a word, please.'

Penny slid out from behind the desk and Ian shut the door abruptly as she stepped into the hallway. They might as well have stayed in the room though, as Amy could hear everything from where she was sitting.

'What on earth is going on, Penny? They're all waiting.'

'Yes, but Sue told me you were going to be late, so I thought I'd better get started.'

'But you knew we were meeting in Room Five. The three of them have been in there since quarter to nine. I've been running backwards and forwards making excuses and Lydia looks like she's going to kill somebody.'

'Well, I merely thought it would be a good idea to go through a few things before we went in there,' Penny asserted. 'We need to know if these people can actually do the job or this whole exercise is pointless.'

'That is for me and the governors to decide too, Penny,' Ian replied. 'Now let's just stop this nonsense and take her in there before they all storm out of the building, shall we?'

There was a shuffle and the doorknob began to turn.

'No, leave this to me,' he said loudly. 'You'd better get down there and tell them we're on our way.'

'Whatever you say.'

Penny's footsteps clicked off into the distance and the door finally opened. Amy smiled politely as Ian walked in. She was silently relieved he had interrupted the grilling.

'I'm so sorry about this little misunderstanding.' He

shook her hand. 'I assume you're Amy. I'm Ian.'

'Nice to meet you.'

'We're going to have to hurry to the boardroom. The governors are waiting for us but don't worry, their barks are worse than their bites.'

Amy followed him into the corridor. He was friendly with a jolly tone to his voice and kind, smiling eyes. As they walked down a small staircase, he filled her in about the school. He seemed very proud of the huge reconstruction it had undergone ten years before, as Amy had seen straight away. On their journey to the meeting room, he described a much happier place than Penny had implied, citing the new buildings as a significant improvement.

Her first impressions were a world away from what she had been expecting. It was like being inside a completely different school and the fresh, white-washed interior brought back no cruel memories of the past. Only a minimal portion of the original building had apparently remained the same. Ian promised to show her around properly later on, but now they had to hurry to the governors.

Ian held the door open, acquainting Amy with two men in shirts and ties. A petite woman with glossy auburn hair sat between them and smiled as Ian introduced her as Lydia.

They were all seated in an intimidating line, but Lydia spoke to her almost like a friend with far more patience than Ian had just described. The more Amy said, the more impressed Lydia looked. Ian barely stopped beaming from ear to ear and the others seemed satisfied with her answers to their questions, but somehow she still felt on edge.

Penny's silence bothered Amy the most. She sat there with the same tight smile, drilling her pen nib deep into her notebook, not looking at her colleagues or responding when they spoke.

After a lengthy session in the meeting room, Amy was left with Ian and Lydia to take a class in their presence. The children were despondent at the start and perhaps shy around someone they didn't know, but with enough effort from

Amy, the animation soon surfaced. Even in this short space of time, her warmth reached out to the loneliest corners of the classroom.

The visit ended with a tour around the school, which Ian conducted hurriedly due to the late commencement of the interview. They ventured into the lower block with its coloured doors and drawstring gym bags. Amy peered into each paint-splashed classroom at the tiny chairs and tables. Every member of staff was a fresh face. Every inch of this school was new. Relief washed over her as she took it in. She was out of the woods after all.

Ian showed Amy the children's gardening area, with flower beds and bulbs that had recently been planted. He led her to the canteen, where the caterers were preparing for the imminent lunch hour, and he finished back at the main entrance.

'Well, I'm so sorry, but we've run out of time. I must dash or I'll be late for the next meeting.'

'That's fine.'

'Of course, you're always welcome to come back another day if you'd like to see the rest.'

'Thank you, I might just do that.' Amy nodded, knowing it wouldn't be necessary.

'Anyway,' Ian shook her hand once again. 'You should hear from us either way by the end of next week.'

'Great. Thank you for everything.'

'It's a pleasure.' Ian stepped inside. 'Goodbye, Amy.'

She bought some lunch from the shop across the road before driving straight back to Popplewell. She would have visited her parents, but they were away seeing relatives. And besides, she was due to arrive home at precisely the time she usually got in from work, so Colin and Rosie would be none the wiser of her whereabouts. They had no idea just how far away she was prepared to go and she didn't plan to tell them unless she got the job.

'You look rather pleased with yourself, darling,' Colin

remarked when she arrived in the kitchen. 'Good day, was it?'

'OK, I suppose.'

She didn't look him in the eye and sat down at the doily-dotted table, upon which Colin had laid out his tea set complete with silver spoons left to him by his grandmother. He always insisted on full-blown afternoon tea whenever he wasn't working.

'Where has Rosie got to?' he asked despairingly, tilting the elaborate teapot over Amy's cup. 'She said she'd be home by now.'

'Don't worry, she'll be here soon.'

'Well, I *am* worried, darling.' Colin looked vexed as he prodded a tray of bite-sized cucumber sandwiches. 'This bread will be like a scouring pad if she takes any longer.'

'Honestly, only you could panic about a few sandwiches and a cup of tea.'

Colin shot her a wounded expression. 'Well, perhaps I won't bother next time.'

'Don't be so silly,' Amy laughed. 'A day without all this is like a day without sunshine.'

His scowl morphed into a grin as Amy stirred a circle of tea with her spoon. Then the front door slammed shut and Rosie's loud sigh floated along the hallway.

'Someone pour me a vodka, I have had one bloody awful…'

She entered the kitchen and stopped talking. Amy's eyes were fixed on the floor and Colin stood dejectedly with arms folded across his elephant-printed apron.

'What?' Rosie frowned.

There was a long pause before Colin finally spoke.

'Vodka?' He shook his head in disbelief. 'How on earth can you want vodka at a time like this?'

'What are you on about?'

He directed Rosie's eyes to the spread on the table.

'Oh, that.' She tutted, collapsing into a chair. 'Can't we have something else for a change?'

'Something *else*?' Colin looked devastated. 'Do you have any idea how long I have slaved away, young lady?'

'A pot of tea and sandwiches,' Rosie sneered. 'About ten minutes?'

Colin's face was like thunder as he whipped a tea towel off a tiered cake stand adorned with eclairs, fruit slices, and scones layered with jam and cream.

'Colin dear, is this really necessary?' Rosie slumped her head into her hands. 'Get a mug, chuck a teabag in it and fill it with hot water. Cup of tea. Done.'

'Fine.'

He headed out of the room, but Amy grabbed his arm.

'She doesn't mean it! She's just had a bad day. Of course she wants your tea.'

'No, I'm serious,' Rosie continued with a yawn, 'I need a stiff drink and a long bath, not Mr Kipling's rave up.'

Colin's lip quivered and Rosie met his pained sideways glance.

'Oh, give me a custard tart then.' She rolled her eyes as he gleefully reached for his tongs.

'That rocky road is mine!' Amy enthused.

He served the cakes and seated himself at the table.

'So, tell me, dearest. What was the cause of that little outburst?'

'Just people. I've had complaints up to my eyeballs all day. They want to move rooms because the view's not good enough. They want new pillows because the others are too saggy. One even said her free shampoo was too small. Can you believe it?'

'That's right, sweet pea, let it all out.' Colin massaged Rosie's shoulders. 'I wouldn't put up with it. Two minutes of backchat from that lot and I'd tell them where to shove their shampoo.'

'Yes, and you'd be out on your ear,' Rosie answered, wiping crumbs from her mouth. 'The customer is always right, remember?'

'Not in my neck of the woods. Treat the staff well or go

to hell – that's my little message for the customers at Broomfields. You should come and work for me, darling, you'd have a whale of a time.'

'One more day like this and I might be on my way,' replied Rosie, turning to Amy. 'Speaking of which, how are you getting on with the job search?'

'Well, to be honest....' Amy looked up as they listened with interest around the table. 'I'm just keeping my options open.'

'Very wise.' Colin patted her hand. 'Just don't set your sights too far away.'

'Sorry, but if I were her, I'd snap up the first thing that came along.' Rosie looked Amy in the eye. 'Don't get me wrong, babe, I'd miss you like mad but with an ex like that lurking around the corner, I'd have to run a mile.'

'I know.' Amy smiled weakly at the reminder. 'I'll keep you posted.'

As they turned their attention back to Rosie and her terrible day at work, Amy's mind was elsewhere. Wondering how she was going to break the news if she ended up getting the job. Colin would be inconsolable and even though Rosie was prompting her to leave, Amy knew the reality would hit her hard too. She had a soft heart through that icy exterior.

***

The days passed by with no word from Woodbrook. Amy had been fairly confident, going by the interview, that she had a chance. But the more time flew, the more she convinced herself that she had overestimated her ability. Either that or Penny had stuck her neck out to make sure Amy didn't land the job.

As she walked home each day through the medley of conifers and the mountainous sycamore leaves erupting from their branches, she told herself that this was a blessing in disguise. The way the elements seemed to wrap themselves around her meant that perhaps she shouldn't leave. Every inch she travelled down the picturesque pathways reassured her all the more. The ballerina peonies in their tutu clusters and the lingering scent of honeysuckle urged her not to go.

So, she was startled when her phone rang on a sunny Friday afternoon, just as she had sat down on a bench in the park. Ian apologised profusely for taking so long to get in touch. He had been away, leaving the task to Penny, but she had apparently forgotten. *Of course she had*, Amy thought, but nevertheless she listened intently as Ian offered her the position. She accepted in an instant, only half hearing the rest of the call as he informed her that an email would be sent that evening.

So that was it. Feeling the rigid lines of wood press into her back, she looked over at the sprawling parkland, the overflow of rhododendrons and the velvety Japanese acers, blowing from burgundy to vermilion through the ornamental beds.

She could hardly believe she was about to leave all this for good. This place, with its comforting arms of serenity, had been the centre of her world for so long. Whether it had been carefree hours of basking in the sunshine or somewhere to contemplate in any time of need, a few deep breaths in the bounteous open air had always provided a kind of therapy.

Her sight drifted over to the old brick wall, running along the edge of the clearing. Beyond its shield, the neatly tended gardens gave way to a straggly carpet of grasses with one solitary tree, reaching out its gnarled boughs as if to conduct the orchestra of greenery.

It was there that Amy had taken refuge, bruised and battered at the hands of Nathan. She had slumped in a heap at the flaky trunk until she'd been sure he'd stopped chasing her. She remembered the terror and the sheer devastation that still left its mark on her skin.

Walking away down the slope, she followed the dotted trail of flowers until the stream could be heard lapping just ahead of the bushes. Beauty poured from every corner. The watercolour petals painted pictures from their stems and the baby-blue sky caved over it all like a silk sheet of protection.

But it wouldn't compare to the new leaf she hoped to turn over in Flintley. At last, she would be free of the daunting recollections creeping around behind her at every turn. Trips to the pub, the supermarket, or wherever she chose to go would no longer come at a price. Somehow, with strength and a good pinch of luck, perhaps she could make this move work.

Filled again with the strange pull of Woodbrook, she braced herself and headed off home. It was time to tell Colin and Rosie.

Four

Amy followed the voices to the garden where three sunbeds were out on the lawn. Rosie was sitting upright with a glass of lemonade in one hand and a blob of sun cream in the other, which she slapped onto Colin's back.

'Will you keep still?'

'Stop tickling then.'

'Wait a minute.' Rosie placed her chilled glass on the ground and returned to Colin with both hands. He clung to his sunbed and shuddered.

'What now?'

'You're freezing!'

'Well, I'll just leave you to frazzle. Pity about your nose though. I think the circus has left you behind.'

Colin inspected the reflection on his phone. 'What a sight! Now I'll have to stay away from the pub for a week.'

'Of course you won't, dear. This will do the trick.' Rosie squirted the tube at him and covered his face in cream.

'And there was I, thinking you loved me,' he groaned as she clutched him, laughing.

'What's up?' Amy cut in.

'At last,' replied Colin, wiping white smears from his chin. 'Long day, was it?'

'I was just in the park.'

'Somewhere quiet, I hope.' Rosie tutted. 'Was it busy?'

'Deserted actually.'

'Well, do join us,' said Colin, nodding at the empty sunbed. 'I was just off to the freezer for some sorbet. Can I interest you?'

'Too right,' Rosie piped up. 'Get me a scoop of mango.'

'Not *you*. You're in disgrace, dearest.'

'Oh, come on.' She puckered her lips. "You know I love you really.'

He ignored her request and glanced over at Amy, who was climbing onto her sunbed.

'What's it to be, my sweet?'

'Nothing for me, thanks, I had a late lunch.'

Colin disappeared into the kitchen, but soon trotted back across the lawn with the sorbet, heaped into two ornate glass bowls, one of which he thudded into Rosie's lap.

As the three of them lay in a line striped yellow and white by the canvasses, there was silence under the warm pool of light. They lounged in the sun-drenched peace while blue tits whistled in the bushes and insects sketched lacy patterns across the pond.

Amy took a breath and felt her body tense. She looked at Rosie, soaking up the weather in her wide sun hat, her hair tied with red bows that almost matched her poppy-lipped smile. Beyond her, Colin had his earphones in and was tapping his feet to the music while he licked the last of the sorbet from his spoon. Maybe another hour, Amy decided, putting off the news for as long as possible.

When the sun had burned out into orange peel flecks that seared the marmalade sky, they began packing up to go inside. Only Amy remained in her place, watching the others as they filled their arms with books, empty glasses, and sweet wrappers. Then just as Colin began to walk away, she jumped to her feet and stopped him.

'Wait.'

He spun around on the spot, seeing the seriousness in her eyes.

'I need to talk to you,' she continued. 'Both of you.'

'What is it?' Rosie sat back down to face Amy.

'Is it that monster again, darling?' Colin's intrigue turned to anger. 'Because believe me, if he has laid so much as a finger on you…'

'It's not Nathan. Well, not exactly.' Amy took her time, hardly knowing who to look at.

Their expressions were eager, pressing her to speak.

'I've been offered a job.'

'That's great!' Rosie grinned and Colin launched forward to embrace Amy.

'I knew you would, you little star,' he said in admiration. 'So, where is it?'

There was a brief silence.

'I'm going back to Flintley.'

'What?' Colin sat down on the grass.

'Flintley?' Rosie's mouth widened. 'That's halfway across the country.'

'I know.' Tears brimmed in Amy's eyes. 'But I can't stay here anymore. Everything reminds me of him. Of what he did.'

'Of course it does, babe. It's just happened so fast.' Rosie's sorrow seeped through as she fiddled with her magazine.

'I had to take the first thing that came up,' Amy replied. 'You understand that, don't you?'

'Come here, baby doll.' Colin flung her into his arms. 'Words can't say how much I'll miss you.'

Rosie narrowed her eyes. 'It's not where you went to school, is it?'

Amy nodded slowly.

'That will be a blast from the past.'

'It's quite different now. I wouldn't have known it was the same place.' Amy had never told them how much she'd hated it as a child. 'You'll come down all the time, won't you? And I'll always be back to see you.'

'Promise, darling,' Colin was too speechless to say much more. 'Promise we'll never lose touch.'

'I don't need to. You know we won't.'

'Good on you, girl.' Rosie slipped an arm around her. 'I'm so proud of you.'

Amy felt a muddle of heartache and relief as the dusk set in around them and crickets chirruped to herald the nightfall.

For the rest of the evening, they sat around the kitchen table drinking Colin's Torchlight Toddies and reminiscing over their years together as housemates and best friends. In tears of laughter, the happy memories came alive and reaffirmed their closeness. No distance would sever their ties and Amy could be sure of that. She might be leaving alone, but she would never be without them.

***

The doorbell rang early on moving day and Amy's heart plunged with anxiety. Opening the upstairs window, she looked down at the doorstep to see her sister.

Vanessa had come on the train to help out. They planned to load Amy's car, leaving the larger items for their father to collect later in a van. Casually dressed in a hoodie and jeans with her platinum-blonde hair flowing loose down her back, she waited impatiently to be let in. Amy tapped the glass as her sibling looked up at her and frowned.

'Come on, I haven't got all day.'

'Give us a chance. I'm still packing.'

Vanessa rolled her eyes. 'Well, let me in then and get the kettle on!'

'Allow me, darling,' Colin's voice rose from the hallway and grabbed Vanessa's attention. 'If you want tea from her, you'll be waiting for a week.'

Vanessa giggled as he led her into the kitchen and their words echoed to the landing.

'Tell me about it,' she said loudly. 'Tortoise is her middle name.'

'Hey,' Amy shouted from the top of the stairs. 'It never takes you long to start on me.'

'Hush now, angel cake,' Colin called out to her as he turned to Vanessa and sifted through his tea collection. 'What takes your fancy, lovely lady? I have Earl Grey, rosehip, camomile, rooibos…'

'I'll give the camomile a try.'

'Marvellous.' Colin was thrilled. 'Much more adventurous than your sister. I can never entice her from a bog-standard breakfast blend.'

'That's her all over,' Vanessa sighed. 'Pizza with no toppings and boring, mild curries. She's just dull really.'

Colin stifled a laugh.

'Thanks.' Amy's voice drifted through the doorway. 'Anything else to add to the list of compliments?'

'Now you've done it!' Colin chuckled to Vanessa. 'That is what you don't want. Her in a bad mood all the way back.'

'Something tells me you're not going to miss me,' Amy joked, leaning into the room.

Colin turned away. She could see the red of his cheeks as he sucked the tears back through his eye sockets. Immediately, she went over to him and draped her arm across his back.

'Come on you,' she said softly. 'I'm a few hours away, not the other side of the world.'

'I know, I know.' Colin sniffed. 'Just tell me you'll keep in touch.'

'Of course she will.' Rosie breezed in and cocked her head to Colin. 'Now perk up and let's not have all this misery.'

'You should thank your lucky stars,' Vanessa said sarcastically. 'At least you're free of the dirty dishes and the towels on the bathroom floor. I know what she's like to live with.'

'She's got a point there.' Rosie smirked, then gasped at Vanessa. 'Wow, I always forget how identical you two are.'

'Like twins, aren't they?' Colin chirped amusedly.

There were similarities between the sisters, but Amy's shoulder-length hair was streaked with natural highlights while Vanessa's was longer and bleached all over. Despite Vanessa being two years younger, she was still over an inch taller than Amy.

'Give me credit.' Vanessa curled her lip. 'I haven't checked in the mirror this morning but I'm pretty sure my head doesn't look like an onion.'

Colin and Rosie guffawed as Amy's jaw fell and Vanessa wrapped her in a hug.

'Seriously, you look great, sis. I can hardly even see the bruises.'

'Good stuff, that little tube of magic. Thanks for the link.'

'Where is your dad anyway?' Rosie asked them.

'Running late,' said Amy. 'He had to wait ages at the van hire place.'

'Probably quibbling over the deposit.' Vanessa slurped her tea. 'Now are you ready, sis? I've got to be home by five tonight. Giles got a pay rise so we're going out to celebrate.'

'All done.'

Amy stood at the kitchen door, her life packed up in suitcases. She looked at Rosie, changing the station on the radio and Colin, deciding whether to spread blackcurrant jelly or lemon curd on his crumpet, and took in a scene she would never see again.

Half an hour later, the car was crammed with luggage and a stack of clothes. Amy stashed the last items under the glove compartment and met Colin and Rosie at the gate. One more tearful hug, a scattering of kisses and a promise of constant contact, and she pulled herself away from her two best friends, too heartbroken to look back.

She steered slowly through the cobbled streets, past the Frog and Fiddle, and over the bridge which curved above the stream, her limbs heavy as the crooked stonework and swathing greenery whizzed away. Onwards she went, taking the main junction off the bedraggled country lane where the smooth stretch of busy dual carriageway swallowed up the scenery at breakneck speed.

Amy's hands gripped the wheel as her moist, uncertain eyes led the way and in an instant, it was gone. The hills rose up to bury restful Popplewell and the last yellow slivers of sun were rinsed out in the sky. Then she surged into the clutches of the coastal clouds and the woolly cape of charcoal, ruffling across the horizon.

Five

Familiar clouds gathered in a haze and fanned their raindrops to greet her. The sodden streets seemed to haul her in with each sweep of the windscreen wipers. Vanessa dozed as they travelled through the town centre, its run-down shops and parish hall slumbering at the roadside. The vandalised bus stops and benches all stood comatose as they headed over the level crossing where the weathered station platform was bleakly softened by hanging baskets.

One last roundabout and Amy turned left down the coastal road, trimmed with duck egg beach huts and a seaside strip of guest houses in ice cream shades of paint. Following the grassy stretch where flats and a caravan park edged cordially to the east, she slowed at the new house she would call her own. Stepping out of the car, her face was fuzzily soaked as she took her first breath of home.

It always seemed to rain in Flintley. Drops were spattering into the car boot as Amy fiddled with the front door key and dragged a cardboard box into the empty front room.

'Here's another one,' said Vanessa. 'Where do you want it?'

'Just shove it all in here,' Amy instructed from the other side of the wall.

Between them, they lugged everything inside and squashed it up in a corner.

'Where's Dad got to? He said he wasn't far behind.'

'He'll be driving like a slug with all that stuff in the van.'

'Suppose so,' Amy agreed. 'Come and look around while we're waiting.'

On the first day it had been advertised, Amy had taken one glimpse online and secured the house without a viewing. Redecorated and affordable, it had come up for rent at just the right time. As she walked around it now, enveloped in the freshness, all her trepidation seemed to fade.

A staircase led to a small open-plan kitchen and a dining area, where her table would overlook the striking sea view. Two magnolia bedrooms sat either side of a classic bathroom suite along a short corridor. The lounge and a utility room were tucked away downstairs and a glass door at the back opened out onto a lawn edged with stone slabs and a row of baby shrubs.

'Great to have you back!' Vanessa sighed. 'I was so worried about you. Thank God you're free of that jerk.'

'Yeah, let's hope so.'

They returned to the front window and looked out at the road.

'Maybe I'll come over at the weekend. We could watch a film and treat ourselves to a takeaway…'

A white van jutted out as it slowed at the driveway. Traffic came to a standstill and car horns drowned out the grating roar as it turned haphazardly to the right and parked up behind Amy's car. The sisters watched as their father slammed the door. Amy hurried outside with Vanessa right behind her.

'Everything OK, Dad?'

'I wanted to hire a van, not a sardine tin,' he fumed, cleaning his glasses with the bottom of his shirt. Vanessa cackled from the hallway while Amy hid her grin. 'I've driven some old bangers in my time but this tops it off. You'd think someone had put treacle in the gearbox.'

'Are you sure it's not just your driving?'

Stan looked indignantly at Amy, his eyes widening under his cap, but as she and Vanessa exploded into giggles, he couldn't help smiling.

'Where's my little sunshine, then?' He held out both arms and embraced Amy. 'You're home now, safe and sound. And if you ever hear from that rotter again I'll…'

'No chance of that,' Amy reassured him.

'Have you phoned your mother yet? She's desperate to hear from you.'

'As soon as we're done unloading.'

'Come on then, Cuckoo, let's get it all in. I want my money back for this heap of junk.'

'Oh, Dad, do you have to? I haven't got time to hang around while you're in there kicking up a fuss.'

He turned to Vanessa. 'I'll drop you at the bus stop. Now, let's get cracking.'

They hauled Amy's wardrobe up the stairs followed by an oak table and four chairs that her parents had bought to help her out. Stan assembled the furniture, then he headed down to the living room where Vanessa and Amy were slouched against the wall.

'Right, all sorted up there. Just watch that shelf in the spare room, it's a bit wobbly. I'll pop back with some decent nails and finish it another time.'

'Are we leaving now?' Vanessa stood up. 'Sorry, sis, I'd help you more but I've got to get ready for tonight.'

'It's fine. You get going.'

Waving them off on the driveway, it was impossible not to smile when Stan hammered the accelerator to no avail. Vanessa cringed from the passenger seat as they chugged away out of sight.

***

Amy ploughed on, putting everything away. As evening fell, she walked around the house with satisfaction. She was slowly settling in.

Collapsing on a beanbag, she reached over to the remaining boxes. Wishing she had bothered to label them, she peeled back the brown tape to check what still needed unpacking. Two leather books were stashed inside one crate with a small pile of photos and more in silver frames.

Opening an album on her lap, she smiled at the first page. It was a little girl with two blonde plaits and navy hairclips to match her uniform. The apples of her cheeks were round and her eyes danced eagerly at the camera. She stood outside the family house, holding her favourite teddy bear. It was Amy's first day at Woodbrook.

More snapshots filled the album. Amy on stage in a fairy costume and another of her winning an egg and spoon race.

She turned a few more pages and her face changed.

Now she was ten and stood hidden in the back row of that year's class photo, blending into the crowd. Instead, the cheery grins belonged to the ones who had called her names and had trodden on her sandwiches at lunchtime. They all knew she was useless. Miss Dixon said so.

In the middle of the group sat the teacher, with her narrow green eyes and gummy smile. She had ridiculed Amy if she ever asked for help, laughing out loud at her answers to the questions. Taking scissors to her work in front of the class and ordering her to *grow up* if she ever shed a tear.

The torture had continued and she'd carried it all within. No one had known the darkest parts of Amy's lonely life.

The next page, a year later. Her last term at Woodbrook, and a ray of hope.

It was a summer camping trip and the photo had been taken on a boat, gliding down a river with swans in the background. Amy was perched with two other girls, smiling at the camera. She wore a pink T-shirt with a faded denim skirt and her lips were raspberry-cold from the lolly in her hand.

To the left was her new teacher, Mr Craven, beaming out at the water as they sailed along in the sunshine. Twenty-six at the time, he was slim and athletic, his sandy hair tousling in the breeze as he leaned on the side of the boat. He had sunglasses on in the picture, but Amy had never forgotten the piercing blue eyes that had lit up his face and were almost overwhelming.

His deep, commanding voice echoed through her mind and she could hear him now, fighting her corner when the bullies had closed in and always praising her for the smallest accomplishments.

She had come to him broken and bruised by neglect, but he'd picked up the pieces and made her feel worthwhile. He knew how she had struggled and was there with open arms, striving to get her back on her feet again.

Memories lingered of the year under his wing. Like the time when she had sat all alone with the bluebells, etching heart shapes on tree trunks with chalk. His gentle wave from the window had flushed her face with warmth.

And one day, for just one solitary minute, her troubles had disappeared. The moment had always stayed vivid in her mind, because she could never remember feeling higher. It was the day when he had timed her to run across the field.

The spring morning had been perfect, with marshmallow clouds whipped into the sky and zigzagged hues of jade and chartreuse bursting from the bushes. As the grassy mass sprawled before her, Mr Craven had stood waiting as she'd walked into the sunlight. She had stopped behind the line and lifted up her head. Squinting through the buttercup rays, her stare had locked tight on his face.

His composure had slipped away as a fire sparked in its place, calling her across the track and willing her to achieve. A slow nod. A signal. Then down had clicked the stopwatch.

Power had pounded through her in unprecedented waves and she had shot like a bullet over the sun-parched earth, like her life had depended on that one vital minute. The rubber of her plimsolls had shredded up the turf, with a muddy scent stealing each snatched waft of air. Every muscle launching her further towards him.

She had hurled herself at the finish line, where his cheers had deafened the silence and he had plunged into clear view, easing her into victory. Caught up in the moment and filled with his praise, she had wanted to collapse in his arms. His smile had enveloped her as he'd scribbled her time on a clipboard, his face alive with glee.

The next morning in assembly, his voice had silenced the hall as he'd made the announcement. That Amy was the fastest girl in the school.

To this very day, no one had ever made her feel so invincible and free. That one treasured time was a thread of happiness and it would always mean the world to her.

She closed the album and went to the window. It was strange to see her Woodbrook days again. Each shot brought the old school frighteningly close, like a dreary backdrop to the times of torment. Amy felt thankful they were gone. She thought of the charmless simplicity which Woodbrook now encompassed, its modern décor cemented over every detail of the past. It might not be Popplewell Primary, but it was enough to lessen the pain.

Gulls flapped around the inky skyline and the buildings stood like wet blocks of clay. Beaded rain slid down the glass, but still she smiled. This murky drench of town, retiring for the night in its foggy duvet, opened up a whole new beginning. She dug her feet into the carpet and thought about making some tea.

Six

Looking at the kitchen clock, Amy wondered if she should leave a little later. It was only just daybreak but she was ready to go, the mug and bowl from her coffee and muesli loaded into the dishwasher and her work bag neatly packed. It was only a five-minute drive to Woodbrook and far too early to set off yet.

But she was doing this for a reason. The school gates were open at the crack of dawn each weekday and she intended to get there well before any colleagues arrived. That way, she could look around the areas Ian hadn't shown her and see them again for herself. She had to know if any memories would be triggered and she couldn't risk a shadow of a reaction giving her away.

The sky seemed to groan with the sponges of cloud as they started to squeeze out the rain. It fell like pins as she drove past the shops and crossed the central roundabout. She headed alongside the Pig and Trotter, a pub and steakhouse with a generous car park which was used by parents during the school run.

Amy turned the corner where the lollipop man usually stood, making her way slowly uphill. She crept past the driveway to the visitors' entrance before taking the next road, a cul-de-sac, on the left.

There, through a tall metal gate, was the new staff car park. It sat at the highest point of the school and took up a small portion of the lower field. She felt her heart drum in her chest. From the driver's seat, she could see the gravel path that descended to the assembly hall. She followed it there with her eyes, then up again, and traced the dead blocks of the top unit building that nestled into the edge. It hadn't even slightly changed in all the years gone by.

Nothing stirred through the shady windows and she longed to see someone there. Any life or movement to break through the deadness and stop the history creeping back in.

She walked through the gap between the assembly hall and the canteen that opened out into the centre. But coldness drenched her as she headed past the swimming pool and traced the bottom of the grounds.

The old wooden classrooms were just visible beneath a slope at the top of which sat a greenhouse and the new lower block. Amy remembered these huts well. Here was where she had spent the middle years of her time at Woodbrook, when all the trouble had begun.

First, there was the raised hut which had just been built when Amy started school. The light fell in generously through the windows and it still looked new compared to the other one a little further on.

She travelled along the stone path, now aged by weeds that peeped through the crevices. This next, much longer hut was at ground level and housed three more classrooms. Going by the exterior, it had not been as well maintained as the raised one by its side. An old coat of creosote was flaking off in places and bubbles of condensation steamed in the windows.

Amy stood opposite the two white doors, where the rusting railings and single step led from the ground to the entrance. She passed the first classroom with only a quick glimpse as she had never been taught in it. Instead, she headed to the second door which was shared between the middle and end rooms.

A strange sensation prickled her body at the musty smell in the cloakroom. She could feel the bumps in the wooden floor through the toes of her heeled boots. Their knotty fibres had pushed against her feet in the flat tread of her school shoes. The varnish was now opaque with wear and the slats were punched with hundreds of holes from decades of staff stilettos.

She went straight inside the largest room, hoping she was alone. A polished flatscreen was central on the wall and the desks were all new. Specks of dust floated in the weak ray of morning sun which stretched in through the wide windows. She moved along the thin gaps between the tables, remembering every part of the old classroom.

But something made her shudder at the small moderations. They did little to disguise the outlines of a place she knew too well. History still died hard under the roof of this little hut, where so much had once gone on. So much she would never reveal to the people who would soon be all around her.

Without lingering too long and letting it overwhelm her, she headed to the exit. If she felt this uncomfortable where she was standing now, she would certainly avoid going next door into the end classroom. It was in there, just metres away, that she had spent her year with Miss Dixon.

Quickly, she left the room she was in, ready to vacate the hut through the main doorway. She went to shut the small classroom door, but before she could turn away, a sign in black lettering caught her eye at the handle: *4H*.

She frowned. Surely it was a misprint. These weren't the Year Four classrooms. Her room was in the new block – one of those that Ian had shown her, with the leafy view from the windows and the bright paint splashed over the walls. Why else had he not brought her down here?

He'd been pushed for time, but obviously he had focused on the refurbished rooms as they were where she would be teaching. She pleaded with her mind, her memory, to tell her that that this had been the case. But the number was there, clear and unmoving. It wasn't going to change.

Then her stomach lurched. Suddenly, the *H* concerned her more. If the room she had just been standing in was *H*, then her room must be…

Nauseating saliva built in her mouth and she turned slowly, like a hand was jerking her around. She faced the end classroom, hardly daring to read the sign. The bold black initials leapt into the corner of her vision. She closed her eyes in the vainest hope that it would rub away what she had read. Her heart plummeted as she looked again and tried to take it in: *4A*. A for Ashcroft.

She was haunted already as she edged up to the door, the feelings flooding back over her before she had even stepped in. The optimistic teacher who had emerged from her car was now fragile and shaky. Weak and scared. Helpless and hopeless, like she always used to feel. She clutched the handle to steady herself and instantly it turned, sending her almost falling into the room with the force of being pushed. Her chest thumped as she glanced around at the confines of the classroom. The very walls that had surrounded her in the worst of her Woodbrook years.

The floorboards creaked at her feet. There was no view from the far windows; the hanging branches of an overgrown tree had blocked out all the light. Like the middle classroom, it had its updates, but it was smaller and dingy. There was something about the ceiling. It was so low, it could have caved in. She felt cold as she eyed each detail she could never have imagined seeing again.

That spot at the back, just a little to the left, was where she had sat every day. Where they had stared before bursting into laughter. Where they had thrown their notebooks in her face. Where she'd cried until the tears had run dry.

And there at the front was a tall table with its chair facing out to the class. Now, she would be teaching where Miss Dixon herself had once towered. Shredding her into small, quaking pieces.

She bolted from the room, not even stopping to close the door. Gritting her teeth so she didn't cry, she panted across the playground and straight to the main entrance, yearning for something to block out the dread. She steadied her pace as she neared the archway, trying to look as unshaken as possible.

The reception area was vacant, but she decided to check the staffroom for any early arrivals; it was getting late and she didn't want to be spotted ambling inexplicably around the school. As she pushed the door open, just a crack, her eyes darted over the soft leather chairs and the small central table holding a stack of magazines.

Her heart pumped in time with the clock and she pinched her hands together in a tight knot. She thought of her friends. Of Popplewell. Of everything she had sacrificed for this. How could she have imagined that this would work?

Here she was, trying to hide the past. Trying to convince the entire workforce of this school that she was a far cry from her real self. But already, just minutes into her first day, it was all falling down. She was still weak and pathetic. Still living in a complete and utter dream world.

If only she had seen those huts again at her last visit and realised how they would spew up every festering memory, then she would never have returned.

Her insides raged as she recalled the interview. The way Ian had rushed her around after Penny had delayed things. And Amy had been so blinkered by the school's new look that she had somehow just expected a similar revamp in the older parts.

Now, the more she thought about it, the more it was sinking in that what Ian had ended up showing her had masked all that had been unvisited. All that was still aching with years of unyielding history. There was the assembly hall, the offices, the little computer room, and so much more she had long forgotten about. They hadn't even gone to the upper classrooms.

Suddenly, her spine jolted as another thought came to life. She got to her feet and made straight for the door.

Just around the corner was a place she knew too well. The entrance to the top unit. One step inside the tunnelling corridor and she was a girl again. She continued along the walkway, not even allowing her footsteps to make a sound.

The doors opened straight into the TV room, where the science lab beyond it was still twinned with the food tech kitchen. She had never forgotten the smell of baked shortbread sweetening the air in her lessons.

Beyond the glass doors, she checked that the car park was still empty before heading straight outside. There, on the edge of an angled slope, was the single hut which had been Mr Craven's classroom.

Something rushed through her as she walked in. It was just the same. The light and the lifting. The freedom.

A panoramic view of the field swept in through the windows and, at last, she felt relieved to find a treasured piece of the past. Here was the place where her work and ideas had been lovingly displayed for all to see. And there, in that very space by the teachers desk, she had stood to receive her accolade as the fastest girl in the entire school.

Almost running, she crept back down the steps, struggling to control the adrenaline that was suddenly filling her body. Up she climbed, up the tuft of hill as the slippery combs of grass squeaked at her feet and fine rain freckled her skin. With each step, the huge field expanded in a wide square ahead of her. She stood there with the same weakened knees, still overcome with a sense of uncertainty.

But the sky was pasty and ethereal. It soothed her as she looked across at the four green corners that seemed to map out the way. Her eyes scanned the ground and stopped directly opposite. There on the empty patch where he had once stood to greet her.

The fear ebbed away. She closed her eyes, feeling the release and remembering how she had achieved it the first time. The soil scuffing up as she had rocketed along with her sight fixed on her one and only target.

She was strong again, knowing that this place was hers and all she had to do was remember. As her feet reunited with the turf, her mind clicked back to the moment when everything had changed with footsteps and heartbeats.

Filled with the spirit of the field's great depths, she was

ready to face the day.

'Amy? Is that you?'

She froze. Then she slowly turned at the familiar voice.

Seven

She couldn't contain her surprise as she looked straight at his face. His gentle, caring eyes.

'Are you lost?' he asked softly.

'No, I got here early. Just thought I'd take another look around.'

'The rain won't hold off for long.' Ian gestured, nodding his head towards the building. 'Come inside with me and I'll introduce you to some of the staff. I don't expect you met them all the last time you were here.'

As more plump raindrops fell from the slab of cloud above, Amy noted the car park filling up behind her and wondered how long she'd been standing there. She followed him to the assembly hall and joined two other teachers at the back door which led through to the staffroom.

'Nigel!' Ian patted the man on the back. His hair was a shaggy strawberry blond and he wore black-rimmed glasses with a tweed jacket. His style of clothing made him look considerably older than he was. 'This is Amy Ashcroft, our new Year Four teacher.'

'Nice to meet you.' He flashed a geeky smile.

'This is Nigel Piper. He has the privilege of teaching Year Five and this year's bunch are quite a handful.'

Nigel raised a sarcastic eyebrow, then reverted to a friendly beam.

'Right,' giggled Amy. 'Rather you than me, I think.'

'They'll be good as gold.' He winked. ''I always have them well trained.'

'Ignore Midas here,' said the other teacher. She was dark skinned and petite with a waist-length braid of black hair. 'I'm Gita Jaffrey, Year Two. Nerve-wracking on the first day, isn't it? I only started last year.'

'It is a bit.' Amy tried to forget about the old classroom she would soon be returning to.

'No doubt you'll lose yourself around here, I did.' Gita rolled her eyes. 'You'll soon get used to it though.'

'I already am…' Amy cut herself off.

'Sharp as a knife is our Amy,' said Ian with a chuckle. 'She's had a quick look around and she knows it like the back of her hand already.'

'Well, I'm getting the idea.'

Her smile fell as she sucked in a breath and followed them inside.

She met some other teachers in the staffroom where Ian left her to chat and Gita put the kettle on. A lively buzz rang out from the playground and as Amy listened to the talk around the coffee table, the tension soon began to ease. The school seemed a different place when it flourished with smiles and life. This was how it had been at the interview, and why she had taken the job.

They soon began leaving the staffroom to settle in with their classes before assembly would start at a slightly later time than usual. Soon, just Amy remained sitting in a chair while Nigel spoke about the curriculum with one of the other teachers.

No one had come to show her to her room. Finding it wouldn't be an issue, but nobody else was aware of that. After five more minutes, she set off on her own. Ian was probably busy and at least she knew where to go.

Just as she turned the next corner, she smacked straight into a woman who looked about her age, with wide green eyes and mousy hair pulled back in a ponytail. Paper went everywhere and she knelt to pick it up.

'Sorry about that.' She tutted, scrambling around on the floor.

'It's OK.' Amy bent down to help. 'I wasn't looking where I was going.'

'Totally my fault, trying to carry too much stuff again.'

'No worries, really.'

Her smile was mischievous with little dimples. Then she squinted with a kind of recognition. 'Are you Amy?'

'That's me.'

'I'm Alison Huckleberry. Year Four, with you.'

Amy grinned. *That's right*, she remembered. *4H*.

'I was out on a trip when you were last here. They told me all about you.'

'All good?'

'I'll say! Ian hasn't stopped singing your praises.' Alison frowned and looked down the corridor. 'Has no one bothered to show you where you're going?'

'I guess they're just busy. First day of term and all that.'

'So, it's fine to just leave you alone? This is Ian to a T, I'm afraid.'

'I don't mind.' Amy kept her knowledge of the layout to herself. 'I'm sure I could find it.'

'Just come with me, I'm on my way there.'

They passed the offices along the reception area. Then Ian stepped out into their path.

'I'm ever so sorry, Amy, I was just coming to find you. The phone has not stopped ringing.'

'I bet,' Alison mumbled.

'Well, I see you have been put in the capable hands of our lovely Alison. She's your fellow Year Four teacher.'

'It's amazing, isn't it?' Alison spoke up. 'Luckily, I just happened to bump into her.'

'Such a coincidence.' Ian jovially missed Alison's sarcasm. 'Well, I'll leave her with you if that's all right, Alison.'

'Absolutely fine, Ian. You just do that.'

'You know where I am if you need me.' He waved, returning to his office.

'Unbelievable.' Alison shook her head as they carried on

walking.

It was getting better already. Everyone seemed easy to talk to and by the time they reached the lower huts, Amy was feeling more positive. Alison introduced her to the class, then she hurried off next door to get familiar with her own.

'Good morning everyone…' Amy sat on the top of her desk. 'I'd like to hear your names first. We'll start with you and go from there.' She pointed to a girl at the front.

'Layla,' she said with a smile.

'Brittany.'

'Elijah.'

This sequence carried on around the class until it was the turn of a boy with dark brown hair and defiant eyes, sitting near the back of the room. He glared at her and didn't speak.

'Yes…' Amy urged. 'What's your name?'

'What's yours?'

'I'm Miss Ashcroft. And you are?'

'No,' the boy pressed. 'What's your first name?'

'I might tell you if you tell me yours.'

'Why should I?'

'Because I have to call you something,' Amy remained friendly. 'And surely you have a name like everyone else?'

The boy sighed loudly. 'If you must know, it's Bertie.'

'No, it isn't!' a girl shouted. 'It's…'

Immediately, she stopped talking as the boy punched the desk with a loud bang.

'That's enough!' Amy's voice was suddenly fierce. She looked at the girl, who recoiled in her seat, then returned her focus to Bertie. 'What do you think you're doing?'

He didn't answer.

'Now, I don't want our first day to start badly but if there's any rudeness, you'll go to Mr Farley. Do you understand?'

Again, he didn't answer.

'Bertie? Do you understand?'

He continued scowling but he nodded resolutely.

'Right, where were we?' She glanced back over at the girl next to Bertie. 'I think it's your turn.'

'Sophia,' she replied.

'Freya.'

'Flynn,' continued a blond boy, whose angelic face stood out a mile.

'And now that you've all told me your names,' Amy looked directly at Bertie, 'I promised I'd tell you mine. My first name is Amy, but I'm Miss Ashcroft here.'

'I wish I was called Amy,' mused Leona, who was sitting just below her.

'Me too!' Freya giggled.

'I don't think so. Your names are lovely.' Amy hovered a finger over her tablet screen. 'Now, there's just time to take the register before we go to assembly. So, Tara Ainsley…'

'Yes.'

'Sasha Archer.'

'Yep.'

'Flynn Branston.'

'Yes, Miss.'

'Avril Creeson.'

'Yes, here.'

'Reuben Daylesford.'

'Yes.'

'India Graham.'

She continued to read out the list.

'Albert Hughes…'

There was no reply. Instead, the class erupted into sniggers and Amy glanced up to see Bertie clenching his teeth. He looked seconds away from throwing something or lashing out at the nearest person.

'What's the matter?' she asked, knowing full well what was wrong.

Bertie's eyes burned into two angry slits.

'His real name is Albert!' cried a boy in the middle.

Laughter swooped around him, stoking more fury into his face.

'Stop it, now!' Amy's outburst even made Bertie flinch. 'You will not laugh at anyone in this classroom. Ever.'

Bertie flicked balls of paper, not caring who they hit. Amy gestured to his ripped notebook. 'Give that to me.'

He slapped it into her hand and she faced the class.

'Albert is a great name.' She looked assertively at the pupils, who smirked back. 'You should be proud of it, Bertie.'

There was no response.

'Think of the famous Alberts in history. Einstein, Prince Albert... brilliant people!'

There was a twitch from Bertie, as if somewhere deep down, there might just be the slightest chink in his metal-hard exterior.

'Of course, you don't hear it too often these days,' she spoke louder through the muffled laughter. 'But you know what that makes it?'

No one said a word.

'Cool. Very cool.'

The chuckling faded.

'But we'll call you Bertie anyway.' Amy grinned, trying to meet his eyes.

Bertie looked calmer, if not totally convinced.

'Now it's time for assembly and then we are going to make name cards. I want you to design them with pictures that say something about you, so give it some thought.'

As the children filed out into the corridor, they met with the other Year Fours.

'Chelsea,' Alison called as she edged to the back of the line. 'Is that chewing gum?'

'No.'

'Out with it.' Ripping a tissue from her jacket, she looked on sternly as the girl deposited the pink stub into her hand. 'Right, are we ready?'

The reply was a half-hearted murmur.

'Off we go then. Single file and slowly.' She stepped out of the hut and walked behind the children with Amy. 'How's it going so far?'

'They seem OK. I can see one or two are going to be quite a handful.' She gave Alison a knowing gesture towards Bertie.

'I meant to warn you. Just about everyone has lost patience with that one. Have you met Debra, Year Three?'

'I might have done.'

'A larger lady with glasses and scraped-back hair,' she lowered her voice to a whisper. 'Quite a bossy voice.'

'Yes, I know.' Amy remembered her from interview day.

'Well, she had him last year and was at the end of her tether.'

'Really?'

'Name-calling, complete failure to apply himself in lessons and then there was the water incident.'

'Water?'

'He took a vase from the cupboard, filled it up from the sink in the toilets and threw the whole lot over her as she walked into the room.'

'You're joking. What happened?'

'She just sat there in a heap and cried. Of course, Penny went crazy. One of the girls told her and apparently she was about to hit him when Ian ran in and stopped her.'

'What did the parents say?'

'They blamed Debra and said the school had let him down. We wanted more to be done but it was out of our hands. Ian just isn't ever firm enough.'

'Well, I'll have to keep my eye on him.'

'I'm here if you need any help. In fact, some of the staff are great to turn to when times get tough.'

Amy just smiled. Bertie didn't seem all bad. Maybe too lippy for his own good, but right now it was nothing she couldn't handle.

The children sat down neatly in their rows as small odds and ends were tossed about in the crowd. Amy checked that her class was in order and then took her seat next to Alison.

Soon, the volume dropped as Ian addressed the school.

He rambled on about the importance of a new year and everything that came with it. Debra seemed enthralled. Penny looked bored. A mixture of amusement and indifference filtered along the line of teachers and ended at two vacant seats by the wall. There was also a wide gap between the last row of children and the back of the room. Clearly the top year was absent.

After a poem and some singing, Ian introduced Amy to the school before bringing assembly to a close.

'Well, you're probably all aware that quite a few of us are missing.' He eyed the empty spaces at the back of the room. 'That is because the Year Sixes are on their Wicker Sands trip. They'll be back on Thursday and we'll be hearing all about their adventures.'

'Odd to be away at the beginning of term, but they had to reschedule,' whispered Alison. 'The lodge had double booked them with another school.'

'Does anyone else have anything to add?' Ian glanced at the staff, some of whom shook their heads. 'Well, that just leaves me to wish you a good year and a lovely first day with your new teachers.'

When he reached for the door, the children began to talk amongst themselves as they prepared to leave for their classrooms.

'Ian…' Penny stood up and beckoned. She ensured she had every teacher's attention. 'I just wanted to let you all know that there will be a meeting in the staffroom on Friday morning before assembly.'

'Before assembly?' Ian squinted. 'Wouldn't it be better to have it later in the…'

'It won't take long,' Penny snapped. 'So, if everyone could be here early, I would appreciate it.'

Her sarcastic smile quickly straightened and she marched out of the door. Nigel tutted behind Amy while Debra tapped a reminder into her phone.

'Who does she think she is?' Alison muttered. 'We don't get paid overtime around here.'

'It must be urgent.'

'It won't be. She calls a meeting just to ask if she can borrow someone's stapler.'

Amy smirked.

'There's organised and there's just plain petty,' Alison continued. 'No prizes for guessing where our lovely Mrs Langtree fits in.'

***

Back in the classroom, the staggered voices merged into one as the children decorated their name plates. They babbled and scribbled, forgetting that their teacher was even there.

She was sitting at her desk, her stare climbing beyond the wave of bobbing shoulders to focus once again on the dismal room. Small coils of cobweb fell drably from the coving and dust clung to them like the sands of time. The walls looked subdued as the shade drenched them and the tree swamped the window with branches like hooks.

Amy turned to look through the only other window, where the edge of the rickety path led away out of sight. She took it in sharply like a suck from a breathing mask. How she wished she could follow it now.

'Miss Ashcroft…'

She jumped.

'I've finished!' Freya lifted her card in the air. She had written her name in capital letters, adding a grinning cat and dog.

'Very nice, Freya. And why have you drawn the animals?'

'I'm going to be a vet when I'm older.'

'Great. So, they're happy because you've made them better.'

Freya nodded and grinned at her friend.

'Has everyone else finished now?' Amy faced the desks.

Yes was the answer, so she went around the room asking each child to explain their drawings. Even Bertie had sketched a very lifelike picture of himself, which pleased

Amy.

'Is that you?' she asked him.

'Might be.'

'Can you tell us why you have drawn yourself?'

'Because you said to draw something that shows who we are.'

'Yes…'

'Well, that's who I am. Me.'

'Good.' Amy frowned, unsure of whether this was stupidity or genius.

When the whole class had talked her through their drawings, she told them to place the cards out so she could see them. But the soft lines of crayon looked insipid from a distance. Nothing seemed to shift the cloud from this doomed little space.

'Now,' Amy pressed on. 'Because it's the first day, there won't be any horrible hard work. So, what would you like to do instead?'

'Go home,' muttered Bertie.

'Oh, come on. There are lots of things to choose from. We can write some funny stories or even play games.'

There was silence, broken only by the scuffing of feet.

'Look lively!' Amy exclaimed. 'I know it's the first day back and you've loved being on holiday, but it's not that bad, is it?'

No, she thought. *Worse. Much worse.*

The quiet became unbearable until at last, Flynn spoke up.

'Miss…'

'Yes Flynn. Any suggestions?'

He paused. 'I don't like this room.'

Then Freya grimaced. 'Nor do I.'

'It's too small,' Avril piped up.

'Dark and scary too,' added Tara.

Amy glanced at their faces. They looked unsure, as if expecting to be corrected again or told to be quiet. But she suddenly found herself filling up with enthusiasm.

'Do you know what? I completely agree. So, let's do something about it. We can't move to another classroom and we can't knock this one down, but guess what we *can* do?' Heads shook bemusedly as thoughts filled the air. 'We can decorate it!'

At last, animation poured over the class like the fast onset of a rainstorm.

'Let's get out the paints and lots of coloured paper. Draw, stick or make anything you want, nice and big and colourful. We'll put everything up on the walls and windowsills. It will feel like a different place.'

At once, the children were on their feet and happiness rang out in their voices. The contents of the art cupboard gushed like a volcano and the tables danced with plasticine, neon tissue and crepe paper. As they all got to work, cutting, scrunching, and gluing, Amy took a rag and began to clean each neglected corner. She dug in her nails, defiantly erasing the cold murk of yesterday.

Reaching the chipped frame of the hut's front window, she traced a row of stepping stones to the greenhouse on the hill. Just visible was the bottom half of a figure in scruffy jeans, leaning inside the door and fiddling around with some pot plants.

'Carry on,' she instructed the class. 'I'll be right back.'

Her heels squelched into the mud as she made her way up the slope. The person was still shifting about in the glass doorway.

'Hello!' she called out.

A trowel clonked down and a balding man with a moustache emerged.

'Sorry, we haven't been introduced. I'm Amy, the new Year Four teacher.'

'Keith's the name. Caretaker, gardener, and doer of most jobs other people can't be bothered with.'

Amy grinned. 'Nice to meet you.'

'Can I help you with anything?'

'Actually, yes. We're all feeling a little claustrophobic in the end classroom.' She gestured to the hut. 'There's a tree hanging over the back window and it's blocking out all the light.'

Keith was already nodding as he shook the soil off his gloves. 'I've been meaning to get at that little jungle. The whole strip needs a good going over. Just leave it to me.'

'It's like a tomb in there,' she said with a shudder. 'But once that window is clear, it'll make a world of difference.'

'I doubt I'll be able to pull the whole thing down, but I can prune it out of the way.'

'Lovely.' Amy sighed. 'Well, I'd better get back now but thanks, I appreciate it.'

'No worries.'

Trying not to slip on the soggy blades of grass, Amy edged over to the pathway and followed the passage through a small row of hawthorns whose knotty branches formed a shelter at the bend.

Through the windows of the classroom, paint was being swirled on sheets of white. Squares and triangles were snipped alive from flat pieces of card and the beginning of a dinosaur was taking shape on a table. Amy turned at the doorway and looked back up to the greenhouse, where tiny new buds were stirring in their pots and a fresh spray of rain clattered away on the glass.

Eight

The first week was unexpectedly pleasant. The old shell of the classroom, caked in its thousand musty memories, was soon beating with a heart of hope. A paint box had exploded in a fluorescent fanfare. Glitter and marker pen lit up the walls until brightness oozed out into the souls of its inhabitants. Even Amy was beginning to feel at ease in the surroundings.

Keith had got straight to work on the tree. He could frequently be seen slogging wheelie-bins full of weeds beyond the newly-cleared back window. Now the room felt like double its size and at rare times when the rain stopped, a tapestry of sunrays wove in.

When lessons finished on Wednesday, Amy headed to her old family home, just a minute away from the school. It was the highest road in the town, where the houses soared from their driveways as if to absorb the distant seascape. Even the bungalows mounted above the ground, capturing views of the building-block town to the sash of sea lapping around the edges.

The lawns of Glynde Avenue gleamed with tireless attention and the neighbours forever outdid each other with countless home improvements. Familiar as Amy was with this stretch of road, something had often changed yet again each time she returned.

A straggly apple tree splayed out its branches behind her parents' front wall. Below it, chrysanthemums flamed against the weeds and a splash of Old Man's Beard scrambled over the leylandii. Her mother was already standing at the door and she pulled Amy straight into her arms.

'Hello, love.' Her eyes danced. 'Here at last!'

'Missed you, Mum.' Amy squeezed back.

They walked straight into the kitchen diner that had once been two separate rooms. Now, the central wall had been knocked through to create a view from the island hob which tumbled out across the town to the blue veil of the beach. In the corner, Pumpkin the cat was fast asleep in the armchair.

Melinda poured the tea and grinned at Amy as she took a plate from the fridge. 'Especially for you.'

It was Amy's favourite dessert. A chocolate crispy rice base covered in a mint mousse. Melinda had been making it for years.

'You did that just for me?'

Melinda brushed a hand against Amy's jaw, where her bruising had become barely visible.

'It's the least you deserve after all you've been through.' Tears filled her eyes as she gazed at her daughter. 'I just wish you'd move back in with us for a while.'

'Mum, I've got too much stuff.' Amy shook her head and dug straight into the cake. 'Anyway, it's nice being near the sea.'

'Well, at least you're only down the road, I suppose,' Melinda shrugged. 'Is the job helping to take your mind off things?'

'It's definitely different.'

'I bet it's changed since you were last there.' Melinda perched on a chair in her pale citrus dress, her hair in its usual soft waves and a dainty opal brooch pinned to her cardigan.

'You wouldn't recognise much of it. There's a whole new lower block now.'

'Is that where you are?'

'No.' Amy's face fell. 'I'm in one of those huts at the bottom.'

'Still standing are they? They looked battered when you were there.'

'They're a bit worse for wear, but we're working on it.'

'So, let's have the gossip then, love. Anyone still around that I might remember?'

'Luckily, no.' Amy sighed, reliving the relief she still felt about that aspect. 'They're all completely new.'

'Good.' Melinda put down her mug. 'Because monkeys could have done a better job than some of that lot who were there when you were young. Who was that one doing Ouija boards at breaktime?'

'I don't know.'

'And the music teacher who had her teeth moulded into that paperweight?'

'Really?' Amy cut another chunk of crispy cake.

'Mind you, they weren't all bad. That Mr Rowntree was a great Headmaster. He went off to New Zealand, you know.'

'Right.'

'Anyway, I'm just so glad you're back.'

'So am I.' Amy contemplated. 'I think.'

'And are you OK?' Melinda took her hand. 'You know, after everything that's happened with Nathan?'

She swallowed at the mention of his name.

'I just want to forget it now. Carry on with my life.'

'Well, you are doing. And you're safe here.'

'I know,' she nodded. 'Strangely, I feel like I am.'

They chatted on until a car laboured up the drive, followed by a screeching handbrake. The cat looked annoyed as she pricked up her ears and grudgingly chewed at her paws.

'Oh, why does he have to come right up the slope?' Melinda left the table and unrolled some foil from a drawer. 'Here, I'll wrap this up for you. If your dad claps eyes on it, he'll eat the whole…'

Stan's whistling burst into the room as he stepped inside and greeted Amy. He guided the couple's wagging terrier through the door and instantly caught sight of the cake.

'Ooh, lovely!'

Melinda held the foil in mid-air. 'Do you want some?'

'I'd love some.' Stan sat down at the table while Melinda

jabbed a slice off with the force of an axe on a limb. Pumpkin raised a claw to the dog as he swooped over to lick her.

'Wolf!' Melinda clapped her hands. 'Leave my Pumpkin alone.'

'Don't be harsh with him, Lindy.' Stan turned his attention to Amy. 'How's our little teacher doing?'

'It's going well so far.'

'Are they pleased with you then?'

'Well, it's too early to know that yet, Dad.'

'You wait until they see what you can do. I'd come down there and tell them myself if I could.'

'Yes, she wants to keep her job you know,' Melinda muttered.

'Guess what, Lindy?' Stan ignored her. 'I'm taking up the double bass.'

'God help us.' Melinda raised her eyes to the ceiling. 'Where are you going to put that?'

'The spare room.'

'And what about my sewing machine?'

'That can go in the garage.'

Melinda swept over to the sink and slammed the taps on.

'You know what this is about, don't you, sweetheart?' Stan asked Amy, gesturing towards Melinda. 'It's because she didn't like the flowers I got her this morning.'

Foam flew into the air as Melinda dunked a bowl into the water. 'They were from someone else's garden, for heaven's sake.'

'Dad!' Amy shot a look at Stan who bit his lip craftily.

'Oh, not you as well. They were hanging over the wall and she wouldn't have seen anyway.'

'She?' Melinda was curious. 'Tell me it wasn't someone we know.'

'Yes, old Mrs Braithwaite. The one with the face like a gooseberry.' Stan's smile was as broad as daylight.

'Oh, Stan!' Melinda shuddered at Amy. 'We got a warning letter from the council because Wolf keeps digging up her garden. Your dad refuses to keep that dog on a lead.'

'Well, that's all right then, I'm off the hook,' Stan chuckled. 'At least it won't be *me* she'll blame for the disappearing flowers!'

He nodded at the dog and kissed his daughter before making his way to the garage.

'Anyway Mum, I'd better go.' Amy yawned. 'Still two more days of work to get through before the weekend. I need an early night.'

'Speaking of which, Vanessa and Giles are coming for dinner on Saturday. Why don't you join us?'

'Yeah, I might do.'

'I hope you're eating well.' Melinda winked as she held out the foil-wrapped cake. 'You teachers need sustenance.'

***

The next morning, a strange spillage of sun gilded the trees as they trembled in the wind. Rainclouds were whittled to fine fishbone streaks under a circular thumbprint of shining primrose yellow.

In the school car park, a gunmetal hatchback cruised into a space and the passenger window slid open. Amy didn't notice until Alison called her name.

'All right?'

'Hi.' She smiled back, locking her car.

'Looking forward to more fun then?'

'Can't wait.'

'No two days are the same. Some people would say that's a good thing, but I beg to differ.' Alison buzzed her window back up and got out of the car, flinging her handbag over the shoulder of her suede jacket.

'It's not so bad right now.' Amy was almost startled to hear herself. 'They're being pretty good.'

'Even Bertie?' Alison glanced at her sideways.

'He seems to be keeping his head down.'

'Well, my lot are driving me insane. Last year's class was much easier.'

'It's just about keeping calm, isn't it? The more worked up I get, the more they seem to grind me down. Easier said than done sometimes though.'

'Mine fight and play up like there's no tomorrow. I feel like tearing my hair out before I even get here each day. Mind you, having a moron for a husband doesn't help.'

'Really?'

'Oh, I love him to pieces.' Alison's voice filled with affection. 'He's just got the intelligence of a burst balloon sometimes. So have I though, to be fair. I guess that makes us a perfect couple!'

Amy laughed.

'Got a Prince Charming in your life?'

'Not anymore. There was someone in Popplewell, but it just didn't work out.'

'Is that why you moved?'

Amy took a breath and felt as if she could tell Alison everything. Then she coughed and came to her senses.

'It was one of the reasons. But I was getting bored anyway and just wanted to come ho... here. Somewhere different.'

Home. She had nearly said home.

'And I'm sure you've got different!' Alison exclaimed. 'Mission accomplished then.'

'Suppose so.'

'Well, here goes another day. Let's do lunch in the staffroom and continue our chat.'

'Sounds good,' agreed Amy, although she hoped they would steer clear of Nathan and anything related to her familiarity with Flintley.

'I've got a TV session in the top unit,' Alison said, backing away. 'But see you at lunch if not before.'

As Amy approached the steps on the way to class, Penny appeared in the opposite direction. She wore a puffball velvet skirt and a pair of mustard boots that looked like wellies. Reeking of the usual stale cigarettes, she smiled at Amy with slightly stained teeth.

'Amy! How is your first week going?'

'Good thank you,' she answered warmly. 'Feels like I've been here for a year sometimes.'

'They're not giving you too much trouble then?' Penny seemed genuinely pleased. 'To be honest, they're always better behaved when you're new. I doubt you'll say the same thing when we're halfway through the term.'

'They're much happier in the classroom now they've brightened it up. Thanks to them it looks so much...'

'Faye!' Penny's attention sprung away to a woman wearing canteen uniform with a brassy head of highlights. 'Your hair looks amazing.'

In a second, Amy was left standing on the spot while the pair rushed away up the corridor. Resolving not to be offended, she put it to the back of her mind.

By midmorning, the classroom was so warm that the windows were flung wide open. Outside, trees jiggled with bouncing birds and every speck of green was coated in sunshine.

Keith had been tending to the vegetable patch and lugging bags of compost from the shed, but now he had parked his wheelbarrow on the grass behind the classroom. He guided a hose around the hut, quenching the earth with fast jets of water where he had just planted a row of new saplings.

'Are you all listening?' Amy asked the class. 'Because today we start our first topic.' The interest sparked, so she continued. 'We're going to find out all about bread.'

Claps and chatter echoed around the room.

'You'll discover when and how it was first made and learn all the history. We'll be looking at types, recipes, and how it is eaten in lots of different cultures.'

'But Miss,' Flynn said with a frown. 'Won't our picture board look a bit boring? All our drawings will be of bread.'

'Who said you're doing drawings?' Amy asked. 'Next

week, we're going to be making a special dough which we'll shape into anything you like. We will paint and glaze it, and then we can hang each one up on our wall.'

Some of the girls cheered and Flynn was deep in thought, as if already imagining what he might make.

'Now, back to today.' Amy handed out the tablets. 'We'll learn a bit about it first. Then you can read these links and get ready for a little test later.'

While the class worked in groups and scrolled through the details, Amy attached a loaf-shaped banner to the theme board and pierced the cork with drawing pins, ready for next week's dough creations.

Lunchtime soon arrived and once the children had scampered away, Amy left the hut to meet Alison. Ian and Nigel were sat at the coffee table, leafing through an assortment of papers while dipping into their food. Nigel waved with his apple while Ian greeted her with a mouthful of pork pie. She smiled and put the kettle on before nestling into a comfy chair in the far corner of the room.

The door swung open at Alison's arrival.

'Sorry!' She perched on another seat. 'Got held up with a few tears.'

'Oh no, what happened?' Amy flipped the lid off her salad.

'Lorna Wilcox, you know, the little redhaired girl? Well, I put her in a group with the Salter twins and they chucked her out.'

'Why?'

'Because they only ever want to work with each other and not with anyone else.'

'So, what did you do?'

'Put her with Molly and Lexie. And I made the twins work separately – they didn't like that one bit.' Alison chuckled. 'Good morning for you?'

'Not bad. I told them about the bread theme.'

'Ah yes! That has just reminded me. There's a trip coming up in a few weeks' time which might be interesting to do as a joint thing. It's…'

Penny's loud laugh silenced the other voices.

'I'd hardly say you're fat, unlike some people around here. I mean have you *seen* Alison lately?'

Faye shot Penny a wary look as they entered the room.

'Alison…' Penny's cheeks inflamed and she glanced down at the floor. 'How's it going?'

'Fine. What were you saying?'

'Oh, nothing.' She waved her hand. 'I was just asking Faye if she'd seen you. I was wanting a word about some… spelling tests.'

'Right.'

'We'll talk about it later.'

She scuttled out, followed closely by Faye, and the door clicked shut. Alison was a perfectly healthy build and Amy was stunned at Penny.

'I can't believe I just heard that.'

Alison forced out a chuckle. 'Oh, I'm used to it. She just has it in for certain people for no good reason.'

But Amy watched as her hungry chews turned to tiny nibbles.

'You've got a great figure,' she encouraged with a knowing look. 'I'd see that as a reason.'

'That's nice of you.' Alison dropped her last square of sandwich back into her lunchbox. 'But I know I've put on a few pounds lately.'

'You're fine how you are.' Amy lowered her voice. 'I'd rather look like you any day.'

Alison still seemed doubtful, but Amy made tea and they changed the subject, chatting through the rest of the break about what they'd been up to in the holidays.

Five minutes before lunchtime ended, there was a loud knock at the door and the sound of a dozen shrieking voices rang outside in the corridor. Nigel hopped up from his seat and put his head out into the commotion before leaning back in and beckoning to Amy.

'Some of your class want a word.' His eyebrows arched

above his glasses as he held the door open.

The cluster of children scurried around Amy and all tried to talk in unison.

'One at a time!' She silenced them quickly. 'Now, what's the matter?'

'Miss!' shouted Freya. 'You've got to come to the classroom.'

The startled girl ran off down the corridor followed by the rest of the children.

'Sorry,' said Amy apologetically to Alison. 'Got to go.'

'What is it?'

'No idea. I've just been summoned.'

'I'll come with you then.'

More children had gathered outside the hut and others were spilling into the cloakroom, their faces visibly excited and shocked.

Water seeped from the entrance and the outer mat was soaked through. Amy immediately skidded to a halt as she reached the open door of her classroom. The whole carpet was inches deep and lifting in places off the ground. Notebooks floated in the growing pool which rippled as it built above the floor. A rapid spray was pouring from the hosepipe that was carelessly draped over the windowsill, pointing straight into the classroom.

Amy raced up the slope, following the line of the hose until she reached the tap behind the greenhouse. She twisted it frantically until the hissing stopped.

Ian sped out of the main building and down the path, his tie flying over his shoulder in an almost comedic fashion. He peered in disbelief through the window and took in the state of the classroom. As if unaware of the mass of water, he trudged all the way to the centre.

'Keith!' he bellowed, emerging seconds later with his drenched trousers sticking tightly to his shins. 'Where is Keith?'

'No sign of him since I've been standing here. Maybe he's still having lunch,' Alison suggested.

'Just wait until I get my hands on...' He noted the children who were gathered before him, some looking serious and others smirking at their Headteacher's sopping wet legs and the liquid squishing from his shoes.

'Mrs Huckleberry, your room has had a narrow escape. We'll get some old sheets down in the doorway to prevent any flooding coming through, but it's still fine.' He turned to Amy. 'Miss Ashcroft, I'm afraid your room is completely out of use for now.'

'Does that mean we can go home, Miss?' Flynn's eyes brightened.

'No, I don't think so,' Amy replied uncertainly. 'We'll just use a different room instead. Is there an empty one anywhere?'

'Now, let's think...' Ian looked glum but then clicked his fingers with a solution. 'Go to the hut on the field. Year Six are back from their residential trip but most have gone straight home. The rest are only doing outdoor games and they won't be using the room today. We'll see where we are on Monday with the state of play down here.'

She smiled gratefully and led her class away, just as Keith came strolling along with his flask and lunchbox. Ian cleared his throat and marched away to the unsuspecting caretaker.

***

As the afternoon crept by, Amy relished every second in her favourite classroom, watching the drops of autumn sun baste the field as it wrapped around the hut. The bushes quivered softly as the wind combed through and the peace seemed to echo across the walls.

A longing tugged within her as memories unhinged themselves from every part of the room, with its soothing afternoon light and comforting acoustics. How she wished she could stay forever and cling to all she remembered here and outside, on the wide green acres. She devoured each second of being there. A snatched piece of heaven, just like it had been before.

The rising pitch of the children's voices snapped her back to the present as the shrill shouting became too much of a distraction. She stood before them and clapped her hands.

'Keep the noise down please. You're supposed to be talking about the story, not what's on TV tonight.'

Everyone sniggered in response and she softened her strict tone.

'Now, it's time for a test.' She handed out the question sheets, ignoring all the groans. 'You can work in pairs but I want it done quietly and the winners might get a treat.'

Enthusiasm peaked in the growing hush of the room and the children set to work on the questions. Amy sat on the high-legged chair, rubbing her temples to ease her slight headache. Now that the endless noise had died down, she could just make out the soft thudding of a ball game and some blurry shouts echoing from outside.

A buttery fringe streaked through the sky and a cluster of older children jostled around on the stretched patch of green beyond the window. Then a tracksuit flashed out from the monotonous ring of PE kits. It immediately captured Amy and she focused straight on the figure.

Tall and athletic, with neat, sandy hair, he was now crouched beside a small blonde girl who was next in line to bat. He nodded to the bowler who gently lobbed the ball, and with a wary pat, it flew into the air. The girl shot around the bases. Blushing at the finish, she huddled into her team while the teacher clapped triumphantly. As he turned, half squinting in the sun, Amy could see the line of his smile as his face filled with pride.

In those seconds, she could have been eleven again as she gazed, dumbstruck, out of the window at a snapshot from the past. The same vast playing field. The same noisy bursts of cheer. And the same gentle man, guiding the class like a flock of sheep.

She looked again and could no longer feel the ground.

It was Mr Craven.

Her heart felt as if the ball had landed in her chest. With hands clenched as white as a sheet, she gripped her desk, desperate for the pupils not to notice. Her knees weakened. She shook and felt sick. All she wanted to do was run, but that wasn't possible. She looked around at the class and the school that was trapping her. Locking her here in this prison.

Mr Craven swung full circle to face the hut and Amy smacked backwards as she ducked away from view. How stupid to think she could have run away from this. To return to her old school with not a soul knowing who she was. What an idiot she would look when he finally clapped eyes on her and revealed to the rest of the staffroom that she was a past pupil. How would she ever explain why she hadn't thought to mention it?

Her insides lurched as the whistle blew outside. The game was over. She rushed around the classroom collecting all the books, unable to escape the dread that poured through her body.

Once alone in the room he could walk into at any minute, she knew she had to be sensible. She was going to have to face him sometime. It was just a question of how. Should she go and see him or was it better to take the coward's way out and let it be spontaneous? The latter thought took over as she hurried to her car and swiftly drove home before he could come flying over to greet her.

Pouring out a large gin and tonic as soon as she reached the kitchen, she sipped gloomily while the sea swallowed up the pebbles under the brewing clouds. Then another thought hit her like a rush of wind. Penny's meeting.

First thing tomorrow morning, she would come face to face with the one person she wanted to avoid. And in the staffroom, clamped within the cosy circle of chairs, she would sit in half an hour's agonizing silence, waiting for his eyes to click with recognition when he saw her, just inches away. She swallowed her gin in one go and reached again for the bottle.

Nine

The alarm clanged at Amy's ear and she rolled hazily out of bed. She washed, dressed, and forced down some toast. Although she wasn't hungry, the thought of her rumbling stomach drawing attention in the meeting was enough to make her eat. She even wore a blouse in a particularly subtle shade in the far-fetched hope that she would blend into the background.

Her mouth felt parched when she opened the staffroom door, eyes fixed on the carpet as she sat down in a chair. Three teachers were already waiting and she stole a glance around the room. There were empty spaces directly opposite and another right next to her. The wait was endless. More staff chatted and made coffee before loitering over the seats while Amy silently willed them to sit down and take up all the options. Alison was next to come in and at last, she took the chair by Amy's side.

'How dull,' she whispered, retrieving her phone. 'I wonder what the silly cow wants this time.'

'Who knows?' Amy replied tensely, her eyes still on her feet.

'Are you OK?'

'Just not a great night's sleep.'

'Who is he then?' Alison winked.

'There is no he. I was just wide awake.'

'You do look quite pale, you know.'

The door creaked open again and Amy swallowed what seemed like a rock in the back of her mouth. Penny swanned in wearing a paisley dress and a mismatched cardigan in a muddy shade of green

Nigel and Gita were next to arrive and they pulled some extra chairs from the stack in the corner. As they sat down, Penny glanced at the clock and smiled tightly over the room.

'Right, I think that's everyone, so we'd better get started.'

There was an instant hush in the ring of staff.

'As you are aware, our retched computers are on their last legs and I'm pleased to announce that a whole set of brand-new machines will be installed next week.' Penny opened a box file and handed out an information sheet. 'Now,' she continued, 'I'm afraid we'll all have to learn new instructions. This information can be found online, but we'll go through each point in preparation. So, first, Step One: Starting up the system.'

Get on with it, Amy thought. Did she have to bother with the verbal drivel when it was all printed out for them anyway? The droning voice drifted over her head as she sat hunched in her chair, pretending to listen.

Five minutes passed. Penny's shrivelled lips were still moving but the sound didn't reach Amy. Everyone looked bored apart from Debra, who was crouched below Penny with her glasses pinned to her nose, chipping in suggestions. Amy's knuckles whitened around her pen. If only Debra would stop talking, Penny might finish quicker and they could all get out of there.

They reached Point Four of Twelve and Amy was beginning to lose patience. Twenty more minutes at the most and they would have to stop for assembly.

Another snatched look at the time. Fifteen minutes to go. They were on Point Six and halfway through. A glimmer of calmness began to filter through and maybe, just maybe, she was off the hook for longer. As the second hand clicked away on its journey around the clock, Amy softened her shoulders into the chair. It was late now anyway. Far too late for anyone else to show up.

The door burst open. Penny glared in annoyance as Ian's

head slid into view. His red-cheeked face broke into a smile which didn't reflect itself in her expression.

'So sorry for the timing.' He breezed into the room. 'We got caught up discussing the swimming tournament of all things!'

He grinned at the door and Amy sat, cold and dazed, as a familiar figure eased his way sideways and followed Ian to stand against the kitchen unit with Amy's side of the circle in full view.

Shaking like jelly, she attempted to focus on Penny, trying with all her might to think about something other than this unimaginable feeling. If luck was on her side, he would be so deeply absorbed in the subject of shiny new computers that nothing could possibly distract him.

She fought with herself as the dark blond hair pushed its way into her vision with each stubborn blink. Forcing him out of her view, she tilted her head in the opposite direction, even covering half her face with a hand while trying to look as relaxed as possible. It was like a time bomb waiting to go off, the second-hand crawling threateningly around the clock.

Now Ian started to add his comments after every sentence Penny uttered, throwing in the odd joke to lighten the atmosphere. All heads kept turning in his direction, but Amy couldn't bring herself to look.

At long last, Penny thanked everyone for attending and the teachers began reaching for their bags. Amy focused on the door, ready to launch through it as soon as they started to leave.

'Are there any questions before we call it a day?' Penny asked.

'Actually… yes,' Debra started up.

Amy could have cried.

'I just wondered if a similar information sheet will be allocated to the children.'

'Absolutely,' Penny answered. 'In fact, if you are around this afternoon, we could go through it together.'

'Great!' Debra looked euphoric. 'What sort of time?'

Amy screamed from within. Why did everyone have to stick around and listen while all this was going on?

'Let's say, two?'

'Perfect. My class is cooking then, so I'm free.'

'See you back here then, Debra,' Penny smiled.

Everyone began to get up and make their way to the door. Amy revelled in the feeling of her feet on the ground as she stood and turned to go. In the corner of her eye, she could see the back of Mr Craven's head as he chatted to Ian. Time to make her exit.

'Anyone else?' Penny's sharp voice barked across the room. 'Amy, you look confused.'

Amy nearly choked on her breath. The bustle of the room fell silent. Debra's gaze widened through her glasses, Alison grinned by her side and it was like slow motion as Mr Craven broke away from Ian and turned to look straight at her.

'Not at all,' she replied as convincingly as possible. 'Just taking everything in.'

Penny nodded and glided out of the room, followed by most of the staff.

'Of course you are!' Ian's voice boomed behind her. 'I have to keep reminding myself that you're new to us, Amy.'

She gulped. What next? Was he going to introduce her to Mr Craven? She threw a quick grin in Ian's direction and bolted out of the door.

The children were already filing into the hall, but she rushed into the toilets to calm down. She let slow inhalations ease into her body and tried to gain some composure. Assembly would be the next trial, but at least the ordeal in the staffroom was over.

Trying to remain discreet, she slipped into the hall where the teachers were all seated in their line. Ian took his usual place at the foot of the stage, ready to begin his story. At least he was the centre of attention now and all eyes were no longer on Amy.

She scaled the length of her class, checking each child

was sitting up straight and listening to Ian. As she reached the end of the row, her eyes rose to the seated teachers. A repetitive outline of profiles was regimental along the curve, but one face at the end stood out from the crowd.

He wasn't focusing on Ian or watching the children. Through the subtle glance she managed to take, she saw that he was smiling and his strong blue eyes were fixed firmly on her. Grinning shyly back, she looked away, but his stare remained glued like a magnet. She checked again from the corner of her eye and he still hadn't stopped looking.

Did he know her so instantly from that distance? Clearly he did. She looked once more in the hope that he'd turned away. No such luck. His face beamed and she shuddered with embarrassment. He blatantly remembered her, but did he have to stare so intensely?

Her cheeks felt hot as she watched the recollection, the memories, ignite his expression. She felt like a child again, small as a mouse and very out of place. It was as if she didn't belong there anymore. Like she didn't *deserve to*.

The smile continued to burn through her. There was no doubt that he recognised her now. The hopeless one. The one who couldn't even do times tables or throw a netball through a hoop. She wished he wouldn't stare like that, but she knew what he was thinking. Why was someone like Amy showing her face around here again? Who did she think she was, trying to educate children when she'd been the worst-performing pupil in her class?

As Ian rounded off his story, Amy glanced back at the still-watching face and took a deep breath of defeat. She felt like a rabbit in the headlights. There was no choice now but to come clean.

Assembly ended, but she didn't make for the door. Instead, she stayed cool and calm, waiting for it to happen. The inevitable voice sounded almost instantly in her ear.

'Amy?'

Pausing for a moment, she took her time and spun slowly around to greet him.

'Yes.' She smiled, feeling her stomach somersault. 'It's me.'

She was met with the same soulful blue eyes she had always remembered, that darted at her now like arrows. He locked her in a piercing smile and she drowned in a puddle of inhibition. She traced his skin down to the base of his neck and could hardly believe twenty years had gone by. He had changed to an extent, but the few soft lines on his forehead did nothing to detract from the vigour of his gaze and the lean physique that he still naturally possessed.

'Joel Craven.' He shook her hand. 'How long has it been?'

Amy didn't know where to look. 'I really have no idea.'

'Too long, I'd say.'

'None of that matters anymore,' she answered almost bluntly. 'I'm all about the here and now.'

His face changed and he looked more serious. 'I've been away on a trip,' he explained. 'That's why it's taken so long for us to meet.'

Amy widened her eyes. He hadn't been referring to the years that had passed since he'd taught her – he was talking about the few days of his absence. And what did he mean by *meet*? She pondered for a moment. Did he really recognise her at all?

'I was surprised to hear you'd got the job actually,' he said matter-of-factly.

Amy's heart sank. He knew her, all right. This was exactly what she'd feared. He'd remembered all her ineptitude and didn't think she was worthy. Her toes twisted in her shoes. Why was she even standing here in this gym, trying to hold an intelligent conversation? It was like being a schoolgirl all over again and scrutinized for her faults. Only he had never made her feel inadequate until this very moment.

'They were considering a guy from Redcott for weeks but they changed their minds at the last minute,' Joel elaborated.

She was thrown again by his response. He really didn't seem to register. And despite the clues she'd given in this scrambled conversation, there was still a chance that Joel hadn't twigged. Amy's face lit up slightly and she tested with a question.

'So, how long have you been here now?'

'Twenty-three years and still counting. It never felt right to move on.'

'You must feel like you're in a completely new school though. It's so different from how it used to be.'

He stared back at her and raised an eyebrow. 'You remember it?'

This confirmed it. Joel didn't have the faintest idea who she was. She could hardly believe she'd been spared the humiliation in the worst way it could possibly have been discovered. A part of her itched to tell him everything. To remind him of all they had shared. But as she looked deep into his unknowing eyes, she just couldn't bring herself to do it.

There was something in the way he was gazing at her now. The smile and the tone. The respect. If she blew it all away by being too honest, she might never live it down.

She had only spent minutes in his company, but the fear was suddenly overwhelming. For some inexplicable reason, she couldn't let this go. She had to carry on like she had never known him and resist ever hinting they had any kind of history. That girl was dead and buried now and here was her chance to be sure of it.

Joel Craven would see her in a whole new light and she would do her utmost to keep it that way. He would never find out the truth. And he didn't need to know. She would take this opportunity and run with it. Then her past would be permanently erased.

'I've seen pictures,' she replied, with more confidence. 'Everything's changed so much.'

Joel's face broke into another grin. 'That would explain it. Anyway, we'd better get to class but if there's anything I can do, just give me a shout.'

'Thank you, I will.'

She watched in amazement as Joel vanished from the room. Unsure of whether to run for her life or delight in her newfound freedom, she slipped shakily up to the top unit, vowing to keep her secret past forever locked away.

Amy's class took up temporary residence in the TV area, which was overlooked by Joel's classroom. She pretended not to notice when he walked down the steps and spoke to his class before leading them to the field.

It was so strange, just knowing she could look him in the eye and he wouldn't see the young girl who had once been his pupil. Before disappearing, he glanced at her through the glass and sent an awkward chill along her veins.

But when he wasn't looking, she couldn't help but stare. It was like she was a thief, stealing images and movements when he had no idea who was watching. She compared him to the picture – the young man on the boat. His smile was as warm as she remembered, with its slightly sideways curve. The deep voice swam around her head for the first time in years. She could still hear the words of yesterday, filling her up with hope. But she was most thankful for his eyes. Assertive yet gentle and always as blue as day. Now, in a secret way, perhaps she could keep them near again.

By home time, the sky was a smoky shadow, clogged up with clouds and pelleting rain. The ground was speckled with the start of the downpour, so Amy dashed to her car. She placed her bag on the passenger seat and then hurried round to climb in.

'Amy?' Her back stiffened. Joel was behind her, his keys jangling. 'Good week then?'

'It's not been too bad.' She instinctively tilted her umbrella to cover part of her face.

'Good. As I said, I'm always around if you need a hand with anything.'

'Thanks, I'll remember that.' Amy forced some warmth into her voice and glanced up at the weather.

'Better get home before the sky caves in. Have a good

weekend.' Joel backed towards his navy BMW with a quick wave.

'You too. See you Monday.'

Sliding into her seat, she breathed away the tension. It was one thing to be confident when Joel was at a distance, but face to face would take more time. The closer he came, the more naked she felt – as if she was being peeled away with every smile. She watched in her rear-view mirror as he drove obliviously out of sight.

***

On Saturday evening, Amy boxed up a carrot cake she had baked for Stan and Melinda. With a slick of lip gloss to match her damson sweater, she set off in the car.

The sky looked murky and metallic as the rows of cloud blackened the world below. Turning down Glynde Avenue, she parked against the kerb and Wolf ran out to greet her when Stan opened the door.

'Hello, sweetheart!' He pulled her over the threshold. 'Give us a cuddle.'

Melinda squeezed past them but soon returned, dragging the dog behind her.

'Good to see you, love.' She kissed Amy's cheek and hurried back to the oven. A huge bowl of salad and a large baguette had already been put on the table.

'My turn to bake something for you.' Amy put the box down in front of Melinda whose eyes lit up as she took the lid off.

'That's lovely, but I'll have to hide it from you know who.'

'Wine, Amy?' Stan called over.

'No thanks, Dad, I think I'll just stick to that other stuff.'

'Pomegranate and elderflower,' he said, pouring some into a glass.

'Done anything nice today then?' Melinda asked.

'Nothing exciting, just cleaning'

'Good to do something different after a busy week at work, I suppose.'

'Definitely, I needed a break.'

'It's still going well though, isn't it?'

'Fine,' Amy replied quickly. 'I'm just getting to grips with everything, that's all.'

As Melinda opened the oven, a knock sounded at the door and voices could be heard beyond it. Amy went to let the others in.

'Hi, sis.' Vanessa hugged her and put a box on the worktop. 'I made this, Mum.'

'More cake!' Melinda enthused.

'Banana bread, actually, I know you love it.'

'Not as much as carrot cake!' Amy nodded smugly towards her tin of iced squares.

'I'll be polishing that off.' Vanessa smiled, then turned back to the door. 'Are you coming in or what?'

Giles fell inside with Wolf gripping his waist. He kissed Amy and Melinda before taking his place at the table. Vanessa pulled her chair close to him and they pecked each other intermittently on the lips while Melinda prepared the last components of dinner.

'Something smells amazing,' Vanessa called out.

'It's just lasagne. Hope that's OK.'

The cheesy topping bubbled as Melinda brought it over and set it down in the middle of the table.

'I'm starving.' Giles's brown eyes widened. 'Load me up, Lindy!'

The meal was delicious and Amy felt glad to be enjoying home cooking for the first time in so long. Vanessa took seductive forkfuls, gazing at Giles with heavily made-up eyes. He returned the gesture all the way down into the plunging neckline of her electric blue top.

'So, how's it going? All settled in?' Vanessa asked Amy as she gripped Giles's thigh under the table.

'It's been a bit crazy,' Amy replied, licking her fingers from the thickly buttered bread. 'But it's nice to be back.'

'What's the school like now? Has it changed much since we were there?'

'Quite a lot, actually. The whole main building has been refurbished.'

'That's good then.' Vanessa seemed relieved for her. 'It would freak me out if it was still exactly the same. All frozen in time like a ghost town.'

'They've done wonders. It's so different these days.'

'None of those old bag teachers are still there, are they? If you ever see Mrs Macleod, tell her I still can't stand her.'

'She's lucky on that score too,' Melinda cut in. 'They're all new, so she tells me.'

Amy opened her mouth to update Melinda, then thought better of it. Vanessa had been in Joel's class just two years after Amy and she would definitely remember him. Her mind went into overdrive, imagining all the extremities that could possibly occur once she'd told her sister that Joel was now her colleague. If Vanessa ever bumped into him, she would soon be revealing all about Woodbrook's newest teacher.

'They're all very nice though,' she said instead. 'I do feel like I've been there for years.'

'Not missing Popplewell much, then?' asked Giles, draping an arm around Vanessa.

'Sometimes.' Amy felt her eyes glisten.

'Really?' Vanessa wrinkled her nose. 'Don't tell me you've still got feelings for that scumbag.'

'You'd bloody better not have.' Stan's cheeks reddened. 'If he comes anywhere near you again, I'll…'

'Dad!' yelled Amy. 'Not if he was the last man on earth.'

'Promise?'

'Of course I do.'

'He doesn't know where you are, does he? You weren't daft enough to tell him where you were going?'

'Do you think I'm stupid?' Amy raised her eyebrows. 'The whole reason I left was because of him and you actually think I would tell him my whereabouts?'

'Don't bite my head off, sweetheart. I'm just concerned,

that's all.'

'No need to be. I've moved on and I will never see him again.'

'Yeah, but don't go all single on me.' Vanessa beamed at Giles. 'There are some good ones out there.'

'I'll always treat you right, babes.' Giles rested his chin on her shoulder. She turned to him and leaned in for another long kiss.

Amy smiled at Melinda as if begging her to change the subject. She could still hear the mouths slapping together and could think of a million things she would rather observe.

As the family feasted on sticky toffee pudding, the conversation switched to the luxury spa break that Giles had booked for himself and Vanessa.

For a moment, Amy's mind slipped away to Nathan. Now that she really thought about it, the pain had become indifference. She had left Popplewell stinging from the heartbreak, but her time with him now seemed like lightyears away. In fact, she was beginning to wonder if she had ever really loved him at all.

But it made no difference now. Her future was just beginning and anyway, did she honestly miss being in a relationship? She glanced over at Vanessa, who was now straddling Giles and sliding dessert into his mouth. No, Amy decided. No, she did not.

Ten

Three weeks later and autumn had arrived. Clouds wisped invisibly against the marbled sky and the mornings were sifted in sugary frost. The bones of trees were jagged against the landscape, their leathery leaves like shrivelled skin in clumps on the ground.

Bonfire ash tinged the air and swirled with the breath of cold lips and noses, so to spend time in the warm school kitchen was a welcome opportunity for Amy. She watched in satisfaction as each child shaped their dough and squeezed it to life with their busy little hands.

Alison came to join her at breaktime while she stayed behind to bake the shapes.

'Looking good.' She took in a sniff of the floury aroma. 'Any leftovers I can pinch?'

'It's not edible, remember? It hardens so they can paint it.'

'I hope my lot will do as well as yours.' Alison peered inside the oven. 'Ah, that reminds me. I've got a brilliant idea.'

'What?'

'Year Six are studying windmills. Just started last week.'

'Right.'

'Well?' Alison held out both hands as if her point was obvious. 'Ties in with our topic, doesn't it?'

'I suppose so.'

'And Joel's taking his class to Punch and Judy, the twin windmills over in Brittlehurst, for a trip. They're going to learn how flour is made and the whole process from wheat to bread.'

'OK.' Amy sounded slightly more interested. 'I'll get him to bring us back some info.'

'No!' Alison rolled her eyes. 'You should go with him and then I could take mine when Martin goes with the other Year Sixes. It'll be great for the kids to mix things up a bit.'

Amy swallowed quickly. 'Oh no, I don't think so.'

'Why not? Amy, you've gone pale. Aren't you feeling well?'

'I'm fine.' She tried hard to smile. 'Maybe it's a bit short notice. I wouldn't want to invade something he's organised.'

'He'd be thrilled, honestly. He loves it when there's a joint effort thing going on. Learning from each other and all that. I'll have a word with him if you like.'

'No, don't!' Amy was shocked at her own harsh tone. 'Sorry, I mean… I'll think about it.'

'OK.' Alison nodded with a look of perplexity. 'Don't think I'm trying to push you. I just thought it would be fun.'

'I know and I appreciate it.' She smiled more meaningfully this time. 'I'll keep it in mind, I promise.'

'Brilliant.' Alison winked. 'Better get down to the playground anyway. Nigel's swapped shifts with me so I'm on duty.'

'Catch up with you later.' Amy waved, concentrating on the gently browning dough.

She felt guilty for rejecting Alison's suggestion, but this was a situation she wasn't ready to get into. It was fine to pass Joel in the corridor. Fine to chat about how she was getting on. But to spend a whole day with him on a school trip? That was unchartered territory and she would be seriously out of her depth. He might ask one too many questions and she couldn't be sure of holding back the truth. Thinking on the spot was not one of her strong points and she would rather not demonstrate this obvious lack of skill.

As the day went on, Amy let it go. Seeing what the class had achieved completely eclipsed her worries. There were toothy smiles with bright red mouths brushed in bold, oily shades onto the dough. Even Bertie's scarecrow figure, with its dark, scowling face, was undoubtedly impressive, even if not quite as jovial as the others.

Alone at home time, she finished the display and was tidying the last of the clutter from the classroom when a tap on the window startled her. Joel waved as he gazed through the glass, then promptly entered the hut.

Amy shivered with equal measures of doubt and unease.

'Hi there,' he put his head around the door. 'How are you doing?'

'Really good. You?'

'Could be better. I don't like this cold weather really.' He gestured towards the hostile breeze and the sparse foliage it mauled outside.

'You always did love your summer sports.' For a split second she watched the sky, lowering itself like a cloak over the daylight. Then reality hit her when she realised what she'd said. 'Apparently… so I'm told.'

'Well, there's always skiing,' he joked.

Amy was on edge. Keeping up this pretence was tiring as well as terrifying.

'Anyway, I just wanted to run something by you.' Joel pointed to the display board with its colourful coating of dough.

She sighed in defeat, knowing what was coming.

'We've got a trip soon to Punch and Judy. They're twin windmills in the countryside at Brittlehurst. One is still in full swing and the other is preserved as a point of interest. I just thought it would be great for your class to do the same.'

'Sounds fantastic. I'll look into it.'

'No, I mean…' Joel stared at her intently, the blue of his eyes igniting. 'Come with us.'

'Joel, I don't know. There's a lot going on in the next few weeks.'

'It's only one day,' he pressed. 'There must be some time

you can set aside.'

'I'd have to look at my diary.' Amy felt her protests weakening by the second.

'This is a great opportunity for your class, Amy.' His voice changed this time. It was more commanding, like it used to be when he had tried to encourage her as a reluctant child. 'Surely you'd want them to get the best out of this, wouldn't you?'

'Yes, of course.' She caved in as he coaxed her to go for it, just like he had in the old days. 'OK, we'll come. If you're sure we're not going to be too much trouble.'

She could almost feel her school tie, tight around her collar, and the growing tint of pink heating up her cheeks.

'The more the merrier.' He glowed, triumphant that he'd convinced her. 'You won't regret this.'

Amy's forced smile disappeared as something familiar tugged away inside. The pride that pumped out of him, just from being able to help, was still as alive as it had always been. Those little kicks of happiness she used to feel were back with the click of a finger.

'You're right. I want them to do well and if this helps them, all the better.'

'Great.' Joel walked to the door. 'We'll get it organised later in the week.'

'Sounds good. And thanks for thinking of us.'

He beamed back at her and vanished from the hut, leaving her to contemplate the agreement she had just made.

***

On the day of the trip, the coach sped down the highway and then edged further inland to the steep, chalky countryside. Excitement buzzed over the engine and the seats were crammed with a sea of multicoloured raincoats. Amy sat at the front, directly ahead of her class while Joel was on the opposite side, scrolling on his tablet.

Wild grass drooped in crystallised mops beneath bushes

that rusted with bronze. Claret blackberries gleamed through brambles and wove intermittently with the glistening remnants of spider webs. Rain fell in dewy sheets against the slate of sky, spritzing patterns on the moving windows.

A huge windmill emerged on the hillside. It had white panels and majestic sails which reached into the air and almost touched the ground. Beyond it, the outline of a smaller mill was visible.

The teachers introduced themselves to the tour guides, Brian and Iris, before leading the children out of the coach in a loud crescendo of enthusiasm. The morning progressed with Amy's class starting off at Judy, while Year Six went to learn all about Punch. Then, they would swap for the afternoon, only coming together at the end. Iris made it fun, taking them through a slideshow and passing large plates of fresh bread around to taste.

Time flew to a lunch break and both classes set off down a path to the picnic area. With the children walking behind, Joel stayed next to Amy. They followed the lines of flint and grass, scuffed grey by the scalp of earth. Barbed wire guarded each side of the pathway, as if to keep the two of them no more than an inch apart.

She could almost feel his breath against her cheek and the rustle of his anorak, rubbing her thin raincoat. But he squinted straight ahead into the mist as it netted over the sky.

They entered a small clearing where the view swept down over the countryside. The hills were a montage of heather and maize, all layered up like they had been spread over with condiments. Tiny cars beetled like toys along an invisible road and the scarf of sea wrapped itself eerily around the edges.

The children sat at the wooden tables and Joel joined Amy on a higher mound of green. As he unwrapped his food, a smile played on her lips. Seeded granary bread stuffed full of cheese and pickle and a packet of salt and vinegar crisps. It was the same combination she had seen many times before, years ago on his desk.

She glanced at him while he looked away. Strands of windswept hair fell like hay over his forehead and his steel eyes lifted as he took in the sights of the landscape.

No words were exchanged as they sat there, ensconced in the noise of the eagerly hungry children, but Amy found the silence hard to swallow. Dread touched her nerves with the risk of recognition. His sudden realisation that he knew her after all. She had to say something. Anything to make him talk and allow her to gauge what was on his mind.

'Cheese and pickle again? Nothing changes, does it?'

'Sorry?' Joel looked her straight in the eye.

The fruit juice strained her throat with a sudden hard gulp. She opened her mouth for a moment but nothing came out.

A snigger of amusement washed over his face. 'Are you usually this clued up about what we colleagues eat for lunch?'

'Didn't you have exactly the same thing yesterday?' Amy answered quickly.

She hadn't even seen him yesterday. She looked bewilderingly down into her napkin. 'That sounded really rude. I just meant...'

But Joel was chuckling. 'I'll have to spice up my sandwich fillings from now on if the food police are going to be checking.'

'Ignore me.' Amy's face flushed with embarrassment. 'I suppose I just get quite fascinated with what people like to eat. It says a lot about them.'

'Really?' he asked curiously, holding a crust in the air. 'So, what does this tell you about me?'

'I don't know. You're... content. Comfortable in your own skin.' She looked confidently into his eyes while her whole body felt as if it would cave in. Inside, she was begging herself to stop talking.

Joel looked thoughtful, his eyes narrowing into familiar slices of blue. 'That's not a bad theory. You've got me figured out, that's for sure.'

'Seriously, I don't stay awake at night analysing

everyone's eating habits.'

'Maybe not, but you're clearly very observant.'

Amy rolled her eyes and glanced out at the steamy swell of coastline.

'I'm impressed,' Joel added, bringing her face to face with him again. He beamed at her just how he used to, when she'd got a good mark in a maths test. She peeled her satsuma with tense fingers and was glad to hear a pupil call for him.

Inhaling as much fresh air as she could hold, she bit her lip tight in disbelief. Every attempt to steer clear of the past was a spiel of absolute nonsense. With sandwich psychology springing to mind, it worried her what would be next.

'Amy...' She turned to see Joel's worried expression. 'There's a problem with one of my girls, Lauren Samson. She wants to talk to you.'

Without hesitation, Amy left her seat and walked over to the girl, whose brown hair fell around a face wet with tears.

'Lauren,' Amy smiled gently. 'Shall we have a chat over there?' She gestured towards some tall trees just a short distance from the picnic spot and the girl followed her.

Once they had arrived under the seclusion of the branches, it took a few moments for Lauren to speak up.

'My stomach hurts.'

'Do you think it might be something you ate?'

'No.' The girl stared at the ground. 'I'm bleeding, Miss.'

'Oh, I see.' Amy put an arm around her, finally understanding. 'Have you had this before?'

She shook her head.

'So, it's your first one. You know all about periods, don't you?'

'Yes, Miss,' replied Lauren, wiping her eyes and becoming more relaxed.

'Are your parents around today?'

'My mum is.'

'Do you think she could come and pick you up?'

Lauren nodded.

'What I'll do then, is get your friend... What's her name?'

'Gracie.'

'Gracie can stay with you while I speak to Mr Craven and then...'

'Oh, please don't...' wailed Lauren.

'I'm just going to explain that you don't feel well and your mum will be coming to get you.'

Lauren gazed at her with red eyes. 'Thank you, Miss Ashcroft.'

'You're all grown up now, so be proud.'

Amy returned to the table, looking considerably more at ease than Joel.

'Did you find out what was wrong?'

'She just doesn't feel too good. I think it's best that she goes home.'

'Are you sure it's that bad? She can't stick it out for the afternoon?' Joel frowned.

'No, she can't.'

Her knowing glare cleared him of perplexity.

'Best for her to go then.'

Amy waited with Lauren until her mother's car arrived. The girl was relieved to be collected and she waved thankfully as she left.

The remainder of the trip was a great success. Brian and Iris cracked jokes as they shared their expertise. Amy felt grateful and a little foolish that she had almost declined to come.

They boarded the coach under a sky wiped with pink, just where the sea thrashed to touch it. The clouds loomed like giant coals, leaving ashy trails in their wake. Amy leaned back in her seat, glad that the day hadn't been such torture. She wished she could kick her boots off and curl up for a sleep.

Rain dashed in watery pockets, splitting into droplets as they shattered on the glass. A gathering of crows swooped from a field and disappeared like smoke into the trees as the coach wheels churned through the wet sludge. *Some warm soup would be nice*, Amy thought. Perfect with her bread rolls from the windmill. She cosied into her lambswool scarf and watched evening fold over the daylight.

'Amy…' Joel had moved across from the window and was now perched on the aisle seat. 'I didn't thank you earlier for how you handled Lauren.'

She shook her head. 'Anyone would have done the same.'

'In all my years in this job, moments like that are always a little tricky.'

'Helps to have a girl around, I guess.'

'Yes, but it's not just that. Some of the other staff wouldn't have had as much compassion.' He gave a sideways expression which hid names he wouldn't mention.

'I just know how it feels,' Amy looked away. 'Embarrassment, self-consciousness and teachers who only end up making things worse. I never want any child to feel the way I did.'

She quickly broke off, unwilling to elaborate. She had said just enough, allowing him to know her motives, but it was time to stop before anything else came out. If only she could always have this much control.

'You had a bad time at school then.' Joel half smiled but with understanding rather than mockery.

'It wasn't great.' Amy hoped she didn't sound snappy, but she wanted to end this conversation.

'Miss Ashcroft!' yelled a voice from two seats back. Amy closed her eyes momentarily before twisting around in her seat.

'Yes, Freya. What is it?'

'We want to sing a song.'

'Right. Go ahead then.'

She began to turn away and Joel slipped back into his window seat.

'No, we want you to start it,' continued Freya.

Amy laughed. 'I don't think so. It'll sound much better coming from you.'

'Come on, Miss,' another voice piped up. Soon the whole coach was cheering her on but Joel stayed quiet, only half listening to the dialogue.

The pressure showered down, shooting tension back into her body. If she wasn't having her schooldays scrutinised, she was being harassed into singing, of all things.

But if there was one thing she could do, that she had always been able to do, it was sing. It was another secret she had kept closely guarded, but here and now, she found herself taking a breath and racking her brains.

'OK.' She stood to face the rows in front of her. Joel let his pen fall into the middle of his lap, intrigued at her show of confidence. 'Do you know Yellow Bird?'

The pupils were unfamiliar with the old camping tune Stan had taught her and Vanessa when they were younger, but it was a happy ditty and when all the parts were sung together, it chimed with fond memories.

'You'll learn it in seconds,' Amy continued. 'I'll sing it to you first and then this row up to the middle will sing the melody. There are two harmonies, so these next three rows will do the first part and the rest of you can do the final bit. So, here goes.'

The notes poured out of her mouth and sailed around the coach. With every line, she loosened up more, loving the release this feeling was giving her. Amidst gasps from the crowd at the richness of her voice, she kept her eyes fixed over the seats of animated faces.

She conducted the two classes to perfection until they were belting out the verses with all the fusion of a choir in concert. It wasn't until she knelt back on her seat, grinning triumphantly as the tune soared high, that Joel caught her sight and she had to look away.

Nothing could take the grin off his face. He looked entranced by how she was shining when she otherwise seemed so insecure. His blue eyes pierced through the dim light of the coach and his beam made her feel abruptly breathless.

Her treasured teacher was here again. The person whose approval had been her whole world was making her feel just the same. Pins and needles pulsed through her hands at the impact she knew he still had on her. It was a power that had never died.

For the first time since they'd met again, she let her smile reach down and touch his face. She held it there boldly, feeling just how much he was still inside her soul. Watching and absorbing how he stared back at her now, full of joy for the girl he didn't recognise. And completely unaware of what he was to her.

Eleven

The lemon lozenge numbed Amy's throat as she checked the prescription on the passenger seat. She'd been held up in the pharmacy after feeling unwell all weekend. Gathering her bags in the car park, the wet morning dripped over her as she emerged from shelter and walked wheezily into work.

Sue was typing away at her desk as she hurried in. The traffic had been heavy too, so she was nearly ten minutes late.

'I passed on your message.'

'Thanks.' Amy knew her pasty face didn't look its best.

'Are you sure you're well enough to be here? I can see you're under the weather.'

'I'm not too bad.' She sniffed. 'Must get to class.'

'Take it easy then,' Sue called after her as she dashed away.

She was glad to have her inhaler though and at least it would help if she felt chesty again. All she needed was an easy day and hopefully the children would behave.

But as she neared the huts, Penny came into view. Her arms were fiercely folded and she frowned straight at Amy.

'Sorry I'm a bit late. I had to pick up my prescription and...'

'In future,' Penny's tone was sharp, 'please keep your appointments out of school hours.'

Amy shook her head. 'It wasn't an appointment. There was a queue in the pharmacy. I've been ill all weekend and really needed my...'

'I don't care. We never use working time to carry out

personal duties here. Everyone else complies with that rule so I expect the same from you. Is that clear?'

'Yes.' She felt her face reddening.

'Get to class. That's ten minutes wasted now.'

Amy opened the door. 'It won't happen again.'

Penny glowered at Amy with eyes lined in white pencil, making them look almost infected. Then she swept off up the hill, her peplum blouse flapping in the cold breeze.

Amy's cheeks tingled. Today's lateness had been a first, yet Penny had still seemed incensed. And going by the noise inside the classroom, the day was about to get worse.

A fight had erupted in the centre, surrounded by a ring of shouting pupils. She swooped in on the pair embroiled in the scrap and pulled Bertie away. Flynn was lying beneath him with a beetroot face and hair fuzzed up by the friction of the carpet.

'What are you doing?' she shouted, despite her raspy voice.

'He's nicked my shoes!' boomed Bertie, making another dive at Flynn.

'Get off him!'

Amy lunged, forcing him out of the way by the back of his sweater. As he struggled to resist her force, he elbowed her hard in the ribs. In a second, he was back on the floor, pummelling into Flynn who could only hide his face while Amy recoiled in pain.

Instantly, a pair of arms flew past her, ripping Bertie away in one swift move. Then Alison marched him out into the cloakroom.

'Don't you move!' she shrieked before coming back inside, where Amy was helping Flynn to his feet. 'And as for you lot, you can sit down and be quiet or you'll all be missing breaktimes for a week.'

Sheepishly, the children slid into their seats and Alison looked explosive as the crowd began to disperse. She beckoned Amy to the cloakroom where Bertie stood in the corner, looking at the grey socks on his feet. Then she quickly returned from her room, dangling a pair of black shoes by their laces.

'I take it these are yours.' She held them out and he nodded. 'Put them on and get to Mr Farley.'

'Where did you find them?' Amy asked, still wincing from the blow.

'Kian did it earlier.' Alison crouched to Bertie's level. 'So, it wasn't Flynn at all. I have had just about enough of you. Everyone has. Let's see what Mr Farley's got to say about this and when you get back, you'll apologise to Flynn in front of the class. Understand?'

Bertie said nothing, but his eyes welled up like two bubbles waiting to burst.

'Now, get outside and wait there for me.' Alison stood up again as she watched him go. Then she turned to Amy. 'Are you OK?'

'It's only a bruise.' She played down the injury as it throbbed through her bones.

'That boys needs a serious kick up the…'

'I think I can handle it from here. Let's not get Ian involved this time.'

'And let that little turd get away with it? Are you mad? He's just beaten someone up, Amy. We don't accept violence here.'

'No, and I'll more than remind him of that but please, leave it to me.'

'Not to mention assaulting a teacher. Just wait until Ian hears about this!'

'That part was an accident. It just happened when he launched back at Flynn.'

Alison stared at her in disbelief. 'Don't make excuses for people like him. That's not doing him any favours, you know. He'll only keep behaving like an idiot.'

'I'm not going to let him get away with it. I just think I can settle this without Ian's help.'

Alison sighed. 'As long as you're sure.'

'I am. Thanks for what you did, honestly, but I am.'

'Your decision. I'd still have a word with Ian though and let him know what's happened.'

'Yes, I probably will.'

In fact, it was the last thing she would be doing. She felt bad enough with her cold and now a battered rib. Bertie might have been bang out of order, but Amy did not need Ian thinking she couldn't control her own class.

'It's your lucky day,' Alison called sarcastically to Bertie. 'Miss Ashcroft has kindly said that you can stay here and not go to Mr Farley.'

Bertie made his way back indoors and looked up, almost thankfully.

'That doesn't mean you're off the hook,' Amy said sternly. 'Believe me, you're going to be very sorry by the time the day is over. Now get back to your desk.' He obeyed and Amy glanced quickly at Alison in the hope that she'd managed to convince her.

Full of relief that the incident was over, Amy was keen to move on. Bertie was made to apologise publicly with the threat of seeing Ian if he misbehaved again. But as Flynn graciously forgave him and had escaped unscathed from the lashing, the issue was soon resolved.

Still feeling groggy and worn out by lunchtime, Amy headed for the staffroom. Peace and quiet at last. Just the clock ticking away on the wall and rain pinging like darts against the window.

The door screeched open and Ian walked across to her.

'There you are, Amy. I've been looking for you.' He smiled and she did her best to reciprocate. 'I thought we should have a chat. Is now a good time?'

She felt her insides sinking as he stretched to get a chair. Of course, this was all about the fight earlier on and the fact that she hadn't handled it properly. Alison must have talked to him because she just couldn't help being concerned. Amy composed herself, waiting for Ian to flag up her incompetence.

'So, how do you feel things are going?' he began. 'We haven't had the chance to discuss it recently.'

'I'm really happy. There can be ups and downs, but nothing I can't manage. Everything's fine.'

Ian smiled awkwardly. He shuffled in his seat before continuing. 'The thing is…'

'What a goal!' Nigel enthused as he burst through the door.

'It was offside,' Joel insisted behind him. He gave a quick nod to acknowledge Amy without interrupting the conversation. She couldn't hide her pale face and the added burden of what Ian was about to say.

'Fair and square,' Nigel raved. 'My boys might be younger than yours, but they're giving them a run for their money.'

'I'll just point out that we were two men down and Ricky Burton is injured.'

'Any excuse, mate.'

Ian coughed. 'Shall we step into my office? I think that would be better.'

He stood up and led the way out of the staffroom. Amy followed, her head starting to ache. She felt like a helpless child who had landed herself in trouble.

'Do take a seat.' Ian planted himself behind his desk. 'I hear you've been having a little difficulty.'

'Not at all. There was a small incident this morning but…'

'Yes, that's right. I understand you had a doctor's appointment and you were very late for class.'

Her blood began to boil. 'No, that's not exactly…'

'Obviously, we all have unavoidable commitments from time to time, but I just wanted to make you aware that our policy requires that they are made out of school hours.'

'It wasn't an appointment. I've been unwell all weekend and needed a new inhaler. I got held up collecting it this morning.'

There was silence and Ian appeared to be totally

confused. 'Oh, I see.'

'I was ten minutes late. I've never been late before.'

'Well, that's different.' He frowned. 'I think this must be a case of someone getting their wires crossed.'

'I explained this to Penny.' Amy tried to contain her anger. 'She knew there was no appointment.'

'That's quite all right. Penny has a lot of work on at the moment. I expect she just got a little muddled.'

'Right.'

'And you're feeling happy about everything else?'

'Yes, I really am,' Amy affirmed.

'Good. As long as you know, I'm around if there are any problems.'

'Thank you, I'll remember that.'

Amy was bracing herself for the next topic of discussion. How dare she have let a physically abusive boy get away with his attack on an innocent pupil.

'Enjoy the rest of your lunch. I hope I've not taken up too much of your time.'

'No.' The surprise sounded in her voice. 'Not at all.'

Quickly, she got to her feet and made for the door.

'Bye for now.' Ian grinned. 'I hope you're better soon.'

She stood there in the corridor feeling utterly cheated. Penny had twisted the whole story in a bid to make her look bad. Now, Ian would be constantly suspicious and always checking up on her timekeeping. It was all becoming clear that Penny was out to get her.

Livid and hurt, Amy turned back to the staffroom, but she thought better of it. With lunchtime in full swing, it would be packed with happy teachers who were free to do as they pleased without anyone trying to bring them down.

Instead, she returned to the classroom and took her overcoat off the peg. Then she slipped behind the huts to the secret spot where she always used to go. As a restricted area, it was unthreateningly quiet as the pupils were not allowed to play there.

Childish noises echoed from afar, masked by the icy whip

of breeze. She settled on a tree stump hidden by reeds that fringed the pond like a broken basket. Beneath the ailing lily pads, there were no other signs of life. But the same stone elf was crouched in the undergrowth, waiting for a catch with his fishing rod.

She scuffed her feet lazily through the grass, watching the horse chestnuts roll over in the leaves. Their lime-green armour was ripped at the seams, baring the smooth mahogany of their hearts.

Tears pushed into her eyes and she hated being so sensitive, but she wondered what she had ever done to make Penny so ready to bite. All that fuss over ten minutes this morning. But in the space of just ten minutes, so much had gone wrong.

A branch cracked as a squirrel darted through, scattering acorns to the ground. She could do without an equally stressful afternoon of probably much the same, but the children were milling back down to the classroom and lessons would soon be resuming. She just had to take it on the chin. Make absolutely sure she was never late again and do her utmost to appear more capable. *Things really haven't changed much around here*, she thought, as she trod away.

Luckily, the afternoon was uneventful and Bertie just stayed quiet, working cooperatively through his sums. All this aggression was a front. She saw that if no one else did. Nothing excused the way he carried on, but the teachers were yet to make a change.

He held the pen tightly and chewed his bottom lip. Anger or nerves? She couldn't tell. But those gestures fought with his deep, dark eyes and that face harboured something contradictory. Amy silently vowed that she would find it.

The end of the day came and she detoured to the staffroom. Penny was chatting to Debra as she walked through the door. She knew she should speak up for herself and set the record straight, but Penny's air of importance made Amy feel helplessly meek.

She hid behind the bookcase and looked for the titles she

needed. There was silence, then a snigger. Through the gaps on the shelf, she could see them whispering. Then they both laughed out loud.

'Where did you get your shoes, Deb?' The sudden change of subject was an obvious act.

'Present from Shane.'

'Love the colour. It's a pity other people don't share your taste in clothes.'

They walked across the room and Penny held the door open.

'By the way, are you busy for the last couple of hours tomorrow afternoon?'

'No, why?'

'Cover for me will you? I'm getting my hair done.'

Dumbstruck, Amy stormed down the hallway, sending paper Halloween shapes fluttering off the display boards. She was no longer thinking straight as she tore away from the building, opening the door with such force that Joel ducked out of her way.

His face changed as he saw the sorrow brimming from her own, but she wasn't going to stay there a second longer today. She hurried across the playground and up the steps to her car.

She patted her pockets for her keys, but nothing. Opening her bag on the bonnet, she rifled through make-up and sweet packets.

'Amy...' Joel's voice was filled with urgency. His breathing had quickened from running and he almost blocked the car door.

She managed a faint smile, hoping that her tears hadn't revealed themselves in mascara.

'What's the matter?'

'Nothing, Joel. I just want to go home.'

'Talk to me. Please.'

'I'm not feeling too good, that's all.'

'You're upset.' Joel's eyes scoured for the details.

'I don't want to make a big thing out of it.'

She continued to root in the bottom of her bag and finally pulled out her keys.

'Tell me what's happened.'

Amy took a few seconds to calm herself and checked that they were alone. Then she looked at him and felt the trust rush back in. He was caring and concerned, like he always used to be. Wanting her to be happy, despite not even knowing he had wished all this before. His eyes coaxed her to speak, and any control she had previously possessed was slowly slipping away.

As she recounted the events of the day, he listened to every word. She could feel the tension unravelling as she relayed all her troubles. He laughed when she said she'd been weak and incapable dealing with Bertie's fighting.

'No one has ever got through to him,' he assured her. 'But you know you can handle it.'

'He's the least of my problems.'

'Is there something else?' He moved closer.

She looked down at her feet. It wasn't going to be easy to disclose this. How long had Joel been working with Penny? Perhaps he held her in high regard. It seemed almost petty to raise a concern, especially being relatively new. She was unsure that Joel would believe anything she was about to say.

'I was late in this morning and… someone… misunderstood where I'd been. I made it clear that she'd got it wrong, but she reported me to Ian all the same. And now she has an appointment in school hours tomorrow.'

Joel folded his arms. 'Who was this?'

'It doesn't matter.'

'Yes, it does,'

'I don't need to name her.'

'No, you don't.' His eyes met hers knowingly. 'Because it's Penny, isn't it?'

Her face showed the truth and Joel looked away, shaking his head in annoyance.

'Has she said something?'

'No. But this is just typical of her.'

'Seriously?' Amy could have melted with relief. 'I thought it was me. I was almost convinced I'd done something out of line.'

'Not at all.' He squinted at her in that way he always used to, when he had been saying something important. 'Between you and me, she's not a nice person. She'll pick a target and make their life a misery.'

'She doesn't like me, Joel. She delayed my interview so she could grill me in her office. She made a huge deal out of what happened this morning and there's snide comments and whispering whenever I'm in the room.'

'I'm not having this.' He began to step away. 'Someone's got to say something.'

'Joel, please. It'll be OK.'

But he was adamant. 'People have left because of her. I'm not letting the same happen to you.'

'I'm not going anywhere… yet anyway,' she half joked. 'Don't do anything. She'll know I've been talking about her.'

He stood on the spot, raging but thoughtful. 'Whatever you say. But if anything else comes up, even if it's irrelevant, you tell me.'

'Promise,' she agreed with a grateful smile.

'Amy…' He moved in closer. 'Can you remember something?'

Her mouth almost fell open. Had this deep discussion finally jogged his memory? She prepared herself for a full account of what he realised he knew about her. As dread crept back in, she waited to hear what a chore it had been to teach her.

'Remember that you are better than the rubbish people throw at you. You are a great teacher, do you know that? Have you seen the difference you are making to this school? You are here because we want you here. So just go home now and believe in that.'

No. She was still safely unidentified. For a moment, she held his gaze and looked, almost daringly, deep into his eyes.

It was as if she was offering him a brief chance to recognise her. He made her feel too calm for words. She took a breath and the next sentence glided out of her mouth.

'I've been here before.'

The confused frown that clouded his face seemed to blot away all remnants of sympathy. She felt a barrier shoot up in an instant. It wasn't right to carry on. Joel obviously cared far more than she deserved, but he was also a no-nonsense man. He might not think so highly of his dim-witted pupil. Then the secret would be out to anyone he chose to tell.

'Just that...' she spoke carefully. 'It's not the first time someone's had it in for me.'

'So, you should know that people like Penny aren't worth worrying about. Yes?'

'Yes.'

He chased away her fears and it made her want to fly, just like it always had. Staring back with restored warmth, his eyes consumed her in a pool of schoolgirl awkwardness.

As the russet sun made tiger stripes against the charred clouds, Joel was constant beneath it all. And just beyond his shoulders, the field sprawled out with unforgotten hope. The secret she would always keep – even from the person who had once shared it with her.

Twelve

'I don't like it.' Vanessa grimaced.

'Why? It's great on you.'

'I look like a sack of potatoes.' She pulled off the parka and returned it to the hanger.

'What about this?' Amy pointed to a camel duffel coat lined with faux fur.

Vanessa inspected it and then shook her head. 'I've had loads like that. I want something different this time.'

'Well, I don't even need one really. There's hardly any room left on my coat rack.'

'You need casual,' Vanessa informed her. 'You're all macs and overcoats.'

Feeling far from inspired by the first two shops, the sisters made their way to a department store. Stan's Christmas present to his daughters had always been a new coat. He gave them the money early every year and sent them off to buy one.

'Look at that!' Leaping to the first rail inside the entrance, Vanessa grabbed a fitted cream coat that was just above knee length. She put it on and gazed at her reflection.

'Lovely!' said Amy, wishing she'd seen it first. The colour was perfect against Vanessa's skin.

'Sold. Now to find yours.'

'Not so fast.' Amy nodded at the price tag.

'How much?' Vanessa groaned. 'At this rate, I'll be stuck in that old dogtooth thing with a hole in the armpit.'

An hour later, and still empty-handed, they were

beginning to lose enthusiasm. Vanessa's taste was far too expensive and any that caught Amy's eye had belts which reminded her of a dressing gown.

They entered the next shop and stopped to peruse the Christmas gifts. While Vanessa disappeared behind the displays, Amy continued to search. She found plenty of coats that were too flimsy or out of stock in her size, before suddenly noticing a dream contender.

It was a vivid royal blue and slim fitting with military-type buttons. There was a poster of a model wearing the same style and Amy could see it looked even better on. Checking the price, she picked the correct size and went to find her sister.

Vanessa was in the footwear department, slipping her toes into a pointed black court shoe with a skyscraper heel.

'I've found just the right match for that!'

Her mouth widened when she saw the coat in Amy's arms. 'Wow! Have you tried it on?'

'Not for me. For you.'

'Are you sure? You'd look hot in it.'

'I'm after casual, remember? 'She held it out while Vanessa slid her hands into the arms.

'Seriously, you saw it first. I don't mind if you want it.'

'No.' Amy stood back and beamed. 'Check that out.'

Vanessa looked undeniably good. The colour struck a chord with her eyes and set off her platinum hair to perfection. She pulled it further around her waist and fastened some of the buttons.

'Do I want to know how much this is?'

'There's change for the shoes.'

'I'm all done then. I'll just get these and we'll have a refuel. On me!'

As they queued in the line at the coffee shop within the store, Amy felt fed up. She loathed shopping for something specific that she just couldn't find.

'We're having caramel lattes,' Vanessa announced, tossing napkins and stirrers onto a tray. 'You'll never look back.'

'OK.' Amy was indifferent.

'Come on sis, don't give up yet.'

'Nothing suits me. I'll just get one online.'

'We're not leaving until you find yours.'

'Fine.'

'Now go and get us a table. I'll be over in a sec.'

Unconvinced, Amy sat down in a booth and watched all the other shoppers going by, their hands full of carrier bags and faces lively with satisfaction that they had found what they wanted. It annoyed her.

After last week's episode at work, she had been looking forward to today, knowing how much clothes shopping usually cheered her up. A new coat would probably have done the trick, but instead she was left feeling deflated. Thanks to the shoddy fit of the few she had liked, she imagined that a bin liner would make her look better. Add to this the harsh lighting on the shop floors and she felt like giving up altogether.

'You want to see your face.' Vanessa cruised over with the coffees.

'Not particularly.'

'You look like the world has ended.'

'It has.'

'Because you haven't found a coat yet?'

'No.' Amy feigned a stroppy pout.

'What then?'

'Because they all look bad on me.'

'"They don't!" Vanessa cupped her hands around her latte. 'I'm going to find you one, you'll see.'

'I've had enough now. Let's just do something else.'

'You're not giving up that easily.'

'I really don't need to spend the rest of the day finding out just how many coats I can look horrendous in.'

Vanessa scowled back at her. 'OK, what's up? You're moody today.'

'I'm not.' She ripped a napkin with her fingertips.

'Come on, I know you better than that.'

Amy's stare dissolved into a less severe expression. 'It's just work, that's all.'

'Manic, is it? Must be hard with all those kids driving you insane.'

'Yes, but it's not that.'

'Then, what?'

'Just some hassle with a colleague,' Amy sighed. 'She's giving me a bit of a hard time.'

'Well, you know what to do about it.'

'What?'

'You are going into school on Monday all done up in a brand-new coat. Women like that can't stand it when you look good.'

Amy laughed dismissively. 'I don't care about all that.'

'You can't beat killer clothes and a bit of war paint, sis.'

'Maybe, but please, no more coats today. Instead let's…' She caught her breath as something grabbed her view in the background. 'Let's look at dresses!'

'Dresses?' Vanessa spun her head around in the direction of Amy's gaze. 'What kind of dresses?'

It was a sleeveless bodycon, dripping in black sequins that gave it an almost wet look. Just the kind of shape that suited Amy's figure and an instant cure for her dejection. She was already on her feet, edging out of the coffee bar towards what was fast becoming her prized possession. Vanessa, still perplexed, hurried along behind her.

'How amazing is *that*?' Amy seized the hanger and held it out in front of her.

'Nice.' Vanessa hardly looked.

'Where are the changing rooms?'

'No, you're not trying it on. We're not here for that.'

'I said I didn't need a coat, and I was right. What I need is this little number right here.'

'That won't keep you warm when Earth freezes over.' Vanessa frowned.

'It doesn't matter. This will make me feel far happier than

any coat could.'

'And where are you going to wear it?'

Amy paused for a moment, registering Vanessa's point. 'I'll think of something.'

'So, you're using Dad's money for that, are you?'

'He won't mind.' Amy turned away from her sister.

'Want to bet?'

'He'll want me to get something nice for myself.'

'He'll want you to get a coat.' Vanessa forced the dress out of her hand.

'Give that back!'

'The money's for a coat and that's final.'

'But I don't need…'

'Out.' Vanessa cut her off.

Her unrelenting face made Amy giggle.

'Don't expect me to talk to you for the rest of the day,' she muttered as Vanessa marched her through the shop.

She hated to admit it, but Vanessa had been right. And not long later, the proof revealed itself. Amy tried on a double-breasted trench coat in a rich redcurrant shade. It wasn't the casual jacket she had wanted, but at least it was practical and suited her well. She took it straight to the till, glad it would be another year before she'd go coat shopping again.

***

As it turned out, a raincoat would have been preferable. Showers bucketed from a permanently grey sky all through the following week. By Wednesday morning, the torrent was in full swing and Amy had to dart inside the school.

'You made it in one piece then,' Alison said in the staffroom. 'I forgot my brolly so that's useful.'

'How long is it supposed to last?'

'The rest of the week apparently. Don't you just love wet breaktimes stuck in the classroom with your little darlings for company?'

116

Amy rolled her eyes. 'I guess the fireworks are off then.'

'Looks like it. Ian's going to let us know later.'

As hard spatters continued to drum, Amy felt disappointed. The display was a longstanding Woodbrook tradition that had always been a highlight of the autumn term.

'Is this going to take long?' Martin, the other Year Six teacher, looked irritated. 'I've got a job lot of new test tubes coming.'

'Not at all,' Penny grinned. 'Ian just has some news.'

She looked remarkably smug about something. Perhaps she was pleased that she could make other plans now that the fireworks seemed unlikely.

More teachers gathered, clearly for an impromptu meeting. Ian arrived in a fluster and hurriedly straightened his tie.

'Sorry to keep you all waiting. I just have a quick announcement.'

'Wake me up when it's over,' Alison murmured under her breath.

'Our Christmas play will be Joseph and the Amazing Technicolor Dreamcoat. An evening performance on the last day of term.'

The smiling teachers pulled out their devices, making a note of all the details.

'Now, as you know,' Ian continued, 'I always select one of you to direct the production and this year, that choice is an obvious one.'

He beamed at nobody in particular, but Penny was smiling from ear to ear, just waiting for Ian to say the words.

'This particular person has a natural gift for the stage. Her ability has been apparent for quite some time and we would be honoured to have her as our theatrical extraordinaire.'

Penny closed her eyes in mock embarrassment, quickly flashing them open again, as if to prepare for the glorification.

'So, without further ado...' Ian bounced on his heels. 'I

am delighted to announce that the person I have nominated is…'

Penny took a bold step forward.

'Amy Ashcroft.'

He held out a hand towards Amy as if to present her to the huddle of excited colleagues. She was stunned to silence. All she could see was Ian's delighted face in the blur of clapping, which drowned out the sound of the rain.

Penny's eyes darkened as rage quivered over her lips. She looked up at Ian in a near fit of betrayal. Amy felt the heat soar into her cheeks as Alison gave her shoulder a congratulatory squeeze.

'Are you sure?' she finally asked Ian.

'Of course. You are happy to oblige, aren't you?'

'Yes…' She regained control of her gaping mouth. 'Yes, I'd love to!'

'Then it's settled. Auditions will be held in two weeks' time, so that's the first thing to organise. Feel free to take a couple of others on board to help out. I'll leave the rest to you and you know where I am if you need me.'

'Nice one!' Nigel winked at her as he hurried off to class.

'I'll help with auditions if you want,' Gita volunteered.

'And me,' added Alison. 'I directed last year, so I'm all clued up.'

A few more teachers wished Amy luck and Ian turned back to her as he reached the doorway.

'We can discuss this properly later and I'll run you through how it all works.' He bid her goodbye with his hand.

'Ian,' she moved quickly over to him. 'You definitely want me to do it? I mean, why me?'

Before he could answer, Penny pushed past them and tore down the corridor in a frenzy of fury.

He chuckled warmly. 'Let's just say, a little bird has been telling me about your skills. It seems you would make the perfect candidate for anything music and drama related. You really do keep it all in, don't you?'

She was stunned as he shot her a knowing look and

glided away to his office. What was that supposed to mean? The heavy thudding that was taking over her ears was no longer powered by the rainfall. Now it was her heart, banging in her chest as the realisation took hold.

It could only have been Joel. He had finally found her out. Their chat in the car park had made him twig that he'd known her all along. Useless, pointless Amy, who didn't have a hope with anything else, but wasn't too bad at drama.

He would probably have been amused as he'd filled Ian in and the two of them would have silently laughed at her for not coming out and revealing herself. Perhaps this nomination was a way of taking pity on her, or maybe it was a tactic which was designed to show her up. Why ever else would Joel have done this? Why hadn't he come to her first when he'd finally realised who she was?

And now that she thought about it, where *was* Joel? He hadn't been in the staffroom just now, so he clearly felt awkward in her company. Panic swelled at the chaos this would cause. She had to find him now, before he told another soul.

Thirteen

Against all odds, the rain finally surrendered and Ian confirmed that the fireworks would still be taking place. When the children had gone home for tea, the teachers headed to the Pig and Trotter to while away the hours before the display began.

Amy and Alison chose a table by the window, where streetlights glowed through the violet clouds of dusk. A welcome waft of steak and chips floated out from the grill and the bar had long changed from the old vintage layout. Now it was stacked with a kaleidoscope of bottles and various brands of artisan snacks.

As Alison browsed the range of food, reading out full descriptions, Amy sat tensely against her chair. She watched the groups of teachers who were already inside and checked continuously at the door.

Debra was by the jukebox, shovelling her way through a loaded burger, while Penny knocked back a second glass of wine. Nigel laughed loudly with Martin as they settled in front of the TV and Gita was on her way over, having ordered her food.

'All right girls?' she asked as she pulled up a chair. 'How's it going?'

'Not bad,' Alison replied. 'I was all set on the scampi until I saw the Tex Mex platter. What are you having?'

'Just a jacket potato.'

'But they're doing them later at school, aren't they?'

'Not with chilli and sour cream. Amy, what about you?'

'Ribs or something.'

Her eyes flitted back to the door and then out across the car park. Still no sign. She had hoped to have found Joel by now, but a hectic day with Bertie hadn't given her the chance.

'Looking forward to the play then?' Gita asked.

'Definitely. Can't wait to get started on the auditions.' Amy tried hard to cover her anxiety.

'We did a modern Dick Whittington last year,' said Alison. 'Your Flynn was the lead.'

'That child is incredible. He's heading straight for Broadway,' Gita added.

Amy nodded. 'Top of the class in everything else, too. I'll be interested to see him in action.'

'No need to look for a Joseph. He's your boy.' Alison smiled.

'You know where the costume cupboard is, don't you? Loads of parents will pitch in, too,' added Gita. 'Ian's wife, Stella, does the props and Keith is a dab hand with the lighting.'

Amy was only half listening as the door swung open and Joel headed down the staircase to join Nigel and Martin.

'Thanks, by the way, for stepping in with the auditions. My round for the drinks.'

'Wouldn't miss that for the world!' Alison laughed. 'You're going to need all the help you can get.'

Amy went down to the bar where her three male colleagues were engrossed in the football match. She wondered how to get Joel's attention without distracting the others.

'What can I get you, love?' the barmaid called out.

'Two vodka and oranges please, and a gin and tonic.' As the vampy-looking woman pumped a shot into a glass, Amy heard Joel's loud objection to a penalty. 'Double,' she requested, slightly louder than she intended.

'I hear congratulations are in order.'

She froze and turned her head in the direction of the TV. Joel had heard her voice and was leaning out to speak.

'Yes.' Amy smiled as thankfully as she could while their fellow teachers were nearby.

'You'll be terrific, Amy.'

As he cast a quick eye back to the game, she took a generous swig of her gin and quickly gulped it down.

'Joel, I need a word.'

She looked serious and he came straight over.

'Sure. Shall we go outside?'

He led the way to a small garden with sleeping flower beds softly illuminated by night lights. A water feature trickled invisibly in the dark and all was calm around them. She held his gaze with decisive eyes, gearing herself up for this first exchange when, at last, everything would be out in the open.

'Look, about the play. It was you, wasn't it? You've been talking to Ian.'

Joel's face broke into a smile. 'You don't mind, do you?'

'So, you know.' Amy stared at the pavestones. 'You know I'm into music and drama…' She looked at him again. 'Don't you?'

His eyes shone in approval. 'How could I forget?'

Her toes bunched into knots. Feeling as if her legs would give way, she perched on the nearest bench and glanced at him, full of insecurity. All at once, her barriers crashed down and she felt exposed to the core.

'How long have you known? All this time, and you haven't mentioned it.'

'From the moment I saw the proof.'

His smile was so confident. Surely she shouldn't feel this safe in his company.

'Really? When was that?'

She waited for him to say it. Would he honestly remember her, dancing on stage in her fairy dress? Maybe it was more likely to be her later Woodbrook plays. She was taken aback by his calm expression. He knew who she was and best of all, he didn't seem to mind.

'The coach trip, Amy. It took five minutes and you had

two whole classes singing like professionals.'

She zipped her lips together to stop another clumsy word from pushing her out of the safety net she had just fallen back into.

'You are happy, aren't you?' Joel asked. 'I just thought the play would be right up your street.'

She felt so stupid. How could she have forgotten about that silly little singsong when they'd visited the windmills? Here she was, ready to reminisce about the schoolgirl hobbies she actually thought he'd remembered, when Joel's only knowledge was a moment he had witnessed just weeks ago. There was no Amy of yesterday in a fragment of his mind and the quicker she acted to keep it that way, the better.

'Of course I am.' She shrugged with relief. 'I'm just surprised, that's all.'

'Why?'

'Well… it's quite surreal how a bit of fun has got me in charge of a whole play.'

Joel sat down beside her. 'You know what you're doing and I believe in you.'

Silence swept over them. Even in this much darkness, his fierce blue eyes were ever clear through the moonlight mist. She ached to tell him everything. To relive the precious memories she had locked up inside.

But he might never look at her in the same way again and the thought of that seemed unbearable. He still had such a hold on her and not a thing had changed.

A shiver stroked her skin and she couldn't fathom the cause. Was it the crisp autumn evening or the presence of Joel sitting next to her? She breathed slowly in the stillness and weakened again under the power of his smile.

'You're getting cold,' he said in a near whisper. 'We should go back in.'

He walked up the steps to the door.

'Joel,' Amy called and he spun around to face her. 'Thank you.'

'My pleasure. And I can't wait to see it.'

'I wouldn't get your hopes up,' she giggled. 'It might be a disaster.'

'Don't forget what I said. You can do it.'

After a hearty meal, coffee was ordered with a sharing platter of doughnuts. Most of the staff had returned to the school, while the three friends stayed behind to chat. They were halfway through their indulgent treat when Alison's phone beeped.

'He wants to know where to pick me up. Does he not listen to anything I say?'

'Is that Nick?' Gita asked, licking sugar from her lips.

Alison prodded at her screen. 'He knows I'm at school tonight so where else would I need a lift from?'

'At least you've got someone to drive you home and keep you warm on a cold night.'

'I wouldn't say that. He just rolls over and takes the covers with him most of the time.'

'Better than having a great big double bed and no one to share it with,' mused Gita.

'Feel free to swap!'

'I suppose I'm just too picky. My knight will come one day.'

Amy listened intently but wasn't keen on commenting. It would only be a matter of time before her own love life was brought up.

'I'll fix you up with someone.' Alison's eyes gleamed cunningly at Gita. 'Who do you fancy at work?'

'No one!' Gita screwed up her face.

'Nigel.'

'Too boring.'

'Keith.'

'Give me a break. Anyway, he's married.'

'Joel.'

'Too… single.'

'What?' Alison's forehead furrowed. 'How can anyone be *too* single?'

'Joel's not with anyone?' The words rushed from Amy's mouth and both women turned their heads. She took on a casual expression and quickly masked her shock. 'I just thought he was married, that's all.'

'Not anymore,' said Alison solemnly. 'It lasted five years and she left him. Went off with a rich bloke overseas. There's been nothing serious since then apparently.'

'He needs a good woman.' Gita's suggestion made Amy's skin prickle. 'But that woman isn't me. He's too into his work, that one, and obsessed with sports. I don't do men who love their football more than partners.'

'He had his heart broken!' Alison said sympathetically. 'After what *she* did, he probably perishes the thought of someone doing it again.'

'I guess so, now you mention it.' Gita considered the point. 'OK, if you swear not to say anything, I'll tell you who really does it for me.'

'Go on,' pressed Alison.

Gita couldn't help blushing. 'Mr Myers.'

'Martin!'

'Shhh! If this gets back to him, I'll never live it down.'

'Oh, come on. He'd jump at the chance to go out with you. Just let me do some matchmaking. Promise I'll be subtle.'

'No way.' Gita shrank into her seat. 'If it happens, it happens, but I don't need anyone doing me any favours.'

'I'll find out if he's taken though, just leave it to me.'

'If you must, but do *not* mention my name. Like, ever.'

'Let's go,' Amy checked the time on her phone. 'We should be getting back.'

The three of them split the bill before making their way out of the pub, which was now glimmering externally in a coat of pin-prick lights. They crossed the road and slipped into the twitten which led up to the lower playground, Alison and Gita walking in front and Amy dropping behind them.

The petrol sky faded fast into the throat of darkness, but the moon peeped through the starry glitz like half a white chocolate button. A lashing breeze ripped at her coat and she pulled it tight to her body, digesting the facts as they slowly sank in.

How could Joel be alone? It didn't make sense that this kind-hearted man had no one to share his life with. That someone once held him in the palm of their hand and had thrown everything away.

She thought of the smile as it filled her up. Of the way he steadied her falls. And his eyes were sensual, caring and calm in their pools of cerulean blue. One shred of his faith made her feel so secure, as if nothing could ever break her. Yet Joel was not in love and perhaps he was even lonely. A wave of sadness hit her just to imagine it was true.

They ascended the sloping playground, where chatter rang out ahead and Keith was preparing the fireworks.

'Good evening everyone!' Ian greeted loudly. 'Welcome to Woodbrook's annual fireworks display and we promise it will be the best yet.' He thanked a few people for helping out with the event. 'Please assemble into class groups and your teachers will stand with you accordingly.'

The children spread out in a semi-circle and each teacher took their place. Then Ian signalled to Keith who struck a lighter to a noisy backdrop of excitement.

Amy's eyes followed the ring of spectators, all the way round until it stopped, directly opposite where she was standing and ended with class 6C. The pupils bobbed and rippled in a sea of knits and hoods while Joel stood quietly behind them.

In an instant, she couldn't look at anything else. The dark blond hair ruffling in the wind as the hazy light hit his cheekbones. The tiny shape where the coat parted against his neck. Shivers returned with a vengeance, brushing like fingers down her back.

And when she had coaxed his eyes to her face, she held them there with her gaze. His mouth curved in a smile and she welcomed it with her own. Her focus remained there, frozen in time, permanently and entirely on him.

Jewels crashed in smithereens, painting the sky with gold. The black was flamboyant with dots, stripes, and shocks of glittering dust. Each spark crackled and fizzed in streaks like a wall of metallic graffiti.

But Amy wasn't watching. Nothing could distract her now as she took in every part of him. The colours of the night shone their spectrum on his skin and she could hardly breathe.

The distance over the playground felt just like the field. A wide-reaching space with a fortune at the end of it. There, through the darkness and the thick plumes of smoke, she held on to this moment as the fire began to blaze.

Fourteen

The hall door clicked shut and Alison let out a sigh. Amy glanced at Gita and was unsurprised by her expression. Deflated, she crossed a line through the next name on the list and sank back in her chair. Auditions had been in progress since the start of the day and the three teachers had just endured another unconvincing performance.

'Hopeless,' Alison said through gritted teeth. 'How many times did we ask him to sing louder?'

'I think he knows he blew it,' replied Amy.

'Well, his parents will be more gutted than he is.' Gita nibbled her pen.

'Don't worry folks,' said Alison with glee. 'The best is yet to come.'

It was the only thing that was keeping Amy's hopes up. Woodbrook's supposed finest were leaving a lot to be desired, but she had a sneaky suspicion that Flynn would save the day.

'Who's next anyway?' Gita yawned, slumping her chin into her hand.

Alison checked the names. 'Kara Swayne, one of mine.'

'Any good?' asked Amy.

'Don't know actually. She didn't audition last year.'

'Interesting.'

'But she's got the confidence, I can tell you that.'

'Good.' Amy smiled expectantly. 'Maybe she'll be audible at least.'

'Just you wait.' Alison nodded. 'I hear nothing but her

voice rabbiting on all day.'

'But can she sing?'

'I would think so. She does have a nice speaking tone.'

'Well, that doesn't mean…'

There was a knock on the door and a girl grinned at the panel. Her dark hair hung messily around her face, but her eyes were lively with intent.

'Hello, Mrs Huckleberry. And Miss Jaffrey. And of course you, Miss Ashcroft.'

Amy chewed the inside of her cheek. Was that a curtsey?

'Welcome, Kara,' Alison greeted her. 'How are you?'

'Fine, thank you.' Kara almost shouted.

'And what are you going to sing for us?'

'Well, Mrs Huckleberry, I have prepared two songs from the musical.'

'That's good Kara,' Amy chipped in, 'but you'll only need to sing one.'

'The thing is, Miss…' Kara said assertively. 'They show off my voice in different ways, so I want to sing both.'

The teachers shuffled in their seats as Amy stared back at Kara.

'No one else has sung more than one, so it wouldn't be fair. Please take your pick and off you go.'

Kara tutted and Amy tensed her eyebrows. Then the girl's face relaxed and she took a slow breath. The three teachers waited as she began singing the notes.

Amy craned her neck to gauge the voice. Not a bad start. Kara did have a good tone after all. She travelled through the verse and stumbled over a lyric. Then another one, but the next line was well recovered. *A definite contender*, Amy jotted down. This girl was giving her hope.

Until her forced pronunciation put the notes out of tune altogether. Kara then repeated another verse, throwing her arms in the air for another rendition of the chorus.

'That's all we need to hear.' Amy held up a hand.

Kara stopped singing and searched them for a reaction.

'So, have I got a part?'

'The cast will be announced on Friday. You'll have to wait to find out,' explained Alison.

Kara left the hall as Amy shot a questioning look to her left.

'What?' Alison was surprised.

'I'm not listening to you again.'

'I said she *might* be good. That is no guarantee.'

'Understatement,' said Gita with a smirk.

'Right,' Amy looked at the clock. 'Lunch. We'll resume at one and let's hope this afternoon is better than the morning.'

'With some of the names on this list, I doubt it.' Gita groaned as they filed into the staffroom.

'Tea?' Amy asked, clicking the kettle on. 'Shame there's nothing stronger around here, I'd be downing it.'

Alison scooped a cracker into her pot of cottage cheese. 'Don't lose heart. If I managed it last year, you'll be flying.'

'But you did have a brilliant Year Six to play with who are no longer with us,' Gita recalled.

'I must admit, I'm getting slightly worried.' Amy filled the mugs and perched on the edge of a chair.

'Let's see how the rest of today goes before we reach crisis point,' advised Alison.

'Which would mean?'

'We make the staff do it instead!'

'Maybe that's the answer,' Gita nudged Alison. 'Hey, who would you cast as Joseph?'

'Ian of course. Can you imagine?' Alison began to do an impression which had the others in stitches. Then they fell to silence as Ian walked in.

He held the door open and Amy's skin tingled as Joel was next to enter. Her heartbeat drummed at double the speed and she sincerely hoped her make-up was still in place.

'So, we're leaving it on the late side, but we should be able to book it in time,' Ian said loudly.

'You don't think they'll be full then?' asked Joel.

'That's where Sue comes in. Her cousin is the events manager there and apparently she can tug a few strings.' Ian moved over to the others. 'Ladies, we are thinking of pulling out all the stops and having our Christmas do at The Spring Lake.'

'Really?' Alison's eyes lit up.

Ian nodded smugly. 'Sue's cousin can wangle it for us.'

'That's brilliant,' chirped Gita. 'I stayed there once. It was amazing.'

Amy just grinned. She knew The Spring Lake well. It was the best hotel around for miles and it had been there since she was little. It was nestled into a hillside on the outskirts of Flintley with a backdrop of open countryside sweeping up behind it. Melinda had even worked there for a time when Amy had been young.

'You probably won't know it, Amy, but it's the most gorgeous hotel.' Gita filled her in. 'New frocks all round!'

'Speaking of Christmas festivities, how are the auditions going?' Ian asked.

'Great!' Alison cut in. 'We've seen some fascinating performances so far.'

'I must say, we are spoilt for choice,' he chuckled. 'They're naturals, some of them.'

'You'd think they were from stage school,' Gita chimed sarcastically. 'We'll have no trouble with the cast list.'

'That's wonderful. Give me the details when you're ready, Amy.' He turned to Joel. 'I'll just get my planner. Then we can have that meeting.'

Amy and the others held their frozen smiles until Ian had disappeared. Once he was out of earshot, they made no secret of the reality. Amy and Gita lamented but Alison couldn't hide her amusement.

'Nice job, Gita.' She winked.

'Stage school?' Amy's eyes narrowed as she smiled.

Joel smirked as he leaned against the unit next to her. 'Not going too well then?'

'Awful!'

She smiled playfully back at him and worked to calm the thudding in her chest. His grey merino sweater made his eyes flash with blue and he sniggered softly at her annoyance.

'Oh, come on,' Alison urged. 'They just need a bit of practice and anyway, we haven't seen the rest yet.'

'I don't think I want to,' joked Amy. 'I've heard cat fights with more conviction.'

'That's where you come in though, isn't it?' Alison reminded her. 'Transforming them into little stars fit for the West End.'

Amy rolled her eyes. 'No pressure then.'

'You're going to work magic.' Joel's voice lifted her eyes straight back to him. 'You are.'

She knew she was starting to blush. His words were so strong and reassuring, they almost vibrated through her bones. It was like swallowing a shot of the most sublime spirit, dripping down like velvet and making her feel alive.

Seconds went by and she allowed herself another glance. The man was so sincere, yet so blinded from the reality. How could he not remember her in a snippet of his mind?

'OK, girls.' Gita's lunchbox clicked shut. 'Time to get back in there. We need to go over our notes before the next bunch arrives.'

She and Alison stood up, but Amy was still drinking her tea.

'Come on, Ashcroft, let's get to it,' ordered Alison.

'Hold on!' Amy exclaimed, taking another gulp.

'A woman in demand.' Joel beamed his sideways smile. 'Easy to see why.'

Amy fixed her stare on the inside of her mug as she sucked up the last remnants. She got to her feet and coyly swilled the crockery in the sink. Then she flashed him one last grin.

She followed the others as his stare burned through her. It was almost a relief to be out of his sight and uncoil her limbs from the pressure, but somehow she missed him from the moment she'd closed the door. Now, this afternoon would be even more of a mission, trying to focus on anything other than Joel.

The day continued and so did the stream of mediocre auditions. The majority either didn't sing loudly enough or they frequently forgot the words. One or two had scope, but nobody had really made Amy sit up and take notice.

'Sorry, Miss, can I start again?'

'One more time when you're ready.' Amy tapped her fingers impatiently. Liam Hagan, a boy from her class, was starting his song for the fourth time. He just couldn't get through without jumbling up the words.

'Sorry Liam, time's up.' Alison said firmly. 'Don't worry, you've still got a chance, just like everyone else.'

Amy bit her lip at the over-ambitious comment and wondered how she was ever going to cast this production. Panic built up as she scanned the list, now with every name ticked off as having been seen. Just one person was left. The one who would undoubtedly walk into the room and turn this whole process on its head. Amy had her fingers crossed three times over that Flynn Branston would steal the show.

Liam made a crestfallen exit and vanished down the corridor. As they waited in a bored line behind the table, Gita turned to Amy and gestured at the list.

'So, who are you going to cast? Any idea yet?'

'There's a handful.' Amy studied the names, trying to muster some optimism. 'I guess the first few weren't too bad.'

'Have no fear.' Alison nodded at the door. 'Your solution has arrived.'

Flynn greeted the teachers politely and walked up to the audition spot. Amy taught him every day, but she treated this situation as if she had never seen him before. As Alison spoke to him and he told her what he would be singing, Amy used the moment to examine his appearance.

To look at, he was flawless. A thick mop of hair and two almond eyes that could hook anyone in. He spoke clearly and eloquently, with the kind of confidence that was assured without being arrogant.

So far so good. Now all Amy needed was for his singing

to match what he offered in just about every other area. He posed with a wistful face as the first few lyrics sounded in the room. It was full of feeling and note perfect. Not a word or line was out of place and his posture oozed a professionalism way beyond his years.

When he ended the song, Alison clasped her hands together to avoid an unfair round of applause and Gita wrote something in large capital letters next to his name on her list.

As soon as he was gone, Alison slapped the desk in delight. 'What did I tell you? How good is he?'

'Amazing.' Gita looked awestruck. 'At last, we have our Joseph.'

'Do we?' Amy frowned slightly. 'That's not been decided yet.'

Alison guffawed. 'You *are* joking, Amy. He brought the house down last year. You couldn't give the lead to anyone else.'

'Doesn't that make it a bit unfair? Shouldn't someone else have a go?'

'Like who? Name one other person who remembered their lines.'

'It's only going to make you look bad if everyone messes up,' Gita added. 'That's why Flynn is perfect.'

'I don't doubt that.' Amy doodled shapes with her pen. 'I need to keep an open mind, that's all.'

There was a long and awkward pause.

'Well, you've only got another day to decide. Ian wants the list by Friday so you can't hang around,' said Alison.

'Honestly, I don't know what there is to think about. Flynn deserves that part hands down.' Gita filed away her notes. 'It's got to be him.'

'It's my choice.' Amy looked at the startled teachers. 'Thanks so much for helping out. I just need some time to think. It's only fair, right?'

'Makes sense, I suppose,' Alison agreed as they got up and left the hall. 'But let's face it, we all know what the outcome will be.'

***

Caviar clouds swarmed in, constricting the oyster-pink daylight, and a lacy mist clung to the fiercely thrashing waves. Away in the distance, miniature ships dipped in and out of view, voyaging on through the cryptic night as it swathed over the coast like a cave. And just below the window, the foamy water tossed and turned as it collided rhythmically with the pebbles.

Amy took in the last glimpse of day before it petered out completely. Between bites of her fishfinger sandwich, she tried to focus on the papers splayed in front of her. On top of the pile, the unfilled cast list sat waiting to be finalised and she read the audition notes for the umpteenth time in the hope that something would become of them.

She thought back to Flynn and tried to get to grips with what was niggling her. He had it all. So why had his performance left her feeling underwhelmed?

When she mulled it over in her mind, she realised what it was. Yes, he was good. But that was about it. To her, it had all been rather mechanical. Bland, even. And the hype from the teachers had been way over the top. In all honesty, Flynn was nothing more spectacular than the best of a bad bunch.

But try as she might to deny it, there really were no options. From the few other possibilities, no one could match Flynn's squeaky-clean performance. It would be a travesty to cast anyone else over him.

Her biro hovered over the blank cast list and she touched the nib to the paper to write down Flynn's name. No. She dropped the pen. Not yet.

Alison and everyone else would be on her back tomorrow, but to make a decision when she felt this way would just be giving in. The production would be average rather than outstanding and all her enjoyment would be lost to the weaker desires of other people. She had spent years succumbing to this kind of pressure and she was damned if it was happening again.

A palpitation flitted in her ribs as she thought of Joel in the staffroom. Memories stirred of the things he used to say. Don't ever be pushed around or do something she wasn't happy with. Believe in herself. And he still believed in her, even though he didn't even know it.

Later that night, she lay in bed, thinking and pondering as the clock ticked on. She imagined him there with her, soothing her mind. His skin on hers, soft as her pillow. She pulled his jaw towards her, as close as she could get and as her lips touched his, she was deeply and peacefully asleep.

Fifteen

The next morning was predictable. Amy had barely set foot in the staffroom before Alison pounced.

'So?' she demanded.

'So, what?'

'Have you done it?'

'If you mean the casting, then no, not yet.'

'Amy, what are you doing? You're cutting it very fine.'

'Yes, I know that. I've just been busy with other things.' She glanced up briefly and Alison's frown hit a nerve. Clearly, she didn't trust Amy to decide things for herself. 'Is there a problem with that? I thought the deadline was tomorrow.'

'It is. But time is getting on and it takes longer than you think to devise a whole cast list. I did it last year, remember?'

She sighed heavily. Alison was starting to get patronising now. Ridiculing even, as if Amy had been born yesterday. 'By tomorrow morning, I promise you, there will be a full cast list. Now, can we just leave it?'

Alison raised a doubtful eyebrow. 'Well, you've got my number if you need any help at one in the morning while you're still trying to get it done.'

'I'm off to class.' Amy slung her bag over her shoulder. 'See you down there.'

On her way out, Gita nearly banged into her.

'Morning!' she squealed. 'Got it all done then?'

'No, she has not,' Alison replied disapprovingly in the background.

'What?'

The shock on Gita's face almost made Amy laugh.

'I haven't had time yet. I'm doing it tonight.'

'But surely Flynn is Joseph. You must have decided that much.'

'No!' Amy's fury was building by the second. 'Please get off my back, both of you.'

'Oh, Amy. You can't do that to him. He'll be crushed if he doesn't get the part and his parents… they'll be down on you like a ton of bricks.'

'That's not the reason I should be casting him. I'll do it because he's right for it, not because his parents won't like it if I don't.'

'Well, on your head be it.' Gita looked almost sympathetically into her eyes. 'No one else is capable, you can't deny that.'

'Just leave it, Gita, she's not going to listen,' Alison said loudly. 'She'll have to find out for herself.'

Amy gritted her teeth. 'Thanks for the support. I thought you wanted to help me.'

'Yes, we do.' Alison got up and stood behind Gita. 'We just know how things work around here and we don't want it to go badly for you.'

'I appreciate that, but I just need more time. The deadline isn't even up yet, so will you both just chill out?'

'Whatever you say.' Alison backed away.

'You're in charge.' Gita looked uneasy and pursed her lips.

Amy took off down the hallway and couldn't help feeling hurt. Alison shouldn't have been so quick to challenge her and as Gita knew her slightly less well, it was all the more reason not to judge her.

But she was sticking to her guns. Something about Flynn just didn't move her enough. Maybe he had been a tremendous Dick Whittington, but that wouldn't automatically fast-track him to Joseph. She was going to make sure of that, even if she did eventually decide to cast him.

As the lessons rolled on, she kept her sights on him in class, trying to connect with the same qualities that everyone else seemed to find. There he was again, with his pristine face and those effortless mannerisms. He was shining through so much today that perhaps she had been unfairly dismissive of his talents.

Deep down, she knew there was no other choice. At least Alison and Gita would be thrilled with the outcome and everyone would think highly of her for doing the right thing. She was going to need all the support she could get with this play and enemies were the last thing she wanted right now.

'How's it going?' Alison appeared as the children left for lunch.

'OK.' Amy smiled, slightly frostily, and continued to tidy around the desks.

'I didn't mean to upset you this morning.'

'It's fine, don't worry about it.'

'I just know how hard it can be to organise the play. Quite frankly, I couldn't be bothered last year, trying to knock the kids into shape. Flynn's an easy option and I just thought you'd benefit from that.'

'I understand, Ali.' Amy gave a warmer smile, but she still disagreed with Alison's thinking. She wanted to make the best of this play and she'd do all in her power to achieve it. 'I'm close to deciding now, anyway. I'm onto it straight after school.'

'Gita wants to catch up with you, too. Coming to lunch?'

'I can't. I'm on duty.'

'Then I'll tell her to find you.'

'Could do with a chat while I'm dying of boredom.' Amy grinned and Alison seemed relieved to have made peace with her.

Halfway through the cold lunch hour, Amy patrolled the playground. Balls bounced, skipping ropes cracked and children frolicked in a cloud of coats. Shouts and screams blended together and rang out in her ears like a clattering brass band.

'Ali said you'd be here.' Gita spoke with wide eyes, her loose hair blowing against her cochineal scarf. 'Look, about this morning, I'm sorry.'

'Gita, don't worry. It's over now.'

'I know but I wouldn't want to fall out over this. We didn't mean to upset you.'

'Everything's under control, OK? I do know what I'm doing.' Amy sounded far more reassuring than she felt.

'I think it was just a case of too many cooks. We all want this play to be brilliant and I guess, because you're quite new, we went a bit overboard. You'll see what I mean about Flynn. He's just so easy to work with and...'

'Wait a minute...'

Amy suddenly craned her neck, concentrating hard on a noise from over the wall. She listened for a few seconds longer, then hurried away.

Goosebumps pricked her shoulders as the sound grew louder until there in the corner, she found the very source. A girl was pinned against the wall as Bertie repeatedly chanted in her face.

Her heart flew like a rocket while she took in the discovery she had somehow managed to stumble upon.

'Get off!' She shouted at the top of her voice. 'Let her go!'

Instantly, Bertie released the crying girl and started to run away.

'No, you don't.' Amy blocked his exit. 'You stand over there and wait.'

Bertie did as he was told and Amy knelt down to the girl. 'Are you OK, Jess?'

Two friends came to comfort Jess and they soon skipped off together. Then Amy turned to Bertie who was staring at the floor, his mouth twitching in anticipation of his fate.

'Get inside.' She pointed to the door. 'Now!'

The entire playground went dead. He walked slowly down the path with Amy marching behind. All eyes were on shameful Bertie and the furious teacher who followed him.

Once they were in the building, he paused outside Ian's office.

'No,' Amy motioned to the assembly hall. 'In there.'

She shut the door and he seemed perplexed about why he was in this room.

Amy sat at the piano. 'Sing!'

Bertie said nothing, but he shook his head and looked down at his feet.

'Do it.'

'I don't want to.'

She stared back at him, her eyes wild. 'Would you rather go to Mr Farley? Have your parents called down here again?'

He shook his head a second time.

'Then *sing*, Bertie. I know what I just heard out there. Now, copy this note.'

She hammered on a key, feeling panic and excitement welling up inside her. He did so, but very quietly.

'Louder! Come on Bertie, you've got it in you.'

'No,' he whimpered. 'Just let me go.'

'Bertie!' She swung around. 'If you walk away, you are going to Mr Farley. So, just do this one thing for me and sing. No one else has to hear it. And maybe, just maybe, I will let you off the hook.'

It was no good. His hands trembled in his pockets and he made towards the door.

'Fine. I've tried to be nice here.' Amy got up from behind the piano. 'I've tried to stop you getting into trouble, but the other teachers are right about you, aren't they? You really are one big waste of...'

Then slowly and skilfully, Bertie kept his back to her and began to sing. One cautious line mumbled its way out and then he was off. His voice floated high around the room, pure, powerful and as smooth as silk. As the song built and cascaded into the chorus, his confidence flourished and he turned to face Amy. His eyes were two balls of hurting, soaring emotion and they melted into tears as the words poured out of him.

Amy's heart somersaulted up into her mouth. She had to sit back on the stool as the tremors prickled down her spine. Her own eyes glistened until teardrops dampened her cheeks. It was the moment she had been waiting for and who ever could have known that Bertie would make it happen?

She watched his posture and the movement of his limbs. His troubled face had metamorphosed into something of beauty. Something she knew no one had ever seen before. This was the real boy, hidden behind a brash, mistaken facade.

He finished on a sensational note, his body quaking with breathlessness. In a second, Amy shot to his side and put her hands on his shoulders.

'I knew it. You're out of this world!' She beamed. 'How long have you been singing?'

'Every day, Miss, as long as I can remember.' Bertie glanced up as if he was crossing hot coals.

'Do your parents know?'

He shook his head.

'Does anyone?'

'No.' He wrung his hands together and looked ashamed.

Amy could hardly contain herself and the wheels were spinning in her mind as she paced across the floor.

'Bertie…' she said finally. 'Would you like to be Joseph in the play?'

His face paled immediately. 'No, Miss. I couldn't.'

'Why not? You'd be perfect.'

Bertie looked out onto the playground, where the children had resumed their lunchtime games. 'They'll make fun of me, Miss.'

'They will not. Don't you know how good you are?'

He thought for a moment. 'Not as good as Flynn.'

'No, you're not as good.' She reduced her voice to a whisper. 'Because you're even *better*, Bertie.'

He quivered with realisation and his watery stare gripped her.

'I mean it,' Amy continued. 'I sat through so many auditions yesterday and no one even came close to having the talent you've got.'

She begged him with her eyes.

'Bertie, if you do this, you will change everything. Everyone will be proud of you. Your friends, your parents. Me. You can be amazing. And I'll be there every step of the way. No one is going to make fun of you. I won't let that happen, I promise.'

She could see that this was his dream and he wanted it more than anyone. But she also saw the fear that was still clouding over his face.

'Come on,' she pleaded. 'Show them what you're made of!'

Bertie smiled. For the first time she had ever known, he smiled and it transformed his whole face. It was as if his soul had been suddenly unleashed and he was trusting her with every last shred of his dignity.

'I'd really like to, Miss.'

She dabbed her moist eyes with her cuff and hurried back over to him. 'You've made my day, Bertie. My year.'

'Miss,' Bertie sniffed and the corners of his mouth turned downwards. 'Sorry I've been bad.'

'Don't worry. You're going to make up for it, you'll see.'

She knew that this day marked the end of all that. He had hidden behind his tough boy image for too long and the staff had only exacerbated the situation. But no more. Soon, everyone was going to see the real Bertie and be stunned by what that meant.

Together, they walked out of the hall and headed back down to the classroom. And she couldn't wait to write his name at the very top of the cast list.

Sixteen

Amy entered Ian's office with a huge smile on her face. He looked up from behind his desk where papers littered the surface.

'Good morning, Amy, what can I do for you?'

'Here is the final cast list. I finished it last night.' She waited for Ian to peruse it.

'So…' He spoke without reading the details. 'Are you satisfied with who you've selected? There's always time to change your mind before I make the announcement.'

'No need for that. I'm more than happy.'

She watched Ian's focus move to the list. In seconds, his eyes widened to their limits and he looked at her in horror.

'Amy, I'm not sure this is a good idea,' he warned softly. 'The boy has quite a reputation, you know. This isn't going to go down well with the staff.'

'I know what you must be thinking, Ian, but he's unbelievable. He sang for me yesterday and I was totally blown away.'

Ian frowned, unconvinced. 'I find it hard to believe that he could be better than someone like Flynn. I mean, *there's* a child known for his talents.'

'He's overrated,' Amy replied flatly and Ian's mouth gaped in response. 'I'm sorry, but Bertie completely outshines him. I was even in tears by the end of it.'

'Why has no one ever known about this?'

'Because he was scared.' She took the opposite chair. 'He thought the kids would ridicule him and that we wouldn't take him seriously.'

Ian looked saddened as he registered what she was saying and he flopped into his seat.

'Let's face it. If he'd dared to approach anyone about this, they'd probably have laughed in his face. No one likes him much, so why would they give him the time of day?'

'Well, there could be some truth in that,' Ian nodded solemnly. 'But how ever did you find out?'

Amy skirted around the episode in the playground.

'I heard him… humming at breaktime yesterday and I detected something in his voice. I managed to make him sing a few lines and bingo. Ian, he's got star quality and, quite frankly, if he's not our Joseph then…' she chose her words carefully, 'then I'd rather not direct the play.'

That did it. Ian looked alarmed at the prospect. It was obvious that he wanted her to drive the production and he would be unlikely to replace her at this late stage. He fixed the list to the clipboard without reading it any further.

'Well, if you're happy then so am I.' He grinned broadly. 'It's only right that we bring out the best in our pupils.'

'Thanks, Ian.' Amy's eyes gleamed. 'Believe me, he'll knock your socks off!'

'Better wear my best pair then,' Ian winked. 'See you in assembly and well done.'

Amy led her class confidently into the hall. Nothing could get her down right now as she sat back in her chair, waiting for the moment to arrive.

'How's it going?' Gita sat next to her in a frilled green tunic.

'Good thanks. You?'

Alison burst in and glanced at the clock with relief. 'That's all right then. I thought I'd had it when the car wouldn't start.'

As she seated herself, there was silence between the three of them.

Amy looked from side to side. 'You can ask, you know.

I won't bite your heads off.'

'I wasn't going to say anything.' Alison feigned indifference.

'Me either,' added Gita.

Amy smirked. 'It's all done. Decided from start to finish.'

'That's good.' Alison eyed Amy's folder and could no longer contain her interest. 'Let's have a look then. Where is it?'

'I'd say it's right there.' Amy nodded her head at Ian, who was just coming into the room.

Gita was intrigued. 'So, who have you…?'

'Good morning, everybody!' Ian took his place at the foot of the stage and commanded all attention. 'I have some very exciting news but for now, let me tell you what happened when the old lady down my road lost her canary.'

He launched into a long story, no doubt with a strong moral to be remembered at the end. But Amy's mind was distracted by other things. Namely Joel, squinting vacantly at the wall. The sleeves of his jumper were pushed up over his forearms and his hair seemed even blonder in the muted light.

She fixed her sight on his chest as it filled and unfilled with his silent breathing. Sliding further and deeper down, she fought the urge to take over with her hands. Then she retraced the path to his eyes, which were now returning the intensity of her stare.

Quickly, she glanced away, wondering how long he'd been watching her. But he locked her in a smile which she couldn't escape from, even if she had wanted to.

Ian finished his tale and began to read the notices, so she peeled herself away and hoped Joel would be accepting of the news.

'Now, at last I can tell you who will be playing who in our Christmas production.' Ian pulled the list from his clipboard. 'So, I'm pleased to say that Joseph will be played by…' He gave what seemed like an endless pause. There was shuffling in the seats around Amy, little coughs of expectation and every ear ready to receive the details. 'Bertie Hughes.'

The children turned to find Bertie in the crowd. A few laughed, not to ridicule him but because clearly they thought it was an error. Bertie the bully boy, taking to the stage? Mr Farley must have read that out wrong.

As he sat in his place, enduring the reactions, Amy's smile tore away the misguided scrutiny.

'The narrator will be played by Flynn Branston, Pharaoh by Phillip Greengage...'

Ian carried on through the list, but no one seemed to be listening. Displeasure began to make itself evident with gasps and whispers of disgust. She turned to see Penny staring back and boiling over with anger. Gita's hand had flown over her mouth and Alison's couldn't stretch wider.

But Amy continued to keep her cool. She had to do it for Bertie.

She looked down the line of horrified teachers and her heart sank when she focused on Joel. He frowned pensively into the distance and his arms were firmly folded. There was no looking back at her anymore.

Amy eyed Bertie again and swallowed as it dawned on her. Joel did not support this and she understood why. She thought back to the days when she was set upon by people like Bertie, and she knew that giving them any reward was against everything Joel believed in. He was by her side in most things, but this was a step too far.

But strength still towered inside her when she looked over at that boy. She could hear him now, singing from the heart and spilling out the years of hurt and secrecy. He glanced at her again and it shot her to pieces, just knowing how much trust he had given her. Smiling again, she saw his spirit taking flight. They were going to do this. Just him and her against anyone who didn't have faith in them.

When assembly came to a close, the teachers gathered in the staffroom. Their grave faces were a chain around her neck and she knew they'd be sniping on the quiet.

Gita was speaking to Alison, whose face was completely aghast. Their whispers were more than obvious despite Amy being present.

'Everything all right?'

Gita turned around slowly. 'Not really. What are you *thinking*?'

'Bertie Hughes, of all people. Are you insane?' Alison seethed.

'You don't understand. He can sing.' She waited for their faces to brighten. 'He can *really* sing!'

'Oh, come on,' Alison laughed. 'He wouldn't know about acting if it hit him in the face.'

'That is where you're wrong.' Amy had to stop herself squaring up to Alison. 'Acting is exactly what he's been doing.'

The two teachers glanced at each other in confusion.

'He was too embarrassed to be open about his singing. He thought he'd just be mocked so he covered it up.'

'And what about how he's made other people feel? It's fine for him to treat everyone else like dirt then. In fact, let's just give him a medal, shall we?' Alison shook her head.

Gita then chipped in. 'I just don't think it's fair on Flynn, Amy. He's never caused any trouble around here and now the part that should be his has been given to someone like…'

'Oh Gita, I couldn't care less about who's been good and who hasn't. I'm casting a play, not dishing out Santa's presents.'

The pair were open-mouthed, like two startled goldfish.

'And anyway,' Amy asserted. 'Bertie is far more talented. His voice knocks spots off Flynn's.'

'How can you *say* that?' squealed Alison. 'It's a known fact that Flynn Branston is the star of the school. I told you that from the start but for some reason, you just didn't want to know.'

'No, he isn't,' replied Amy bluntly. 'And you can't make that judgement when you've never heard Bertie.'

Alison snorted. 'I think I'll pass on that one!'

Amy gestured a hand at her. 'You see, this is just what I'm talking about. He's been damaged because of attitudes like yours.'

'Right, so now it's my fault?'

'I didn't say that.'

'Well, good luck to you.' Alison pursed her lips. 'And when Bertie lets you down and the whole thing's wrecked, don't say we didn't warn you.'

'He's not going to ruin this play. He'll be the making of it.'

But her plea was useless. Alison and Gita turned away and refused to continue the conversation.

'Suit yourselves then.' Amy stormed across the room. 'But that boy is going to prove you wrong.'

She shut the door with a hard bang and swept off down the corridor. She knew the whole room would be up in arms now she wasn't there to defend herself. But what did they know? Her head was still swimming in the warmth of Bertie's voice, revelling in the secret that only she had been privy to.

It was quieter than normal down the walkway, no doubt because everyone was caught up in the commotion. But a shuffle sounded ahead of her and someone stepped into her path.

'I want a word with you.'

'Penny!' Amy raised a hand to her chest. 'I didn't realise you were there.'

'Believe me, you won't forget it.'

Amy looked blankly back as Penny smiled sarcastically.

'You've got a nerve, Amy Ashcroft. Who do you think you are?'

'If this is about the play...'

'Giving the lead role to the lowlife of the school. That's your idea of a job well done, is it?'

'He's best singer we've got.' Amy looked into her eyes. 'And he's not a lowlife.'

'You poor, naive little soul,' Penny smirked. 'You

thought that by doing something nice for him, he might just have a personality transplant and leave everyone alone. Well, I'll give you an A for effort.'

'You'll see, Penny. No one believes me yet, but…'

'No one believes you because you're wrong.'

'I wish you could hear him. We're rehearsing next Tuesday after school. Why don't you pop in and…?'

'You're fooling yourself. This production is going to be a disaster and unless you ditch Bertie, you can consider it cancelled.'

'I don't think so. Ian knows all about it. He wouldn't have read out the list if he…'

'Ian is a bumbling idiot! Just one word from me and he'll change his mind.'

'You can't do that.'

'Watch me.' Penny looked down her nose at Amy. 'You're clearly not capable of managing something like this if you're casting out of sympathy. Bertie Hughes! I've heard it all now.'

Amy tried fiercely to hold herself together. 'You can't just shatter his dreams like that. He had a hard enough time opening up to me in the first place.'

'The boy should be locked up, not showcased on the stage.'

'How can he ever be expected to improve if no one believes in him?'

'I'm beyond caring,' Penny snapped. 'But he will be starring in that play over my dead body.'

'No way. I cannot and will not stop Bertie from playing Joseph.'

'Why ever would you do that?' The voice at the top of the staircase made both women look round. 'Not having second thoughts, are you?'

'No.' The tears in Amy's eyes smudged everything out of view. 'It's just that…'

'I'm giving Amy a little advice about the ups and downs of managing a production.'

'Good idea, Penny,' Ian chuckled. 'Because if anyone learned the hard way, it was you! I mean…' He tried to control his laughter. 'How you could mix up two different musicals is beyond me.'

'Yes, Ian. I don't think we need to say any more.' Penny stared coldly out of the small windows along the top of the wall.

Ian leaned into Amy. 'It was supposed to be *Annie*, but half the songs were from *Annie Get Your Gun*. We had a whole stage full of orphans in cowboy costumes!'

Amy's eyes dried as she watched Penny shrivel in the face of Ian's glee.

'We didn't get the best reviews that year, but at least she tried. Didn't you, Penny?'

There was no reply. Penny just stood drilling her foot into the floor.

'But don't you worry, Amy. I'm sure things will run much more smoothly for you. I can't wait to see the fruits of your labour!'

'Excuse me.' Penny began to skulk away. 'I've got a class to teach.'

Ian guffawed after her until she was out of sight.

'Ian,' Amy caught his attention with her serious expression. 'You are still happy about Bertie, aren't you?'

'Yes, Amy, surprisingly I am. I saw his face when I made the announcement. I've not heard him sing yet of course, but there's a change in the lad. I can at least see that.'

'Rehearsals start on Tuesday,' Amy smiled. 'We'll be in the hall if you want to come and listen.'

'I may well just do that.' Ian nodded as he backed away. 'I may well.'

Relief rushed over her as she headed to the huts, full of anticipation as she stepped into the room. Nothing else was going to bring her down today. There was a new boy in this class now and she couldn't wait to teach him.

***

When the day ended, Amy clicked off the lights with a hefty pile of work to mark. It would usually bore her to tears after a long and arduous day, but the change in Bertie had left her feeling joyous. Even his classmates had given their approval. If only the teachers weren't such hard nuts to crack.

The staffroom was dark, but as most of her colleagues had now gone home, it was peaceful at last and heat still circulated from the radiator. It wouldn't be locked for a few hours yet, so Amy decided to stay. If she got everything marked while she was still at school, she could head home for an early night.

Twenty minutes in, she was leaning over the coffee table, furiously penning corrections. She tried to concentrate through the loudening footsteps and in an instant, Joel appeared clutching a pile of exercise books. She covered another page in biro, hoping he wouldn't mention the play.

'I didn't expect to find you here. Looks like we had the same idea.'

Amy was surprised by his friendliness. 'I'm just trying to get it over with.'

'Long day?'

'Good, actually.' Her smile faded. 'Not the best morning though.'

'Let me guess. You're getting stick for casting Bertie in the play.'

'Come on then, I've had it from all the others. You might as well have your say, too.'

'There's no need.'

'Yes, there is. He isn't worthy. I shouldn't be rewarding him for months of bad behaviour. I should have given it to Flynn…'

'Who says?'

'Just about everyone! Ali and Gita aren't talking to me. Penny said I was incapable…'

Joel bowed his head in dismay. 'I'm so sorry. I should have stuck around after assembly.'

'It's fine, really. I can't expect anyone to understand right now.' She turned back to the marking.

'I do.'

Joel's words made her look straight at him. He was smiling so gently, chasing away her solitude.

'So, you've seen it too?' Her face lit up. 'You know what he's really like?'

'Rude, conceited, disruptive and downright lazy.'

Amy shook her head and glared at the floor.

'But I know you've done the right thing.'

'That doesn't make sense.'

'Yes, it does.' His gaze nearly drowned her. 'Because I believe in you. I told you that before.'

'You don't think I'm crazy?'

'The passion you have for that boy… it's clear there's more to him than anyone else realises.'

'I promise you.' Amy nodded. 'And everyone's going to see it for themselves.'

'I said you'd work wonders, didn't I? Nothing's changed.'

'But you didn't look happy in assembly.'

'I was just thinking.'

Amy tensed up, feeling warmth hit her cheeks. 'What about?'

'Not one single member of staff would have had the balls to do what you've done.'

She smiled. His faith empowered her so much, she wondered how she had carried on all day without it.

'I hope you're going to keep holding that head high.' Joel's expression was radiant as he lifted the first book off his pile. 'Because everyone who doubted you will be eating their words when this play is over.'

'You think?'

'I know.'

A good hour passed and her eyes needed a rest. She blinked away the pencil lines that flashed in her tired vision. Joel was crouched over the table, almost halfway through the work. She watched him rest the pen between his lips, his hand splayed out across the open book. He etched a note on the last line and Amy smiled to herself as his curvy handwriting took on its familiar shape. She was sure she still had exercise books of her own marked in identical squiggles of red.

But here she was sitting closer to him than she'd ever imagined she would. Here in what had once been the out-of-bounds staffroom. As their bodies missed each other by inches, she almost felt forbidden. Like she wasn't allowed to be there.

Subtle shadows wove in bands across the room and her concentration dwindled with the slightest of Joel's movements. As she reached her last section of marking, she slowed down, noting the small chunk of books he still had to get through. She was none the wiser at the end of each sentence. Joel just kept eating into her mind.

'Right, that's me finished,' she said softly. 'I guess I'll get going.'

Immediately, he dropped his biro and eyed the papers in Amy's arms. 'Can you manage all that?'

'I'll be fine.'

She tried not to let a single page slip from under her elbow but he sprung straight to his feet and as she reached the doorway, he was right behind her.

'I'll get this.' He slid his arm around the curve of her waist, with the narrowest gap possible between them, and grabbed the door handle. 'It always seems to jam when your hands are full.'

'Thanks. See you tomorrow, then.'

'Yes, see you.'

She took a last look at his smile and his hair, frayed from the concentration, and walked further towards reception.

'And Amy…'

She stopped as his voice echoed out behind her.

'If anyone else can't keep their opinions to themselves, I want to know about it, OK?'

'Thank you,' she replied softly. 'Bye for now.'

She hurried around the corner, but her pace slowed when Joel was out of sight. A grey haze was settling outside and the hedges brushed their bristles against the lilac wash of sky. The staccato clicking of her heels on the tarmac pierced through the silence and Keith was the only other person in sight.

Amy continued in almost slow motion, out of the playground and past the canteen. She couldn't seem to fight another glance over her shoulder in the strange hope that she was being followed. Reaching the top of the path all too soon, she allowed her keys to lose themselves deep in the clutter of her handbag. She stared once more behind her for any sign of life, but her view was only swamped by the cold night.

Across the car park, Joel's car sat motionless. This evening had been as good a chance as any, but his interest in Amy was nothing more than professional. Reality took over as she sat behind her wheel, wishing he would stop her at the very last moment. But slowly and cautiously, she edged her way out of the car park as the faint glimpse of window light faded into darkness.

Seventeen

It was good to wake up the next morning without being deafened by the alarm. Amy rolled over and turned on the TV to a weekend cookery programme. She made a bowl of porridge and got straight back under the duvet.

The clouds were piled like mountains through the window and the thinning daybreak didn't extend into the room. Perhaps she would stay right where she was, with the addition of a hot water bottle.

She'd had a thoroughly draining week and she still felt exhausted from the backlash. Add to this a large stack of work which had taken up most of the evening ,and she was surprised to be awake at this reasonably early hour.

A weather report came on the screen and a blue blob expanded over the entire south coast on the map. The rain would be in full swing by midday, so it was final. She would have a lazy day and maybe not even get dressed.

The packed car parks and bedlam-filled shops would just have to wait. Today, her only Christmas shopping would be online. She pulled her tablet off the floor and balanced it on her knees. Praline chocolates and some music books for Stan, perfume for Melinda and a gift set from Vanessa's favourite cosmetics brand. It was all going well so far. She bought Giles a grooming kit and treated the pets to some toys and biscuits.

Then her phone rang and Alison's name flashed up. What did *she* want? She had never phoned Amy on a weekend before. Perhaps it was best not to answer. The last thing she needed was another battering about the play.

But she answered the call regardless and turned down the TV. 'Hello.'

'Amy, it's Ali.'

'Hi.' Amy sounded pleasant enough, but she wasn't overly warm. 'How are you doing?'

'Fine, well… not really. I just wondered if you fancied meeting up for a coffee.'

Amy glanced at the brooding storm, ready for the imminent downpour. 'Today?'

'That's right. Sorry, are you busy?'

Yes, she was actually. She was busy having some time to herself for once. She was busy not getting dressed and maybe not even getting up. She was busy trying to clear her head of people like Alison, who hadn't given Amy's feelings a second thought before launching into a tirade at the drop of a hat and humiliating her in the process.

'No, not really. Where do you want to meet?'

'What about Camari's in Burling?' Alison suggested. 'That's the big café on the corner of the seafront road.'

'Suppose so. What time?'

'Shall we say, eleven-ish?'

'OK then. See you soon.'

Amy threw the phone down and filled her cheeks with a sigh. Now she had to drive to the next town and sit around in a rainy beachside coffee bar with someone she didn't feel like talking to.

But it would have felt wrong to refuse. They had built up a good friendship and Amy didn't want to lose it. She hoped that Alison wasn't trying to change her mind about Bertie, but perhaps it was something else.

She grabbed a warm jumper and pulled her fur-lined boots on over a dark pair of jeans. With a quick dash of make-up and a brush of her hair, she left the house in a waterproof mac, stuffing an umbrella under her arm.

After a brief stop-off for petrol, she began the dreary drive to Burling. It was three miles west along the seafront and the closest town of any use. If there was shopping to be done or coffee to be enjoyed, Burling was the nearest place to go.

A brewing sea rumbled in a long spearmint stretch and the clumpy beach weeds floundered under the wind's force. The buses moved sullenly in and out of the shelters, carrying one or two passengers at most. No seaside snack bar looked complete without its rainbows of rock and barley sugar lollipops. The cafes and outdoor restaurants were ideal in the summer, but all of that was wasted now as heavy rain soaked the town.

She passed the domed structure of the old pavilion theatre, where the pantomimes of her childhood had played out. Beyond it, the pier dipped its feet into the ocean near the nightclub at the end that had been her favourite teenage haunt.

Camari's cafe was right on the corner just as she remembered it, but the retro logo had been replaced by a modern brown frontage. A giant plastic ice cream was displayed optimistically outside with a full list of flavours scrawled in bright liquid chalk.

She walked through the door and easily spotted Alison in her pale pistachio gilet over a white cotton top. Her smile was warm, hopeful almost, when Amy sat down at their table.

'How are you doing?'

'Fine,' Amy nodded. 'You?'

'OK, I guess. Sorry, hardly the best weather to be out of the house.'

'I don't mind. Might as well just carry on Christmas shopping as I'm here.'

'I'm all done with that. Finished last week.' Alison tightened the elastic in her hair and paused before she spoke again. 'What are you having to drink?'

Amy didn't even need to think. The classic Camari hot chocolate had been her favourite since she was little. She hadn't had one for literally years.

'I'm going for the hot chocolate,' Alison said. 'You really should try it. This place has been around since time began and it's one of their signature recipes.'

Amy bit her lip. 'I'll go for that then.'

She unzipped her handbag to fish out her purse, but Alison waved her to stop.

'I'll get these.'

'Are you sure?'

'Of course. I dragged you here after all.'

She returned with two mugs full of steaming, rich chocolate and some miniature biscotti on the side.

'Thanks for this.' Amy savoured the taste in her mouth as she waited for Alison to speak.

'Look, the reason I wanted to meet you… I just thought it would be a nice change to get together out of that staffroom for once.'

'Yes, it is.'

Alison looked straight into her eyes. 'I'm so sorry. I was way out of line yesterday.'

'That's OK. I know the whole Bertie thing is a bit unexpected.'

'You can say that again. But I shouldn't have rubbished your opinion.'

'Ali, everyone's got the right to say what they think, including you.'

'I know, but not the way I did. I mean, you're not a complete idiot. You must see some sort of talent in the kid.'

Amy looked back at her, the proof of Bertie's voice fuelling her grin. 'I do. And everyone will.'

'Well, at least I can take your word. If you say he's good, I believe you.'

'That means a lot.' Amy was touched.

'You're such a great friend now. I don't want to fall out with you.'

'Don't worry, it's all over.'

'So, I'm forgiven?'

Amy laughed. 'You only had a bit of a go at me, that's not the crime of the century.'

'Truce though?'

'Truce.'

They clinked mugs and took generous swigs before moving on to more trivial topics.

'So, you've finished your Christmas shopping? I'm far from done.'

'You'll get there. I just didn't put much effort in, especially with Nick. He's got a tool kit. That's my hint for him to get off his backside and fix everything that has been broken for the past year.'

Amy giggled. 'I guess I just take too long deciding. I should grab a leaf out of your book.'

'Well, it's given me more time to choose a dress for the party. Can't wait to see how they deck out The Spring Lake.'

'Seen anything you like yet?'

'A few. I might go and have a look in a minute.'

'Come on,' Amy scraped her chair away from the table. 'I'll walk round with you and then press on with gift ideas.'

Amy left Alison at the entrance to some fitting rooms, holding a selection of dresses. She browsed for a few more presents, but the rain pelted down so she swiftly left for home. And as the weather continued its foggy descent, she was only too glad to be back in the warmth with TV, pyjamas and that furry hot water bottle.

***

Things at school were better now that Amy and Alison had cleared the air and, by Tuesday, even Gita was being pleasant. They were yet to be swayed by Amy's decision, but at least they were beginning to accept it.

Bertie was changing fast. He was more involved in lessons and even helping others if they needed it. Amy felt so proud of him already. She was looking forward to this evening's rehearsal and couldn't wait to share his voice with the cast.

But first, Ian had asked the staff to stay behind for what he had assured them would be a very quick meeting. As usual, time was getting on and he still hadn't shown up.

'He's always doing this,' Nigel tutted. 'Just when there's a match on.'

'And Nick's parents are staying. I've got to get home and do dinner,' Alison added with a yawn.

The door flew open and Ian hurried in.

'Ever so sorry to keep you all waiting.' He looked at the rows of fed-up faces. 'Anyway, just a few quick points. Firstly, the staff Christmas party will be at The Spring Lake. There'll be a slap-up meal, dancing and free drinks, so plenty to look forward to. Here is the menu, so please hand this back to Sue when you've selected your three courses.'

He gave everyone a copy and then waited until they were all listening again.

'Right, moving on. The Christmas play is the following week and I need some volunteers. Stella is starting on the props tomorrow, Amy. Keith is on lighting and Sue is doing ticket sales, but I need someone on front of house.' He looked around the room and Alison raised a hand. 'Alison, thank you. And make-up. Gita, would you like to repeat last year's efforts?'

'I suppose I could.'

'Gita on make-up.' Ian jotted it down. 'Programmes? I need someone to compile the information and someone to design it.'

'I can do the layout,' Debra offered.

'And Penny,' Ian glanced sideways. 'Can I ask you to do the content?'

'I'd love to!' she enthused. 'Count me in.'

Amy looked down at the back of Penny's head. It was baffling that she would want any involvement, especially after Ian's mockery of her own stint in the director's chair. But Alison and Gita were making more effort, so maybe Penny was too.

'And last but not least, I need two people on traffic control. There'll be mayhem in that car park if the visitors are left to their own devices.'

'Go on then.' Nigel raised a hand.

'Anyone else?' Ian looked around.

'If there's a cup of cocoa at the end of it.' Martin lifted a finger.

'I think we can do better than that,' Ian said with a wink. 'Well, I won't take up any more of your time. Have a pleasant evening.'

Amy headed straight into the toilets with her gym bag. Once there, she changed into a pair of joggers, some new trainers and a stretchy T-shirt in a light candy pink. She pulled her hair back in a loose ponytail and freshened up her face. Then she made her way to the hall, where Bertie and the other cast members were waiting.

'OK, everyone.' She sat down at the piano. 'Come and gather round.'

The children all got comfortable, some on the floor and some on the edge of the stage nearest to Amy.

'We're going to practise the dances and go through some of the scenes but first, I think you need to hear something.' She looked with delight at her leading boy. 'Now Bertie, I'm dropping you in at the deep end here, but will you just let everybody know why you're our Joseph?'

He glanced around at the expectant faces. 'OK.'

'Do you know this song?' She opened the music score at one of the best-loved songs and Bertie nodded. 'Great. Here we go.'

Amy keyed out the introduction and gestured to bring Bertie in. The sensational voice sailed out, working the same magic it had done that day when she'd first discovered his talent. Amy watched as the listeners eyed each other in complete disbelief. Every bar he sang reaffirmed how right she had been to select him.

When he finished, he lowered his eyes to the ground, but the room was filled with cheers. Amy turned to face the joyful children.

'So, what do you think to him?'

'Brilliant!' said one.

'The best Joseph ever,' shouted another.

'Good,' Amy smiled. 'So, if you really want this play to be great, you've got to work well with your leading character. Concentrate on your faces, your emotions and reactions to every word he sings. It'll be fun, so are you ready?'

A resounding 'Yes' was the answer.

'Now, let's get on the stage and do our first big number. Bertie, stand there, Brittany there, Flynn over there and this group of you… about there.'

Amy proceeded to demonstrate the actions, initially with Bertie and Flynn, and then moving outwards to the more minor characters. It was rather a muddle at first, with some children being far better movers than others, but before long they began to get the gist of the routine. After well over an hour, the scenes and songs were starting to take shape.

She was so excited inside. Here they were, on an empty stage in their PE kits, but the way their talent seemed to come together was like someone had flicked a switch. This evening, they were shining. Bouncing off Bertie and coming alive with him.

'You've got it!' Amy clapped. 'One last time, all the way through from the beginning.'

She walked over to the sound system and started the track, then she got into position and guided the cast through the song. The upbeat music and happy vibes soared around the room and the wide-eyed faces were the driving force.

In the darkness of the window, Joel's smile caught her eye. As she moved over the floor in precise shapes of symmetry, she felt his approval shining through it all. The children leapt across the stage, their voices towering above the tune as Amy led the way.

Knowing he was watching sent waves through her limbs with each mirrored step in perfect time. It was as if her feet were inches from the ground as the thrill of his attention showered down on her. The same look of pride he had once given the girl was staring back at her now. She danced in the spotlight of his vision, never wanting the moment to end.

Eighteen

Hair up or down? She couldn't choose and Alison was about to arrive in the taxi. Taking another sip of gin and tonic, she stepped back from the mirror to check her full reflection.

She couldn't have resisted the black sequinned dress she had seen that day with Vanessa. Clingy and flattering in all the right places, it nipped her in at the waist and finished just high enough above the knee to show her legs off to perfection.

Her glittery eyes were coated in thick mascara with a rosy dusting of blusher and nude-pink lips. The light spray tan had paid off too, polishing her skin with a golden glow. She scooped her hair up in her hands one last time before letting it fall onto her shoulders. Definitely down, she decided.

A car horn tooted outside, so she quickly slipped on a pair of heels and grabbed her clutch bag. Alison smiled from the back of the cab and handed Amy a can of spirit and mixer. She looked even better with her hair like that, sitting in soft waves around her face. Her dark coat revealed a burgundy dress and a delicate garnet necklace which brought out the green in her eyes.

'You look gorgeous!' she enthused. 'Please tell me you're faking the lashes, though.'

'New mascara,' Amy smiled worriedly. 'Is it too much?'

'No, it's amazing. I'm useless with those chunky wands.'

'What are you talking about? Your eyes look huge. Definitely do the liner thing more often.'

'Nick just laughed at me. Quoted a phrase out of some

horror film.'

'Probably just doesn't like you being all done up and on the loose without him.'

'Well, he's the one with a hot date this evening. Video games and a curry.'

'Typical.'

'Speaking of dates, we're setting Gita up with Martin tonight.'

'But I thought she said...'

'A couple of drinks and he'll be all over her. Then she can thank us.'

'Don't get me involved! We're only just back on track after the whole Bertie thing.'

'I know, but matchmaking is so much fun.'

'Not for the victims.' Amy giggled. 'Unrequited love is not a good thing.'

The taxi drove in darkness along the main road until they reached The Spring Lake in its scenic hillside spot. The surrounding glasshouse was softly illuminated and solar lamps climbed the alfresco seating area as it twisted up the slope.

Vivid lighting fell across the bar and out over the glass like a blue curacao waterfall. Bartenders bustled around a decorative display, while loud music blended with the noisy clinks of ice.

Bellini and bucks fizz lined the front table, so Amy and Alison helped themselves, watching more colleagues arrive. Faye's tiered dress was reminiscent of a wedding cake as she stood downing shots with the rest of the canteen staff. A hand grabbed her shoulder and she turned to face Penny, who immediately complimented the outfit.

Penny wore a chinoiserie-style jumpsuit and her bare feet were squashed into a pair of pointed mules. She and Faye sat down at a nearby table where Debra was dipping into various bowls of crisps. Her make-up was stronger behind her glasses and two shimmering earrings dangled from her lobes.

'All right ladies?' shouted a voice, causing Amy and

Alison to turn around. Nigel wore a smart suit accentuated with a purple shirt and he held a glass of lager in each hand. There was just a drop left in one of them and the other was full to the brim. 'Looking very nice, I must say.'

'Thanks,' Amy grinned. 'Been here long?'

'About half an hour. Just getting stuck into these.' He held up the emptiest glass.

'Pace yourself, Nigel,' warned Alison. 'Your table dancing isn't much of a turn-on.'

He pretended to look insulted. 'But I've been practising all year, just for you.'

'I'd stick to teaching, it suits you better.'

'Ah, you don't mean that, Ali!' He drained his glass and began to slurp from the other one.

'Trust me, she does,' said a woman behind them, turning her head to speak. A gold slide clipped her hair sleekly off her face and she wore a one-shouldered peacock gown. Her blue and gold eye make-up glowed against her skin and it took a few seconds for Amy to realise it was Gita.

'Not you too.' Nigel was comically open-mouthed.

'A little advice…' Gita sauntered across and spoke loudly over the music. 'Check out your moves in the mirror some time.'

'Plenty of those down there.' Nigel splashed beer from his glass as he pointed at the staircase to the function room. 'Are you girls coming?'

'In a minute,' said Alison. 'More cocktails first.'

'Later then.' Nigel waved as he disappeared downstairs.

'You look great, Gita,' Amy praised.

'I was going to say the same to you. What a dress!'

'You think it's OK?'

'Stunning. You too, Ali.'

'Thanks.' Alison finished her Bellini. 'Come on, let's get some more drinks.'

'Where are the loos?' asked Gita. 'I've got to check my face.'

'Let's all go then,' Alison sighed. 'I need borrow that

166

mascara.'

Gita smeared her cheekbones with a bold magenta blusher while Amy's mascara worked wonders for Alison. With her skin and eyes still vibrant and dramatic, an extra slick of lip gloss was all Amy needed. Just another drink and she'd be flirty and tipsy, but not stupidly drunk.

They ordered cosmopolitans and stayed in the area for a while as more staff caught up with one another in a whirlwind of eveningwear and laughter. When most of them drifted downstairs, Amy and the others followed into the function room.

Even though she was lightheaded from the drinks, Amy fluttered below her ribs as they began to descend the staircase. Joel had to be down there somewhere. She walked with Alison and Gita into the impeccably adorned room, where the ceiling was dotted with speckled lights and the tables looked set for a banquet.

An empty dancefloor and a second bar were edged by a mirrored wall and growing gatherings of people were forming around the side lines. Amy scanned the whole place for a hint of him. Amidst the throng of bodies and faces, she soon saw Nigel and Martin, standing in the queue for the bar. Then, looking across to a small crowd near the tables, Ian came into view. He was wearing a tuxedo and linking arms with his wife, whose shoulders were covered by a spangled mohair stole.

The other woman talking to them had her back turned, but she continuously flipped her auburn hair and it shone in each flash of light. It was Lydia, one of the governors from her interview. Amy hadn't seen her since that day and had forgotten how attractive she was. Her petite frame was hugged by a silver dress with spaghetti straps and a plunging neckline. Platform court shoes made her legs look endless as she laughed with Ian, Stella, and another man. Joel.

He wore a simple black shirt and his hair had its usual tousle, but right now he looked incredible. Tonight something fiery was unwinding. He was sensually loosened up and whatever he was chatting about didn't seem to be work-related. It was the side of him that Amy had longed to discover more of and had somehow always known was there. While Alison and Gita continued to admire the scenery, the image of Joel with this carefree disposition was enough to make her weak.

But his focus didn't move from Lydia, who swished her hair and held her pose with such an air of confidence. They moved closer together and Amy's insides plunged as he leaned right over to whisper in her ear. It was too much to take and she shifted her eyes to the other side of the room. Suddenly, all the excitement seemed to drain away.

'Come on,' Alison shouted. 'Let's go to the bar. On me.'

'I'm all right for now,' replied Gita. 'We've got all that wine at dinner to get through.'

'So? We're not even sitting down yet.'

'Gin and tonic, thanks.' Amy refused to look in Joel's direction.

'Just get me a spritzer then.' Gita winked.

As soon as the drinks arrived, Amy gulped away drearily.

'What's up with you?' Alison asked.

As Amy opened her mouth, Gita beat her to it. 'Nothing. I just haven't seen Martin yet.'

'He is here, I saw him a minute ago.'

'Did you?' Gita's eyes widened.

'Well he was... hang on,' Alison squinted through the crowds. 'Over there.' She nodded at a table of nibbles in the direction where Amy knew Joel was.

Gita glanced subtly over. 'Where?'

'Look,' Alison pointed. 'See? Where Ian is in the suit.'

'Yes...'

'Just behind him, look. Stripy shirt.'

'Don't point!'

Gita bashed Alison's arm down, but it was too late. Martin hadn't seen, but it had been enough to distract Joel from his discussion. He immediately stopped talking to Lydia, his eyes clocking Gita's gentle swipe at Alison, and was stunned to silence as his gaze fell on Amy. She couldn't bring herself to look straight at him, but her heart leapt inside. Now, she could do nothing else but try and look her best, even if someone far more model-like was standing right next to him.

Feeling his stare burning away at her, she sipped her drink, lifting her eyes around the room but not letting them make contact with his. While Alison spoke, Amy pretended to listen, blinking softly so her eyelashes fluttered and parting her lips in the prettiest pout possible.

Chills were bursting through her body and her glass would have smashed if she were to clutch it any tighter. She flicked her eyes sideways, over some more, just enough to see him without being obvious. Lydia had turned away. Ian was busy having his bow tie straightened by Stella, but Joel was still looking at nothing but Amy. Like fingers down her skin, she could sense his gaze sweeping over her hair, her face, and the way she looked in the black sequinned dress.

She worked to steady her breathing, but the alcohol and the pounding in her chest made her feel heady and fierce. Seconds later, her eyes were on his and she saw a deep breath fill his lungs. She could still feel the blueness piercing the dark as he held her there in his sight.

Suppressing a breath, she looked away in case she was imagining this. Perhaps her hair was out of place or her dress too far up her thighs. Did he think she was drunk and unruly or being too loud with her friends? She braced herself and returned once more to face the power of his gaze.

It was unmistakable and she knew it now as she smouldered in the line of his vision. The seconds turned to minutes and he couldn't look away, as if she would vanish if he dared.

'Ladies and gentlemen!' The voice of a waiter called out over a ringing glass. 'If you would like to take your seats, dinner is served.'

Gita and Alison snapped her out of the stupor and hurried her away to find their places. She peered back at Joel, but he was no longer there. Scanning the throng of partygoers, she tried to track him down. The idea of him lost in the mass of heads was making her increasingly anxious.

Amy kept her eyes well peeled as she laid a napkin in her lap. To her left, an unrecognisably smart Keith was already getting stuck into the bread basket as Gita took her place on his other side. Alison sat down one chair away from Amy and they both read Martin's name on the card between their seats. They glanced at Gita, who flushed when he arrived and made himself comfortable at the table.

Keith wittered on about plants to Gita while Alison dug Martin for details of his personal life. But Amy was miles away. The waiting staff rallied around pouring wine and soon the starters were served. She blew on the roasted red pepper soup, watching scrupulously for a trace of Joel.

She picked her way through the venison, piled high on a bed of root vegetables and shallots. It was tender and flavoursome, but she could barely taste a thing. He must have left without staying for the meal, she concluded. No matter how hard she looked, he was nowhere to be seen. No one was trying to get her attention. No eyes were calling across the room. She pushed her plate away and sat back in the chair, washing down the torture with her cold white wine.

Bring on dessert, she thought. Because once that was over, she'd be out of there. Time to call a taxi and get off home to wallow in the agony of the evening. Yes, he had noticed her and yes, he had stared, but Joel looked the same way at everyone and she had to remember that. She tried to see sense as the drink took hold.

Taking another swig, she tipped her head back and there, just visible over her glass, was Joel. Picking two beers up from the counter, he walked back to a table not far from her own. He handed a drink to Nigel, who was busily talking to Debra, and his seat was angled at such a slant that the view had been masked by Stella.

The mood changed completely from then on at the table. She was alive with conversation and back in the highest spirits. Chatting to Keith and Gita, she amusedly observed Alison's probing of Martin. And when a mocha cheesecake was put at her place, she relished every mouthful as it crumbled on her tongue. She was merry from the wine but drunker than ever on bliss. Just knowing he was there did inexplicable things to her soul.

A speech from Ian ended the meal, thanking The Spring Lake for its hospitality. The music started as people spilled onto the dancefloor, some modestly shuffling their feet and others like zombies in the middle.

'Come on,' said Gita, grabbing Amy's hand. 'Let's dance!'

She pulled her through the crowd, smacking into various staff members who were too bleary-eyed to notice. Alison followed, clapping her hands as they reached a clear spot off the centre. Amy felt every muscle loosen up as the music took control of her limbs. She was a naturally impressive dancer, but as the wine surged into her, she was numbed of all inhibition. A few teachers turned to watch as she captured their attention and showed a different side to the calm, level-headed colleague that they thought they knew.

Her two friends strutted around with her. Gita waved her arms while Alison head-banged through the tunes. Stella was unamused to be twirled around by Ian as he peered over at Amy and the others through the whole song.

Nigel sashayed up to them, rolling his arms in a routine. His quiffed hair was in disarray and his glasses appeared to be frying in the heat. The jacket and tie were long gone and his shirt was unbuttoned just a little too far down. Gita fell into him and giggled as he twirled her. Then he shimmied over to Alison, stamping with his fists in the air. By now, a circle had formed around the group, watching as Nigel took on the three female teachers.

Alison spun away from him and he boldly side-stepped to Amy. As plastered as he was, even he raised his eyebrows at her risqué dancing. For a few minutes, she allowed him to sway with her and they glided through some intricate footwork before he swung her around.

Smoothly turning out of his grasp, she came face to face with Joel. He had joined the edge of the circle and was watching her move with a face full of glory. Nothing could have prepared her for the pride in his expression and knowing she was now under the spell of his stare.

The next song was one of Amy's favourites and she stepped up the dancing to a soulful, sensual grind. Now was her chance to show Joel that there was more. More beyond the composure she always held at work and more than the inept schoolgirl she hoped he would never remember.

Feeling his eyes pouring down on her now, she began to mouth the words. Throwing back her head, she teased the hem of her skirt, tossing her hair to one side of her face with another sensuous look.

The group closed in and Amy found her back inadvertently pressed into him. She reined in her more provocative moves with softer swaying to the music. With each brush against his clothes or a wisp of breath on her neck, something unimaginable shot through her.

She would crack under the strain if he didn't touch her soon. Slowly, her fingers slid behind her waist, an inch away from his own.

But the hands she felt were not his. Nigel had flown from the other side of the ring, squashing her in a suffocating cuddle. She smiled awkwardly while he breakdanced at her feet and hoped Joel would soon step in. But as she looked desperately around her, waiting for the moment, he faded away into the crowd.

Overheated from the exertion, she walked through the bustle of slurring staff members and back up the staircase to the main bar, noticing that once more, he was nowhere in sight. With a pint of cold water, she headed outside the glasshouse where the garden lights glistened down the spiral of the hillside.

She filled her chest with the nippy fresh air and took a long drink. One minute, Joel was all over her and the next he had disappeared. Perhaps this was just what he was like and he wanted to keep it that way. A single man who'd grown too used to the lifestyle and didn't wish to be tied down. Her heart could have smashed at the possibility that she had just misread this whole night.

'Are you OK?'

Her back stiffened at Joel's voice and the sound of him coming towards her.

'I'm fine. Just cooling down a bit.'

'I'm not surprised.' His smile almost touched her shoulder. 'You're quite a dancer.'

'Wine does crazy things to me. I'll probably be sorry in the morning.'

'I hope not.' Joel moved closer. 'I won't forget it.'

The words fizzed through her like she was dreaming. Inching ever nearer, she turned around to face him and all at once, she was reeled in through the darkness. The heavy bass thumped out from below and drowned in the clarity of the slower song just inside the door. Above them, the outlines of sleeping clouds formed a bilberry arc over the moon. She felt as if she could reach out and touch it, like a solitary piece of chalk on the sky's vast blackboard.

Her head began to spin, but the drinks had nothing to do with it. His hand was there again, resting centimetres from her fingertips. She just knew that in seconds they would be woven into one.

'Amy.' He glanced out into the acres of blackened countryside before bringing his eyes back to her face. 'There's something...'

A crash sounded out behind them and a panel of glass flew in lethal chips onto the pavestones. The arm of a bar chair jutted out of the window and Amy gasped at Gita, lying face down on the floor. She raced inside to help her up with Joel right behind. Gita screeched with laughter while Alison struggled to support her.

'She's overdone the sambuca,' she explained. 'I tried to stop her but she's beyond listening.'

'I heard that!' Gita just managed to get back on her feet.

'I'll go and tell someone about the damage. Ian's going to lose it when he hears.'

'Leave it with me,' Joel instructed. 'Just call her a cab.'

With Gita safely inside the taxi, Alison climbed in next to her and dialled Nick on her phone. Amy confirmed their destinations to the driver, still standing outside in the cold. She was just walking around to the passenger seat door when Joel emerged from the porch.

'So, you're off then.'

She stepped back into the lamplight. 'Got to get her home safely. We were all planning to leave together anyway.'

'See you Monday,' he said softly, nodding back in agreement.

'Definitely.'

Amy's gaze was one of sadness. She turned away and her heart stopped as he reached out and gripped her arm.

'And I meant what I said. I won't forget.'

Her eyes met with his for the last time that evening.

'Hurry up,' Alison shouted. 'It's like an igloo in here with that door open.'

Amy watched Joel slip away through the window. But as the taxi pulled out of the car park, her view to the doorway was blocked.

A dark shadow glowered at her with eyes as feral as a cat's. Gita was out like a light and Alison strained to hear Nick through the bad reception. Only Amy could witness the force of this stare and the loathing that brewed within it. Penny faded fast into a distant fleck of dust, but her imprint dug much deeper into Amy's puzzled mind.

Nineteen

There was no time to ponder the events at The Spring Lake. The next week brought hardly a moment's peace, with rehearsals for the production occupying every minute of time. Amy was breaking her neck to get Joel alone, but the pressure was on to deal with the show.

Things were not much better for Gita. Not only had she landed on the wrong side of Ian, but Martin was steering well clear of her.

'Someone's feeling sorry for herself. What's happened now?'

It was Thursday, nearly a week after the event, and Gita's dejected face had still not lifted.

'Just saw him again. He blanked me.'

'Ian?' Alison asked in half jest and Gita looked unamused. 'Joking, sorry. What did you say to him?'

'Nothing much.'

'He's probably just embarrassed,' Amy suggested. 'Not because of you. Maybe the others are winding him up.'

'Exactly, because of me.' Gita sighed regretfully at the sky. 'I have well and truly blown it.'

'There's a chance I could talk him round.'

'You've done enough damage thanks, Ali.'

'That's rich.' Alison couldn't resist. 'I think it was you hanging out of a broken window with a chair on your head.'

'Hey, come on,' Amy smirked. 'Go easy on her.'

Gita looked weary. 'Nor do I need to be slapping face paint on who knows how many cheeks this afternoon.'

'You're not pulling out are you? It's the dress rehearsal.'

'Don't worry,' Gita shook her head. 'Got to keep Ian sweet at least. What time do you want me?'

'We start at one, so eleven would be good. Then you can get the chorus made up, too.'

'Can't wait.' She grimaced at her watch. 'See you there.'

She skulked off inside the building leaving Alison chuckling discreetly. Amy hid a grin and waited until Gita was out of sight.

'You are cruel!'

Alison frowned playfully. 'Self-inflicted, I think.'

'I know, but can you imagine what it's like for her? If everyone knew that *I* had feelings for…'

She trailed off and Alison snapped into action, urging her to finish the sentence.

'Had feelings for who?'

Amy bit her lip. She looked at Alison's eyes, wide and ready for the name, and vowed not to tell her. Alison had played a big part in messing things up for Gita, so heaven only knew the havoc she could cause with Joel. She quickly tried to retract what she'd said.

'Someone, just… someone.'

'Amy, you little minx. How can you not have told me about this?'

'About what?'

She felt the security slipping through her fingers. One word from Alison and everything would be ruined.

'Who have you got your eye on? I *need* to know!'

'What I meant was, if I liked someone… anyone… I'd hate the world to know about it before I'd even…'

'But you don't fancy anyone specific?' Alison's eyes narrowed slyly, making Amy feel uncomfortable.

'No!'

And that was no lie. This was far from a fleeting crush. When she thought of her history with Joel all the way up to now, nothing she had felt for anyone could ever compare to this.

'Hmmm…' Alison smiled. 'You're hiding something.'

Amy shook her head, concentrating on the children arriving in the playground.

'Look at those eyes! Amy, you can't fool me.'

'Right.' She nodded casually. 'Anyway, I've got to get started in the hall. They're putting up the scenery and I don't want them making a hash of it.'

She left Alison standing by the swimming pool and made for the door into the lower block.

'I'll get it out of you. Just you wait and see!'

'Ali,' Amy stepped inside and shouted back from the doorway. 'Get it into your head will you? I'm not interested in anyone around here.'

She shut the door before Alison could utter another sentence. Then she spun around and froze. In the empty corridor, Ian was opening packets of books and filling the shelves with their shiny new covers. And standing next to him, slashing scissors through the boxes, was Joel. Amy felt the colour draining from her face. There was no question that he hadn't heard her last assertive statement.

'Morning, Amy,' Ian called out.

'Hi, Ian.' She winced inwardly and glanced at Joel. He smiled faintly, but his eyes didn't. As she walked towards them, he looked back down and carried on slicing away the parcel tape.

'Some of these are on the way to your room.' Ian flapped a book in her direction. 'The new Spell and Tell series.'

'Great. I'll have a look later.' She tried to sound keen, but Joel seemed so despondent that it was impossible to feign such optimism.

'All set for tomorrow?' Ian asked.

'I think so.' Amy watched Joel again and welled up inside. 'I'd better get a move on.'

'Of course,' replied Ian, turning back to the shelves. 'Good luck and I hope they all break their legs! Well… not really, obviously.'

'Let's hope not.'

Guilt showered down on her and she longed to put Joel right. Reassure him that she hadn't meant anything she'd just said to Alison. If only Ian weren't around, then she could tell him the truth. How her bones ached for him to hold her and how she had never felt like this about anyone.

Later that day, Amy sat in the hall watching the dress rehearsal. Not a line was forgotten or a note out of tune and it thrilled her to think that she had done all this. But despite all the efforts that were fast paying off, she still felt heavy. It was impossible to wipe Joel's crushed expression from her mind.

Another shameful wave plunged over her as she remembered what had happened in his past. Someone had walked all over him once and now she was doing just the same. Her attention swayed from the play to the clock and she counted the hours until she could find him.

When the last song was over, she ushered the children to the science lab, which was being used as the dressing room. She stowed away her script and stacked up the chairs. Then she was ready. She switched off the lights and headed to the staffroom.

Nigel chatted to Joel with a coffee by the microwave while Alison marked homework on the table. Amy started watering the plants and loitered behind the tallest yucca, hoping Nigel would soon make himself scarce. And with any luck, Alison would be too preoccupied to notice Amy beckoning Joel away.

'So, when do you go?' Nigel asked.

'The first Friday of next term,' Joel replied. 'The apartment's all booked.'

'How long is it this time?'

'Two weeks, as usual.'

'Can I come?' Alison joked. 'I'd kill for some sun after the Christmas I've got in store. Nick's family always do my head in.'

'Seriously, Joel mate, consider me first.' Nigel took a sip

from his mug. 'An entire season of my mum's festive cooking and I'll be begging to get in your suitcase.'

Amy felt uneasy from where she stood. What was all this talk of a trip? She listened in for longer to try and find out more, but the subject seemed to be over.

'How's it going, Amy?' Alison asked loudly. 'Was the rehearsal OK?'

Amy paused before speaking and still stayed hidden.

'No, it was terrible. The worst one yet.'

She heard Alison drop her pen.

'Why?'

'It just went to pieces.' She came out from behind the plant. 'The set fell down, they forgot their lines… just about everything went wrong. I don't know what I'm going to do tomorrow.'

'Please tell me you're joking.'

'Of course I am. It was fine!'

'Thank God for that.' Alison's hand slammed against her chest. 'I thought you were serious for a minute.'

Amy walked behind her chair and looked straight at Joel, making sure she had his undivided attention.

'Well, don't believe everything I say, Ali.'

She smiled so fully and held his eyes to hers until she was sure he'd understood her meaning. His face lit up and it made her feel lightheaded.

'I wouldn't speak too soon,' Alison replied unsuspectingly. 'Your make-up artist is hardly on top form and how can I do front of house without any programmes?'

Amy frowned. 'They're not done yet?'

'Actually, I think that's all in hand,' Nigel said. 'Debra was printing them last time I looked.'

'Is she still in there?' Alison finished her marking and stashed it in her bag.

'Should be. It wasn't long ago.'

'I'll go and find her then.' She looked intrigued and rushed out of the room.

Amy took her mug from the cupboard and got some milk

out of the fridge. Now all she needed was for Nigel to leave.

'So, should I be jealous?' she asked boldly. 'Did I hear that you're going somewhere nice after Christmas?'

'Oh, that.' Joel smirked. 'Just an annual PE conference abroad. All the Heads of sports go along. I suppose it's good once I'm there.'

'Costa Navarino,' Nigel added. 'A hidden gem, right out in the Med. Great climate for all the demonstrations.'

'Sounds like fun,' Amy enthused.

'Sometimes,' agreed Joel. 'But I do work at the apartment too.'

'Do you… stay there on your own?'

Joel nodded. 'We book the same one every year and I get it all to myself.'

Amy felt happier. That was good at least. A whole fortnight would be hard enough without him, but the idea of Joel having company might have pushed her over the edge.

'You should have a word with Ian.' Nigel said with a wink. 'Surely two heads are better than one. We'd have a ball, mate!'

'Exactly,' Joel laughed. 'I'd never get anything done.'

Amy searched for the teabags, wishing Nigel would go. Joel shot her a glance and she knew he was thinking the same. Her skin flushed rose as his eyes soaked her up and she couldn't wait to be near him.

All silence broke as the door creaked and Alison entered gloomily. Debra followed her with a mortified face. Placing a programme in Alison's open palm, she chewed her bottom lip as if she dared not come any closer.

Alison was full of remorse as she opened the cover of the booklet, then handed it to Amy who perplexedly studied the contents. It was information on the cast and crew, with photos and bios of each actor. But right at the top, under the heading of Director, Amy's picture was absent next to her name. Instead, in the frame where her image belonged, a gold death mask sat vulgarly in its place.

She didn't know what to feel. Perhaps it was the children

playing a prank. But Debra must have noticed when she had worked on the layout, so why had it not been corrected prior to this?

'Amy?'

Joel's voice travelled over her shoulder, so she stepped aside to let him see the page.

'What's going on here?' he asked calmly, but Debra wouldn't look his way. 'Did you submit a picture?'

Amy didn't hear that he was now questioning her. She stared blankly at the wall.

'Amy,' he asked, more firmly this time. 'Did you give them your picture?'

She looked at him, still stunned, and nodded in response. 'It was a print. Penny was going to scan it.'

'So, where is it?' Joel took a step closer, the rage ripping into his eyes.

Debra fiddled frantically with the cuffs of her cardigan and she scrunched her nose to hitch up her glasses. 'Penny wasn't given one. She found an image of the mask thing and she told me to use that instead.'

'This is absurd.' Joel pointed at Amy. 'Do you know how much effort she's put into this thing? How many hours she's spent working with those kids?'

'Joel, it's OK,' Amy almost whispered, her face burning from the shock.

'No, it isn't!' he shouted, squaring up to Debra. 'Remember that brat who threw water in your face? The boy no one ever thought would change?'

Debra nodded, clearly not knowing where to put herself.

'He's a different child now and it's all because of her. No one wanted to believe her. Some of you still don't. But Amy knew what she was doing. She's changed this school for the better and *this* is what she gets in return?'

Amy's vision blurred with tears. Joel glanced back at her again and she saw how her distress had immediately become his own.

'I'm sorry,' Debra said sincerely. 'I didn't want to do it,

but…'

'Where's Penny?' Joel asked her.

She scuffed the floor with her foot. 'In her office.'

Wasting no more time, Joel snatched the programme from Amy's hands and shot out of the staffroom. She followed, just catching sight of him.

'Wait!' she cried. 'Please, Joel, you don't need to do this.'

He reached Penny's office and slammed the door behind him. There was a loud smack as the programme landed on her desk.

'What the hell is this?'

'I don't follow.' Penny's voice was muffled behind the wall.

'*This*, Penny.' His hand smashed down on something hard. 'Where's Amy's picture?'

It was a while before she answered. 'There wasn't one.'

Amy widened her eyes in disbelief.

'Oh, yes there was,' insisted Joel.

'I kept asking her to give it to me but for some reason, she didn't. I had no choice but to find something else.'

'Don't give me that.' Joel sniggered softly and although it was with anger, Amy's neck bristled at the sound. 'You've got that picture somewhere, I know you have.'

There was shuffling and clanging in different areas of the room and Amy realised that Joel was physically searching for the photo.

'You're wrong, Joel.' Penny's voice weakened and her chair scraped across the floor. She had obviously leapt to her feet and was becoming more defensive by the second. 'There is no picture. I'm telling you.'

'Step away, Penny,' Joel demanded.

'You don't know what you're talking about!'

'Step away!' His voice boomed louder than Amy had ever heard.

Then the noise of something hollow and metal rang out inside the office. Joel was going through the bin. Paper rustled until something made of stronger material could be heard being pulled from the bottom. There was a loud crackle and he opened whatever he had found. Amy's heart pumped in fast motion. Joel was holding her picture and she knew what he was seeing.

The black and white image had been taken on Stan's professional camera and the light fell flatteringly on the contours of her face She had smiled into the lens like the proud director she was. Although Amy wasn't usually keen on herself in pictures, this was a rare photo she'd have been pleased to see in print.

'So, what do you call this?' Joel almost panted.

'I had no idea it was there. The cleaner must have thrown it away before I even saw it.'

'You're a liar!'

Amy sucked in a breath. No one had done anything on this scale for her before.

'Don't you dare speak to me like that.'

'You've had it in for her since she's been here.'

'Oh, please, you're being ridiculous,' Penny cackled. 'This is a silly mistake.'

'You can't stand it, can you?' His voice grew louder as he neared the door and Amy took a step backwards. 'She's good at her job, she's kind, she's talented… all the things you're not.'

'She's a nobody. A nothing!' Penny howled.

'She's everything!'

Amy collapsed back against the wall. It felt as if her heart would surge up into her throat. She didn't know where to go. She had no idea what to think. Her head throbbed with a thousand thoughts, pulling her feelings in too many directions.

Just to hear Joel in there, defending her to the end, was making her shatter with emotion. So many years ago, he'd done all this before. And here he was, obliviously doing it all over again. Making her feel bulletproof. Worthy and alive.

'*You're* nothing.' He lowered his voice. 'Nothing but poison.'

The door handle turned and Amy sprinted back to the staffroom, her mind clambering for calmness. Alison was there, sitting tensely at the table while Nigel was making fresh drinks. Debra got to her feet as soon as she set eyes on Amy.

'I'm so sorry.' Her lips trembled as she spoke.

'It's not your fault.'

'It was out of my hands. You understand, don't you?'

'I know it's nothing to do with you.' Amy attempted a smile.

'Are you OK?' Alison asked worriedly. 'Come and sit down.'

'I'm fine.' She flopped into a chair. 'I'm not so sure about Joel, though.'

'What happened?'

'He went to Penny and completely let rip. The picture was there in her office too, he found it.'

Alison's face was full of compassion as she gazed at Amy. 'She deserves every bit of it. I just can't believe she did that.'

'I can.' Nigel wrinkled his nose. 'She's a nasty piece of work. It's about time she got it in the neck.'

'Is he still in there?' Alison asked.

'I don't know. I think he was coming out.'

'Maybe he's gone to tell…'

The door swung open and Ian scanned the room. By the look on his face, he had clearly been informed.

'Amy…' He caught his breath. 'If I could have a word. We can talk in private if you like.'

She glanced sideways at her colleagues and shook her head. 'It's OK. Here is fine.'

Ian sat down in the chair opposite hers.

'I know about the issue with Penny and the programmes.' He gave a wary look to the other teachers. 'Without going into too much detail, she won't be attending the play tomorrow and neither will she be back here until next term. I will review the situation when we've all had a break.'

Amy nodded.

'But there's nothing we can do about the programmes at

184

this late stage.' He gazed at her sympathetically. 'We'll just have to print plain text copies. I'm ever so sorry.'

'I suppose there are worse things that could happen.'

'Now, I suggest that you get yourself home. You'll need all your strength for tomorrow.'

'Thanks Ian, I'll do that,' Amy agreed, almost forgetting about the play.

'No, thank you for being so understanding.' He started to leave the room. 'And best of luck with the play.'

'Ian… where's Joel?'

'He's gone home. I have to say, he was very concerned, but I advised him to get some rest and assured him that this would not be overlooked.'

'As long as he's OK.'

'Oh, he'll be fine.' Ian relaxed his face. 'I'm sure he wouldn't miss tomorrow for the world.'

***

Amy dropped her bags on the floor as soon as she got into the house. She sat down on the stairs, trying to make sense of what had just happened. She was stinging from the blatant spite that was now in permanent print. The grotesque mask could never be erased, even if it wasn't made public.

Tomorrow could not come fast enough. At last Bertie's talents would unfurl on that stage and tonight would pale into the background. It was Amy's chance to prove herself and to thank the one person who had supported her. The show would unquestionably go on. And as long as Joel was there, she knew she would survive.

Twenty

As darkness fell around the school, it gave the hall a different aura. Soft lighting was draped onto the closed stage curtains which hid all the secrets that would shortly be revealed. The seats were getting filled as more parents took their places and the musicians were striking melodious chords as they tuned up with the piano.

The science lab was buzzing with noise as the children scurried around, some unrecognisable in their full make-up and wigs. Gita worked face paint onto the last of Joseph's brothers while Stella hurried in and out, transporting more props where needed.

With five minutes to go, Amy gave a final pep talk and checked that everyone knew what they were doing. Excitement and hairspray filled the air and the chitchat of the audience blended with the whispers of the cast.

Bertie turned to face her and butterflies stirred within. His skin was rich against the costume and his eyes bewitchingly bright under the vivid kohl liner. He looked nearly as impressive as his voice but nothing, in Amy's opinion, could top that. In just minutes now, he was going to blow everyone away with a transformation beyond any recognition.

'How's the leading man?' she asked him. 'All ready?'

Bertie nodded, taking a hopeful breath.

'Give it your best out there. I know you'll be brilliant.' She looked at everyone else. 'You all will.'

With one last smile, she headed into the dim corridor,

contemplating all that was waiting. A gathering of families, all eager to see their children. Bertie's unwitting parents, about to be staggered by their son. An expectant line of staff, anticipating the mystery of the last few weeks. And the one person who had been her rock every step of the way.

After tonight it would all be over and finally she could be with him. No more glances in vain across the staffroom and no more interruptions keeping them apart. Her pulse galloped, knowing the splendour that was about to be unravelled. Knowing Joel would be brimming with pride to see what she had done.

As she entered through the doorway, an array of heads turned. Every seat was full now, with coats hanging across the backrests and jewellery glinting intermittently in the crowd. Just below the stage, a chair had been specially positioned for Amy, where she would be viewable by all in the room.

People clapped softly as she took her place, feeling the fascination in everyone's stare. Reaching for her script, she glanced at her colleagues who were wondering what was in store.

Ian was cheery as usual and he gazed earnestly at the stage. Nigel nudged Martin as Gita took a seat looking radiant in the persimmon dress she'd been wearing under her make-up smock. Alison winked supportively at Amy, even though she too was unsure of what would happen.

And there at the end of the line, was Joel. He showed not a hint of apprehension. In a sea of unfamiliar people who fixed their attention on her, his calm smile kept her afloat. She thought back to the old days, when he'd washed away her tears with his words. She had sailed across the grass with her heart in the sky and the same was happening now.

Shaking inside, she smiled at him and he curved his mouth to return it. Her ruby red lipstick matched her rich crimson blouse and her crystal earrings twinkled as the lights dropped, fading the room out to a black canvas. There was no going back now and nothing to bear thinking about. But dark and blinding as the hall had become, the force of his eyes scorched through it all like flames.

She nodded to the orchestra and the rousing overture filled the air. The curtains parted ways and the stage poured with light, revealing the chorus and Flynn, right in the middle. He wove in and out as he led them into the story. The music built around his words and Amy knew the drill.

Every fibre in her body tensed as Flynn brought his first part to a close. As graciously as Amy could ever have hoped, he stretched his arms over to the side of the room, where the spotlight hit a figure and lit it up in glory.

The introduction rolled for the song he was about to sing and his face begged to be filled with a love he had never known. The look of a stranger who had just come home.

Bertie sang the first line and the room quaked. Astonishment ripped through the hall at the impact of his voice. He glided through the crowds like an apparition before their eyes. Like this heavenly sound they heard could not possibly be coming from this boy. The chorus fused with the power of his song and Amy could barely see for tears.

Ian was on the edge of his seat, unable to contain his pleasure. Alison stared in complete awe and Gita's hands were covering her mouth as she gazed in utter wonderment.

Down in the shadows of the front row, a man hugged a woman to his side. She sobbed at the echo of every word, stunned and overwhelmed. And Bertie's vocals transcended even more when he saw the effect on his parents.

As he finished, the applause was deafening and he basked deservedly in the praise. From tonight, his life would be different and no one could regard him in the same light again.

The interval lights flickered on and a woody hint of nutmeg filled the room. With no water to be found at the refreshments table, Amy settled for eggnog and a mince pie for good measure.

'Miss Ashcroft...' A woman with a curly blonde bob stood nearby, her eyes red from crying and a crumpled tissue in her hand. 'I don't know how to thank you.'

Amy smiled back at her, remembering how she had felt when Bertie had first sung at the piano. His mother was much newer to the experience. 'Mrs Hughes...'

'Hannah.'

'You don't need to thank me. It's all down to that son of yours.'

'Without your help, we might not have known. He never said a word, did he, Ray?'

She tilted her head to a tall man who handed her a glass of mulled wine. He could only manage a silent head shake, as his boy had left him dumbfounded. Amy looked at his face and immediately saw Bertie staring back at her.

'He's a superstar. You should both be very proud.'

'Wait until I get my hands on the blighter.' Ray bunched his mouth up tightly before his face broke into a delighted grin. 'I might even kiss him!'

Amy laughed wholeheartedly, feeling thrilled for Bertie. Now he could walk with his head held high and do what he loved deep inside. She could hardly contain her happiness as she stared over the room, only to stop at Joel.

Teachers and parents chirped all around him but he wasn't remotely interested. Nothing could distract him and his proud smile made her shiver. How much more time did she have to spend unable to be near him? She pulled her sight away for yet another time and hurried out of the room for a last talk with the cast.

The rest of the play was sensational, gripping everyone to the end. The music climbed for the finale, sending the room into an ovation. Whistles screeched like rockets when Bertie took his bow and both parents beamed adoringly at their very own star of the show.

Ian then had the final word, thanking everyone involved. He heaped the praise on Woodbrook's talent and Amy was surprised when he invited her up to the stage.

'And finally, I hope you will all join me in congratulating our newest teacher, Miss Amy Ashcroft, for her painstaking work and commitment. We've only had her with us since

September but I think you will agree, she is a most valuable asset to this school.'

Heat rushed to her cheeks but she was grateful to be appreciated.

'So, Miss Ashcroft,' Ian gave her a large poinsettia and a bottle of expensive wine. 'I hope you will accept this small token of thanks on behalf of us all.'

She smiled at the palms clapping together in her honour, making all her tension drain away. And as she flashed Joel a secret smile, she hoped that she had reaffirmed the reasons he'd stood by her.

***

One hour later, the hall was empty. The teachers and children had gone home for the holidays. Only Amy was left clearing up while Keith finished off outside. After a final check of the science lab, she wheeled the clothes rail down to the walk-in storage space in the assembly hall.

She parted the curtain doorway, being careful not to knock the mistletoe. Resting her handbag on the side, she began to put the clothes back in their places. With the portable rail just outside the door, she reached for each item before sliding it back into the rows of colourful costumes.

Leaning out of the cupboard door to grasp another hanger, she smacked straight into something. A person. She looked up to see whose chest her chin had banged against and Joel stepped into the room. Everything pulsed inside, from her spine to the pit of her stomach. They were so close in this tiny space, just an inch between their bodies as his eyes fell onto hers.

'I thought I'd missed you.'

He kept his voice low and beamed a half smile. She could smell the scent of him with every movement.

'No. Too much clearing away to do.'

'You must be tired.'

Amy rested her back against the wall and rolled her eyes

to the ceiling in mock exhaustion. 'I'm going to bed tonight and I'm not getting up for a week.'

'You were amazing.' Joel almost cut her off. 'Do you know that?'

She shook her head modestly. 'It was all down to Bertie and the kids. They did the real hard work. I just...'

'Put the whole thing together.'

'I had a great time doing it though.' Amy lifted her face to his. 'But thank you. I wouldn't have had the chance if you hadn't put in a good word for me.'

'And I was right.' He gazed at her with a deep, concentrating squint. 'I knew you could do it.'

Her insides fluttered as he smiled.

'I'm so proud of you.'

His sentiment made her look away. He had no idea how many times he'd said this in the past to the little, troubled Amy who still kept him in her heart. But tonight, it pulled her deeper than it ever had before. She took this moment and shifted daringly nearer. Now their faces were achingly close and his eyes ripped their way straight to hers. She willed him to keep going, desperate to hear him say more.

'I owe it to you,' she almost whispered.

'Amy...' Joel looked so ardently into her eyes that his face weakened with the strain. His breathing was fast and heavy, but he managed to pull himself back. 'We'll be locked in if we don't get out soon.'

'I know.' She slowly came to her senses as the seconds slipped away.

'Are you finished in here?'

No, she thought. *Far from it.*

'Just one more thing to put away.'

Joel stood back to let her pass and she carried her silent torture to the doorway, where she reached out to the clothes rail once more, dragging the last costume backwards into the cupboard.

The multicoloured coat was bulky and heavy, and Joel stretched out his arms to help her transport it through. He heaved it up into the air with one hasty move, skimming her handbag which was resting on the ledge. In an instant, the open bag fell onto the floor, spilling out everywhere.

'Sorry.' Joel hung the costume up as quickly as he could and bent straight down next to Amy. 'Let me help.'

'It's fine, I've got it.'

She scrambled around gathering everything up. Her blusher case had cracked, her diary was creased and the back had dropped off her phone. Joel picked up the parts and got to his feet to fix them while Amy checked that nothing else had fallen out of sight.

'I think it's still working.' He pressed the power button.

'Doesn't matter if it's not. I could really do with an upgrade.'

She stopped talking as she caught sight of Joel. He looked stunned. Sickened and devastated. His hand trembled as he gripped the phone, like he wanted to smash it back to pieces.

'Joel... What is it?'

Looking as if someone had knifed him in the chest, he slowly turned the screen towards her. One glimpse and her eyes flew shut at the picture of herself last June, sitting in her bedroom back in Popplewell. Her skin was bruised purple and jabbed around the jaw with red, bloody scratches.

Joel's voice cracked as he found the strength to speak.

'Please...' He refused to let his eyes slip from hers. 'Tell me this was an accident.'

'It was months ago. And I'm fine now, see?'

But Joel shook his head, unsatisfied with her answer. 'Tell me, Amy.'

Shame filled her and she stared down at the ground.

'Oh no.' He covered his mouth with a hand. 'This can't have happened.'

'Joel...' She grabbed the phone. 'Just forget it. I didn't even know I still had the pictures. My friends made me take them in case...' She hesitated for a second. 'In case I went to the police.'

'Who was it?' Joel snapped with fury. 'Who did this to you?'

There was a roll of carpet at the back of the dull room. Amy slumped down on it and took a few moments to think. This was the very last thing she dreamed of discussing, but she finally stared back at him and found faith there in his eyes.

'His name was Nathan. We were happy for a while, it was fun...' She glanced up at Joel's grave expression. 'He started being distant and I thought there was someone else. His ex again or someone new. Then one day, he cut himself off. Stopped answering my calls, ignored my messages and no one knew where he was.'

She didn't know if she wanted to go on. She shuddered at the thought of unearthing the full details and her stomach lurched just to remember them. But as she winced up at Joel, she knew she was going nowhere. Not until she'd told him how she had come to be battered and broken.

'Then I knocked at his door and he sprung on me. He told me to leave him alone and said he didn't want me. That I wasn't a patch on her and never would be.'

She stopped again as the pain of the past caught up with her.

'I went in after him to get an explanation.' She swallowed hard. 'He grabbed me round the throat and pushed me. I fell and hurt my arm. My face hit the table, I was bleeding... but I just got up and ran away.'

There was silence in response. She peered at Joel's face, buried in his hands. Then he revealed his eyes, welling up with tears. It hit her like a stone, just how much he cared. How it wounded him to imagine that someone had laid a finger on her.

'And you didn't take it further? How could you have let it go?'

Amy shook her head, like it would have been all too much. 'I just wanted to forget about it. Erase him, and everything, from my mind.'

'What I would do to him, Amy.' Joel narrowed his eyes. 'I just can't tell you what I'd do.'

'I just wanted to get as far away as possible.' She blinked softly. 'That's why I came here.'

'Thank God you did,' he whispered, kneeling beside her on the cold floor. 'Because you belong here. You...' he bowed his head down, then raised his eyes to face her. 'You're worth more than you could know.'

Tears trickled down her face, just to hear him say those words. It had felt like a lifetime, waiting to catch him alone. Her heart filled up at his voice in her ear, revealing he wanted her too.

'I'm here now.' Joel's hand slid over hers. She held it, felt his skin and quivered. 'And I'll never let anything happen to you,' he soothed. 'I'll never leave you.'

She smiled through her watery eyes and couldn't believe this was happening. She pushed her face close to him, her hands clamping his like she never wanted to let go. His mouth curved and her bones shook at the sideways grin that turned her upside down.

'How can I stop those tears?' he asked, dabbing them with a thumb.

'Kiss me, Joel,' she whispered at his lips. 'Just kiss me.'

He took her face in his hands and planted his mouth onto hers, breathing helplessly and silently in the dark. She leaned backwards, pulling him over her body, her hands gripping shirt, skin, and soul as he wrapped himself around her. She brushed his face with her fingers, touched his hair and dug at his neck, buckling in his arms as he devoured her heart. Their lips grinding, pounding together like nothing could tear them apart.

'Anyone there?'

A voice made them jerk back to their feet. They stared in a daze at the doorway as Alison frowned.

'You haven't seen a clutch bag lying around, have you? I thought I'd left it on my chair.'

Amy quickly neatened her hair. 'No, I don't think so.'

'Honestly, I'm going mad. I thought I'd lost my keys this morning until I checked my car boot, of all places. Nick couldn't believe it when I told him. Lucky me, he said. How did I end up being married to such a...'

'Toilets?' Joel interrupted her loudly.

'What?'

'Have you checked them?' he asked. Amy could sense the annoyance in his voice.

'Oh, I see. Well, I did go in the interval, so I'll try there.' She hesitated. 'Can one of you come with me? Those corridors freak me out when it's dark.'

'Let's get this over with then.' Joel stepped away from Amy and she ached at the distance, even if it was only a metre.

'Won't be long, Joel.' Alison's voice petered out ahead of him. 'Then you can walk us to the car park.'

He turned back to Amy in the half-lit doorway, his face a perfect mixture of ecstasy and frustration. Then, seconds later, he was gone.

She crouched on the pile of carpet, still warm from their feverish unity. What a night this had been. Fighting to steady her breath, she could hardly believe this was real. All she could do was wait for him now in the hope he would come back alone.

Thanks Alison, she thought, wondering exactly what Nick had called her that morning.

Twenty-One

The lights glimmered in sequence on the spiked branches, their gemstone colours blurring into the glass as Amy stared out from the living room. The road was heavy with the parked cars of visiting relatives. Two doors down, a boot was being unloaded while people embraced on the driveway.

Celestial rays splintered the sea's distant pulse and from the height of Glynde Avenue, Flintley looked microscopic. Everything was moist from the early morning dew and each rooftop glistened as if it had been touched by magic dust.

She couldn't see the school from where she stood, but she knew just the spot where its grounds stretched out. Now it would be locked up without a soul in the vicinity. The image left her feeling cold.

How empty it would be without him there. A chore to get through each day with not even a glimpse. All at once, she missed everything. The way the faintest smile lit up his face and the soft laughter that made something give way in her knees.

Her cabled sweater clung snugly to her arms and she wished she was feeling his hands. She had been so blind. Just a few weeks back, wrapped up in her embarrassment, she had done her utmost to avoid Joel. Now her heart clawed out for him.

She closed her eyes and was back there in the darkness for that last hurried moment in the costume cupboard. The brushing of his clothes as he came up close, his gaze burning through the dingy lamplight. How concern bled so deeply that desire had rapidly eclipsed it, only to be snatched away.

'Get over here and open some presents.'

Vanessa's voice put a swift end to the heady climb of Amy's thoughts. Once again, the cold day stared back at her. Nothing but swollen cushions of cloud and the rogue sparrow flitting along the hard, deserted ground. She turned away to focus on the scene indoors.

Giles had just started his second shandy while discussing cars with Stan, who lounged around in a Santa hat, tossing treats to Wolf. Vanessa was busy distributing gifts from the brightly-wrapped mass below the tree. Her pompom slippers matched her tunic and she wore a band of tinsel in her hair.

'Come on, these are yours.'

Amy eyed the small pile allocated on the sofa. 'But I thought we weren't doing them until after lunch.'

'We're saving the main pressies. These are just little ones.'

She sat down next to Stan and began to tear a small one open.

'Wait!' commanded Vanessa. 'Not until everyone's here.'

Amy rolled her eyes, 'But you just said…'

'Mum!'

The unmistakable aroma of stuffing and roast potatoes drifted through the air as pots bubbled and the oven hummed.

'What is it, love?' Melinda called out.

'Come on. Time for some presents.'

'I've got to watch the meat now. Just start without me.'

'Please, it won't take long.'

A whisk clattered and Melinda hurried in, panicked to be leaving the cooking at such a crucial time.

'Quickly then.' She motioned to everyone. 'Or it's going to end up getting burnt.'

Amy unwrapped some aubergine gloves in a soft angora yarn. 'You got them!'

'Of course, love.' Melinda beamed. 'You haven't already bought them, have you?'

'I so nearly did. What do you think?' She slipped one onto her hand.

'Very nice. The colour suits you.'

Stan handed Melinda a package which she hesitantly opened. From the plain white carrier bag inside, she pulled out a second-hand paperback book and raised her eyebrows.

'One Thousand Species of Snails.'

'What's wrong with that?' He was stung by her reaction. 'You love animals.'

'I have a soft spot for cats. That doesn't include the creepy crawlies slithering around in the back garden.'

'That's a pity. Bargain, too.'

'Looks like you'll have to take it back to the pound shop, Dad,' Amy grinned.

'Boot sale, actually.' He winked at Melinda, who pursed her lips in response.

Vanessa pulled silver paper from a thin rectangle shape and her eyes lit up at the set of lip colours. 'Wow, thanks sis.'

'Try one out.' Amy went across to her. 'Let's see how they look.'

Using the mirror in the lid, Vanessa brushed on a bubble gum pink and turned to Giles, who was wriggling his way into a new pullover. 'What do you think, babe?'

Giles looked dubious. 'Not sure. You know how I feel about lipstick.'

Amy frowned at him.

'It just makes you even more irresistible!' He pushed Vanessa backwards onto the sofa and sank on top of her as they engaged in a very public canoodle.

Melinda coughed and stared down at her book. 'Anyway, I must get on. You'll only moan if dinner is late.'

'Want a hand?' Amy asked, getting to her feet.

'If you don't mind setting the table. Vanessa, an extra pair of hands would be nice.'

She giggled loudly from somewhere under Giles as he dived in for another smooch.

'No chance,' mumbled Amy as she followed Melinda out

of the room.

An hour later, the tablecloth was spattered with gravy and cranberry sauce. The leftover turkey sat on the sideboard, littered with parsnips and pigs in blankets. Everyone was slumped in their chairs with crackers snapped open and paper hats sliding over their brows. The smell of cloves and steeped fruit punched the air from the Christmas pudding that was almost reduced to crumbs in the centre of the table.

'I'm stuffed.' Vanessa sighed. 'That was amazing.'

'Glad you liked it.' Melinda started clearing away. 'I was going to do goose for a change, but your dad wouldn't have it.'

'You can't beat a good turkey, Lindy.' He gave her hand an affectionate squeeze. 'The highlight of my year and you've just done me proud.'

Melinda turned away as she loaded up the plates. 'Shame it's not reflected in your choice of presents.'

'Leave all this, Mum,' Amy ordered. 'We'll do it later.'

'Come on, let's get back to the big ones!' Vanessa got up from the table and massaged Giles's shoulders. 'Bring the wine, babe.'

'Coming right up.' He took two bottles from the sideboard and followed her back into the living room.

By the time the others had joined them, a music channel was blaring out Christmas songs while Vanessa had covered the carpet with boxes, bags, and other objects, all concealed by decorative paper.

More presents circulated until at last, they had all been given and received. Stan nodded off on the end of the sofa while Giles fastened the necklace he had given Vanessa. She smiled in gratitude as the fiery orange topaz flashed and caught the light.

'I'm off to do the dishes then.' Melinda headed out of the room.

'Mum, wait.' Amy retrieved a square present from behind the tree. She quickly read the tag. 'It's yours.'

Melinda glanced at Stan when she saw the handwriting. Vanessa nudged him awake just in time for him to see his wife tearing away the wrapping. As the paper fell to the floor, she looked in awe at the gift in her hands.

'Stanley!'

The logo on the box was Pearson Wells, an expensive pottery firm. Melinda had always dreamed of owning a piece of the sought-after china, having spent years leafing wistfully through each new catalogue and collection.

Her face was a picture of disbelief as she released a mound of tissue paper. Easing it away, she welled up at the sight of the vase inside. Beautifully curved and polished to perfection, its design was a fusion of florals and leaves in bold swirls of plum and amethyst, crowned with a matching lid. She gazed at it in all its magnificence and was rendered completely speechless.

'Well, you do like it, don't you?' Stan examined her reaction.

'Like it?' She drew in a gasp. 'I didn't think you had it in you.'

'King of the old romantics, Lindy, that's me.'

'Stanley Ashcroft, you have surpassed yourself.'

'So, does that mean I've earned next year's turkey?'

'On one condition,' she pointed a finger. 'No more of those tatty old books.'

Stan laughed and slapped the space next to him on the sofa. 'Come over here and give us a smacker!'

As she sat down beside him and leaned in for a hug, Pumpkin barged in between them, knocking Stan's glasses off his face.

'Bloody cat,' he groaned, much to everyone's amusement.

The evening soon drew in. After a stroll round the block with Wolf, the family felt peckish. Melinda brought in two large trays packed with cold meats, cheeses, and chutneys along with fresh bread and some crisp white grapes.

A tin of chocolates was cracked open, and glasses of sherry and port were refilled in plentiful amounts. The board games came out and competitive spirits were in full swing until the festivities began to wind down to the sound of a televised carol concert.

Then everyone else went to bed, leaving Amy to peruse the TV guide for what Boxing Day had in store.

The fire blazed incandescently, its gold aura lavishing the holly at each side of the mantelpiece. Amy watched the flames blushing the coal with molten licks as she sat there on the rug, wishing she wasn't alone. Feeling the roasted air on her lips, she remembered what it felt like to kiss him. How sensual his voice had sounded when he'd whispered in her ear.

Gazing out at the night sky, she wondered where he could be. Whether he was thinking of her, too, right at this very moment. She watched the last sparks melting deep into the grate and felt her heart plummet with the ashes.

Twenty-Two

Two weeks later, everything was invisible under a crust of snow. It looked as if angels had swept over the earth, turning it into a feather bed and sculpting art from the ice. Branches were loaded with cotton wool tufts as snowdrops peeped over granules of grass.

The heavens shimmered with mother of pearl as they churned out their supply of unsullied winter dust. Clouds swirled in an alabaster quilt and shook down their shavings on the bleached world below.

Amy's car heater took a while to work as she steered cautiously through the streets. For once, she admired the gloomy little town in all its glacial charm. She smiled at the icicle fences and the windows engraved with nature's complex needlework.

A robin stopped pecking and dashed away when she pulled up at the school. Joel's car was nowhere to be seen and it filled her with unease. It had been a gruelling holiday with next to no contact. Her phone was still temperamental since it had broken after the play and Joel had been staying with family where there was scarcely any reception.

Tomorrow he would be gone again on the first flight to the conference, but one way or another they would buy some time. After all, there was still tonight.

Amy stepped outside and the air stung her face, but she was wearing her new redcurrant coat which staved off the worst of the freeze. She padded against the snow-covered tarmac, thinking of the last time she'd been here in the black of night with Joel. Of their parting in a wrench of suppression with a million unspoken words.

Any minute now, he might pull up in the car park. At any random corner, she could walk straight into his path. She had no idea when the moment was going to arrive, but if one thing was for certain, she knew it would.

'Here she is!' Ian clapped his hands as she entered the staffroom to a round of cheers. 'We were just talking about you.'

'Really?'

'Yes, my dear, you're a genius and the show was a complete triumph.'

'You want to check your pigeonhole.' Nigel nodded in the direction of the hallway. 'It's rammed with cards. No doubt all the parents bombarding you with fan mail.'

She gasped back at him.

'Guilty conscience alert,' said Gita sheepishly. 'I feel like such an idiot for not listening to you.'

'No worries,' Amy waved dismissively. There were far bigger things to think about.

'Did you have a good Christmas anyway?'

'It was nice, but I missed it here.'

'OK, forget what I just said. You have lost the plot after all.'

'I hope you're not suggesting you'd rather loaf around in the comfort of home, Gita,' Ian said in mock disapproval.

'And forsake my ice-cold classroom and a bunch of squabbling kids? Never!' She smirked back.

'I must say, I'd sooner be sat in front of the TV with a whisky for another two weeks,' mused Ian. 'And we did have an excellent Christmas dinner.'

'All right for some.' Nigel turned down the corners of his mouth. 'Sprouts, sprouts, nothing but sprouts and lumpy custard in the trifle.'

Amy giggled. 'Your mum was on top form then!'

'Beans on toast for me next time or a one-way ticket to Jamaica.' He shuddered, hugging his knitted green tank top.

Alison breezed in and tossed down her things.

'Happy New Year!' She dipped into a tote bag. 'Anyone for a hot drink?'

'Count me in.' Ian pointed to a giant mug he must have received as a present.

'Yes please,' added Amy. 'I need warming up.'

'You should be drinking bubbly.' Alison winked. 'I think you've got plenty to celebrate.'

A chill shot through Amy as she recalled the interruption in the costume cupboard. 'I don't follow.'

'The play! I mean, what can I say? Phenomenal.'

She sighed inwardly with relief. 'It seems to have gone down well.'

'Oh, and I'm really sorry about… you know. What happened later on.'

'What?' Amy tensed.

'Well, I was so caught up in finding that bag, I didn't even congratulate you at the time. Anyway, I'm saying it now. Sensational. The best production ever.'

'Thanks, Ali.'

'And after all that, guess where my bag was?' Alison turned to make the drinks. 'The car boot *again*! I'm going to check there from now on whenever I lose something.'

'You found it, that's the main thing.'

'Come on then.' She beckoned to Amy after handing out the mugs. 'Let's go and get settled down at the ranch.'

Ian followed them out of the room. 'The radiators might take a while to work, so if you need electric heaters, just ask Keith.'

'We might have to,' replied Alison. 'You'd think Jack Frost had taken up residence while we've been away.'

Instantly, the three of them slammed into Penny, who was draped in a leopard-print faux fur coat with a slap of bright red lipstick. She glared as she passed them and narrowed her eyes at Amy.

'Or maybe it was the Snow Queen,' Alison whispered, shooting her a bold look of disgust.

Ian's face darkened. 'Apologies, ladies. You'll have to excuse me. I have an urgent matter to deal with.' He faced the other way with his arms folded. 'Penny...'

She turned on her heel and looked back, annoyed that her journey had been interrupted.

'My office, please.' He headed away to his room, not waiting for her to accompany him.

Penny paused and retraced her steps past Amy and Alison, who watched from where they were standing. She slunk off behind Ian with her glare fixed ahead.

'Bet she wishes she'd never slithered out of her hole this morning.'

'Yesterday's news. Anyway, I doubt anything much will become of all that now.'

'I guess,' replied Alison. 'And Ian's got all the disciplinary skills of a wet dishcloth.'

But Amy could not have cared less about Penny or what was being said in Ian's office. She only had to remember how vehemently Joel had defended her the day before the play. Just knowing she had an ally in him was enough to keep her strong. And now she knew how it felt to be buried in his arms, to look deep into his eyes and kiss him. Nothing else could enter her mind now it was filled with these sensations.

'So, did you see anyone else in the car park?' she asked, as they reached the hut. 'It seems so quiet around here.'

'Deserted.' Alison held the door open. 'They're probably all snowed in or stuck at home with a cold.'

Amy felt a pull deep inside her. The blizzard was quickening in the wind and either of Alison's scenarios could ring true.

When lunchtime came around, there had still been no sign. But her undercover searching had to wait as she was due for duty outside. She fastened the buttons of her new coat and put on an aubergine beret and scarf that matched the gloves she had received for Christmas.

The playground glinted like a skating rink, far too

dangerous to set foot upon. Today, the children would be up on the grass, making the most of the fleeting Flintley avalanche. She took the gravel pathway to the fields and slowed down to scan the car park. But Joel's car was still not there.

Frosty specks pirouetted like moonflowers and she anxiously brushed them from view. She looked over at the woollen dots of colour, jumping and laughing in the giant blankets of white, and her eyes ached from the strain.

A line of hedges separated the upper and lower fields with a path that ran along the middle. From here, she could watch the top three years as they frolicked noisily over the space, kicking up the powdered mass and lobbing giant snowballs. And to her right, the younger classes could be seen over the hedge, foraging for arm-like twigs and lending their scarves to snowmen.

For the rest of this long breaktime, she would walk up and down the path, trying to find some sense through the turmoil misting her mind. Fresh from the parchment sky, more snow began to descend as if ripped out of a pillowcase. The slivers of winter parachuted down, wafer thin and as bisque-white as doves.

She could barely see through the billowing gusts as they flew around her face, clinging to her knitwear and dusting over her eyelashes. Reaching the end of the path, she turned on her toes to walk back. But through the tumbling bursts, something was just visible. Something dark and definite within the blinding pallor. Amy stepped closer and her heart was in her mouth. A charcoal coat. A ruffle of sandy hair and a smile that warmed her spirit for the first time in weeks.

Even though the maddened snowflakes blurred her vision, his face blitzed the frozen pinch of ice. She blinked the fluffy atoms away, trying helplessly to breathe. Her feet moved before her body could catch up and in the next moment, he was already surging towards her. Whirlpools of whiteness parted ways until there was just an inch between them. But, face to face, they grappled for restraint in the company of the oblivious children.

'Where were you?' Amy stared into his eyes as joy bubbled up inside her.

Joel was already shaking his head. 'Stranded. I couldn't get the car off the drive… no buses, no trains…'

Amy frowned with confusion.

'So, I walked.'

'From Burling?'

'Of course,'

'Why didn't you stay home? You might have got ill.'

He laughed and then straightened his face. 'I would have walked to the ends of the earth.'

She softened at the darting of his eyes, straight into hers.

'I missed you,' he whispered, clenching his hands at his sides as if battling to keep them away from her. 'I still do.'

'I'm so glad you're here.'

'I can think of better places to be.'

Amy smiled and bit her lip. 'Do you know how hard this is? Just standing here and not being able to…'

'Don't.' His voice quivered. 'I've thought about nothing else.'

'And you've tortured me all day. I was so worried about you.'

'I'm fine.' He beamed. 'At least, I will be later.'

'What's happening later?' Amy teased, half knowing what Joel had in mind.

'You and me together. And no interruptions.'

'Don't you have to pack for tomorrow?'

'There's plenty of time for that.' His ocean-blue gaze shone at her. 'We've got all night.'

She grinned and looked away. The thought of a minute alone with him made every hair on her head prickle.

'As long as you don't mind driving.'

'Where to?'

'Who knows? Anywhere but here.'

She pushed her lips as close to his as she dared. 'Peace. And wine… and you. I just want you.'

Their coats smacked together and his mouth hovered a fingertip's length from hers. His jaw moved in to cover it and her eyes closed in readiness. Then he drew in a steadying breath and tore himself away.

'I've got to go.' He eyed the noisy crowds. 'You have no idea what you're doing to me.'

'After school then, in the car park. Don't make me wait.'

She sizzled within, despite the whole world freezing around her.

'Wild horses…' He stared back at her face. 'I'll see you.'

He edged further down the path and the snow blustered over him until he was out of sight. She stood, ecstatic on the spot, as the sleety flecks turned to droplets on her clothes.

The afternoon was the slowest ever. Amy looked at the clock every five minutes, wishing the time away. After writing about the holidays, her class joined Alison's on a winter nature trail, returning to make snow scene art in the last hour.

As she watched Bertie making an imaginative picture, she couldn't help staring far out of the window, where the greenhouse was translucent and a sword of platinum sunlight pierced the sky. Dusk hung over the clouds and soon it would be time. She would be warm with Joel in the cold, dark night and sharing the things she had dreamed of.

Lessons finally ended and she couldn't wait to get out. She hurried along the corridors and glanced into the reception area. It was all clear. Safe to rush out of the building and leave, at last, together.

'Amy?'

She spun around just as she reached the exit.

'Sorry to delay you, but I wonder if you could just spare a few minutes in my office.'

Ian sounded pleasant enough, but he couldn't have picked a worse time. She knew her expression was less than thrilled but she struggled to hide it.

'Actually, I'm in a bit of a…'

'It won't take long,' he replied firmly.

As he strode to his room, Amy stayed rooted to the spot. Should she even follow him? This felt like life or death. If she went in there now while Ian waffled on, she could lose this one chance with Joel.

But as close as she was to racing out of the door, she knew she had to give in. Hoping and praying it would only cost five minutes, she launched herself back down the corridor and into Ian's office.

There was Penny, slouched in the chair opposite the desk. She wore a mustard shirt over baggy tweed trousers and her long nails were varnished in a glossy carmine red. As she turned sideways, Amy took in the taut bones and a nose as sharp as a woodpecker's beak.

'Penny has something she would like to say regarding the incident before Christmas.' Ian nodded to prompt her. 'Penny…'

She angled her head just enough for a quick glance at Amy. Coughing lightly, she pursed her lips into a smile.

'Yes, about what happened…'

Amy could hear her own teeth gritting.

'I maintain that it was an innocent mistake.'

Of course it was, Amy thought. But as if she cared about any of this right now.

'I have no recollection of you giving me that photo.'

She chuckled and Amy was ready to bite. She could have it all out now if she liked and give back as good as she got. With the things she had ready on the tip of her tongue, she could pull Penny to pieces and tarnish her reputation for good. But her need to see Joel was too strong now. All the injustice could go up in flames, as long as she reached him in time.

'Obviously, I wouldn't dream of upsetting you, Amy.' She laid a hand over her chest. 'I hope you can find it in yourself to get over this.'

Amy nearly laughed. *That* was an apology? Nevertheless, she responded with calmness.

'That's fine, Penny.' Anything to end this absurd

conversation that jeopardised all that was waiting for her.

'I'm so glad you are willing to move on.' Ian smiled, as if they were all ensconced in a rapturous group hug. 'Penny's been beside herself since Christmas.'

'Right.' Amy forced a grin. If he didn't let her go in the next ten seconds, she was going to break out of the window.

'Well, I'll let you both get off.' He beamed, seemingly delighted with his peace-making abilities.

Penny got straight up and pushed past Amy in the doorway. It would probably have bothered her a few weeks ago, but right now, she couldn't give it a thought. She bid Ian a hurried goodbye and finally walked out of his door.

'Oh, Amy…' he called.

She could feel her knuckles tensing up and she tried to keep her composure.

'Thank goodness I remembered.' Ian shook a finger as she glanced back into his room. 'I've got a message for you, from Joel.'

Her heart thudded into her mouth.

'Apparently, you had a meeting with him after school?'

She nodded, hoping that was as much as Ian knew about their plans.

'Well, unfortunately he's had to go. His flight has been cancelled tomorrow because the weather is set to get worse. There's one going out this evening that he'll have to take instead. He tried to contact you but couldn't get through. It was just after lunch when he left and asked me to let you know.'

'No problem.' Amy looked the opposite way as her eyes were piling with tears. 'We'll just do it some other time.'

She bustled out of the building but couldn't run for the ice. Pulling herself up the banister of the steps, she rushed uphill along the frozen gravel path, as fast as physically possible.

Driving out of the car park, she was unable to see for crying. Mascara seeped down her cheeks and she felt the tears on her scarf. She couldn't even look at the passenger seat.

The place where he should be.

Managing to get home safely, she unzipped her boots and sank into a chair, her sobbing masked by car tyres as they squelched outside through the snow.

She wished she hadn't seen him for those few minutes at lunchtime. That she hadn't been able to indulge in his fervent blue eyes. It had only enticed her, brought her to the brink and then all turned to dust in her fingers.

Looking ahead to what the fortnight had in store, she perceived two weeks of gloom. She'd have hankered for him anyway, but now it would be even harder.

The streaming make-up was irritating her eyes, so she went upstairs to remove it. She grazed her way through dinner and ran herself a bath. As the water gushed into the tub, she sat on the edge of the bed feeling cheated and deprived.

It all ran through her mind again. The moment Ian had told her and the shock she'd felt at the news. And then, she was suddenly confused.

Ian said Joel had been trying to reach her, but how had he not been successful? She knew he wouldn't have found her when she'd been out on the trail with Alison, but surely a call or text would have done.

She froze.

Opening her handbag, she found her phone and tried the power button. Dead again. She let out a scream and hurled it across the room, imagining the missed calls and messages that might have shown up if only it had been working.

With more tears relentlessly flowing, she went to get a tissue from the kitchen. Splashing cold water over her face, she caught sight of a red light, indicating a voicemail on the landline. Without hesitating, she swooped over to the answerphone.

'Amy, it's me. It's about half past three. I'm in a cab on the way to the airport. My flight got cancelled so I have to leave tonight. And after all that, there is a flight tomorrow. It's too late though, I've got to go now. Your phone's turned off and I couldn't find you, so I had to leave a message with Ian. I'm so sorry. All I wanted was to be with you. When I saw you today... I've never felt like this. It's going to be hell without you now.'

Sitting on the window ledge, it killed her to listen knowing she hadn't been there to hear his words in the flesh.

'I can't spend another two weeks like this. Just come, Amy. Get on that flight tomorrow. Call in sick if you have to. And don't worry about the money, I'll see to that. But please. Just come to me.'

Twenty-Three

Wide awake in bed, Amy traced the outline of her suitcase and tomorrow's clothes on the chair. How she wished she could wake straight up to dawn. Instead, she stared at the bedside lamp and listened to the slow ticking of the clock until the sky turned from black to blue-grey and at last, the soft gold of daylight.

Her alarm wouldn't ring for a good while longer, but she was already up and heading for the kitchen. After a shower, she applied her make-up before slipping into jeans and a black camisole vest, which she was bound to freeze in on the journey. A final spray of perfume and she was ready to go, twenty minutes before her taxi arrived.

The train rolled over the tracks and she watched Flintley ebbing away, hardly believing that she was doing this. She had chosen a discreet seat at the back of the carriage where she was almost invisible to anyone, yet that didn't make each stop along the line any less excruciating.

But slowly and surely, the shapes of the coastline disappeared until the train sped into reams of unfamiliar countryside. A dreamy panorama was swathed in white and kissed by the morning sun as it thawed gently from the harsh midnight freeze. She was thrown into the wonderland as it knitted its way around her and she felt her tight head unwind. Her intuition calm and trusting in the choice she had made. This felt so right and real. And she was going to live it.

She closed her eyes, remembering the sound of his voice on the answerphone begging her to drop everything and go to him. Within an hour, the flight had been booked and she was sitting tensely in a lukewarm bath, trying to believe that she was actually about to do this.

As the train catapulted on, the towering layers of frigid snow began to evaporate and diffuse away. The colourless sky raced into a rinse of icy blue and the soothing sunlight caressed the ground into a fresh and earthy revival.

The memories came alive with the motion. She saw him in the back of her mind, standing in the spot, right where she remembered. Waiting for her on the field. She felt her young self, standing there before him, about to run for her life. She could see herself looking at him through wide, unquestioning eyes and letting him command her with his faith. There was the cue, the stopwatch. Like the ticking of their hearts, beating against time for the moment she would reach him.

Nothing had ever changed. And now, as she lost herself in the whirling greens of the frosted scenery, she could feel that day happening all over again. She was running now. Risking everything. Lunging over land, air, and sea to get to him. Her eyes grew moist and her breathing was patchy, just imagining how things would be. How it would feel to be there, finally together. Just the night and the silence. And them.

Once at the airport, she was lost and yet comforted by the busy crowds, coming and going from every corner of the globe. The smell of espresso and freshly baked bread seeped out of the snack bars as she made her way to the check-in desk and reached the long queue.

As she charged into the sky, climbing higher than the eiderdown of magnolia clouds, something free and rapturous oozed into her body. Like a butterfly shaking off its chrysalis, she felt everything below her drop away. The chaos she might have caused at the school by phoning in sick. Penny in a bubble of smugness, having got off lightly with her antics. And the manic, interrupted life there which had kept her and Joel apart.

The hours trudged by. She read for a while and ate most of a noodle salad, followed by a coconut protein bar. A light sleep passed the time away after all her unrest from the night before. Then she watched the colours transforming through the window as the hundreds of miles glided past. A wintery white to a promising pale blue. And as the hours crept on, the blue changed again to a vibrant cyan, lit by the glow of a gilded sun.

She could just sense that he was near. Somewhere under that titanic, tropical haze. Everything that had weighed her down was lifting and fading away. It almost seemed as if a different person would be stepping off this flight.

As the plane prepared to land, she topped up her bronzer and dabbed on a lipstick. She quickly neatened her hair and slung everything back in her bag. There was nothing left to do now but fasten her seatbelt and feel the touchdown as she reached the ground where Joel would be.

Having reclaimed her luggage, she headed to a quieter area and held her breath, hoping her phone would turn on. With a grain of hope, she held the button down.

As if by magic, it came to life and the logo popped up with an automatic welcome. She accessed Joel's number, her chest beating wildly while the line connected to his. A few moments passed and there wasn't even a ringing tone. She frowned. It was taking a long time to get through.

But she checked the screen and her heart sank. The power had gone and this time, it really was lost. Amy turned away and headed outside. There was one thing for it. She would go straight to the apartment and just hope that Joel was there.

The heat met her in a wave at the exit and the sky was rippled with a pink, syrupy sunset, melting the vivid blue of the day. Several taxis were queuing outside and she took the next one available.

Those first few minutes of the drive were dull as the car zoomed along motorways and main roads, but it soon reached the aquamarine sea, laced with an endless line of rocks which led the way for miles.

Gently swaying palm trees hung over the deserted beach. The silhouettes of graceful birds dipped their wings in the still water. Foamy waves licked the shoreline, leaving a wet stain over the sand and the sun was immersed in a nectar smudge low down on the horizon.

Tall houses stood like royal iced cakes finished with exotic flowers. Gleaming cars were parked in the driveways and turquoise pool lighting was just visible from the gardens.

The cab entered a desolate stretch of beach, where apartments shone in the moonlight that knifed through the sky. The driver slowed at a stone building in a circle of trees with a balcony running along the width. All the indoor lights were out and only a faint glow could be seen.

Amy paid the fare and followed the lamplight up a high flight of steps. She put her suitcase to one side and peered through the glass. All was dark inside and she began to wonder if she was at the right place. Clutching her handbag, she slowly tapped the knocker.

At last, she saw a shadow and heard the latch release. The door opened a few inches and Joel's face appeared through the crack.

'Amy.'

She smiled.

Twenty-Four

He pulled her through the door and she fell into his arms, watching the rapture take over his face. She felt every breath course through him and raggedly, helplessly, he cupped her jaw, drawing further in towards her. Her palms slid down from his chest until they linked around his back, every bone crammed tight against the shape of him until their lips collided.

Feeling weightless in his hold, she closed her eyes as he kissed her, numbing the sting of every ordeal and obliterating the pain of the past. Her cheeks hot against the cold wall, he slipped away her straps, dipping low, releasing her and tasting her. She stiffened as he trailed back up, counting the seconds until he faced her again.

His gaze burned through the light and dark of the hallway and she hung on it, hands inside his shirt, bathing him in the intimacy he had not known for so long. Uncaging him, she crawled up his body, bare legs coiled around his waist and her open mouth on his skin, awakening each nerve, each flame as it alighted with her touch.

In a moment he paused, eyes interlaced with hers. She trembled at his fingertips, smoothing her flushed cheekbones. The same hands that had lifted her up from a cloakroom floor. That had steadied her and given her new life. She grasped them to her now, as fearless as she could ever be, enlivened all around him and ravenous for more.

He carried her into the candlelight and laid her down on the bed, but she pulled him to her, grazing him with kisses.

Nothing could feel righter than the weight of him, stripped and in fusion with the beating of her heart. She opened herself up to him, their lips pressed together as he eased between her thighs.

Full of emotion, he moved hard and slow, his head against hers as their breaths echoed each other. Tears of relief rained on the pillows, with every minute better than the last. She looked up at him, his striking eyes as bright and alive as she'd always known them to be, but now they were hers.

She took over, unleashing her passion like lightning through his veins. He couldn't even keep her an inch away and drew in, crushing her down on top of him. Taking her face in his palms, he kissed her endlessly and turned her back over, brimming with bliss and hunger.

In seconds, she was sprinting through the grass on that balmy day, her body glistening with heat as she advanced towards him. As the waves throbbed through her, she cried out, clinging to him tighter than ever.

She whispered through soft, open lips, arching her back until the grinding built up again. His breath was hot as he groaned into her neck and immersed himself in her eager body.

The candles burned and oozed as she drank him in. Then they stayed, cocooned in the sweltering euphoria. The calm after the storm. Tired and elated, she curled up in his arms and their dark shadows merged under the flickering light. The last bud melted on the smoky candlewick and trickled into the hot pool of wax.

***

Morning arrived. Mingled scent surrounded her as she gazed at Joel, who was still fast asleep. She smiled as she watched him and thought of the last few hours, hardly believing that she was really there, living out the illusions that had filled her mind. He shifted slightly and she waited, anticipating every pause in his breathing, but he still slept on so she went to find her suitcase.

With her thin dressing gown around her, she glanced in the hallway mirror. Her hair was tangled and her make-up had faded, but her skin was fresh and illuminated. She touched her lips, still warm from him, and could hardly wait until he woke.

The apartment was far bigger than she had expected. A large kitchen filled the back of the room, with thick oak cupboards and a polished granite worktop. Two leather sofas sat in the middle of the space around a large glass table. Pictures of seascapes adorned the walls and double doors led the way to the balcony.

Amy stepped out to behold a stunning view, relishing the wispy breeze infused with bursts of sea salt. The ocean shimmered gold as the risen sun stroked it and the sky was an array of white and aqua drizzled with honey. The waves frothed and bubbled on the brown sugar shore while gulls frolicked in the shallow water.

A plaintive boat drifted in the mellow dawn as it swirled over the deep line of ultramarine. Placid air embraced the terracotta garden as she took in the stillness of the atmosphere, her bare feet warm on the paving slabs.

'Morning.'

She jolted at his gentle voice and in a moment, his arms were around her. As he nestled into her shoulder, she grinned.

'Did you have a good sleep?'

'Not the most peaceful of nights, no.' He tightened his grip on her.

'That's me on the sofa tonight, then.'

He pressed his lips onto her neck. 'As if I'd let you.'

'It's for the best.' She fixed her eyes on the smeared blue shoreline. 'Must have been the mattress. I just couldn't drop off for some reason.'

Tensing her shoulders against him, she felt the shape of his smile on her skin.

'Now, you just listen to me...' His forceful tone was the

exact way he spoke in the classroom. 'You set foot out of my sight and I'll have no choice but to carry you, kicking and screaming, back to bed.'

'I might be too heavy.'

'Then I'll have to drag you.'

Laughing, she turned around to face him. His usually groomed hair was straw-like and dishevelled, and he wore a grey T-shirt and shorts. His smile diminished and he looked deep into her eyes.

'I've got you now. I'm not letting you go.'

His gaze followed the apricot sunlight glowing across her skin until he touched his mouth to hers. Then he held her as they watched the decadence of morning.

'Hungry?'

'I'm starving.'

He pulled out a chair from under the table. 'You just sit down and leave it all to me.'

Reluctantly, she took her seat and looked up at him. 'Are you sure?'

'Of course.'

Joel turned to enter the living room, but she pulled him back playfully, tugging his clothes. 'Don't be long.'

He crouched and kissed her on the forehead. 'I'll be right back.'

Tempting smells wafted out onto the balcony and oil hissed in the background as he moved around the kitchen, taking plates from the cupboards and shaking the pan every now and then. She revelled in the sight of him, deliciously unruly and fresh from bed. The chinking of cutlery rang out behind her before he emerged with a piled-up tray.

Amy was amused by the concentration on his face as he launched at the table, eager not to drop anything.

'This looks amazing!' She eyed the toast, gleaming poached eggs and crispy bacon.

'It's bacon and eggs. Anyone can do that!'

She shook her head. 'Not me, I'm useless with eggs. I can only do scrambled and that's not difficult.'

'Well, you make good coffee. I know that much and I'm very particular about my coffee.'

'You are.' Her mind flashed back to the pungent aroma that had floated from his mug years ago. 'You've always had it very strong…' She cut off and he glanced at her. 'I mean, you always… have it very strong.'

'It's got to be,' he continued, coating a piece of toast in egg yolk and not noticing how her cheeks had flushed. 'Too much milk completely spoils it.'

Joel frowned in mock disgust as she whitened her coffee and stirred it to a pale beige. She couldn't hide her smile between sips when he took back his comments on her skilfulness.

Satisfied from breakfast, they reclined in their seats, looking out at the glittering sea and breathing in the cool air.

'So…' Joel beamed. 'You got my message.'

Amy nodded with a grin.

'I am so sorry. I tried to ring you but…'

'Don't get me started.' She held up a hand. 'I had to call in sick from a payphone yesterday.'

'Were they OK with it?'

Amy raised an eyebrow. 'I don't care.'

Joel seemed impressed by her rebelliousness and it thrilled her. How indignant he would have been as her teacher. But how waywardly he was smiling at her now.

'You know I don't condone that kind of behaviour.'

'Really?' She played along and ruled his eyes, despite weakening inside. 'Well, I hardly approve of yours. Cancelling our date, leaving without a word and getting Ian to break it to me.'

Her reminder visibly stung him. 'I'm sorry for all that. I really am.'

'You'll make it up to me,' she asserted. Then her face softened into an overwhelmed smile.

'I can't believe you're here.' Joel breathed. 'I didn't think you'd come.'

'Why?'

'It's a bit of a tall order, asking you to travel all this way with no notice. Even if you decided to, you might have changed your mind at the last minute.'

'Changed my mind? I'd have come if it was the last thing I ever did.'

His response was a radiant smile and his eyes were alive with the same blue as the band of ocean before them. He looked at her as if he was soaking up her whole body from head to toe. Shifting backwards in his chair, he reached out his hands.

'Come here.'

Drawing her closer with need in his eyes, his succulent kisses tantalised her mouth. He ran his fingers across her like water down a rock. The edge of her robe fell away and he covered her shoulders with his brisk, delicate lips. She closed her eyes as the amber sun shed its rays over the balcony.

***

That afternoon, they took off for a long drive, passing patchwork fields of green and ochre stitched together with hedgerows. Rivulets wove in strips between the meadows, where portly pigs and goats trotted merrily over the valleys. An ancient church stood deserted, its motionless bells echoing out the silence.

Further into the countryside, the acres of nurtured landscapes lapsed into a wilderness of grassland and enormous archways of branches. Golden rays flickered through the foliage and wildflowers peeped from the ditches along the roadside.

At last, they entered a clearing under a dazzling pool of light. Amy gasped as she looked over the edge. The rugged hills dipped and merged as they intertwined with the flaxen wheatfields. A cornflower blue was brushed on the sky and a deep wash of cobalt glinted underneath it.

The road sat below a slope of ferns and mossy groundcover. Grasshoppers sang out from the bushes and birds fluttered their brilliant plumage among trees studded with luscious fruit. Amy looked at the scene in amazement as Joel pulled up near a ledge.

She stepped out towards the precipice but he guided her backwards onto safer ground, taking her hand as they walked further along the track to a tier of grass at the top of a higher slope. Jagged rocks formed wedges down one side and they climbed to reach the platform, collapsing beneath a leafy canopy and a sprinkling of bright yellow flowers.

Lying flat on her back, Amy turned to look at Joel. He was staring up at the clouds with the widest smile. Those eyes were bright under strong brows and his cheeks were ruddy with the heat as he fixed his sight on the sky.

'I told you we'd make it.'

'Don't be so sure,' Amy rubbed the scrape on her knee. 'We've got to get back down yet.'

'We could get even higher if we keep going.'

'I'm not moving from here.' She shook her head at Joel, ever the sportsman.

He sniggered at her stubbornness. 'We can't stay for long. This whole slope could crumble.'

Amy sat bolt upright. 'How do you know?'

'Didn't you see the cracks on the way up?'

She thought of the colossal drop below them, right on the very edge. The idea of plummeting into its depths filled her with dread. She planned to be back at school on Monday in one piece, not lying paralysed in a far-flung hospital.

'This is too scary. Let's go back down.'

Joel rocked with laughter. Amy knew how worried she looked but she couldn't hide her fear.

'I risked enough just getting on that flight. I'm not breaking my neck as well.'

Smiling, he pulled her until she was lying back down beside him. 'There are no cracks.'

'Don't do that. My heart stopped beating for a second.'

'I think you know I wouldn't put you in danger.' He stroked the tips of her fingers.

'Actually, I don't.' She smiled from ear to ear as he curled up tightly against her back. 'Can you imagine the trouble I'd get into if anyone knew where I was?'

'We're safe here,' Joel whispered.

Something flipped inside her at his body, pressed against hers, and his voice tickling her earlobe. She couldn't help feeling that they were years back in the past. In the bright little hut on the field, where he was looking into her face after another brush with the bullies, telling her she would be fine now. That he would always be there for her, guarding her with his life.

Amy turned to face him. 'I'm always safe with you.'

His smile slowly diminished. She was sprawled in a slovenly twist so that the hem of her dress had ridden up above her knees and her parted mouth was stained from the faded lipstick. Joel shifted onto his front with an expression that sent waves through her bones.

'Amy...' He stopped. 'Nothing. This just feels... so right.'

'I know.'

She bit her lip and then released it to breathe him in. He could barely look back at her.

'Having you there at school is really not a good idea.'

'Mr Craven,' she grinned. 'Are you thinking of breaking some rules?'

Joel studied her face. 'I don't know that I'm going to be able to pass you in a corridor and not...' He smirked and shook his head.

'That's fine by me.' She inched closer. 'I've waited long enough.'

'I can't count the times I tried to do something about it. Too much kept getting in the way.'

'We got there in the end.'

'We did.' Joel smiled. 'No going back now.'

They lay silently for a minute. Then Amy spoke.

'When did you know? About how you felt?'

'You've always been special to me. It's like... a

connection.'

She stiffened. Could it be that he was beginning to realise?

'You get me in here.' He pressed her hand on his chest. 'I can't explain it any other way.'

Her heart started to pound and she homed in on his face, gauging his reaction as she lowered her voice.

'There is a connection. There's a reason.'

Joel drew back slightly, hanging on her words. She took a breath, wondering how he would take it. This could be the last time she might be so close to him. She questioned what would happen if he suddenly changed his mind. If he would be unwilling to take things further with an ex-pupil. Or worse, that his feelings would be soured by recollections of a gawky child who had been too hopeless to help herself.

She swallowed hard and strained her throat, unable to ruin this moment. Not here and now, a million miles away and alone at last with him.

'It's more than a fling, Joel. It's... so much more.'

The honesty of the words echoed in her voice. He lifted her face like a flower in his palms and breathed so close, she thought she could burst.

'You mean everything.' He touched a finger to her mouth. 'My world.'

He kissed her so heavily that all was forgotten in the seconds, then minutes. They were up on their knees, pulling in like the tide then falling and rolling in a knotted heap onto the straggled bed of grass. Locked up tight and there to stay until dusk began to fall over the clifftops.

***

That evening, the sun smouldered in a line of lava, seeping tangerine into the clouds. Under a palm tree, a blanket was vacant on the soft sand and an open bottle of wine sat in a bucket of ice. The magnetic breeze blew over the scattered clothes as two figures splashed in a sea of serenity.

Amy plunged deep into the water, trying to swim away from Joel as he glided effortlessly towards her. He grabbed her with both arms and buried his face in her neck, laughing triumphantly as he pushed her down until just her head remained above the surface. She screamed as he gripped her ankles and worked his way up to her waist. And the protest faded away as he held her against him in the stillness of the ocean and ran his lips over hers.

He carried her to their tree where they drank the cool remnants of wine until the sky was just an inky mass, lined with a rim of bronze. Then they headed back to the apartment and straight into the shower.

Joel stepped under the trickling jets and pulled her in by the hand. He squinted through the moisture, watching as the stream rushed down the contours of her body. She surged at the feel of his skin on hers, pressing her mouth onto his collarbone and working her way up until she reached his lips in a spell of kisses.

With water flooding over them, she leaned back on the tiles, moving against him in a slow, wet rhythm. Their bodies welded through the steam as they fought to catch their last breaths. And then his soft smile consumed her once again.

Twenty-Five

On her way back into school, Amy's happiness was almost too much to contain. Two perfect days with Joel were hardly conducive when she was supposed to be under the weather.

She had covered her face with a layer of pale foundation, trying to avoid highlighting her rosy glow. Her chunky jumper was more than enough to detract from her light tan and she hoped it gave the impression that perhaps she was still feeling the chill.

The rain had made a comeback, washing the snow to a muddy sludge as fog screened the sky. She wrapped herself up beneath it all, discreetly bathed in the dandelion sun and still prickling all over from the heat of Joel's touch.

Passing his classroom, she blushed at the image in her mind. Beyond that very door, their history still stayed covered but her one nurturing teacher was now the love of her life. She momentarily closed her eyes, having not yet allowed it to sink in. Every part of her shivered when she thought of what they had done. How it really felt to be hot against his body and holding him through the night.

The spring in her step was obvious, as if she could grow wings. Never before had it been so hard to mask such a burst of bliss. All she wanted to do was jump on the roof and tell the whole world. But no one was going to know. Not yet, and possibly never.

Until Joel knew everything, their togetherness would be under lock and key. Secret lovers stealing time in the sultry shade of the building.

As she neared the hall for assembly, she prepared to be greeted. Tissues and cough sweets at the ready and a very convincing sniffle.

'You're back.' Alison smiled sympathetically. 'How are you feeling? You don't look too great.'

'Better than I was, that's for sure.'

'It's going around, isn't it? Gita had a sore throat on Friday and I've been sneezing this morning.'

'Go home if you start to feel worse,' Amy advised. 'You don't want to spread it.'

She hoped Alison would do just that. And if Gita was off today, it made Amy's case all the more believable.

'Did you go to the doctor?'

Amy shifted in her chair. 'No, I just... stayed in bed and kept warm. It did me the world of good.'

'Sounds like that's just what I need.' Alison sniffed and Amy passed her a tissue.

A pang of emptiness hit her at Joel's unoccupied seat. The next fortnight felt like it was going to be a lifetime.

Alison chatted on at her side, reassuring her that she hadn't missed much, but once again her mind was elsewhere. Skipping back to that last day, when she'd lain with him under the hazy sun. Her head resting against his body as she'd pushed her toes into the sand. His fingers winding in her hair and his limbs encasing hers.

A loud sneeze from Alison snapped her back to the present and as time went on, it was clear that Gita wasn't going to show up. When Ian welcomed her warmly, she breathed an inner sigh of relief to have got away with her absence. Now all she had to do was concentrate on work. She turned her focus to assembly in the vague hope of distraction.

'Well, everybody, it's Monday. Your favourite day of the week. I'm sure you've had fun settling back in, but now we must all knuckle down.'

He was met by a unified groan.

'But it's not all dull and boring,' he encouraged. 'Next

month is Open Day. Now, this is our big chance to show the visitors just how great this school is.'

Intrigue stirred in the children, although the rustiness of the holidays still hadn't quite worn off. But Amy was happy to hear about the plans. At least this gave her a slight diversion through these next tedious weeks.

'This year's theme is all about being ourselves and you will be creating some wonderful displays around the school. So just keep thinking of what you like about Woodbrook, how much you have learned here and how you can show that to others.'

'Forgot to tell you about that.' Alison's voice was nasal. 'I'll fill you in later.'

Amy subtly turned away. How would it look if she were to catch the real cold now?

As they left the hall after assembly, Alison stopped off to look through the first aid kit.

'Pastilles and some spray,' she said, tossing them into her bag. 'They'll have to do for now.'

'Do you think you'll manage all day?'

'Probably, it's just a stuffy nose.'

'Was Gita like that on Friday?'

'Come to think of it, she was. But I can't be off now, not with Open Day to think about.'

'So, what did I miss in that meeting?'

'Basically, you and I need to come up with a task for the kids to do based on the Being Yourself theme. They'll start working on it next week and it needs to be something that will display well. We could have a think at lunch if you like.'

'OK.' Amy opened her door. 'They'll appreciate doing something different after this morning. I'm giving them a maths test first thing.'

'How kind,' Alison scoffed. 'You'll be popular.'

'See you in a couple of hours then, if you're feeling up to it.'

'Don't worry about me. I'll be fine,' muttered Alison as she stepped into her room with an earth-shattering sneeze.

For the first hour or so, the morning seemed to go well and Amy was pleased to hear that the children had missed her last week. A wave of guilt hung over her momentarily, but her innermost thoughts of the weekend soon put an end to that. When the test finally got underway, she absorbed herself in organising the week's lessons.

She scrolled through the pages for the fortnight ahead. There was nothing much of any interest to fill her time. Nothing to divert her from the constant pull of Joel. If only she was as busy now as she had been just before Christmas. Two weeks of rehearsals would have easily passed the time and at least kept her focused on something else. But these days were going to be long and lifeless. And the slow, teasing hands of the clock told her she was in for a long wait.

A chair shuffled. Amy looked up and Freya hitched her seat slightly to the left. Then there was a loud tut, which disturbed the rest of the class. Amy watched the room until everyone returned to their work. Then Freya raised her hand.

'Miss?'

'Yes, Freya.'

'India's copying me.'

'No, I am not!' cried India, making her classmates turn their heads.

'You are. You keep looking at my answers.'

Amy was perplexed. India was one of the cleverest girls in the class and always got good marks.

'I'm sure India wasn't copying,' replied Amy. 'Perhaps she was staring at something else.'

'I saw her reading my work.'

'I was looking at your Sunshine Street pen.' India smiled. 'Look, we've got the same one.'

Freya wanted to say something more, but it was clear that she had been overreacting.

'Very nice.' Amy noted the disruption that this was bringing to the test. 'Well, I think you can see that India wasn't cheating. Back to work now, please.'

'I've got the pencil case!' Avril cried, waving it above her head.

'It's lovely, Avril. Now, back to work.' Amy said sternly.

'I'm collecting all the figures and stickers,' Freya added.

India sat back in her chair. 'I got the Roxie Rainbow doll for Christmas.'

'My favourite is Cassie Cloud,' replied Freya, instantly on better terms with India.

'I'm getting Millie Moon for my birthday,' said Tara, turning around in her chair.

'Girls!' Amy clapped her hands. 'You've got five minutes left on this test before time's up. This isn't fair on the others.'

'I want the Star Car with all the Planet Pets.' India blatantly ignored Amy.

'My sister's got that,' Avril continued. 'But she won't let me play with it. The other day she hid it, so I went and told my mum. She was really angry with Karina and said she had to share it, but secretly she told me she never would. So, I…'

'Right, that's enough,' Amy snapped, getting up. 'If you haven't finished because you've been talking, that's tough. I just hope you haven't ruined it for everyone else.'

She slapped the papers into her arms, giving unamused glances at the giggling girls. It was understandable that they were settling back into school, but she was surprised at India's attitude today.

At least there had been no fights so far, though. No tussling on the floor or any unacceptable behaviour. And certainly not a whisker out of line from Bertie. He'd been happy and attentive, getting stuck into his maths test. He seemed closer to Flynn now too, working with him and spending breaks together. Their shared love of the stage had struck a chord between them and to see this playing out was the highlight of Amy's day.

At lunchtime, she dismissed the class and stepped into the sleet, which had liquidised the snowy debris to a cold, dirty mush. It was the kind of rain that soaked her immediately in the short time she was outside. She jogged up the path and got under cover as fast as she could.

Alison was huddled in the staffroom breathing menthol from a tissue. Her nose was a flaming red and her colourless face shivered into her shawl.

'Oh, Ali, you're really coming down with it.'

She nodded, dabbing her chapped nostrils.

'Let's talk about Open Day some other time then.'

'It's OK,' Alison said with a sniff. 'It won't hurt to bounce some ideas around.'

'Well, if you're sure.'

Amy got her lunch and noticed that Alison wasn't starting hers.

'Aren't you eating?'

'Well, there's only that.' She nodded at her cheese straw, the only item under the clear plastic lid. 'I didn't have much appetite when I packed it earlier.'

'Have some of this.' Amy reached for two bowls and poured out equal amounts of soup from her flask. Then she split her buttered roll in two and handed one half to Alison. 'Keep your strength up.'

'Are you sure?'

'Of course. Now get it down you before it goes cold.'

Gratefully, Alison polished off the food, sinking back in her chair when she had finished. Amy found a hot drink sachet in her bag from the time when she really had been unwell. She made it up for Alison and took out her notebook.

'Anyway, I've been thinking about this theme. Maybe we could get them to do something with clay.'

'But we'll have the dough people on display anyway, right?'

'Probably,' Amy agreed. 'It's the best creative thing they did by far.'

'Exactly, but if there's clay as well, we'll have modelling overload.'

'I guess so. I didn't think of that.'

'They could write some thoughtful verses about

themselves. Even make stamps to decorate it with, like they've put their own stamp on their poems.'

'I like that, but...' Amy looked underwhelmed. 'It needs to jump out at people visually.'

'Point taken. Actually, how far have you got with the art project?'

'I'm just about to do shading techniques, starting with dark paint and paling out. We're doing sky scenes in lots of different colours.'

'That's it!' Alison's watery eyes widened. 'Why don't we do silhouettes?'

'It would surely look good. But what about the theme?'

'That's where the overhead projector comes in. They could pose in whatever way shows their personality and we could trace their shadows. Then, we'll cut out the shape on black paper and mount it against the painted skies. It'll look eye-catching, it covers the theme and it even touches on a present one.'

'I think we're onto something here, Ali. You might feel like death warmed up but you're on form with the brainstorming.'

Alison rubbed her throat. 'Well, I can't promise I'll be keeping that up for much longer.'

'No better, then?'

'Not really. Some fresh air might do me good though.' She stretched and walked across the room.

'You know where I am if you need anything.'

'A good book, a cuppa, and a big chunky blanket please.' Alison sneezed as she walked out of the door. 'And a whack around the head with a mallet.'

The day trudged slowly on and Amy couldn't believe it was still Monday. Two whole weeks exactly until Joel's return. And now that Alison wasn't likely to be around, the time would be even slower to pass by.

As the lessons progressed after lunch, it seemed that the children were finally getting into gear and departing from the excitement of the holidays. They began reading a new book together and expanded on some French vocabulary, which took up a good chunk of the afternoon.

But as the last session was PE in the hall, it wasn't long before her mind caved back in. Swarming with images of Joel, dashing around in his sports kit. Throwing all his energy at his class and helping every pupil to be the very best. So much passion filled his heart and all of that came through so fervently now.

When school finished, she was too maudlin for words and it was a relief to head anywhere that might divert her thoughts. Without bothering to phone first, Amy drove through the evening rain and made her way straight to Vanessa's flat. She rang the buzzer, hoping that Giles might let her in if Vanessa wasn't back from work. But nothing. Feeling fed up, she waited for a while in the car.

But the time slipped away as darkness began to fall and the soaking wet pavement shone orange under the streetlamps, so she started the ignition and prepared herself for another lonely night.

Then suddenly, she had a thought. The fortnight ahead might not be such a slog if only she had something to look forward to. Something fun to get her through the next empty weekend. What she needed right now was some serious cheering up and there were just two people for the job.

Twenty-Six

The bell rang on Friday evening and Amy raced downstairs. As soon as she opened the door, Rosie flew into her arms.

'Babe, it's so good to see you!'

'You, too.' Amy clutched her and smiled. 'You look amazing. What have you done to your hair?'

'Not a big deal, I've just gone slightly more chestnut.'

'It really suits you.'

'Do you think? I needed a break from the boring brunette.'

'Very nice, dearest,' a voice called from the boot of Rosie's car. 'But high tea would be a more appropriate time to discuss cosmetics and enhancements. Some assistance, if you please, before I freeze to death.'

Rosie rolled her eyes. 'You want to see the state of *him*. Dressed for the Bahamas, not post-snow Flintley.'

Colin stumbled to the doorstep with two large suitcases and three supermarket bags for life. He dropped them in the hall and threw his arms around Amy, kitted out in sunglasses and a palm tree-printed shirt.

'My darling, come hither at long, long last!' He grabbed her and squeezed away, rocking from side to side. 'It's so wonderful to see you.'

'Have I missed you!' Amy nuzzled into his shoulder. 'I'm so glad you're here.'

'Not in that outfit, surely?' Rosie came up behind them with the last of the bags. 'I begged him to wear something easier on the eye.'

'Nonsense dear, we're on holiday!' yelled Colin, as they made their way up the stairs. 'Let's get this party started. Tequila slammers all round.'

'I think coffee will do for now,' replied Rosie, curtly.

'Lighten up, pretty kitty, this is a celebration.'

'Yes, I know it is.' She yawned. 'But there's so much to catch up on, I don't want to be blind drunk before we've even begun.'

'Very well. But mark my words, you two will be off your faces after a sip of my Vacation Vodka.'

Once they were gathered around the table, Colin unpacked the bags and filled up the kitchen with food. Then he made three swirly coffees and served them up with a plate of iced biscuits, buns, and macarons, which he had baked at the crack of dawn that morning.

'This place is great.' Rosie gazed at the scenery out of the window.

'It's not quite Larkspur View,' replied Amy. 'But I could have done a lot worse.'

'Well darling, I'm all ears,' Colin said, biting into a frosted finger. 'How are things going?'

'Really good.' She looked at both of them. 'I made the right decision.'

'I'm so pleased for you. I mean, babe, life's never going to be the same without you in Popplewell, but if you're happy, that's a load off my mind.' Rosie paused for some coffee. 'So, how's the job going?'

'I love it.' Amy smiled. 'I never thought I'd say that, but I do.'

'Must be strange working at your old school. Mind you, I suppose it's quite different now, isn't it?'

Amy nodded. 'Most of it is. There are still a few reminders of the old days, but I guess I've just got used to that.'

'Good for you,' praised Rosie, breaking up a biscuit coated with a fancy sugared topping. 'I bet your mum and dad are pleased you're back.'

'It's good that they're only five minutes away. There's always something on the go at Mum's when I haven't got any food in!'

Colin looked into her eyes and raised a brow. 'And how's the love life? I hope you're not still moping after Nathan, young lady.'

'Who's Nathan?' Amy beamed a radiant smile.

Colin trod carefully. 'So… you're not still traumatised by it all?'

'Ancient history, folks. I'm just indifferent to the whole thing now.'

'Wow!' Rosie glanced at Colin and then back at Amy again. 'You really have put everything behind you.'

'Behind me? I can't even remember being with the guy.'

The pair were almost speechless at her new attitude.

'This is tremendous. You seem like a different person, darling,' noted Colin.

'I'll say,' Rosie agreed. 'What's your secret, sweetie? Got a new man?'

Amy grinned bashfully.

Rosie slapped her hands down on the table. 'You have!'

'Spill them… now.' Colin leaned inwards, the delight ringing out on his face. 'Every last detail.'

Amy couldn't stop smiling. This was the first time she had told anyone and she felt her heart flip over. 'He's called Joel. He's a teacher at the school and we kind of got it together at Christmas.'

Rosie was open-mouthed. 'How can you not have said anything before? All those video chats and you didn't even hint!'

'I don't know. I just didn't want to speak too soon.'

'So, come on, what's he like?'

'He's just…' She shook her head and looked away. It was impossible to put into words.

'Well, I say, darling.' Colin was startled. 'After everything you went through with that piece of filth, I never thought I'd see this day. Look at her, Rosie, she's head over heels!'

Tears swelled in Amy's eyes but she carried on smiling as if to confirm his observation.

'You really are serious about him, aren't you?' Rosie marvelled.

Amy glanced down at her hands, remembering how they had tangled up with his.

'He's changed everything. Knocked me sideways, completely.' She looked back up at the two thrilled faces. 'I'm so happy.'

'I'm over the moon for you, sugar plum!' Colin gripped her arm. 'You deserve every bit of this.'

'So, do we get to meet him?' Rosie's eyes lit up.

'Unfortunately not. He's away on a trip right now and he's not coming back for another week.'

'That's a shame. I want to check out this dream lover who has come along and rocked your world.'

'You will.' Amy nodded confidently. 'All in good time.'

'Speaking of dream lovers...' Colin exaggerated a cough.

'You?' Amy threw him a stunned look and he nodded back with a slight blush. 'How can you not have said anything?'

'Likewise! Anyway, we're just keeping it casual right now.'

'Casual?' Rosie chuckled sarcastically. 'He's practically our new housemate. I hardly see Colin anymore without Fabian attached to his hip.'

'Fabian, eh?' Amy winked. 'So, it's going well then?'

'It's only been a few weeks, but I dare say, things are rather joyful.'

'Well, when are you going to introduce us?'

'Actually, darling,' Colin tapped his phone and handed it to Amy. 'I think you've already met.'

Sure enough, the wallpaper on the homepage was a picture of the barman, who Colin had been set on since their last visit to the Frog and Fiddle. He looked just the same in his photo, but this time he was out of uniform.

'*Him*!' Amy gasped. 'How did you manage that?'

'I went for a jog late one night and just happened to pass the pub.'

'As you do,' Rosie mumbled.

'And would you believe it? He was coming out of the door there and then after finishing his shift.'

'Of course, he was.'

'Obviously, we recognised each other from the night when we first clapped eyes…'

'Obviously.'

'So, naturally, we just got talking and then, well…' Colin looked flattered. '*He* asked *me* out on a date.'

'Cool.' Amy widened her eyes and gave a nod to Rosie. 'So, it wasn't you he was after in the end.'

'No way.' She covered her face with a hand. 'Can you imagine me with him? A classic example of chalk and cheese.'

'You keep your hands to yourself, darling.' Colin inhaled dreamily. 'He's all mine.'

'How devastating,' Rosie snorted. 'I was looking forward to my pastel bedsheets getting caked in Tango orange.'

'Not got your eye on anyone then?' Amy asked her.

Rosie shook her head. 'To be honest, I'd rather go to bed with tea and chocolate. Relationships are way too much hassle.'

'And on that note, how are we kicking off this love-free weekend?' Colin's eyes flashed at Amy. 'Show us the way to the bars, sweet cheeks.'

'I'm exhausted,' whined Rosie. 'Can't we do all that tomorrow?'

Colin rolled his eyes. 'Time is precious, dear. How often do we get to do this anymore?'

'We've got the whole weekend. Try and take it slowly for once.'

'Come on, let's stay in,' Amy agreed. 'We can pile into the lounge and chill out all night.'

'Girls, I am a slave to your slovenly ways.' Colin shook his head as he cleared away the plates. 'But I may just be available for the catering, as long as we stick to the dress code.'

Amy and Rosie questioned him with a glance.

'Strictly nightwear. We're partying in pyjamas!'

After organising the luggage, they pulled out the sofa bed and brought in extra cushions and blankets for sprawling across the floor. Colin made a large speciality pizza accompanied by salad and garlic bread. Then they chose a film and talked through most of it, catching up on the last few months. Amy filled them in on more about Joel and they were stunned to hear of her bold weekend trip.

Accompanied by mint juleps, they carried the chatter on into the night, like a re-run of all the happy times they had spent together. It reminded Amy just how much she still needed them in her life. They huddled up under a duvet and the TV blared out to no one while they bantered, gossiped, and laughed.

It was well after midnight by the time Colin was snoring on the sofa bed and Rosie had gone up to sleep in the spare room. But Amy was still wide awake. She sat at the window by the dining table, watching the slender raindrops conjoin like necklaces and slide in slow motion down the glass. The sea's edge was ragged in the wind as if it heaved with pain. She stared all the way out to its stonewashed line where it blurred beyond the horizon, knowing that somehow it led to where he was. She hugged her legs, warm in her flannel pyjamas, and couldn't wait to wake up with him again.

***

The next day was kicked off with breakfast burritos. Then the trio went for a stroll along the seafront to blow away the cobwebs. They all walked arm-in-arm, taking in gusts of the salty coastal air. With the exception of his sunglasses, Colin had decided to ditch the holiday outfit in favour of his long faux fur-lined coat. To his side, Rosie squinted as the icy winter sun flickered in her view. Her hair was tied up in a loose bun and her chunky boots flattered her legs under the flared hem of her fitted cream overcoat. Her fruity perfume carried in the breeze as Amy directed their sight to any vague points of interest.

Under a sky as grey as the pigeons, they took shelter in a carousel of beachside benches and tucked into fish and chips, watching over-keen surfers crunching across the pebbles and the dim colours of boats dipping along in the sea.

They crossed the road and visited the pleasure park which had been there since Amy's childhood. Grass fell at all angles down to a large lake, which was the main attraction. Amy had many a happy memory of Melinda bringing her and Vanessa here to have fun in the adventure playground or to splash about in the concrete paddling pool whenever the weather had been hot enough.

Settling by the water, they shared a packet of bonbons and threw food to the passing ducks. Rosie set her phone camera on a tree branch and the three of them cuddled up on the bank for photos of their treasured time together.

As the late afternoon diluted the sky in a flush of periwinkle, they headed off to get ready for the evening. While the girls each showered and washed their hair, Colin got busy in the kitchen. By the time they had dried off and painted their nails, he had laid out a homemade buffet on the table, with mini spring rolls, bite-sized onion bhajis, jalapeno cheese melts and mini chicken skewers, all served around a selection of colourful dips.

'My darlings!' He beamed as they entered in their bathrobes. 'Welcome to the VIP room.'

'Tell you what,' said Rosie, launching towards the food, 'I could eat the lot. Thanks for doing this, babe.'

Amy took a handful of deep-fried vegetables and widened her eyes at the first bite. 'What are these?' She held one up to examine the middle. 'They're delicious.'

'You are currently sampling the Titillating Tempura, madam.' Colin winked. 'Hits the spot every time.'

'Aren't you having any?'

Colin shook his head. 'Not just yet, dearest. There are seven possibilities for tonight's attire and I really must make a decision.'

'Leave that to me.' Rosie licked her fingers. 'I'll soon tell you what not to wear.'

'Put this in your pipe and smoke it.' He covered a breadstick in taramasalata and held it up to her face. 'Believe me, honey bee, whatever goes into that cakehole of yours is far better than anything that comes out.'

Rosie's mouth fell open in protest and Colin shoved the food in between her teeth, then smiled contentedly and left the room.

Amy and Rosie finished eating and headed off to get ready while Colin freshened up in the bathroom. With a base of shimmering eyeshadow and lashes coated in mascara, Amy finished off her look with beige lipstick. As she tonged her hair in soft waves, she admired Rosie's made-up face, complete with perfect strokes of black liquid liner and a blood-red topping of her favourite evening lip gloss.

'That's me done.' Rosie checked her reflection one last time before taking two tops off the back of the door. 'So, which of these shall I go for?'

The black option was one-shouldered and embellished with a band of silver diamante around the neckline, while the other was shocking pink with glitter of the same colour accenting the sleeves.

'Definitely the black,' Amy advised. 'It'll go better with your lips.'

'Right you are,' agreed Rosie. 'Back in a minute.'

While she was next door getting changed, Amy slipped into a gold beaded top with skinny trousers and heels.

'How does this look?' she shouted out to Rosie, who came back into the room fully dressed.

'Stunning, babe. Me?'

'Drop dead gorgeous.'

'Come on then.' Rosie led her out to the hallway. 'Let's get some drinks while we're waiting.'

'Right…' Amy tried to remember what she had stock of. 'Well, we finished most of it last night. There's not a lot else to get started on.'

'Au contraire!' Colin grinned as he reached the top of the staircase in a bird-printed shirt, fitted trousers and a pair of polished brogues in a rusty shade of red. He waved them into the kitchen, where three martini glasses stood packed with crushed ice, each one adorned with an origami flower and an impeccably round slice of lemon. A sangria-coloured concoction filled a glass bowl that Amy had never seen and Colin lifted the dainty ladle that hung from a hook on its side. 'Time to get down and dirty with something you've never tasted before.'

'Looks lethal.' Rosie raised an eyebrow.

'I created it in special honour of our trip.' He poured it over the ice and handed each drink out. 'Cheers, my dears.'

'So, what have you called it, dare I ask?' Rosie inquired before she and Amy took a simultaneous sip.

'Forget Sex on the Beach.' Colin beamed. 'This is a Gleesome Threesome.'

Twenty-Seven

Half an hour later, their taxi cruised into Gliston. To be only twenty minutes away from the cosmopolitan resort was one of Flintley's assets. Sitting right by the sea, it boasted a wealth of shopping, a diversity of restaurants and a buzzing night life, ranging from the large commercial venues to the alternative hangouts along the beach. It was the obvious place to bring Colin and Rosie to get a real taste of south coast culture.

As the moody evening met the glittering lamps, the arms of the city welcomed them in. Music pumped from the rowdy bars, where disco lighting flashed beyond the burly doormen, and some already-tipsy revellers were working their way around the busiest hubs. The cab stopped at traffic lights where the concert hall and cinema were positioned on the corner and the main street of pubs and clubs ran uphill from the seafront. They hopped out into the bustling breeze and straight to the first bar that Amy suggested.

'That's more like it.' Rosie sighed after the first slurp of a cooling mojito. 'You need to revise your cocktail-making skills, Colin. Maybe add some mixer once in a while.'

He laughed back at her and stirred the straw in his generous glass of Sea Breeze. 'Oh, darling, I do pity you. There must be a fault with your palate.'

'Is it such a crime that I don't want to be hammered after just one drink?'

'There's a cure for your condition, pussy cat, and trust me it's not tonic water.'

Rosie just frowned in response.

Colin turned the other way and focused on the bar. 'Speaking of which…'

He nodded at the barman who was balancing several tumblers under different optics and pumps while throwing flirty glances at the customers. He had large dimples in his cheeks and two sleeves of colourful tattoos.

'Don't start that again!' Amy slapped Colin's arm. 'You're taken now, remember?'

'Yes, yes.' He rolled his eyes. 'But I can still admire from afar.'

'I'll just tell Fabian what you've been up to,' teased Rosie. 'I'm sure he won't be thrilled to learn he's just another link in your growing chain of bartenders.'

'I'm hardly planning to go over there and get off with Goldilocks. Although, given half the chance…'

'You'll probably be single again after this. Fabie Baby won't be sticking around when he hears about your antics.'

'He'll never leave me now.' Colin glugged his drink. 'He's got too much to lose.'

'Who do you think you are? God's gift?'

'Far from it, dearest.' He grinned. 'But he'd never get better than my toad in the hole.'

Amy noticed that Colin's gaze had attracted the barman's attention and he was looking over to their table and smiling now and then.

'OK.' She swallowed the rest of her daiquiri. 'I think we should move on.'

'Everything all right?' asked Rosie.

'Fine. There's just a few more bars to get round before we go to the club.'

'Very abrupt of you, darling. I was enjoying it in here.' Colin looked disappointed.

'You're not the only one,' smirked Amy, alerting Rosie to the action behind the bar.

'Drink up then,' Rosie ordered. 'It's happy hour at that place down the road. Three for two drinks. What more could you want?'

In a flash, Colin downed the rest of his cocktail and followed Amy and Rosie to the exit. He stopped to give the barman a dazzling smile but was swiftly pulled away and bundled out of the door.

By midnight, the club was in full swing. They had chosen La Mer, with its multiple themed rooms, each dedicated to a different type of music. As all three were merry from their cocktails, they decided to ease off with some cold pints of cola. Standing in a circle to the side of the bar, they watched the crowd pile into the centre where the DJ was blasting out plenty of upbeat tracks.

A group of men occupied a seating booth and were sitting around the table with a fresh serving of beer. Rosie's mannerisms changed and she batted her eyelashes over Amy's shoulder as she continued to chat away. It became so clear and apparent that Amy stopped her mid-sentence and forced her into eye contact.

'What's going on?'

'Nothing.' Rosie swayed slightly, playing with a thin lock of hair.

'You don't fool me. What do you keep looking at?'

Rosie ran her tongue over her teeth and smiled. 'Over there.'

'What?' Amy tried to turn her head, but the view was obscured by people passing by.

'He's fit. *And* he's looking at me.' Rosie gestured discreetly at the booth of men. 'Him in the middle. Reddish hair.'

'Right.' Amy nodded with as much enthusiasm as she could muster, but darkness shrouded the table and people continued to bump past her. 'Can't really see much from here. Shall we go somewhere quieter?'

'No. We can't move now!'

'I'm not standing here all night while you...' Amy looked to the empty space at her other side. 'Where's Colin?'

For a second, Rosie scowled at the interruption. Then she scanned the room and pointed to a space on the dance floor. Colin was in the full throes of a complex routine and he was already surrounded by a clapping troop of onlookers. He caught sight of his two friends watching him and he strutted over, holding out his arms to them.

'Come along, my knickerbocker glories! Let's bring the house down.'

'Not right now.' Rosie flashed another glance at her admirer.

'What's up with you?' Colin curled his lip.

'She's eyeing up some bloke,' Amy explained. 'Come on, I love this song.' She took his hand and shouted above the music into Rosie's ear. 'We'll just be over there, all right?'

Rosie nodded, but wasn't even looking. She remained where she was, working her sultriest expressions on the man in the booth.

Meanwhile, Amy and Colin glided onto the dance floor, twirling each other around and shimmying to the tunes. He picked her up and she waved her arms, mouthing the lyrics and letting her hair down. Nights out with Colin and Rosie were some of the best times she'd ever had and tonight was making her wish they didn't live so far apart.

Others joined in with their boisterous dancing, but the two friends took centre stage, entertaining everyone with their obvious chemistry. They moved in, face to face and then back to back, slowing down as the beats softened and then throwing their bodies into the swing as the choruses boomed out again.

When a few more songs had been played, Rosie still hadn't come to join them, so Amy beckoned to Colin and they both went to find her.

'She's not there,' Colin said, looking over at the empty space where Rosie had been standing. 'Perhaps she's gone to the loo.'

Amy tried to see her through the moving mass of people and the constant altering light which flickered deceptively in the darkness. Rosie wasn't at the bar or anywhere on the dance floor, so perhaps Colin was right. She walked across the seating area where the toilets were situated at the other side, but she stopped and eyed the booth. Two of the men were chatting in the outer edge seats, just away from Rosie, who was deep in conversation with the one she'd had her sights on. Amy could just see the outline of his head and the back of Rosie's as they giggled over the table.

'I see she's getting stuck in.' Colin rested his chin on Amy's shoulder as he caught up with her from behind. 'Let's leave her to it and get another drink.'

They perched on the bar stools with glasses of gin and tonic, enjoying the draught as the door swung to and fro.

'Having a good night, then?'

'It's an absolute ball, darling!' Colin laughed. 'We'll have to come back soon. Fabes would love it.'

'You tore up the dance floor. I forgot how good you are!'

'Ever the superstars!' He stared into the drink and his eyes glossed over. 'We always were.'

'Are you OK?'

Colin squeezed her hand and sighed. 'I just miss you so much, sweetheart. Oh, I know I've still got Rosie but…' He thumped his chest with his hand. 'There's a hole right here where you should be.'

'I miss you, too.' Amy flung her arms around him. 'Maybe we'll live closer together again one day.'

'Not maybe.' He kissed the side of her head. 'For sure, no matter what.'

'Am I missing out on a love-in here?' Rosie pushed them apart and wedged her face in between their heads.

'I wouldn't say that, dearest. You were knee-deep over there.'

Rosie shoved forward until she was leaning on the bar and took a small mirror from her bag. 'He'll be back in a minute.' She licked her finger and rubbed away a tiny smear of eye make-up. 'How do I look?'

'Fine.' Amy grinned. 'Having fun?'

'Sex on legs *and* single.' Rosie fanned her face. 'Must be my lucky day.'

'Given you his number yet?'

'Of course.'

'And his name is… or haven't you got that far?' Amy took a sip of her gin.

'Lionel.'

The drink nearly flew back out of her mouth. 'Lionel?'

'What's wrong with that?' Rosie frowned. 'I think it sounds sophisticated.'

Amy nodded thoughtfully. 'Anyway, we're going upstairs in a minute. Coming?'

'I might catch up with you later.' Rosie glanced swiftly over her shoulder. 'Right, he's back. I've got to go!'

She scooted into the crowd and they watched as her swishing hair disappeared out of sight.

'Charming,' muttered Colin. 'I thought tonight was all about the three of us together.'

'I know, but at least she's enjoying herself. Let's go and check out the other room.'

'Whatever you say.' He sighed as they got up and walked to the double doors. 'Time to bust some more moves and don't you dare outshine me.'

'You know that's impossible.' Amy laughed. 'If Rosie doesn't turn up after half an hour, we'll go and grab her, OK?'

Colin suddenly jerked her arm and stopped her from walking any further. 'Somehow, I don't think half an hour is going to cut the mustard.'

Amy followed his gawking eyes over to the far corner of the room. Rosie had her back turned and was locked in a lingering kiss. Two arms were running up and down her body, with hands all around her face. It was hot and heavy, with no signs of stopping anytime soon.

'She must be so drunk.' Amy looked knowingly at Colin. 'When has she ever gone for it like that before?'

'It's most ungainly.' He angled his head to get a better view. 'And about time, too.'

They smirked and watched for a few seconds, then Amy nudged Colin when it started feeling awkward.

'Come on, let's give them some privacy.' She linked his arm. 'But we'll keep coming back to check on her.'

A good hour passed by and every time they kept tabs on Rosie, she was either flirting wildly or engaged in yet another kiss. So, Colin and Amy had no choice but to enjoy the night while it lasted.

Colin was in his element upstairs, with the kind of music the three of them used to dance to on a Saturday night when they had first moved in at Larkspur View. It brought back so many memories, and the pair went to town in a display of frenzied moves, some that they still remembered from routines and others energetically freestyle.

At last, Rosie appeared and they both cheered, pleased that she had joined them for some dancing at least an hour before closing time. But instead of swaying to the music, she stood on the spot and motioned for them to come away. She had guilt and mischief written all over her face.

'What's up?' Amy asked.

'Nothing, it's just…' Rosie took in their waiting faces and hesitated to continue. 'Do you mind if I go?'

Both mouths flew open, but Amy was first to respond. 'Are you sure about this?'

'Just a bit.' Rosie tried to neaten up her smudged lipstick. 'He's amazing.'

'How will we know where you are? Does he live nearby?'

Rosie paused. 'On that note… I wondered if I could have your keys.'

'Well I never,' Colin gasped. 'Your inner dirty stop-out has finally emerged.'

'You didn't come home when you got with Fabian,' she quickly reminded him. 'All-nighter of tea and scones, was it?'

Colin chuckled and looked away. 'Actually, we…'

'Don't go there.' Rosie held up a hand and turned her attention to Amy. 'So, babe, is that OK with you?'

'As long as you know what you're doing.' She examined Rosie's demeanour. 'How much have you had to drink? You're not going to regret this in the morning, are you?'

'If I do, I'm an idiot,' she assured her. 'I'm onto something good here.'

Amy pulled out her keys, removing the one for the house from the ring. 'There's a plant pot by the front door. Put it under there when you've used it and don't forget, otherwise you'll have to get out of bed and let us in.'

'I wouldn't rely on that, darling.' Colin gave a sarcastic sneer.

'Thanks a million for this.' Rosie's face willed them to forgive her. 'Sorry I'm abandoning you guys, but he's just too good to resist.'

'See you in the morning, I guess.' Amy smiled. 'We've got our phones if you need us.'

'Bye then. Wish me luck!' Rosie kissed them both and hugged them tightly before vanishing into the darkness for the last time that evening.

For a moment, Colin and Amy were stunned to silence. Then they looked at each other in amusement.

'This is turning out to be quite a night.'

'She's got it bad,' agreed Amy, setting a loud vibrate on her new phone. 'It's probably for the best that she took the key. I'd worry if she went back to his.'

'As long as you've got strong ceilings, darling. And two good pairs of ear plugs.'

***

Amy woke to the sound of the radio playing easy listening tunes just beyond her door. The room blurred slightly when she first opened her eyes and she felt the chink of a faint headache. Starving and in need of painkillers, she wriggled out of bed and threw on some tracksuit bottoms with a stretchy purple vest. She tied her hair up in a rough topknot and shuffled into the kitchen.

The kettle was coming to a bubbling boil, a large frying pan was smoking on the cooker and a heap of rolls had been freshly buttered on a chopping board. The fridge door slammed shut to reveal Colin with his arms full of milk, sausages, and other groceries, his casual clothes covered by a flowery apron which Melinda had given Amy as a house-warming gift.

'Morning,' she moaned, flopping down at the table.

'Colin's Cafe at your service.' He bowed to her and came straight over. 'Are you ready to order?'

'Water.'

'Of course.' He poured some out from a jug and handed it to her, complete with two pills. 'It comes with our complimentary starter.'

'Thanks.' She threw the capsules into her mouth and drank them down.

'Now, allow me to get you a coffee.'

Colin filled a mug from the cafetiere and left it black. He brought it to her and set it down with a smile.

Amy puckered her face. 'I can't drink that without milk.'

'It's customary on these premises, dearest.' He folded his arms. 'So, please respect and obey.'

Grudgingly, she took three quick gulps and forced herself to swallow them.

'You may dabble in a café au lait at some point after breakfast,' he assured her. 'Now, have you decided on your main?'

'Anything will do.' Amy hunched forward and let her head drop into her folded arms. 'I'm famished.'

'Then permit me to make some recommendations.' He rubbed his hands together. 'Our Stacked like a Stallion breakfast baps are a real favourite with customers. Or there's...'

'Yes, that.'

'But you haven't heard the other options.'

'I want a bap. Fully stacked.' Amy looked up wearily. 'Now.'

'Coming right up, darling.' Colin darted away to take a pan off the heat before it burned. 'So, feeling rather worse for wear, are we?'

'Not too bad,' said Amy, slipping Colin's sunglasses on. 'Just tired. It's been a long time since I had a big night out.'

'But what a blast it was! If only Her Highness had stuck around.'

'Have you seen her yet?'

'Not a peep. I can only assume she's run out of steam.'

'Well, at least we know she's in there.'

'Yes, so thoughtful of her to chuck her shoes right in the middle of the stairs.'

Amy giggled softly. 'She wasn't thinking straight. I can't believe they even made it home in one piece.'

Colin fried the sausages to a crisp brownness and laid them on the base of a roll. He topped them with buttered mushrooms, a slice of grilled beef tomato, a thin square of cheese and finally, a flawless egg white with a skilfully centred yolk.

'Any topping, ladybird?' His hand wavered along a line of sauce bottles.

'Got any guacamole?'

'You wouldn't.' The lid of the roll drooped between his fingers. 'It'll taste like dirt, darling.'

'I don't care. Load it on thick.'

He did as instructed and cringed as he presented it, sitting on a bed of hash browns with a sprinkling of herbs and an arty flick of baked beans to the side. He anticipated Amy's rejection after taking the first bite, but she shovelled it away as if she hadn't eaten for a month.

Colin joined her at the table for his sticky pancake pudding, served with chopped banana and a modest spoonful of ice cream. Then to finish, as promised, he whipped up his famous Coffee Dash, which was sweet, milky and much more to Amy's liking.

'That was so good.' She licked her lips. 'I wish you weren't going today. Can't you stay here forever and do breakfast all the time?'

'It could well be on the cards, dear, if she doesn't come out of that bedroom soon.'

Amy looked suddenly anxious. 'Maybe I should see if she's OK.'

'I wouldn't be too hasty,' Colin warned. 'Who knows what you might come face to face with on the other side of that…'

The door of the spare bedroom clicked open and silence fell over the table. Their eyes froze on each other while footsteps padded steadily along the landing and then a yawn met their ears as someone entered the room.

Amy looked up and blinked, unconvinced by the reality of the image in front of her. Forcing her mouth to close, she tossed Colin's sunglasses away and stared straight ahead into the light, which fell fiercely through the blinds making everything seem distorted. Either her hangover was worse than she'd thought or Nigel really was standing half naked in her kitchen.

He smiled innocently, then his face began to flush as recognition set in through his squint. 'Amy?'

'Nigel!' She pinched her lips together in amazement. 'You look so different without your… glasses on.'

'Sorry, I thought this was the bathroom.' He rubbed his eyes, trying to hide the embarrassment.

'It's next door to your room.' Amy frowned at herself. *Your room?*

'Right!' He laughed. 'Can't see very well.'

'This is Colin.' She nodded towards him. 'Colin, Nigel.'

'Nice to meet you,' Colin smiled. 'I can't believe you know each other!'

'I can't believe you know Rosie!' Nigel raised his eyebrows at Amy.

'What's this about me?' Rosie asked in a low voice as she breezed into the kitchen in her bathrobe and wrapped her arms around Nigel's chest.

'Nothing, gorgeous.' He kissed her on her temple and

they both turned their faces to Colin and Amy in a bubble of bliss and headiness.

Amy looked at Nigel, grinning down at Rosie and then witnessed how soft Rosie's eyes had become as she cuddled into his body and he locked his chin over her head. This was no one-night stand. Immediately, she could sense something stronger.

'Anyway,' Nigel coughed. 'Do you mind if I just use your shower?'

'Go ahead,' Amy said with a smile.

He gave her a thankful nod and managed to vacate the room just before the towel flung itself from his waist. Then Rosie stood there facing them, blushing, bedraggled, and looking like the cat that got the cream.

When the shower began spraying in the bathroom, Amy stood up and hurried out of the kitchen.

'Downstairs, now!' she shouted under her breath and both Rosie and Colin rushed after her into the living room.

'What's the matter?' Rosie looked thoroughly confused.

'That's Nigel!' Amy hissed.

'OK, so I got his name wrong. What's the problem?'

'I know him.'

'You're joking.' Rosie was amazed.

Amy shook her head. 'He's a colleague.'

'He said he's a teacher, but I had no idea he worked with you!' Rosie grinned, then paused. 'I still don't get it… why are you so wound up?'

'What have you told him about me?'

'Nothing… why would I?'

'You must have mentioned you were coming back to my place.'

'I don't think I even said your name, babe. Just that this was my friend's house.'

'And nothing else?'

Rosie shook her head.

'You're sure?' pressed Amy, the panic rising in her face. 'Even though you were blind drunk, you're sure you didn't talk about me?'

'Of course not.' Rosie was beginning to get frustrated. 'I think we had other things to concentrate on.'

'OK, listen…' Amy kept her voice down and made sure she had Rosie's attention. 'Not a word to him about me and Joel or Woodbrook being my old school.'

Rosie gazed back blankly. 'It hadn't even crossed my mind.'

'No, probably not,' Amy realised, now she thought about it. 'But swear to me you won't say anything.'

'I won't… I wouldn't. Why not?'

'Because…' Taking a breath, Amy looked at both intrigued faces. 'Joel was my teacher when I was eleven and he doesn't even know it. He doesn't remember me and I want it to stay that way.'

'Darling.' Colin looked perplexed. 'Why ever would you feel like that?'

'I don't talk about this very much. I'd rather just forget it, but… I had a really hard time when I was there. I hated it.' She blinked away a stray tear. 'I was a waste of space and I'm not very proud of that. When I got the job and realised Joel was still there, I was all prepared that he would recognise me but… he didn't.'

Colin and Rosie were both stunned and silent.

'I'd probably have told him sooner or later, but the more time I spent with him, the more I fell for him and then… I've just carried on trying to pretend I've never met him before. And the longer I go on pretending, the less chance there'll be that he'll know.'

'Hey…' Rosie took Amy's arms in her hands. 'This isn't fair. On you or him. Come on, you've got to say something.'

'She's right, sweetheart,' soothed Colin. 'And you're a treasure. This wouldn't change a thing between you, I'm sure.'

Amy looked away. 'You don't know that. He might not want to be with one of his ex-pupils.'

'Babe, you're thirty-one, not fifteen. We're talking twenty

years ago,' Rosie tried to reassure her.

'But I'm scared.' Her voice shook as she held back her sobs. 'He's so good to me, just like he always was. He respects me, he praises me… and now he's falling for me. And if he found out who I really am, I know he wouldn't feel the same. He's better than that.' She breathed sadly. 'He wouldn't be interested in someone with my history.'

'Rubbish!' Rosie said firmly. 'No man worth his salt would desert someone over this. Especially not someone like you.'

'Please, just sit him down and get it all off your chest. Promise us you will,' urged Colin.

Amy's lip trembled slightly. 'I can't. Not now. We're just too happy and… I don't know what I'd do if I lost him.'

'You just take your time,' Rosie advised. 'Tell him when it feels right. But whatever you do, don't harbour everything. It'll kill you.'

Amy nodded and flicked her eyelashes to dry them. 'Maybe. But anyway, please don't mention this to Nigel. If he blurted it out to Joel…' She closed her eyes, unable to contemplate what could happen.

'I swear to you.' Rosie hugged her. 'Your secret is safe, you know that.'

'So…' Amy exhaled deeply and cracked a smile. 'I take it last night went well?'

'Look at her.' Colin gave Rosie a playful push. 'I've never seen her so doe-eyed.'

'I can't help it,' she whispered. 'He's only in the shower and I miss him already!'

'Long distance love, then,' Amy beamed. 'Do you think you'll see him again?'

'I'm not letting him get away that easily,' Rosie said, stubbornly. 'We'll work something out.'

Just then, the bathroom door opened and Nigel's whistling drifted along the hallway.

'Sounds like Super Stud is ready for round two,' Colin mumbled in Rosie's ear.

'Right.' She let out a feathery breath. 'Better get back to it… I mean… him.'

She ran out of the door and up the stairs with Colin following slowly behind her. Amy took a moment, then began the climb herself. *They were right*, she thought. There was no other way out of this situation than to reveal all she was hiding. Each time the idea came to mind, her heart seemed to soar as she imagined how things would be if, on the off chance, it didn't change a thing. That Joel just couldn't be without her, even with everything out in the open.

But it was just a fantasy. If Joel had known better in the first place, there was next to no chance they'd be together now. She felt like she was cheating him through every moment they had shared. But she couldn't let go of it for anything. And she didn't have the strength to take that risk.

Twenty-Eight

Keith dug his spade into the cold soil and tore through a knotted clump of roots. All around him, the Year Four children were busily tending to the school's front garden after its heavy spell of snow, their bright wellingtons lightly misted with dewdrops as they trod across the turf.

An inkling of spring was pushing through the frost. Crocus heads were parcelled up like pupae, waiting to release the beauty that hid inside. Early primrose stems had emerged from the ground to blast out their smatterings of pale sunshine yellow. But the thin hem of bordering was deadened and brown, congealed by the chill and starved of warmth or light.

Within the boundary of the picket fence, Amy and Alison sat on the bench, pouring nut mixes into the bird feeders. It was mid-morning on Wednesday, and Ian had nominated their classes to help Keith with the garden before Open Day arrived.

'So much nicer, isn't it?' Alison glanced at Amy. 'Doing joint lessons like this.'

'They're a happy bunch today. I guess it makes a difference when they've got the others to have fun with.'

'And at least we can chat while they're all occupied.'

Amy nodded. 'How do you feel anyway?'

'Much better. It must have been proper flu, I think. You got off lightly, only being in bed for a couple of days.'

Responding with a brief and pensive silence, Amy tried hard to push the memories out of her mind. There was still too much time until Monday and she had resolved not to get caught up in such bittersweet thoughts.

'Nick didn't get it then?' she finally asked.

'He was quite sneezy last night. He'd better be well for the weekend though, we're supposed to be going to his brother's.'

Amy looked up at the grizzly sky, teeming with more relentless rain. She might have asked Alison to join her for shopping or the cinema, but now that was out of the question. Unless Vanessa happened to be free, she'd have to pass the time in some way by herself.

'Mrs Huckleberry!' squealed a girl from Alison's class, pointing under a bush.

'What, Fleur?' Alison asked. 'I can't see anything.'

'It's a mouse! It's got its leg caught.'

Most of the children gathered round to see it, but Alison kept her distance and stayed where she was.

'Shhh!' ordered Amy at the noisy pupils. 'You'll frighten it.'

'Keith, can you deal with this?' Alison called out. 'Small furry things make me go all...'

'It's fine,' Amy lowered her voice. 'Move away and let me in.'

She caught sight of a shivering rodent, stuck in a small pile of twigs. It didn't bite as she put out her hand, so she gently freed its trapped leg. There was a chorus of adoration as she returned to the lawn and two little eyes peeped timidly out from her fingers.

'Now, if you don't make a sound, you can all come and look before I let it go.'

'Steer clear of me when you do that,' Alison glared.

Everyone flocked around Amy as she waited for the hush to fall and gradually opened her hands. But quickly, she brought them together again and raised an eyebrow at Alison.

'Don't you even think about bringing that over here.' She flinched, then registered the puzzled look on Amy's face. 'What?'

'It's not a mouse.'

'Of course it's a mouse. What else could it be? A guinea pig?'

'It's a hamster.'

The children reached out to stroke it and nagged Amy for a cuddle, but she kept hold of the frightened creature and made them stay away.

'What are you going to do with it?' Alison was getting jittery.

'There's an old cage in the shed,' offered Keith. 'It'll do until we find out where it came from.'

'Just tell Ian.' Amy handed him the hamster. 'He'll do what he can to find the owner.'

'Looks like someone smuggled it into school.' Alison shrugged as Keith took it away.

'That's not fair,' whimpered Fleur. 'I wanted to hold it.'

'So did I,' whined a boy, inducing a wave of protest from the crowd.

'Back to work!' Alison clapped her hands. 'You've got twenty minutes to make this garden look good enough for Open Day. Now jump to it.'

The children retraced their steps to where they had been weeding, digging, and neatening up as best they could.

'Speaking of which, we really need to get on with the silhouettes.'

'We do,' Alison nodded. 'As soon as possible.'

'Friday afternoon? That'll be a good way to end the week.'

'Lovely. I'll reserve the hall so we can do all the projections, then we can go back to our rooms to paint.'

Amy smiled in agreement. At least something fun and easy was in the pipeline to round off what would probably be a long and arduous rest of the week.

As breaktime approached, the children tossed their tools into a large crate and began to file out to the playground. Then the main entrance door creaked open and Ian's face appeared over the wall.

'Hello gardeners.' His eyes brightened. 'You have worked hard!'

'Nothing to do with them,' Alison joked, gesturing her head towards the last few children who were still clearing away. 'The two of us did it all ourselves.'

'No, they didn't,' murmured a girl.

Ian chuckled. 'I wouldn't worry, Bonnie. I think Mrs Huckleberry is just after some of that chocolate I promised you! Anyway, does anyone know where I can find Keith?'

'In the shed,' Amy beamed. 'And I think he might have a present for you.'

'Fascinating,' he said with mock intrigue. 'I'd best go and find him then. Well done Year Four and I shall be mentioning this in assembly.'

***

Later that afternoon, Amy had a break. Her class was in the lab with Martin while he took them through some science experiments, so she used the time to mark papers. But images of Joel poured through her head as she stared out of the window. She drifted into the helium clouds as they layered like shale on the grey. A weakened butterscotch seeped its way out where the sun remained hidden from view.

Two blackbirds took flight from a tree, their wings almost touching as they soared so high, they were out of sight. If only she and Joel could be like that. Gliding away together without a care in the world.

She put her pen down and got up from the desk, trying to find something else to get on with. Something that wouldn't need such quietness or contemplation. There was a shelf in the corner which needed rearranging, so she knelt on the floor and began to take the books out.

But suddenly in the pin-drop peace, a voice she recognised spoke loudly beyond the window.

'Hey lover, it's me.' There was a pause and he laughed softly. 'No, I don't want to talk about me. How are you?'

Nigel's volume grew even louder as he trod across the grass in the secluded space behind the huts.

'Not as much as I miss you… yes, of course I do… oh, nothing much, just work and stuff. You?'

Amy smiled, knowing exactly who he was talking to.

He laughed again. 'Are you getting paranoid? There is no way I would even look at someone else… yes, I'm sure!'

She couldn't help staying where she was, just for a few minutes longer.

'I had the best weekend. I just miss you, my Rose.'

Amy grinned at his words, although going by their chemistry on Sunday morning, it was no surprise that he was smitten.

'I know. I feel the same… OK, gorgeous, I've got to go. Ring you when I get home… you too. Bye.'

She got a rush of happiness that two people she knew had come together in this way. Thinking that Nigel had gone, she continued to stack the books in alphabetical order.

'No, you do it…' he cooed. 'Come on, just hang up! OK…' he made a quick kissing noise. 'Bye baby, speak tonight… bye.'

The footsteps scrunched away and a few seconds later, she watched Nigel walk off up the path.

As time went on and she finished doing odd jobs around the classroom, she thought again about Rosie and Nigel, and her feelings began to alter. An envy took over from the gladness she'd felt before. They were completely free, with no lurking secrets threatening to ruin everything. No guilt on either conscience of something they hadn't revealed. They had each other now, all above board and completely openly. Nothing, not even distance, could get in the way of that.

***

Amy was wide awake as the clock struck midnight on Friday morning. By four o'clock, she gave up trying to sleep and instead sat at the table with a warm cup of tea in the lonely darkness that buried everything outside. She reached across to the answerphone and played Joel's message again and again, feeling her chest swell. Just the weekend to go and she would finally see him.

It was beyond early when she got ready for work. She chose a maroon tank top with a blouse and tailored trousers, pulling her hair loosely into a simple low ponytail. Blackness still blindfolded the waking hours of daylight and at just after five, she didn't yet feel like breakfast. Packing some fruit with a yoghurt and granola, she took off in her car, somehow unable to rest or breathe until she had reached the school gates.

They were still locked as expected, but she pulled right up to the railings and sat behind the steering wheel, staring straight out ahead as sunrise stirred over the desolate field. A soft yet volcanic orb began to blaze, kindling the fog with melted mandarin. It dipped down to the wintered grass, torching a line on the most precious spot and making it glow like a million strands of barley.

How could he not remember? That he'd stood right there on that one perfect day, willing her to reach where he was. Desperate for her to get there as fast as ever was possible. How could he not know her face? The girl whose only freedom had been his words, his unexplained faith and the hands he held out to her, was still there, right in front of his eyes.

The sun faded to a grapefruit pink as daybreak transformed the sky. Its soft creases trickled over the clouds like a deep network of arteries. Hot on cold. Full yet transparent and blending together like flesh tones, all moulding into one.

And at that moment, she knew she had to tell him. He was all that had ever been good and he needed to know. She would face it. Let him look at her for who she really was and allow him to make a choice. If he turned away, it would destroy her. But heartbreak, no matter how severe, was better than deception.

It turned out to be a pleasant morning, beginning with a more interesting assembly than usual. Ian strolled in with the hamster on his shoulder, officially adopting it as his own. There had been no luck in solving the mystery, so Hector, as he was now named, had a new place in Ian's office.

After a long computer session and a reading task, it was soon time to break for lunch. Then Amy and Alison headed into the hall to set up the projector for the silhouettes, putting out a pile of tracing paper, some pencils, and a photocopied sheet of ideas to inspire the children while they decided on their poses.

The eager pupils waited in a line for the shadows to be drawn and their imagination even took the teachers by surprise. One girl turned her head to the side and stuck her thumb cheekily to her nose. Another used her fingers to make little horns on her head and Freya made whiskers and ears like a cat.

Then they all went back down to the classrooms to cut out their silhouettes on black paper. For the final part of the project, they painted their striking backgrounds of the sky using the techniques that Amy had been teaching them in art.

Within minutes, the room was alive with colour, capturing morning to night and every conceivable weather condition. Amy wandered up and down the rows of busy children, admiring each piece of profound individuality. There were cool blues of day and darkest navy nights. Blushed washes of the rising sun and purple reflections of dusk and moonlight. But one particular painting really caught her eye. One set of colours that made her mind fly straight to Joel.

Avril's work sizzled like an evening in a heatwave. There were shades of burnt orange and the crushed red of watermelon. Calm, rosy pinks and a hint of limoncello. And instantly, Amy was back there to that night on the beach. His eyes sinking into her body and burning over her like the sun. She lost herself now in the paradise, miles away from the classroom and the brushes slapping with paint, as she thought of the way they had breathed each other in, absorbed in that bounteous moment. Their own silhouette stamped there like wax against the bubbling magma of the sky.

A tap on the door snatched her thoughts away.

'Come in.'

'Miss Ashcroft.' The voice made her heart jolt. 'Can I have a word?'

She turned full circle, fighting to control every unexpected emotion. Because right there in her classroom, beaming from the gap in the doorway, was Joel.

Twenty-Nine

The second she reached the cloakroom, Joel clicked the door shut and pushed her against the wall. He took one look at her face and his lips plunged into hers. They kissed for a few deep seconds, then stopped to find each other's eyes. He held her neck in his hands, pressing his thumbs to her jaws, and pulled her back in like he wanted to do this forever.

Her spine flattened up against the plasterboard as the taste of him coursed into her mouth again. Stroking her hands through his hair, she could hardly believe he was back so soon. And here to stay this time.

He edged his face away until he could see hers.

'I've been wanting to do that for so long.'

'What are you doing here?' Warmth tinted her cheeks as she smiled. 'You're supposed to be away until Monday.'

'I finished early. Did everything I had to do.' He nudged his forehead against hers. 'And I just needed to see you.'

Amy shivered in his arms. 'I can't believe you're back.'

'Two weeks was too long,' he whispered, frowning into her eyes and kissing her again. 'This is it now. I'm not going anywhere.'

'They're just finishing off in there.' She gestured at the sprightly voices mounting beyond the door. 'We can go as soon as I'm done.'

'The thing is…' Joel looked down tiredly. 'Ian wants me to go through some work with him now I'm here and I've not even been home yet, but maybe later on we could…'

'No.' Amy was hardly able to say the words. 'Get some

rest tonight. You need to sleep.'

'Are you sure?'

The next twenty-four hours would be harder than the last two weeks put together, but the time had finally come to set him straight and if there was any hope of getting this right, she needed preparation.

'Come over tomorrow night. It will be worth the wait, I promise.'

'Whatever you say.' He traced the outline of her mouth with his finger before touching it once more with his lips. 'I'll see you then.'

Hard as it was to tear herself away, she smiled effervescently and slipped back into the unsuspecting classroom.

It had been the second sleepless night in a row, but this time for very different reasons. She rolled out of the duvet, unable to stop smiling. The weekend would no longer be agony, because he was here now and nothing was going to take him away from her. Nothing except a secret that could ruin all they had. She would tell him everything he needed to know, but right now, her head was high up in the clouds.

And this evening, unhinged and with no disturbance, they would explode. She had so much to do, with the house to tidy up and the meal to plan, but today was going to be blissful, getting everything ready for the minute he would finally arrive.

She drove to the superstore to buy fresh ingredients for a meal she simply had to pull off to perfection. Browsing the aisles for ideas, she decided on steak. Juicily tender meat in a rich sauce with perfect chunky chips, some crusty bread and salad on the side. It was one of her ultimate favourites and hopefully Joel would like it too.

With the best organic cuts from the counter, she loaded her trolley with mushrooms, shallots, potatoes, and cream. She chose the finest tomatoes, leaves and dressing, picking up a rustic loaf which was still warm from the bakery. Two bottles of expensive red wine and some brandy for the sauce. Croissants, more coffee, everything for breakfast.

To finish, Melinda's chocolate and raspberry pudding cake recipe would definitely fit the bill. Adding liqueur and cocoa to the trolley, she headed off to pay for the shopping, pausing just once again for a small tub of luxury vanilla ice cream.

With dessert in the oven, she tidied the house, changing the bath towels from pink to pure white and putting new linen on the bed. She laid the table with her best crockery, placing two small candles in the holders and her glass salt and pepper mills in the centre.

Once she had prepared the salad and sliced all the vegetables for dinner, it was late afternoon – long enough to get ready with a little time to spare. Dismissing several garments for being too dressy and others that were not smart enough for an evening look, she finally pulled out a midnight-blue top with a frilled neckline. Clingy without being too revealing and subtle rather than plain, its colour would bring her eyes to life and sit flatteringly well against her skin.

Once she had showered and blow-dried her hair, she sat at her mirror, taking her time with her make-up. Brushing bronzer over her cheeks, she lined her eyelids to match her top, finishing with mascara and glossy rose-pink lips.

A few sprays of perfume and some thin hoop earrings and she stood back to check her reflection. She looked at herself, satisfied and relieved. When she had last been with Joel, she had come straight off the flight with no time for freshening her face. But tonight, she was ready. Fully made up and glowing all over.

Back in the kitchen, she unwrapped the steaks and seasoned them, ready for cooking. She uncorked a bottle of wine and took it downstairs to the living room with two large glasses. Then she brought the salad and bread to the table and checked that her homemade chips were crisping up nicely in the oven.

She was about to pour herself a drink when a car slammed shut outside. Her stomach flipped and she ran to the window. Joel was just locking up as he headed to the front door. Even though she was expecting it, her spine still jerked when the chime sounded in the hallway. She held her breath at the top of the stairs and made her way down to the door.

Her eyes locked with his and electricity sparked. He wore a dark shirt which made his eyes look astonishingly blue. A holdall was slung over his shoulder and a bottle of wine dangled in his other hand. Rain fuzzed in the porch light behind him and he was only just sheltered where he stood.

Amy shot him a flirty grin. 'You made it.'

'Not a moment too soon.'

She had to look away. His eyes were smouldering.

'Come on. You're going to get wet.'

'Is the car OK there? I've totally blocked you in.'

Amy raised an eyebrow. 'I'm not going anywhere, am I?'

'Absolutely not.' He dropped his bag in the hallway and edged closer to her.

'I opened some wine.'

Amy led the way into the lounge where the bottle was waiting on the coffee table. Feeling him right behind her, she nestled down on the sofa and filled the two glasses with the aromatic liquid. She handed one to him and took a long sip from her own.

As it fell down her throat, he gazed from her face to her shoulders and back up to her eyes again.

'You look stunning.'

'Thanks, but… you look better.'

'I don't think so.' He sniggered like he had always done and a line tingled down the centre of her back as his arm slipped behind her and he moved a little nearer. 'Anyway… how have you been?'

'Just getting on with things at school. The time has flown by.'

'Really?' He nodded.

'No!'

His face broke out into a broad grin.

'It's been slower than ever. I've hardly eaten, slept...' She looked at him scornfully. '*You've* done that to me.'

He cocked his head so his face met hers. 'I hated it when you went back. It wasn't the same when you weren't there with me.'

'It's been crazy.' Amy turned to meet his stare. 'I was sitting at the school gates at five-thirty yesterday morning.'

He frowned. 'Tell me you weren't that eager to get to work.'

'No, I was just thinking about things.'

'What things?'

'Just...' She chose her words carefully. 'Memories.'

Joel seemed suddenly tense. 'You mean, your accident?'

'Oh, no!' Amy reassured him with assertive eyes. The last thing she wanted was for Joel to think she had given a moment's thought to anything that had happened with Nathan. 'Nothing like that at all.'

She could feel him relax again as she spoke.

'I mean...' Taking a breath, she looked deeply at him. 'The school just reminds me of so much.'

She examined his reaction, but he just seemed intrigued. 'Like what?'

'Just, how things were before I met you.' She glanced to the ground, but then brought her focus back to his face as the water rushed into her vision. 'And how you changed everything when you came along.'

'You did too.' He nodded gently. 'From the minute I first saw you.'

She stared back at him, both desperate and dreading to have this out in the open. But she suddenly came to her senses. Here they were, rekindling this living, breathing flame, finally in a place together where time and other people were completely non-existent, and she was just about to throw everything out of the window. It was too soon. Far too deep a conversation to be having from the minute he had walked through the door. Perhaps later, she thought, taking in his gloriously stifling face. Or never.

She grinned dismissively. 'Anyway, I just couldn't sleep and the dawn was lovely. I was getting some inspiration for the art we were doing in class.'

'I'll watch it with you next time.' He ate her up with his smile.

'Good.' She reached over and covered his hand with hers. Every pore prickled as she touched him. 'Because I've lost count of the amount of mornings I've had to wake up without you.'

'There's a lot of lost time to make up for.' He ran a finger across her chin and she knew that in seconds they would be kissing.

'The chips!' Amy got up and raced towards the door. 'They've been in the oven all this time.'

Joel laughed as she tore up the stairs with her wine glass in hand and lunged at the oven. But it was fine. They were browned and crisp on the outside with a soft, fluffy centre.

'Everything OK?' He stepped into the kitchen with the half-drunk bottle of wine.

'Panic over. They're rescued.'

Joel refilled their glasses and leaned back on the worktop. He watched her with amusement as she flapped around with a tea towel.

'Looks like you've gone to a lot of trouble.' He glanced at the table and all the ingredients she had laid out next to the hob.

'Well, I hope you like steak.'

'My favourite.'

'That's good,' she replied, heating up a griddle pan. 'But the bad news is, now you've got to watch me cook.'

He grinned so warmly it made her knees go limp.

'I'd love to.'

'Watch and learn,' she said in a sultry tone, her stomach fluttering as he fixed his eyes on her. She could feel, even from a good metre away, how hard it was for him to stay back.

The brandy flames flicked up from the pan and she felt alarmed for a moment, wondering if they would stop. But they soon died down and she added a glug of cream before returning the steaks to cook just enough, until they were left with a mouth-watering middle of delicate pink.

She placed them onto two plates and dripped the sauce decoratively over the top. Then she took the tray of chips and divided them up, serving Joel slightly more than herself and ensuring he was given the biggest of the steaks. He followed her to the table, bringing the wine with him.

'It looks delicious.' He smiled, picking up his knife and fork. 'Thank you for all this.'

'Just make sure you like it, OK?' Amy sat opposite him at the table, giving him the best view of the dusky ocean.

He took a bite of the steak, smothered in the warm, flavoursome sauce, and creased his face with delight. 'Yes, you can definitely cook. It's unbelievable.'

Amy beamed gladly, having nearly finished the next glass of wine. She too was enjoying the meal, but the intensity flowing across the table was getting in the way of her appetite. They ate in a comfortable silence but every now and then, Joel looked up at her like he was killing to get closer. The chills flew as she felt his gaze each time she shifted and at every word she spoke.

Joel devoured every bit and washed it down with a good gulp of wine. 'Well, what can I say? My compliments and much, much more to the chef.'

'Don't be so hasty.' She took the plates over to the dishwasher. 'There's still dessert to get through.'

He drenched her with his eyes. 'You really are spoiling me tonight.'

'I don't know if you're going to approve of this though.' She sliced through the warm cake and laid a wedge on each plate, adding a scoop of ice cream and a garnish of fresh raspberries.

'Why wouldn't I?'

Amy giggled. 'It's a PE teacher's worst nightmare. Pure,

unadulterated stodge on a plate.'

'Right up my street, then.'

'If only they knew.' She glanced from the corner of her eye as she placed a portion in front of him.

'I'm capable of worse behaviour.' He grinned as she settled back down at the table. She wasn't sure how much longer she could keep that far away from him.

He didn't look up again until he had polished off the plate. 'You really have made such an effort. I'm impressed.'

She laughed, tossing a scrunched serviette into the middle of the table. 'Joel, you sound like you're marking me.'

'I couldn't ever mark anything you do.' His soft smile faded. 'You're beyond it.'

Amy looked away, knowing he had. More times than she could remember.

'My turn next anyway. I'll take care of breakfast.'

'If it's anything like the last one, I'll be happy with that.' She slid out of her chair and stacked up the dishes. 'Actually, that's not true. The last cooked breakfast I had was eventful. You'll never guess who stayed over at the weekend.'

Joel turned around in his seat to face her, looking lost and even slightly irked. Amy held his stare with a wicked smile.

'Nigel.' She winked and opened a drawer to find the corkscrew.

There was a long pause and she struggled to hide her delight.

'*Nigel?*' He still maintained the hint of a smile, but confusion got the better of his expression.

'More wine?' Amy removed the cork from Joel's bottle and filled both glasses again.

'What was he doing here?'

'My old housemates came to visit and Nigel was out in Gliston at the same time we were. He instantly hit it off with Rosie and ended up staying over here.'

Joel sniggered again and walked over to pick up his wine glass. 'Well, he kept that one quiet. I got a couple of emails from him last week too.'

'They seem really serious though. I don't think it's a one-off.'

'Interesting,' he mused. 'They'll have a tough time with the distance though. I mean…' he sipped his wine and eyed her over the rim of the glass. 'I couldn't have lasted another day without you.'

'Did you really miss me?'

Amy rested her back on the worktop to take the weight off her feet. Then she froze as Joel put down his glass and moved across to her. He ran the softest fingertip along her hairline and drowned her in the torrent of his gaze.

'Did I miss you?'

He pressed his chest against her and let his hand fall, brushing down to her neck. Then his lips dusted against hers, just skimming, teasing with the slightest touch and leaving her throbbing for more.

'Did I miss you?' he said again in a whisper.

His breath quaked against her skin as he worked his way along her jaw, slipping, tugging her skin as he sank further and further down, making her bristle as his warm mouth reached her collarbone. Then he travelled back up, and further up, and she stiffened as they kissed again, their bodies pushing fiercely together as their lips spoke in a language far more lucid than words ever could.

Clinging to him, she slid up onto the worktop, legs wrapped around his waist. With their mouths still grinding, his hands glided down her back, edging up inside her top and pulling it off over her head.

Gasping for breath as his palms rubbed against her, she pulled his shirt apart without hesitating to undo any buttons, and squeezed herself tightly to him, their bare torsos clenched together, feeling the bursts of heat and coldness swirling between their skin. For a few minutes, they savoured the moments, ticking slowly by. Both caught up in the heaven of each other, feeling the torment ebbing slowly away.

And Amy couldn't open her eyes. With every inch of

body and heart she was consuming now, she ran another metre across that field, getting closer, ever closer to the very depths of him. Feeling the release as she closed in slowly, surely and dangerously. And on such an ecstatic knife edge, there could be no turning back. She could have him now. Submerge herself in the joy of him. The one who had always kept her going. The figure who had waited at the end of the green journey.

But it would be so much better if he knew. If she were to tell him, right now, exactly who he was about to make love to. Suppose he were to look straight back into her eyes and proclaim it made no difference? That he still wanted her just as much. The mere thought made tears glisten out in secrecy as she clung to him and dreaded how it would feel if she had to let go. But the thought of having him, wholly and completely, in full awareness of her past was suddenly intoxicating her mind. Nothing in the world could ever make her happier.

She felt his breathing deepen as he buried his face between her ribs and caressed her upwards in a stream of kisses that waved like shocks under her skin, ending on her lips where his mouth covered them again. Shuffling out of the rest of their clothes, they fused together from head to toe. He took her breath away with the power of his eyes as he relished a last look at her before launching straight back in.

He urged her backwards out of the kitchen, supporting her as they edged towards the bedroom. Before they could even get through the door, he was leaning her against the frame and pulling her up around him. She shivered and gripped him, feeling as if she would die if he waited a second longer. But regardless, and with all her might, she exhaled in resignation and pushed his neck softly away from her face.

She could sense his frustration at her suddenly distant touch, but still, she looked straight into his two agonised eyes.

'Joel…' Her insides shattered as she hung on the very last thread of control. 'There's something I've got to tell you.'

Thirty

Unravelling herself from their torrid knot, she guided him into the room and sat down naked on the cool edge of the bed. While she paused a few moments, Joel knelt on the floor below her and held both her hands in one of his own.

'What is it?'

She gazed at his unkempt hair and the way his bones chiselled in the lasered moonlight. As each of his breaths steamed on her shoulders, she forced herself back, gritting her teeth through the growing waves of urgency that continued to strike all over her body. She hardened and peaked as he brushed against her skin, so open and ripe to submit to every part of him. Yet bewildered as her mind swerved her away.

'You and me...' Her heart flitted like a bird in a cage, just moments from release or a lifetime of imprisonment. 'There's more to this. More to us.'

'We're soulmates.' He nodded, holding her to him. 'And every inch of you amazes me.'

'But it shouldn't. All these things you think about me... I'm not any of them. Not really.'

'I'm not hearing this.' He raised a stern eyebrow. 'You do something to me that no one ever has before. I can't take my mind off you, I can't stop looking at you and I've spent the last few weeks... no, make that months... going insane through not being with you.'

A tear sped down her cheek and she shook despite his warmth. He made her feel so much worth and his eyes showered over her as if she possessed some kind of immortal beauty. She shifted closer into him and rested her hand on his jaw. It still left her speechless to know how strong his feelings were.

As she faced the option of letting it all crumble away, she thought of everything he had built her up to be. And as much as this was all just an illusion, the pressure to live up to it – to be it just for him – was just too highly charged to back away from. She couldn't bear to destroy his fervent, yet overblown perception of her. To be like this again, her spirit akin to his as they collapsed into togetherness, was something she could no longer live without.

'Please trust me here.' His lips crept over hers. 'I believe in you and I want you. And nothing is ever going to change that.'

Her muscles went limp as he leaned onto her, his mouth and hands fuelling her as only he could. She tilted backwards slightly more, awakened and moist from his body and fingers as they caved her in, numbing her fears and ripping away her reluctance. Bringing her to a shuddering edge as she surrendered weightlessly, prised and ready.

She watched as his head made its way to her shoulders and slowly dropped further down across her chest. And with one last fibre of sanity, she lifted his face to her pleading gaze.

'Don't ever leave me.' She breathed. 'I can't lose you now.'

The response in his eyes was one of absurdity stabbing at the pinnacle of pleasure. His look said it all as he shunned the very suggestion. She could see the desire burning through him almost painfully. So, ending the torture she fell helplessly back, taking him with her as she plunged against the pillows. He lost himself within her, tangling as their bodies merged, hot with perspiration and raw against the sheets.

He dug into her furiously, whispering her name. And then she buckled with him as the tremors quivered through her, deeper than ever was possible and higher than the sun.

'You know me,' she slurred into his neck.

The words were impassioned yet muffled all at once and she had no idea whether they had even registered. Joel just kissed her and sprawled over her body, breathless with exertion and spent to the limit from hanging on the cusp. She pulled the covers over them and embraced him into calmness, listening as his breathing slowed until he was slumbering in her arms.

At last her bed was warm and full, and shaped by their braided heap. Although his limbs stayed clasped around hers, she couldn't stop checking to make sure he was there. But every nuzzle was met with his grasp and he kissed her tenderly, even in his sleep.

***

The kitchen tap woke her and she pulled on a chemise from somewhere under the duvet. Calm lights of midnight poured through the room and Joel was sitting on the window seat, looking out into the faraway depths of ocean.

'What are you doing awake?'

His smile lit up in the dead of night. 'Just thirsty.'

'Aren't you cold?' She eyed the outline of his body, still bare with the exception of his trunks.

'Not at all.' He took her hand and she sat beside him, her shoulders shimmering in the gentle starlight. 'Why, are you?'

Amy nodded and shivered slightly. 'That bed's too big just for me.'

'We'd better get back then.'

'It's a little late for that.' She crawled over him without letting her weight fall on his body.

Travelling across him, she inhaled each breath that was quickening from his lungs. Keeping the smallest gap between them, she drew him in magnetically, watching his expression liven under her command. This still so surreal. So secretly empowering. She had sat in so many classes where he had been the one in control, but here she was now, climbing lithely over him. Feeling him relent with her every move.

She smiled as she closed in on his lips, just missing them with her mouth. Instead, she pressed on the bottom of his neck, feeling the tension fluctuating. He tilted his head but she slid to waist level, hearing the pleasure straining in his voice.

He clutched and enveloped her like it would be fatal if she moved. As he reached down for her, she brushed each knuckle, every fingertip, as it coaxed her to the part of him she wanted most. Nothing could compare with being face to face, feeling his smile bring shivers to her bones and knowing that his softest kiss would melt her.

Arms and fingers were intertwined with tendrils of light from the black sky. His strong, searing, perfect eyes were deeper in their blueness than this mass of night. Their bold integrity outstripped the dark, like they would overcome any obstacle to find her.

There could be no better feeling. Nothing more treasured than having him near, and so near that his breathing ripped across her skin. No emotion could be stronger than how she felt right now, rooted firmly against him, happier than ever.

Pressing his mouth in sensual strokes, he came gently forwards in a trail. Her eyelids closed at the first hit and she thought back to earlier that evening. Of the way she had nearly lost everything in the heat of a desperate moment. Just one foolish word could have made him see her in the humiliating light of her past. And they wouldn't be here now, doubled over in pleasure, the embers of the last fire igniting once again.

He edged up to the corner of her lips and in a flash, she was under. Bursting inside as he clambered over every erogenous curve. The time would come for revelation, head on and completely. But for now, she had no choice but to be taken. Swept away and hypnotised in this real but impossible dream.

As the earliest hours of morning came and the

monochrome sky was unchanged, their bodies melded against the glass, watched only by the wild, nocturnal sea.

Thirty-One

School had become a different place in the three weeks since Joel had been back. There was no need to count the hours or combat the loneliness any longer, knowing he was just a few corridors away. The anticipation of seeing him at any time in the day added fuel to the fire behind closed doors.

It was Tuesday assembly in the week before Open Day, and Amy was quietening the raucous children. She wore an olive-green blouse with a stretchy black pencil skirt and by the look on Joel's face, it had been a good choice. Assemblies had become almost excruciating, trying to appear interested in Ian's rambling anecdotes when all she really wanted to do was jump a few seats down the line.

But Ian entered the room more solemnly than usual and the chatter faded at his demeanour.

'Good morning, everybody.'

The audience babbled a questioning response and Ian sensed the tension.

'Well, I do have some rather sad news.' He unexpectedly chuckled at the worried crowd. 'The time has come to tell you all that I will be leaving Woodbrook at Easter.'

Groaning filled the room as the children aired their disappointment, but the teachers were perplexed.

'That's right,' Ian continued. 'Mrs Farley and I are off to enjoy our little villa in the sun and this can only mean one thing. You will soon have a terrific new Headteacher and you won't miss me one bit.'

'Who will it be?' shouted a child, before being quickly

silenced by Alison.

'You'll have to wait and see.' Ian winked. 'But you'll be delighted when you find out.'

'Did you know about this?' Gita whispered behind Amy.

'Not a clue,' replied Alison under her breath.

Amy thought it strange of Ian to tell the whole school before the staff. But then again, he was always unpredictable, so perhaps it wasn't that shocking after all.

'Now,' he continued, 'as we have all been thinking about ourselves for Open Day and how Woodbrook has helped us to be who we are, I want to share everything I have learned in my time here.'

She leaned back in her seat and attempted to concentrate on Ian's words of wisdom, but with Joel only metres away, that was never going to happen. It was as if he didn't even care that his pupils were sitting right in front of him by the way his eyes were constantly drifting over to her. She tried not to return his stare too often, aware that anyone could notice, but it tore relentlessly through the silence and was impossible to ignore.

The collar was turned up on his oatmeal sweater, hugging his neck exactly where she would touch him if she were closer. She gazed at his neat hair, now she knew how it tousled in the morning. Knowing the beauty of his face when he was next to her, fast asleep.

She was sure that Alison would soon notice her stare. It felt as if everyone already knew. That they could all feel the chemistry as evidently as it was sparking now. Ian's words blurred into nothing, overtaken by the echo of Joel's voice as she thought of every whisper. Every crackle of desire that had sounded in his throat. The soft sinking of his lips onto hers.

After assembly, Amy joined the colleagues who were swarming over to Ian at the lectern. Soon, a familiar body pressed into her back. She clenched her fists and looked ahead as he continued to shadow her, tightly and enticingly, until he was pulling her apart at the seams.

She burned inside to be wrapped in his bareness and warmed by the spice of his skin. Each time she tried to edge away, he only pushed up harder against her spine.

'I want you now.'

'What?' Alison glanced sideways.

Her mind scrambled for words. 'I want… to get out of here now. It's too hot.'

'Have you been outdoors recently? It was bucketing down with sleet this morning.'

'I know, but I'm burning up.'

'Not coming down with another fever, are you?' Alison asked half-heartedly as she stretched forward to see where Ian was.

'Probably.'

Amy stuck an elbow out very slightly behind her and jolted as it touched Joel's ribs. He grinned into her hair and she could no longer resist him. As soon as she was sure that Alison's attention was diverted, she made illicit contact with the brazen blue of his eyes. His hidden smile swallowed her up and she wondered how long she could last, having to keep this far away.

She looked down at their fingers, just itching to link, and let the scent of him ooze into her mouth. Finding his chest, then the top of his neck, her gaze rested back on his face.

If only no one else was in the room. There she would be, leaning back on his body as he dragged his hands along each piece of hers. He would be loosening her clothes, kissing every flushed particle of skin and driving her to distraction with the agility of his fingertips.

Tearing her sight away from him, she looked for a gap in the crowd. Involuntary tingles lapped their way from head to toe and she was filled with impatience for the staff to start dispersing.

'You certainly know how to keep a secret.' Alison's statement caught her off-guard.

'Well, I thought I'd be cunning and surprise you all,' replied Ian, who had just joined them. Amy composed herself and smiled in agreement with Alison.

'The whole villa thing sounds nice. Where are you off to?'

'I've left that in Stella's capable hands. That way, I can't get the blame if it all goes pear-shaped.'

'So, come on...' Alison lowered her voice. 'Who's taking over?'

'Nobody as yet.'

'I thought you just said we'd be delighted with your replacement.'

'And I'm sure of it.' He put a finger to his nose and backed away to the exit. 'No matter who that turns out to be.'

Alison shrugged at Amy and the pair made for the door, following the other teachers who were filtering from the room. Amy walked slightly ahead, eager to get out in the fresh air, but there was a hold-up at the doorway. Debra was blocking the path while she spoke in depth to Ian, just as he was heading back to his office.

'Let's have a cup of tea while we're at it, shall we?' said Alison sarcastically. 'And throw in a bun or two.'

Amy swung around in surprise at the comment, but instead she found herself thudding against Joel. He moved further in until they were just a blink apart. There was that knowing gaze again, making her wither under the power of its promise.

All that seemed to make sense was him, and him alone. And the blistering, frantic force that continued to weld them together. Time stood still as their heads drew in, moments away from pounding hearts and gently crushing lips.

But his were not the only eyes drilling into Amy. Something snapped her away from him and blitzed the moment to pieces. Penny scowled though her straggly bob and her front teeth glared from a questioningly-parted mouth. She looked suspiciously from Amy to Joel, clearly seeing what they couldn't hide.

Amy turned away and concentrated on the door which Debra had finally stepped away from. She could hardly bear to walk on, wondering what might happen. But the last few teachers drifted out of the hall and Penny simply strolled away behind them.

***

Just a few minutes into the lunch hour, Alison and Amy were up in the top unit preparing the TV room for an afternoon lesson. The oven whirred in the background, sending an oaty smell flowing out from the cookery area.

They didn't realise that anyone was there until a clatter sounded over the divide. Amy put down a stack of chairs and headed across to find the source of the noise.

'Don't worry, it's only me.' Gita lifted a tin from the rack. 'I nearly dropped a tray. Just got it on the worktop in time!'

'What are you up to?'

'We've just made flapjacks. I'm a great advocate for safety in the kitchen, I almost burned my hand off!'

'Nice.' Alison immediately joined them. 'Any going spare?'

Gita nodded to a plate on the table. 'Go ahead. I'm just about to put those in the staffroom.'

'And what about all that?' Amy glanced at the pile of labelled boxes sitting in a large cardboard tray.

'They're for the class to take home. Just off in a minute to give them out, but I'm in a hurry. We've got that storyteller coming in at two.'

Amy watched as Gita balanced the plate on top of the boxes. 'Do you want a hand with that?'

'I'm fine.' The top level wobbled as she moved. 'I think.'

'Hang on,' Alison said. 'I'll just get these chairs out and we'll walk with you in case you drop anything.'

'Cheers girls, that's good of you.'

'No problem. We're going now anyway.'

When Alison was ready, the three of them began their descent down the sloping corridor. They were just passing the fire exit as Martin pulled it open and came to a standstill when he saw them. He looked straight at Gita, struggling to keep everything together, and smiled shyly at her tense face.

'Hi,' he said, casting a cautious eye at the others. 'Can I help you with those?'

For a moment, Gita was lost for words and her cheeks blushed a rosy pink.

'Thanks, I'd like that. I mean...' She giggled. 'That would be great. I'm getting no offers from these two here!'

As Alison and Amy reined in their reactions for Gita's make-or-break moment of flirting, Martin took the boxes from her hands.

'To your room?' he asked, holding the door open and allowing her to lead the way.

'To my room,' she grinned. 'See you later, girls.'

They waited for Gita and Martin to disappear down the steps to the playground.

'Well, that was a turn-up for the books,' Alison remarked. 'I wonder what's changed his mind.'

'Maybe he's just after a flapjack.'

Laughing, they turned the corner of the corridor to find Joel leaning against the railings, talking to Nigel. He was wearing his padded coat and a woollen hat, having just returned from his Year Six games session.

'And here she is now.' Nigel gestured at Amy and Joel's face lit up. 'We were just talking about you.'

Amy narrowed her eyes and smiled. 'Anything I should know about?'

'What a place Popplewell is. You must have been crazy to leave.'

'It's nice.' She beamed at Joel. 'But I prefer it around here.' Then she stared at Nigel in astonishment. 'How do you know?'

Saying nothing, he grinned unashamedly back at her.

'You've been to see Rosie!'

He nodded in confirmation.

'I'll be having words with her. She never told me.'

'Wow!' Nigel raised an eyebrow at the look on Amy's face. 'She's in trouble now.'

Joel couldn't hide his feelings. 'And don't you just love her when she's angry?'

'Never get on the wrong side of me,' Amy shot him an icy smile. 'You of all people should know that.'

She caught sight of Alison squinting from one of them to the other. The silence that followed was just a few seconds too long.

'Looks like you're in with a chance, mate.' Nigel winked at Joel. Then his phone began ringing and his face was all smiles when he saw who it was. 'I'll leave you lovebirds to it. My lady's on the line.'

He raced outside the building, leaving Alison observing Amy and Joel with more than a growing suspicion.

'Nigel has not stopped banging on about your Rosie since they got together,' she grinned.

Amy looked out of the window in the direction that he had gone in. 'He's all she talks about on the phone now. Not that she ever rings me anymore!'

'He's a lucky man,' Joel added smugly.

'What do you mean? You haven't even seen Rosie.'

Joel gazed at her, unabashed. 'He stayed over at your place before I did.'

Alison cleared her throat.

'Well, on that note, I'll get going.' Her expression was pure amusement as she began to walk off, turning to Amy just before she vanished. 'And I'll catch up with *you* later.'

Once she was out of sight, Amy continued teasingly down the corridor past Joel. 'I can't talk now, I've got too much to do.'

But he reached for her just as she knew he would. Sure that no one was around, she allowed him to pull her straight into his arms.

'Come here, you.' He moved in with a gentle but irresistible kiss.

She savoured it for a second, then pulled away, gripping her hands around the unzipped collar of his coat. 'You are playing with fire today.'

'I don't care.' His breath was feathery as he made the most of the split seconds. 'I want everyone to know now how I feel about you.'

He stroked her lips with his again, making the temptation too much to bear and in the next moment, she lost all consciousness as she plunged into him, unable to stop the rush of stolen kisses. She slipped the hat off the back of his head and ran her hands through his hair. The coarse mass of sandy strands she had wanted so fiercely to touch.

Inside, she was pining for more. More unspoilt time to be with him right now. More of everything that was fastened under his coat. For a few spiralling moments, ideas crept into her mind as she thought of the places they could go. Somewhere they might lock themselves away and nip this in the bud.

'Joel,' she whispered. 'You're making this so difficult.'

'I knew it would be.' He kept his eyes dangerously on hers. 'It's impossible to just look at you.'

She eased his mouth away and pushed it down onto her neck, but the tickle made her giggle louder than she'd anticipated. His smile was alive as he drew her close and held her in a happy embrace.

'How long do I have to put up with this?' she asked. 'Seeing you from a distance and trying to leave it there.'

'Let's think about that,' he said into her hair. 'How about forever?'

She jerked, first at his words as they melted in like chocolate, but very quickly again as a door hinge squeaked from the vicinity of the staffroom. She stepped away an inch, pausing to hear if they had company, but she still kept hold of his hands.

Everything went quiet again, so she eased herself back to him, taking his knuckles and nuzzling them. 'Better go. I'll see you after school.'

'I'm counting the hours.' He leaned in and kissed her, over and over again, until she ripped herself out of his clutches and they parted ways in the corridor.

She hurried down the slope, unable to lessen her smile. But the moment she was about to turn, Penny blocked her path. Her lips were pinched tightly, showing all their papery lines.

'Sorry Penny, I didn't see you there.' Amy was instantly annoyed with herself for apologising.

'I gathered,' Penny replied in disgust. Her skin appeared worn against her drab knitted top. 'And now I know what you've been up to.'

'I don't understand.'

'Don't play innocent with me. I know about your little fling with Joel.'

'Yes, you're right. Me and Joel, we're… together.'

'How long has this been going on?'

'A few weeks.' Amy gritted her teeth. There she was, grovelling again. Feeling intimidated by questions she wasn't obliged to answer.

'And you think it's appropriate with a colleague?'

'Appropriate for who?'

'For *me*.'

Amy began to get defensive. 'Sorry, how does this affect you?'

'We don't permit relationships between staff members at this school.'

'Really? Well, this is the first I've heard of it. I'm sure Ian wouldn't make a rule like that.'

'Ian is insignificant.'

'He's the *Headteacher*.'

'Not for much longer.' Penny sneered callously back at her. 'And when I take over, there will be no staff relationships. In or out of school.'

'You can't do that!' Amy laughed. 'You seriously think you can tell us what we can and can't do in our own private lives?'

'I can and I will.'

'And anyway, Ian said the replacement hasn't been decided yet. So how do you know it'll be you?'

'I have my ways, let me tell you. And if I find out you are still seeing Joel, you can kiss this job goodbye as well as him.'

Amy took a breath, trying to figure her out. 'Why do you really care, Penny?'

'What?'

'Why are you so bothered about me and Joel?'

'What a ridiculous question.'

'No, it isn't. You might think I'm stupid…'

'What do you mean, *think*?' Penny smiled, with nostrils flaring.

The question stung Amy, but nevertheless she continued.

'Look, I really don't know what your problem is, but anyone would guess…'

'Guess what?' she cried.

'That *you* want him instead!'

Amy could see she had touched a nerve. She watched Penny's face break into a cunning grin.

'Want him? He's been after me for years.'

'You're kidding yourself.'

'Am I?' Her confidence was unsettling, like nothing could break her down. 'Well, you just go away and believe that if it makes you feel better. But Joel's an honest man. I'm sure if you ask him, he'll tell you the truth. Go on, next time you see him, just try it.' She pushed her face close up to Amy's. '*Ask him*.'

'She doesn't have to.' Joel stepped out of the corridor and he had never looked more furious. 'She knows I wouldn't touch you with a barge pole.'

Penny's complexion whitened. 'Oh, give me a break, Joel. You've always had a thing for me.'

'You've lost your mind.' He glared at her like she was pathetic. 'And I've had just about enough of you.'

'Joel,' Amy steadied him. 'It's OK. I know.'

'No! I'm not having her treating you like this anymore.'

'Forget it. She's not going to.'

Seeing her this empowered and so strangely unflappable, Joel stood back to let her talk but he refused to leave her side.

Then Amy turned her attention to Penny.

'I've had this from people like you all my life…' She eyed Joel, warily. 'And I'm not putting up with it for another second.'

Penny grinned provokingly, now she was in Joel's presence. 'Don't be so silly, Amy. You're getting yourself very upset over nothing.'

But Amy wasn't about to back down.

'You've had it in for me since my interview. You tried to ruin that for me, then you undermined my decisions about the play.'

'You're imagining all this.' Penny flipped her head back and laughed.

'And you threw my picture away deliberately and replaced it with that… thing.'

'You're off your rocker!' screamed Penny, bending over almost drunkenly. 'You're a lot of things, but I never had you down as a liar.'

'You're the liar,' said a voice from further along the corridor.

The three of them turned their heads to see Debra, slowly edging towards them. Her face was more assertive than Amy had ever seen and her eyes were determined behind the frame of her glasses.

Penny's discomfort was only too visible. 'Get lost, Debra, this has nothing to do with you.'

'You did throw it away, and you know it.'

'Has the whole world gone mad here?'

'Tell Amy.' Debra took another step forward. 'She deserves to know.'

'What are you trying to do here, Debra? You know the kind of consequences you're going to face if you say any more.'

'Are you threatening her?' Amy asked Penny.

'She always does,' Debra admitted. 'She chucked your photo in the bin saying she didn't want your face in the programme. Then she…' Her cheeks grew red as she snivelled into her hand. 'She…'

'*What*, Debra?' pressed Amy.

'She pushed me against the wall and swore she'd fire me if I said anything.'

'I'm getting Ian. You're finished!' Joel shouted, waving a finger at Penny.

'Please don't.' Debra looked agonised.

'It's a serious matter. I've no choice but to report her.'

'There's no need.' Debra took a deep breath. 'I don't want any more trouble after this.' Then she stared meaningfully at Penny, regaining her previous composure. 'But you'd better leave Amy alone now or everyone, including Ian, is going to know what you really did.'

'I'd clear off if I were you.' Penny curled her lip. 'What have I told you about sticking your nose in where it's not wanted?'

'You're not going to tell me anything anymore. You have no power over me.'

'Or me,' Amy spoke up. 'You've done enough damage over the past few months, but you can't break us.' She glanced possessively at Joel and then straight back to Penny, her eyes full of defiance. 'We're solid and it's staying that way.'

Debra gave them a subtle smile of approval.

'You're nothing but a stuck-up little tart.' Penny glared daggers at Amy. 'Swanning around here plastered in make-up, pushing your chest out and thinking you're it.'

Joel made an incensed leap forward but Amy held him back, allowing Penny to continue.

'You make everyone feel uncomfortable. You should be in the gutter, not teaching in a school.'

'I think you'd better go,' replied Amy as calmly as she could, despite being pained by Penny's tirade. 'And believe me, if you put one more foot out of line, I'll be going to the authorities, never mind Ian.'

'How big of you,' chortled Penny as she slowly backed away. 'Well, you've far from heard the end of this. Just you wait until I am Head. You'll all be out on your ears.'

'Oh, about that…' Debra glowered with her hands on her hips. 'I wouldn't expect a promotion any time soon. Not when the governors hear what you've been up to.'

Penny stared back at her, attempting an innocent smile. 'You don't mean that… you wouldn't. Come on, Debs, we can work this out.'

'Watch me. Whoever gets the job, it's not going to be you.'

'Maybe we can talk about this later. We're still friends. We'll always be friends.'

Debra slowly shook her head. Overcome with shock, Penny turned away from the three teachers and stumbled out of sight.

The minute she was gone, Amy rushed over to Debra, who was clearly shaken by her own bold actions.

'Are you OK?' She put a hand on her shoulder. 'That took a lot of nerve.'

'I'm sorry about the programmes.' Debra looked sincerely into her eyes. 'I would have told you in time but…'

'You thought you'd lose your job!'

'I was going home crying every night and I realised I had to stand up to her. I thought she was my friend but… not anymore.'

'You can do a lot better,' Amy grinned.

Debra shrugged back.

'I'm going for a pub lunch with Ali and Gita tomorrow. Come with us, OK?'

'Sounds good.' Her sad eyes brightened.

'And anyway, I think I owe you a drink.'

'I'd better get to the store cupboard before class.' Debra nodded ahead of her. 'Open Day mosaics this afternoon.'

'Have fun,' said Amy as she watched her walk away. 'And see you tomorrow.'

'See you.' Debra paused just before she disappeared. 'You make a great couple by the way.'

Amy stood there on the spot, marvelling at Debra and

the way she had tackled Penny. Then, she found herself enfolded in Joel's arms and she turned inside them to face him. He looked so utterly proud of her. Like she'd answered a question or passed a test. Like she had just raced over the field in a record time fuelled by his faith.

'I knew you had it in you.' He scorched her with his gaze. 'And nothing can come between us. You do believe that.'

'Of course I do.' She kissed him then rested on his shoulder, wishing she could really mean the words.

Thirty-Two

On the morning of Open Day, the school was hushed and spotless in the hour before the children arrived. The interior had never seen so much paint and glue or bursts of glitter and string. Innovation poured from every wall in shapes, swirls, and splashes, lighting up the walkways as daylight trickled in.

Down in the huts, Amy glanced over the display of silhouettes. Squares of zesty orange and yellow, midday blues and sunset pinks were stamped with the drama of their foregrounds. It was a wallpaper like no other and it showed so much that her class could do. Each outline told a different story and spoke of every new skill. And they echoed all Amy had accomplished since becoming their teacher. How Woodbrook was somewhere different now to the place she had dreaded in the beginning.

There was still time before assembly, so she ventured into the main building to peruse the decorations. The lower school corridor was a moving explosion, splatted and dripping with the work of little hands. There was fake food on paper plates, all stuck up high on a gingham backdrop. Shimmering fairies and woodland folk were playfully scattered along the way, and a strikingly designed map of the world was an eye-catching centrepiece.

Opposite the library, the Year Three hooks were all connected by a clothes line, running along the back of the wall as if it held them like pegs. Each shoe bag was embellished with a child's bare footprint, which had then been finished with a stitching of their name. Road markings ran through the middle of the corridor with models of the pupils' own houses as if they were all neighbours.

Amy wandered past the music room and up the staircase to the offices, where the large noticeboard opposite the fish tank was shining back like a reflection, brimming with three-dimensional sea creatures and plants. She stood on the spot, mesmerised and proud of all that Woodbrook offered.

But the largest display board, just outside Ian's office, immediately grabbed her attention. Under the banner, *A History in Pictures*, something made her stomach lurch. Shoulder-length hair pushed back in a headband and a stifled identity she was too scared to show. A slight smile that was the best this girl could do against her two large eyes that couldn't deny the reality.

A group of classmates posed tightly together in the middle of the picture, while ten-year-old Amy was pushed out at the back. They happily held out their dolls and cars, while she hugged her cuddly puppy as her only form of comfort.

She looked closely now at her younger face, puffy and tear-stained from another bout of crying, and she wondered how she had been feeling at that moment. Petrified? Useless? Alone.

Standing there now in the hallway, it hit home just how far she had come. Under the very roof where she had suffered the greatest was the place where she had grown the most.

Now, nobody could put her down; she would stand up to them as she had to Penny. No longer was she an underachiever; this had been proved through the efforts of her work. And just a year after the photo had been taken, she'd had Joel in her life and she still did. The constant spirit that had pulled her through and the only jewel she had ever treasured.

Amy knew that the time had arrived. As soon as today was over, she would tell him every detail she had kept trapped inside. It would take every last piece of courage to look him in the eye and hope that she still had him once he finally saw her for everything she was.

But the picture had to come down before anyone really looked at it. Before they spotted the familiarity in the young, blue-eyed girl. With hardly any time to spare, she tried to pull out the drawing pin which was rigidly fixed to the cork.

'Amy!' Ian's voice startled her and she froze with her back against the wall. 'You've done a fine job with the display.'

'Actually... I didn't do it, Ian.' She smiled innocently, wishing he would turn away.

'Well, someone has captured the school in all its years of glory,' he beamed. 'Some of these are even from before my time.'

'Yes, I remember...' Amy stopped. 'I mean, I know. Look at the old canteen in that one!' She motioned with her neck, still refusing to uncover the picture that was stuck behind her shoulders.

'The visitors will love these. Perhaps one or two of them might even recognise themselves!'

Amy stiffened. 'Sorry?'

'We always get a few old faces showing up each year. They love a good delve into the archives.'

'How old?'

'From way back sometimes.' Ian's eyes turned saucer shaped. 'Some as ancient as the founding year and others who have only just recently left.'

'Do you...' stuttered Amy. 'Do you know who's coming?'

'It's always a mystery,' he retreated back inside his office. 'That's the magic of Open Day, and indeed, the magic of this school. No one ever knows what could be around the corner.'

Amy snatched the picture off the wall and scrunched it into her handbag. Why did this have to keep happening? Why, whenever she felt secure, did something always get in the way? The very thought made her flinch as she took off towards the staffroom.

Opening up her bag again, she retrieved her compact mirror, being careful to keep the rest of the contents zipped well out of sight. Then, noting her paleness, she made a quick grab for her blusher brush.

Alison emerged from behind a shelf, making Amy jump.

'Ali! You scared the life out of me.'

'Don't let me interrupt you. I can see you're busy.'

'I'm not,' she clicked the case shut. 'I just didn't think anyone was in here.'

'Getting all done up for Superman, are we?'

'That's not necessary,' Amy joked, far more confidently than she felt. 'He's into me no matter what.'

'I'll say,' agreed Alison. 'I've never seen him like this before. On top of the world since you came along.'

'Do you think?'

'Oh, it's obvious.'

Amy felt a rush of warmth as she put away her compact, but she touched the picture in her bag and the tension rapidly returned.

'Tea?' Alison asked.

'Lovely.'

'I think Debra made some brownies. They're here somewhere.'

'The tea will do nicely, thanks. I'm really not hungry.'

'You need to keep your wits about you. Open Day always takes it out of everyone.'

Amy said nothing, feeling gradually more uneasy.

'Well, if it isn't Mrs Craven!' Gita breezed in and propped her shopping bag on a spare chair.

'You're a fine one to talk. By the looks of things, you'll be married way before me.'

Gita's face fell. 'Nothing's even happening with that one.'

'Why not?'

'One-way traffic. He doesn't want to know.'

'But the way he helped you carry all those boxes…'

enthused Amy.

'And I was talking to him yesterday,' Alison gave a sly gaze to Gita. 'He was asking about you.'

'Was he?'

'No!' She laughed loudly at Gita's scowl.

'I'll get you for that, Huckleberry.'

'He helped you for a reason,' Amy insisted. 'I wouldn't give up just yet.'

'Amy,' Gita said, rolling her eyes. 'I saw him in the car park just now and all he did was wave. He's not interested.'

'I'm willing to bet otherwise.'

'Enough of all that.' Gita held her hands up. 'I've got other things to think about. Namely today and how I am going to pull off this poetry presentation when my class don't even know the words.'

'Sounds like fun,' chimed Alison as she stirred the mugs of tea. 'What time do you get to embarrass yourself?'

'It keeps changing.' Gita pointed to a list on the noticeboard and Amy could see it was an updated schedule. 'It was eleven, but now it's eleven-thirty.'

As soon as the others were distracted, Amy looked more closely at the list. From what she was reading on the first few lines, it all seemed fine and above board. It would begin with the Headteacher's welcome and some singing from the Reception class. Then a puppet show followed by the poetry recital. A morning tour would commence around the school while lessons resumed as normal.

The only items listed for the afternoon were Martin's science experiments and Joel's sports demonstration. And the day would end with speeches – from a group of past pupils.

She suddenly lost her desire for the tea and headed over to the door.

'Are you off?' Alison asked.

'Just a couple of errands to run before everything gets started,' she replied, her smile dropping away the minute she left the room.

She stepped outside for calmness, but the sky was already fuming. Cluttered clouds enrobed the sun and were speedily reducing it to blackness. The rain slapped with force onto the ground and pelted at her skin as if each drop was deliberate. Hurrying back inside, she stepped under cover just seconds before everything dissolved, pouring down the gravel path and knocking like fists on the glass.

Amy spent the morning on tenterhooks and there was no escaping in the hideaway of the huts. It was as if Ian had plucked a classroom out of the sky to stay in for the bulk of the tour. He arrived five minutes into Amy's reading session accompanied by people in a flurry of ages and faces. Over-cheerful parents with timid prospective pupils. Chirruping, gabbling relatives who had probably come along for the drive.

She kept her eyes on the book, hoping no one would clock her. While Flynn and Bertie read out the passage, she silently urged them to steal the attention and free her from anyone's memory. But her panic was undue and as Ian finally led everyone away, Amy rejoiced in the emptiness of the classroom.

As speech time loomed, she couldn't have walked any slower on the approach to the assembly hall. Peering cautiously ahead, she could see that the number of visitors had grown significantly from earlier. The room was buzzing with a cacophony of chatter and eyes widely soaking up the décor all around them.

But Amy wished she could tear away the trimmings. Then they would all stop exploring this place and examining every last detail. Her stomach jerked at the turn of each head and the sound of every laugh that seemed out of place. The impending weather was dizzily cloying as it clashed with the artificial strip lights. Feeling faint in the atmosphere, she rested quietly on her chair.

Ian was smartly suited and poised at the foot of the stage. It was now set up with a microphone and a wedge of stapled paper, which was probably a copy of every speech that had to be forcefully sat through. Penny stood by Ian's side wearing a gold and black tasselled dress. She gleamed a winning smile, framed by the red swathe of her lipstick.

The teachers took their seats and the visitors formed an audience. Amy scanned over them all, looking for the ones who were about to gain attention. Just like before in the classroom, no one stood out.

She ground her back harshly against the chair, not wanting to be seen. Feeling unsteady in the presence of these strangers, any one of whom could reveal all before she could do so herself. Trembles coursed incessantly from her chest to her fingertips and she knew her complexion was as pasty as the sky. Her secret was still untouched, but nothing could disguise the way it plagued her at this moment.

A head craned in the corner of her eye and she looked up to see that it was Joel. The anxiety had consumed her so much, she hadn't even noticed he was there. He compelled her to look at him. To fight through the commotion with a smile that confirmed all was well. But she didn't want to face him – not if all he believed about her was going to come crashing down.

When their eyes finally locked, he frowned. Amy watched the worry taking over his face and knew that she had failed to bury the tension. There was no fooling him when it came to hiding her troubles; he could always sense them immediately. It was obvious now that something was wrong. He knew her too well. And any minute now, he might know her even better.

'Are you OK?' he mouthed.

Amy forced her lips into a faintly convincing curve and looked away, hoping that this had been reassuring enough. But he raised a doubting brow and coaxed her back into eye contact.

'Are you sure?'

This time, she paused. Every nod was a lie.

'Amy…'

The whisper succumbed to the chaotic voices and Ian's hands clapped like an earthquake. As everyone fell to silence, he addressed the visitors, looking every now and then towards the door. The mystery speakers were queuing up outside, ready to make their entrance and find Amy's face in the audience. The person in question would race up to her afterwards, or worse still, they would tell the entire room the minute they made the discovery.

'Good afternoon,' Ian began. 'I hope you have enjoyed your day at Woodbrook and it's been a pleasure to welcome you. But now, we have a very special treat.'

He beamed out at his listeners, revving up the anticipation.

'Five of our very own past pupils are lined up just outside that door and they are going to tell you all about themselves, where they are now in life and just what they feel Woodbrook did for them. So please would you welcome our eldest speaker, Mr Trevor Sandford.'

Applause filled the air as a balding man with the remnants of ginger-grey hair marched up to the lectern wearing an adult-sized version of the full Woodbrook uniform. He soon had the room in fits of giggles. Amy kept her eyes firmly on him to avoid the scrutiny of Joel's.

Next on the stage was a nurse. She squinted through thick glasses and spoke proudly about her challenging career. Her speech was short but meaningful and Ian soon introduced another woman, who Amy worked out was around five years younger than herself. She didn't recognise the name and she was sure she had never seen her face before.

Soon, Amy began to relax. These people were appearing in order of age, and the two who were left must be even younger.

A man in his early twenties strode up to face the visitors, smirking confidently in a rugby shirt, fresh out of university. He talked about keeping fit and how he was now training in sports science.

Amy could have cried with relief. All that panicking for nothing, and just one more speaker to come. She was almost looking forward to seeing who it would be. Now she eyed Joel again and saw the burden erased from his face when she smiled wholeheartedly back at him. It was going to be all right.

Sure enough, a teenage girl with bright red hair and ripped jeans gave a goofy smile to the onlookers and reached for the guitar on her back. She had valued the music classes at Woodbrook and now she was a songwriter, having even penned tracks for a few well-known names.

Glancing at Joel again, Amy couldn't wait to be near him and finally unleash what was on her mind. No more faces to swerve and avoid, and nobody threatening to invade her deepest secrets. His gentle grin swept her away and she felt bad now for making him worry. All he wanted was her happiness and she hung on to the hope that this would never change.

As the guests got to their feet and the teachers began to mingle, Ian blocked Joel's path and reacquainted him with the sports science graduate. Alison vanished into the crowd and Martin looked flirty with Gita as he closed in for a chat.

Waiting patiently for Joel, Amy listened to the rain cracking wildly against the window and felt all her tension drip away. She now gazed warmly at the people in the room, knowing that the truth was hers to tell.

But from a gap within the bobbing heads, somebody shot into view. A fierce and determined expression on a tall, statuesque frame. The woman had gaunt cheekbones and a thin line for a mouth. Her dyed hair was greying at the roots and a barrelled throat protruded from her neck. The movement of a hundred bodies impaired her line of vision, but through all the frenzied motions, she kept her eyes pinned to Amy. Eyes that were as round and green as marbles, wide until they reddened at the corners.

These were the eyes that had glared across the classroom. The mouth that had smirked at each stumble Amy made. The chortling had rung out from the pit of that throat and so had the shouting that had followed. There was the teacher who had once dragged her down, revelling in the mockery of the class. The very reason why her life had been shattered and she had fought so hard to overcome it all.

Time stood still as her world drowned around her. Cassandra Dixon knew exactly who she was.

Thirty-Three

It hit her like a stone and she felt as if her heart would crack. She looked over at Joel, who was deep in conversation, while she slowly surrendered to Cassandra's recognition.

Alone in this thronging hall of people, she collided with the facts that had never gone away. She was nothing but helpless, weak and pathetic, and she didn't deserve to be there. She was worthless, just as she had always been, and nothing she had was her own.

She wasn't fit for this job or for the life she was living. And there was no way in the world she could be good enough for Joel. All she could do now was wait for him to find out. To be told every word of it in the next few minutes.

Cassandra sidled to a gathering on her left, putting her hand on Penny's shoulder and guiding her away from the group. Then she leaned in with her fingers to her mouth and whispered into her ear. Penny's face ignited. Her triumphant eyes clambered around the room and froze as they fell on their goal.

Amy could no longer feel gravity. She took a final glimpse at her colleagues, knowing she was about to lose all of their respect. Her mouth dried out as she studied Ian's grin, anticipating the reaction he would have about her dishonesty. And as her eyes crept away to behold the other man, she could hardly focus on his face.

Joel stood obliviously, chatting to the graduate. Encouraging and praising, like she had always known him to do. Feeling faint and sick, she looked into his eyes, knowing it was the last moment he would still want her. She had failed him and cheated him by running away from the past. She had allowed him to fall for a fantasy of herself and had betrayed him with the depths of all this secrecy. But history had finally caught her. Now she would pay and get what she deserved.

She took another look at the two gawping women, their faces fully powered by this unexpected knowledge. Laughter and voices swirled in her head, groggy and incoherent. And everything faded away. Her image and reputation. Her hope and integrity. The home she had built here and the person who had called her his soulmate.

Tears spilled bitterly from her eyes as she gripped the back of her chair. Penny glanced over to where Ian and Joel stood and began to edge towards them, Cassandra following at her tail. And Amy could take no more. Making no excuses, she burst through the crowd and fled straight out of the door.

She tore off into the black afternoon and the drenching downpour that smashed onto the ground. Darting alongside the assembly hall in complete view of the full-length windows, she skidded over the playground tarmac, not knowing where she was going.

Running through the sloping twitten, she followed the reams of water as they cascaded in patterns down the drain. She flew past the lollipop man and the parents outside the Pig and Trotter, sprinting on until she reached the park.

She emerged from a small cluster of trees and faced the eye of the storm. The pewter sky was streaked with violet, like steam rising up from a potion. Silver lightning lashed out in the distance and the thunder's deafening cymbals brooded from beyond.

Mud spattered on her clothes, which were now unrecognisably soaked. Her blouse was shrivelled against her skin, the bare flesh of her neckline wide open to the cloudburst. Hair clung to a face rinsed of make-up with only smudges remaining under her eyes. She scrambled to higher ground, where the ancient flint wall ran along the edge and matted clumps of pampas grass cowered with the force of the rain.

Over at the far side of the park, she scarpered under three tall trees whose branches scratched at the sky. Then she mounted a hilly clump of grass and waded into seclusion.

'Amy…'

She bristled at the voice, trying desperately to reach her through the wild wind and the barrage of rainfall, but she still staggered ahead to the concrete path where she would hopefully be able to run faster.

'Amy!'

He was closer now. Fast catching up and unable to let her escape. She ran through the decaying wall where it halted at the entrance to the rose garden. Twisted thornbushes clawed threateningly, as if to stop her going any further into the wilderness. But she carried on, just knowing that it was all too late.

'Amelia!'

She stopped dead. The quickening of her heartbeat had nothing to do with the running. Footsteps whipped through the grass and the urgency of his breathing swelled as he finally reached her side.

Amy shook, not wanting to turn around. Not wanting to witness the fury that would be bubbling over on his face, now that he knew what she had dreaded he would discover. She paused for what seemed like a lifetime before she finally spoke.

'I see they've jogged your memory. Couldn't help themselves, could they?'

Joel looked perplexed as he squinted through the rain. 'What do you mean?'

'Cassandra Dixon, of course.' Amy kept her back turned, letting the stream of raindrops blend with her tears. 'She knew it was me. She and Penny couldn't wait to fill you in.'

'But I haven't spoken to anyone. I saw you run past the window and I was gone. No one had the chance to catch me.'

Her bones knocked with the cold and she stared down at the muddy pools of water. 'There's no need to pretend. It's not going to make me feel better.'

'You don't get it, do you?' Joel stepped up behind her, snapping twigs under his feet. He gripped her hand and turned her body to face him. 'I know who you are.'

'Yes, *now* you do. Now they've told you everything I didn't.'

He shook his head dismissively and locked his gaze on her face. 'I've always known.'

Amy trembled at his words. Then she backed away under the bough of a tree.

'Do you expect me to believe that? That you've known all about me and still actually cared?'

'What's so bad about you then?' A stern expression darkened his face. 'Come on, enlighten me.'

'As if I need to remind you,' she cried defiantly. 'Pathetic little Amelia Green. The one who everyone hated. The loser that no one wanted to be around. I was the one in the corner. You know, the thick one who failed every test. The kid who everyone picked on, and hit, and laughed at. I was nothing, Joel. Nothing but stupid and worthless, and...'

'And the fastest girl in the school.'

His eyes glistened bright blue through the deluge and her heart knocked a rhythm in her ribcage. Cassandra would never have come out with that. This was something only Joel could know.

She finally looked straight at his vehement expression. Rain trickled off the contours of his face and his chest heaved under his wet shirt.

'You remember?' Her throat choked her voice. 'You really remember that?'

Joel sniggered softly and she quaked as it echoed into the thunder. 'How could I ever forget?'

He gazed at her with inexplicable awe and she winced as her clothes groped her body. She thought of the state she must look at this moment, the black smears of make-up and her tendrils of hair, tangling down in a mass. Her heart leapt as he paced again towards her and stopped when their hands almost touched.

'That day on the field…' He shook his head slowly and briefly looked away. 'Do you know how much that meant to me?' Tears brimmed over in his own eyes and she longed to kiss them away. 'You were bruised and beaten at the hands of all those bullies and you put your last shred of trust in me. The look on your face as you ran to me… the way you raced across that track. How proud I felt when you got there! That was the day I made it as a teacher. You did that for me. No one but you.'

'It was all because of you.' Amy shivered as metallic lines slithered like serpents over the sky. 'You were the only good thing I had.'

Joel scowled and silenced her. 'Your heart was like gold, no matter what everyone else put you through. I could never have hoped for better. Then or now.'

'But all this time, you've known me and you've never said?'

He sighed in response. 'Because I was waiting for you to come out with it yourself. When we first talked, that day in the hall, I could see you weren't comfortable with the past and I didn't want to hurt you by unearthing it all. Then it got complicated. The more I fell for you, the more I couldn't bear to push you away by making you talk about it. You had to tell me in your own time.'

Amy stared back, dumbfounded as Joel continued with his outpouring.

'But now I realise what all this has been about. The things you've kept from me and how down you still are on yourself. You're so much more than you realise. Please believe me as much as I believe in you.'

'I tried to tell you, I really did. But I just couldn't. I was… scared.'

'Of what?'

'Losing you.' She glanced up timidly and blinked the rain from her lashes. 'I thought you'd never look at me twice if you realised who I was. And once I had you, I couldn't let you go.'

'Then you're really not so bright after all,' he replied straight-faced. 'If you think I'd change my mind because of something like that.'

'So… you wouldn't?'

Joel raised his eyes to the heavens, stunned and baffled by the level of her doubt.

'That's what makes this special. You were the best student I can ever remember and now…' His words filled her up with a ray of hope. 'Now, you're the love of my life.'

She leaned back on the tree and sobbed away her fears. The flood gushed over her shoulders and all the way down to her soaking wet toes. 'And you still want me? You honestly still want me, after this?'

He grabbed her wrists and slammed her into his body, pushing her hair back with his fingers. Then he beamed with the clarity of a calm, endless ocean, shivering as their eyes met and drying her cheeks with his breath.

'I love you. Please know that. I love you.' He smiled at the bewilderment that lingered in her eyes before lifting her face into his hands. 'My beautiful girl.'

She clutched him frantically, feeling the freedom being kissed back into her lips. As water showered down on them like fountains from above, she swaddled herself in his ever-constant shelter. Her hands rushed into his damp hair and kneaded a trail over the depths of his skin, knowing for the first time that it all belonged to her. She saw his eyes locked eternally on hers until that very last moment when she could taste his mouth. She had him now. She had all of him. He knew her and he still loved her.

The sky's percussion erupted through the clouds and splitting cracks severed the mauve. Rain washed over them in a blinding haze as she stood in the crook of the straggly tree and held onto all that was hers. She blotted her tears on his shoulder and rested her soul in the security of his hands.

Thirty-Four

Apart from the whispering ocean and the wings of a seagull gliding over the shore, the beach was silent from the open window. Gentle breaths of wind made the waves pleat like petticoats, reflecting the mellow tones of the lemon chiffon sky. Amy sat at her table, staring out at the view. She followed the minty froth as it chased after the sand and her gaze climbed high to the platinum threads that were stitched to the barely-there clouds. Not one raindrop dared to fall on this warm spring morning. For a place that came packaged with downpours and floods, today she would never have known it.

The sun brought a peachy sheen to her skin as it fell under the drape of her dressing gown and the diamond on her finger sparkled in the rays. Her face was a picture of perfection, with shimmering eyeshadow and lips in a rose gold glaze. A few stray coils of hair fell loosely to her jaw while the rest was scooped to the nape of her neck and adorned with petals and pearls.

She wondered why she felt this way. Why the nerves had somehow deserted her. Instead, she was nothing but calm and serene, just like the day that was unfurling. She stared in a trance at the fresh coastal glow, knowing she always could. Marvelling at how she had ever held back when now she just wanted to stay here.

'Get this down you, darling.' Colin positioned a tall sundae glass in front of her, piled high with strawberries, passionfruit, and cherries. 'A juicy little way to kick-start the day. And I won't allow you to leave so much as a pip.'

'I won't,' she grinned. 'I'm starving.'

'Good. Then you'll have plenty of room for my Off With the Garter frittatas.'

'Maybe.'

'And you wouldn't refuse a modest helping of First Night Love Bites.' He threw her a warning glance.

'That might be pushing it.'

Colin looked crestfallen as he swirled crème fraiche on top of the fruit.

'Oh, go on then.' Amy rolled her eyes. 'I'll do my best.'

'That's music to my ears!'

'Wait until you try it!' Fabian winked as he poured shots of grenadine into a row of iced glasses.

Colin scowled at his handiwork. 'Do keep an eye on the time. There are more urgent matters to be dealing with than the post-breakfast cocktails.'

He frowned blankly in response.

'The champagne?'

Immediately, Fabian stopped what he was doing and pulled a chilled bottle from the ice bucket. He made his way over to top up Amy's glass, dressed in a smart suit that was identical to Colin's.

'Don't mind if I do!' Melinda beamed as she arrived at the top of the staircase in a kingfisher blue dress and matching knee-length jacket. A nest of gems and feathers glittered in her hair as she turned to look at Amy. 'Your dad's driving me to distraction down there, fretting about the cars.'

'They'll never fit on the drive, Lindy,' called Stan from downstairs. 'I'm going out there to make some space.'

'Well, don't ruin your waistcoat, Stan. We could do without a replacement from your wardrobe, thank you.'

She wandered into the kitchen and filled up a small watering can.

'I say, Mrs A.' Colin glanced between Melinda and Amy. 'It's hard to know which one is the daughter.'

'That's very kind of you, Colin.' Melinda tended to a

wilting pot of cyclamen on the windowsill. 'But I'm still not sure about this necklace.'

'Take it off at your peril, madam.'

'Well, if you really think so…'

'You shouldn't change a thing,' agreed Amy as she finished her last forkful of food.

'We don't need your opinion at the moment.' Colin took her plate away and served the final course. 'You just concentrate on filling your face.'

After her lavish breakfast she sipped her champagne, watching as everyone rushed around the house. Fabian resumed his preparation of the cocktails while Colin loaded the dishwasher and wiped down the worktop. Stan called upstairs asking for Melinda, so reluctantly, she left the room to find out what he wanted.

Amy sat alone with her thoughts, enjoying the experience of having everyone she loved in the same place. Just one more hole remained unfilled. She traced the hem of the sea again as it snaked in Verdigris all the way out to the shadowy dot of Burling pier, where the sunlight pooled in droplets like a liquid chandelier.

'They're here!' Melinda cried as she and Stan came up the stairs carrying a package between them.

Amy pulled back the wrapping paper, gasping at the contents. A waterfall bouquet of blush and coffee roses sprigged with white pinpricks of gypsophila sprawled out from the opening. By its side were two smaller posies in a cream variation, a corsage for Melinda, and some buttonholes for the men.

'Let's see,' Vanessa emerged from the bedroom followed by Rosie. Both were wearing the same strapless dresses, ruched at the bodice in the palest sugar-pink satin. Their hair was swept up in mirroring styles and woven with a scattering of rosebuds.

'They're divine.' Rosie beamed, picking up her bunch and twirling it around.

'How do they look?' asked Vanessa, holding hers and

posing with Rosie.

'Incredible. Now, put them down or you're going to make me cry,' replied Amy with a wave of her hand.

'And how are you doing? Feeling OK?' Rosie asked.

'Yes, strangely fine.'

'Good. Not too stuffed after all that food then.'

'What do you mean, all that food?' Colin challenged.

Rosie pursed her lips. 'It was verging on excessive. One more mouthful and she'd have popped.'

'Lucky you weren't in charge then, dearest,' he sneered. 'Otherwise we'd all have been confined to the cornflakes.'

'That's far more preferable to dining like a dumper truck. No one wants to be bloated on a day like this.'

'Well, it's a bit late now if I am.' Amy grinned. 'I guess we're about to find out.'

'Are you ready?' Melinda took her hand.

'As I'll ever be.'

Accompanied by Vanessa and Rosie, Amy headed through into her bedroom. Melinda took a padded hanger off the curtain rail and pulled down the zip of the long, translucent cover.

Then Amy stepped carefully into the realms of layered fabric. And as Melinda tightened the cording to fasten her in at the back, a flowing, slimline gown took its shape around her body. With cap sleeves and a sweetheart neckline, it was embellished in antique lace over swathes of vintage netting which fell in ivory clouds from her hips to the ground. The bodice was bedecked in a spillage of floral applique, pouring out behind her in a frilled chapel train.

Feeling her way into a pair of peep-toe shoes, she took a last glimpse of her reflection. The lustre of her skin that was healed and radiant again. The anticipation in her glistening eyes and the spidery lashes that framed them. Release flooded into her face and every last blessing was etched there in her smile. She shivered at the echo staring back at her in the glass, the same as it always had been, yet almost unrecognisable.

She moved like an illusion across the floor and swished

down the landing in soft, careful footsteps until she appeared in the doorway of the kitchen, where everyone looked on. Their rapture sounded out from the instant they saw her, stunned at the first sight beyond all expectations.

'Look at my little chick,' Stan praised. 'She's turned into a swan.'

'You're breath-taking, darling!' Colin bawled on Stan's shoulder until Fabian prised him away in an effort to curtail the blotches.

'Belle of the ball if ever there was one,' added Rosie.

'You really think so?' Amy asked.

'I just knew it,' sniffed Melinda. 'I knew you were going to look like that from the day you were born.'

'Only one other person could look better than you do, sis,' Vanessa teased.

'Who?'

'Me, obviously.'

'Funny.' Amy shot her a sarcastic smile.

Colin clapped his hands together. 'Well, I think this calls for a toast.' He nodded to Fabian. 'Do the honours will you, dear?'

Fabian popped the cork on more champagne and filled the glasses that were behind him on the tray. Then, when he had handed them all out, he stepped back and allowed Colin to take his place in the centre of the room. As the excitement faded to a hush, Amy's phone beeped with a message. She hoped it wasn't from a guest who either couldn't make it or had got lost, but as Colin was about to speak, she decided not to check it until afterwards.

'Well, permit me to state the obvious. That my wonderful best friend…'

Rosie coughed deliberately in the background.

'That one of my two wonderful best friends looks like heaven on earth today.' He began to well up again. 'So, please raise your glasses everyone, and let's drink to…'

His speech was interrupted by a crashing sound from the worktop and by the look of doom on his face, he knew full well what it was. He left his drink on the table and raced over to where a small platter of party food had fallen into the sink.

'My Blissful Blinis are soaking wet!' he howled, turning to reprimand Fabian. 'What on earth possessed you to put them there?'

'I didn't... it was you.'

Colin's brows knotted. 'Was it?' He paused for thought, before continuing to flick the soap suds from the smoked salmon topping. 'Well, we'll have to work fast. The mousse is supposed to be chilli and lime, not antibacterial lemon.'

The two of them rescued what canapes they could before making a start on some new ones. So, while they were distracted in their dash around the kitchen, Amy reached for her phone.

'That reminds me,' Rosie said. 'I just need to ring Nigel and find out if he's left yet.'

'Giles is already there.' Vanessa grinned. 'And he said that today I just have to catch the flowers.' She prodded at Melinda's arm. 'Mum, do you think that means...?'

'Sounds very much like it,' Melinda replied with excited eyes. 'Don't you think, Amy?'

But she had her back turned and said nothing in response.

'Amy, love? Is everything all right?'

She spun on her heel, coming face to face with Melinda. Vanessa and Rosie stopped their conversation mid-flow. Tension took over Amy's expression and her cheeks felt warmer than the shade they had been brushed with. She looked up at the three pairs of eyes, all rooted to her and the phone she held in her hand.

'I have to go.'

'The cars won't be too much longer,' Melinda reassured her. 'Don't worry, you're allowed to be late, remember?'

Amy shook her head. 'No, I have to go now.'

Melinda stared back at her, horrified. 'Go where?'

'I can't explain.' Her eyes pleaded with everyone else's.

'What's going on?' Vanessa tried to sit her down. 'You

were fine a minute ago.'

'I still am. I just…'

'Am I hearing this right?' Colin marched over with a piping bag in his hand. 'You're going?'

Amy nodded.

'Now?'

She nodded again.

'Just like that? Darling, it's insanity!'

'I don't get this.' Vanessa started to become annoyed. 'Why can't you tell us?'

'Babe, listen…' Rosie stepped in and put an arm around Amy's shoulders. 'It's just nerves, that's all. Colin, get her a shot of something, will you?'

'Please!' She rushed away from the anxious crowd that was forming all around her. 'I'll be back, I promise you. But for now, just let me do this.'

She hurried down the stairs and past Stan, who gazed bewilderingly from where he stood in the hallway.

'Wait!' called Melinda after her. 'What about your veil?'

But she had long rushed out of the front door and was already walking briskly down the road, feeling the wind as it bustled around her skirts and the weight of people's eyes on her as she glided in a flurry over the pavement.

Halfway along the noisy highway, she hailed down a taxi and jumped in the back, taking up most of the seat in her billowing souffle of lace. Glimmers of guilt flashed through her mind when she thought of the commotion she had just created. Everyone was fraught now and in a state of panic, yet she still felt so unperturbed. This was like a dream. So alarmingly sudden and completely unreal, but all the same, she trusted it.

She watched life carry on out of the window as the cab took her further away. The cyclists tasting the great outdoors after a long and enduring winter. The families crossing over to the beach and the postman wearing shorts at the first sign of sun. Had their lives all changed in such a small space of time, just like hers? Did they finally know what happiness was after having their fair share of hardship? For every person who stared at her, wondering where she was going, she looked straight back into their gaze and pondered the same about them.

The taxi turned into the high street and somehow, it didn't seem quite so tired. The shop doorways were wide and welcoming, now that the last gusts of cold had disappeared. But so much more had altered what it meant to live in Flintley. All the things she'd been forced to part with were now at arm's reach once again. Colin and Fabian had just bought a house only a few doors down from Amy, and long-distance love had proved too much for Rosie who had moved straight in with Nigel.

Sitting back as comfortably as she could, she smiled with fulfilment at the strange fortunes of her hometown. The place she had never really left. Somewhere that had once been dead and empty had turned on itself and reclaimed her. Here was the safe that now held all the possessions she could need. And the most priceless of their kind had always been a part of it, just waiting to be rediscovered.

The cab headed over the roundabout, climbing straight up into the northern border. Wafts of perfume circled around the air as she froze in her seat and shivered. Edging down the road which ran along the park, the scenes outside were idyllic.

Cricketers clamoured to catch the ball as it soared above the wickets. Dogs wagged ahead of their owners, diving after sticks that were tossed for them to fetch. The landscape unfolded like a cloth, stretching far out to the tennis courts and around the bamboo hedges that enclosed the bowling green. She listened to the car as it hummed gently on, knowing that beyond this sound there was nothing else but peace.

Arriving at the Pig and Trotter, the taxi stopped near the crossing to the twitten. She stepped out onto the kerb, her tiers hitting the pavestones like a thousand splashes of milk. In the silence of the deserted space, she inhaled the last moments of solitude.

She looked at the road as it parted three ways. There was the direction she had come from, winding back alongside the park. And just beyond the corner, the path continued to the gothic church which soared up imposingly to the very top of the clock tower.

But it was the third road that stole all her focus. The one that led away gently uphill. She followed it with her sight until it swerved out of view, and in the next moment she was chasing it. The cobbled walls swathed a pattern along the roadside, rising and falling with the rickety shape of the path until she reached the final bend that would lead straight to her destiny. Her footsteps tapped through the quietness and she could hear nothing else. Nothing but her quickening breath and the swooshes of ruffled hem.

Changing colours swirled above as she took her first steps down the road. The road that held everything at its end. The sky had never looked more pristine, with clotted cream clouds like motifs on a cameo. Sugar-spun vapour was smeared over the horizon, as if it could be wound into a giant roll of candyfloss.

Trees were laden with fluffy blossom and the single blooms fell like confetti in her hair. Greenfinches flickered in clusters of leaves as her presence stirred through the shrubbery. There was calm, silky air and the heady scent of lawns, while the honeyed sunshine bathed it in a sumptuous opalescence.

All at once, the pavement ran out and finally she was there. Where railings marked the way into the empty staff car park. Slowly, she crept over the gravel, staying hidden by the pillar of the far wall. Then she took a steadfast breath as her toes touched the grass, feeling the way it was leading her, beyond all control.

The magnetic pull lifted her up the familiar slope. Then she stepped out of the shadows and into the shimmering sun that fell forwards in a crystal-clear pathway. It stretched for what seemed like a mile, fine and opaque like a carpet of organza, flowing straight over to the other side of the clearing.

And just where this stream of light faded beyond her vision, a watchful figure replaced it. There was the hair of sandy blond and the posture, defined and expectant. Black tails and a waistcoat were tailored to his frame, surpassing anything she could imagine. She squinted closer at the new Headteacher and saw his face change, taking in the image of the way she looked right now.

Soft flickers of breeze freed her curls from their fastening in gentle spirals as they fell. Her skin dipped into the flood of ivory lace, which was now exquisite in the jewelled shafts of sunlight. The strength of his stare pounded deep into her middle as she gazed back at him, her cheeks rosily flushed.

There were no cones to mark out the track. No brightly coloured gym kit or clipboard under his arm. But he stood there now in that very same spot, the urgency on his face sending waves through her body. Longing for her to get there as fast as she possibly could.

The same adrenaline coursed inside as the memory rose again. Her eyes were determined as she stopped at the outer corner, taking her position directly behind the line. Her feet over the footprints that had never left this place.

Like history, he looked out under the visor of his hand and waited once more until her sight fused with his. No stopwatch. No signal. Just two outstretched arms, spread wide to pull her in.

Then she kicked away her shoes and she was flying. Racing in a white mist as she jetted over the ground. Like a bullet in the air, she thundered across the soothing stretch of lush, tranquil grass. The thudding of her feet boomed in double time with her pulse and her dress whipped out in a pillow fight of fabric. With each step closer, her spirit was restored, and now the past was sacred as it led her back to him.

She leapt into his arms with a crash of tulle, submerged in the depths of his smile. Even the entire, encapsulating sky could not have been bluer than those eyes. Gripping lace between his knuckles, he breathed into her neck holding all he had cherished years back on this very day.

Hands slipped together and mouths flowed into one. And she locked hearts with her lifeline on the wide, constant field.

Acknowledgements

Many thanks to the brilliant Sub It Club members who helped me breathe life into this concept, keeping me afloat through the querying process and celebrating my publication news with such joy.

To Stuart and all at SRL Publishing, I am so proud to be a part of this diverse, forward-thinking, and environmentally conscious company. Thank you for believing in me and making my dream come true.

Heartfelt gratitude to my amazing mother, Margaret, my rock in life, who has always been behind me, encouraging me to write.

And finally, my husband, Andy, and my children, Blake and Scarlett. Your endless patience while I was "on the laptop again" has made this possible to achieve. Now you finally know what I've been doing all this time. I was writing every word for you.

SRL Publishing don't just publish books, we also do our best in keeping this world sustainable. In the UK alone, over 77 million books are destroyed each year, unsold and unread, due to overproduction and bigger profit margins.

Our business model is inherently sustainable by only printing what we sell. While this means our cost price is much higher, it means we have minimum waste and zero returns. We made a public promise in 2020 to never overprint our books just for the sake of profit.

We give back to our planet by calculating the number of trees used for our products so we can then replace. We also calculate our carbon emissions and support projects which reduce C02. These same projects also support the United Nations Sustainable Development Goals.

The way we operate means we knowingly waive our profit margins for the sake of the environment. Every book sold via the SRL website plants at least one tree.

To find out more, please visit
www.srlpublishing.co.uk/responsibility

J2